MISSED
SIGNALS

A Novel About Life, Love,
Loss, and Football

Paul E. Wootten

Grebey Creek Publishing

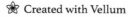 Created with Vellum

"The art of life lies in a constant readjustment to our surroundings."
   Kakuzo Okakura, The Book of Tea, 1906

"Change before you have to."
   Jack Welch, 2001

"Junior college football isn't glamorous, but it's important."
   Alex Kirshner, SB Nation, 2018

PART I

1

*T*hey kept coming.

"Sorry for your loss, Coach."

"Miss Linda was real special to Herman and me."

"Did you get the plant we sent, Coach?"

The queue seemed never-ending. Respect-payers, condolence-offerors, and the peculiar few who regularly turned up at the A. S. Robinson Funeral Chapel to gawk at the dearly departed.

"You doing okay, Coach?"

"Miss Linda got us sixty-one-three for our split-level out on Dexter Road. Me and Grace didn't think it was worth more than fifty-five. That woman could sure sell a house."

The visitation was three hours in, and Dale Fox just wanted it to be over.

"Dad, does anyone call you by name anymore?"

Dale considered Susan's softly whispered question. He couldn't remember the last time someone from Mozarkite had called him anything but Coach. Come to think of it, even Linda, his wife of thirty-three years had, at some point, stopped calling him Dale.

Of course, she wouldn't be calling him anything now.

"Damn, she was a good woman, Coach."

"It's so tragic, Coach. Did you have a clue that she might be ill?"

None. Linda had succumbed to a massive heart attack while driving between appointments. She somehow maneuvered her two-month old Cadillac Escalade to the curb before losing consciousness and collapsing onto the passenger seat. Merkle, the EMT who arrived on the scene first, made a point to reassure Dale, "Coach, you can probably get most of what you paid for that Caddy. Everybody knows how Miss Linda took care of her cars."

Dale smiled appreciatively as the mourners passed but kept his responses short. Better to keep the line moving. A few minutes earlier, Albert Robinson, the funeral chapel operator, had sidled up and whispered, "Longest receiving line I've ever seen, Coach. They're circling the building twice and snaking all the way back to Benny Smoot's place. Longest line we ever had before was when Reverend Booker passed away back in ninety-six, but his line only went around the building once." Albert paused, then added, "The Reverend's widow went all-out, though. She buried him in the *Corinthian*. You saw that one in my showroom, didn't you, Coach? The *Corinthian*?"

He had indeed. The *Corinthian* was top-of-the-line. Albert had returned to it several times during his presentation, explaining how fitting it would be as Miss Linda's final resting place. Even in his dazed and confused state, Dale had been jolted by the *Corinthian's* price tag. Albert's disapproval was obvious when he settled on the more economical *Sprint* model.

"Dad? Did you hear that?"

"Sorry, Susan. What did you say?"

Susan rolled her pretty green eyes and said, "Mrs. Magnuson was just talking about how she and her husband were the first friends you and Mom made here in Mozarkite."

"Of course," Dale smiled as he extended his hand to the pasty, obese redhead. "It's good to see you again."

"I've always regretted how we grew apart after Wayne and me moved to Potosi," Mrs. Magnuson said, the fat on her upper arm undulating as she pumped his hand. "Wayne died you know. Two years ago."

"I... I did know. Linda and I were sad to learn of his passing."

Mrs. Magnuson nodded. "It's been hard, but I'm getting by. Now, Coach, if you need a friendly ear, or anything else, you give me a call."

"I'll remember that, Mrs. Magnuson."

She laughed, a jarring sound that brought disapproving glances from the other mourners filling every corner of the somber chapel. "Call me Toots like you and Linda used to."

"Of course, uh... Toots. Thank you. We appreciate you coming."

"You don't remember her, do you?" Susan whispered when Mrs. Magnuson was out of earshot.

Dale shook his head. "I don't remember anybody named Toots. When did you say that Evan was bringing Max? I thought they would be here by now."

"We thought it would be better if Max didn't come until after the funeral. He's still wrestling with the fact that Mimi's gone." Susan peered over her shoulder at her mother's waxy form. "Her makeup looks like it was applied with a paint roller. And her hair? Geesh, she looks like an Amish sister wife. That updo is four decades out of style."

"How can you say that, Susan? I had Darcy come over and fix her hair and makeup like she always does."

"Mom hasn't stepped foot in Darcy Fannon's shop since the nineties. Bonnie Willing's been cutting her hair once a month since I was in junior high. I wish we could just close the lid and display a few pictures of her from better times."

"People in Mozarkite come to funerals expecting to get one last look."

"If anyone does that to me, I'll come back and haunt them from the grave. Hello, Mrs. Camper."

"Sweet Susan, you look stunning."

Dale had always thought that Effie Camper looked like a bunch of pillows stuffed under a dress the size of a pup tent, and the sight of Susan being pulled into the midst of all those pillows might have been funny on another day. Susan wasn't bothered at all. And why would she be? Effie Camper's freshman class had ignited a love for U.S. history that led Susan to pursue a bachelor's degree at Mizzou and a master's at St. Louis University. Her master's thesis on the changing role of women in the 1920's had led to offers of employment from several small colleges, including Dale's employer, Mozarkite Junior College. She turned them all down.

The line grinded to a halt as Susan and Effie began discussing some recent documentary they had viewed. Dale looked past Effie to where Bridget and Jackpot Jones visited with the Corydons while waiting patiently for their turn.

"I'll be right back," Dale whispered to Susan, who barely took note. He caught Albert Robinson's attention and pointed toward a small side room reserved for family members. Albert had mentioned that Patsy Werner dropped off some leftovers from the Goldrush Diner. Thursday was liver and onions day at the Goldrush, but Patsy knew of Dale's disdain for liver, so she probably substituted country ham and mashed potatoes left over from Wednesday. His mouth started to water as he opened the door to the family waiting room. Sure enough, country ham and mashed potatoes. And a coconut cream pie missing one piece.

And a man Dale had never seen before. Helping himself to all of it. Like it was his.

A priest.

"Hello."

The priest was just about to shove a forkful of potatoes into his mouth as Dale entered. He turned, but only after finishing the task at hand.

"Hey," he said. "You're Dale, right?"

The man was about Dale's age, taller, with a full head of gray hair. Dale did a mental rewind through his past, trying to remember a point when their paths might have crossed, but like his recollection of the woman called Toots, he came up with nothing.

"I'm Father Clark," he said as he set aside his fork. "I drove straight through from Sioux City to get here. There wasn't even time for dinner, but that nice mortician, Mr. Robinson, invited me to enjoy a light supper before seeing Linda."

The food wasn't Albert's to offer, Dale thought. Instead, he said, "Sioux City's got to be an eight-hour drive."

"Nearly ten, but as soon as I heard, I knew I wanted to be here." He remained seated but offered his hand. Dale shook it. "My full name is Clark Smith. Perhaps Linda spoke of me at one time or another?"

"Doesn't ring a bell. Did you grow up together in Oklahoma?"

The priest laughed. "Do I sound like I'm from Oklahoma? I'm a Jersey boy. Still would be if the Catholic Church had any common sense. Sadly, they think I can do more of God's work in Sioux City."

"Sioux City's a fine town. I had a player from there a dozen or so years ago, a lineman named Rasmussen. Know him?"

"I've only been there for five years, so probably not. And you're right, Dale. Sioux City is an okay place unless you've known the Jersey Shore. I was born in Freehold. I guess you've heard of it?"

"Sorry, no."

"Bruce Springsteen?"

"I know of him. Singer, right?"

Father Clark shook his head and blinked several times. "*Born to Run*? Don't tell me you didn't own that album, Dale. Everybody our age owned *Born to Run*."

"I was always pretty busy with work and football. I didn't have time for music. But back to Linda?"

"Oh, yes, we met in college."

"Linda went to Stephens in Columbia. That's a women's school, Father. Are you sure you have the right person?"

A look of bemusement crossed Father Clark's face. "Fix yourself a plate, and I'll tell you all about it. I went to Westminster College in Fulton, about twenty miles from Columbia. Basketball scholarship." Father Clark laughed. "Talk about culture shock. Big Macs and near-beer on Sundays was as crazy as Fulton got in those days. My buddies and I started going to Columbia on weekends. It wasn't Jersey, but at least they had a couple good bars. I met Linda one night in Booche's, the best burger place west of Asbury Park. Ever had a Booche's burger, Dale?"

Dale sat his plate across from Father Clark's and took a seat. "Never. I've been to a few games at Mizzou, but most of my time is spent here in southern Missouri."

"You've missed one of the greatest culinary delights on God's green earth. In fact, I plan to stop through on my way home and get a dozen for the road. By Saturday night Mass I'll be breaking more wind than a Kansas tree farm, but what can you do?"

Dale flashed a smile he wasn't feeling. The guy was loud for a priest. Not that he knew many. Mozarkite was a Baptist town with a few Methodists and Lutherans tossed in for good measure. The one Catholic church in town had been overseen by Father Frank for more than twenty years. Father Frank was a man of few words, and those he did utter were usually reserved for his parishioners.

"Linda was very special to me," Father Clark said, breaking a silence that had taken hold. "Every guy in my fraternity had a crush on her." He shook his head ruefully. "They couldn't believe it was me who caught her."

"*Caught her*?" Something in the pit of Dale's stomach told him to drop it, but he didn't listen.

Father Clark's face turned crimson. "Gosh, Dale, I didn't mean like... caught her, like... we... I just meant that we went out a few times. She must've seen pretty quick that I wasn't the one, because after a couple months she called me at the dorm one night and told me she was breaking things off. Man, I was in bad shape for weeks."

The tension in Dale's gut receded a bit. It was still there, but not as much. "I can't believe she never mentioned you."

"She moved on pretty quick. I heard she was at a Pi Kap mixer the very next weekend. She was out of my league, anyway."

"A girlfriend would have made it tough to pursue your present calling."

Father Clark laughed. "Linda dumping me actually pushed me toward the priesthood. I finished senior year at Westminster and enrolled in seminary back home at Seton Hall. We exchanged letters for a couple years. The last one she wrote was all about this guy she met. His name was Dale, and he was going to be a big-time football coach."

It was Dale's turn to blush. "I don't know about big-time, but I'm in a good place. The local junior college has treated me pretty well." He took one last bite of ham, wiped his hands with a napkin, and got to his feet. "Thanks for coming, Father. It would've meant a lot to Linda."

Back out front, the receiving line had moved along at a faster clip during Dale's absence. Susan, who possessed the same take-charge personality as her mother, was handling things with her typical aplomb, efficiently receiving visitors, listening to personal remembrances, and accepting hugs and condolences.

"Sorry," Dale whispered as he reassumed his spot. "I ran into an old college friend of your mother's. Did she ever mention someone named Clark?"

"Clark Smith? They had a thing in college, but Mom broke it off."

"He's in back. Eating my country ham. He came all the way from Iowa."

"Who's in back?"

Dale had missed Fran Tompkins's approach. He turned, expecting to also see her husband, his longtime friend and assistant coach, Willis, but Fran was alone. That meant Willis was having a bad day. Lately the bad days outnumbered the good as the dementia deepened its hold.

"Hey, Aunt Fran," Susan said, giving her a peck on the cheek. "Dad was asking if I had ever heard of Clark Smith."

"Clark Smith is here?"

"Why am I the only one who never heard of the guy?" Dale asked.

Susan squeezed his arm. "Girl talk between Mom and Aunt Fran, probably. Mr. Smith and Mom must've been *really* good friends."

"Why would you think that?"

"He came to Mozarkite, didn't he?"

"But, Susan, your mother was—"

"Look, Dad, it's Mr. Packwood. Hi, Mr. Packwood, how are you?"

● ● ●

JUST BEFORE EIGHT the atmosphere in the chapel received a sudden jolt of energy. Glancing over the heads of mourners who filled every seat, aisle, and corner while they visited and gossiped, Dale realized why. The Mozarkite Junior College football team, his Polled Herefords, had arrived.

All fifty-five of them.

Like most young men their age, they were unaccustomed to somber surroundings. Try as they might, they couldn't resist joking and playing grab-ass among themselves as they waited in line. Most wore ill-fitting sport coats and ties over dress shirts stretched to the max. As they edged toward the front of the chapel, Dale overheard snippets of inappropriate conversations, along with occasional bursts of flatulence. They were a breath of fresh air. The boys, not the flatulence.

Most checked out Susan as they would any attractive female. More than a decade older and long used to the attention of her father's players, she paid them scant notice. Then, one-by-one, they approached and offered awkward sentiments. Most had at least a passing acquaintance with Linda from home games and the occasional team meal. There were a few tears from the handful who had made the effort to get to know her. They gawked at her lifeless form in the *Sprint* casket. For some, Dale suspected, it was the first time they had experienced death up close.

The last in line was the team captain, Quarterback Jeff Devereux. The son of a Little Rock surgeon who had spent hundreds of thousands on personal coaches and clinics, Jeff's self-confidence far exceeded his playing skills.

"We're having our best week of practice all season, Coach," he said quietly as he looked Dale in the eyes. "The guys have dedicated Saturday's Homecoming game to you and Miss Linda."

"It'll be tough, Jeff. Iowa Western is seven and three."

Jeff shrugged. "Don't underestimate this bunch. I've stepped in and led the offensive unit's practices. We've got some plays Iowa Western won't be expecting."

"Straight and simple, Jeff. Remember that."

Jeff winked, pulled Dale into a tight embrace, and followed his teammates toward the exit.

"Your players are coaching now? And *hugging* you?" Susan's tone dripped with sarcasm. "Did somebody kidnap my father, or have you changed?"

Dale shook his head and offered a brief smile. "I'm too old to change now. Jeff is more talk than anything else. Come Saturday he'll be doing just what he's supposed to. They always do. And speaking of football, you remember Mr. Shockley from the *Messenger*, don't you?"

Susan's gaze followed her father's to a well-fed, cherry-cheeked man in his late forties. "Sure, I do. Hey, Mr. Shockley."

"You're all grown up now, so call me Randall like everybody else. Good to see you again, Susan. Sorry for the circumstances, though." He grew somber when his eyes met Dale's. He tried to speak but struggled for words. Dale saved him.

"Randall took a job last month with the daily paper in Cape Girardeau. How's it going so far, Randall?"

"Not bad. I'm covering the large-class high schools. They're talking about having me report on the college team during basketball season, maybe even go on the road with them." Shockley turned his attention to Susan.

"Where are you living these days, young lady? Last I heard you were in Bangkok or somewhere."

"Botswana, but that was two years ago. We've been in Chicago since then." She paused to glance at her father. "But I'm planning to move back to Mozarkite."

Dale made no attempt to hide his surprise. "What?"

Susan nodded. "It's time to put down some roots. Max needs stability."

"And Evan is okay with this?"

"It doesn't matter, Dad. We've been living apart for five months. Mom's passing was the push I needed to finally file the paperwork."

"And you're moving back *here*? Why? What's here for you?"

"You."

Dale considered his daughter for a moment. They never were particularly close. He searched his memories for highlights of Susan's childhood, but the best he could come up with was her junior year of high school when she scored thirty-eight points in a varsity game against West Plains. Had she gone to prom? Maybe. She was popular enough, but as far as her dating life was concerned, he had no clue. That was Linda's area.

And now she was telling him that she was coming back to Mozarkite to be closer.

To him.

To him?

"But... what will you do? Are you thinking of teaching? Because I don't expect the college will have any openings for—"

"We can talk later," Susan said as she cut her eyes toward Randall Shockley, who was hanging on every word.

"Sorry, Randall," Dale said.

"Don't worry about it. Have you had a chance to meet my replacement at the *Messenger*?"

"I didn't know they had hired anyone yet."

"I mentioned it to you before I left. She's a very talented young woman, fresh out of Mizzou's journalism school. She did the write-ups of your last two games. Did you see those?"

"I try to avoid reading about our losses, Randall. Does she know football?"

"She has an excellent grasp of sports in general. I've read some of the stuff she wrote for the student paper at Mizzou. A real go-getter, too." Shockley smiled at Susan. "She reminds me of this one when she was that age."

"It's hard to get used to women covering football," Dale said. "I mean, Randall, you were free to come into the locker room after games. If some young kid—a girl—tries to come in, I'm not sure how the players would react."

Susan laughed harshly. "Seriously, Dad? Could you be any more behind the times? Do you think this is a problem at UCLA or Florida?"

"Mozarkite isn't California or Florida. It's a conservative Midwest town with conservative Midwest values. People don't want girls in the players' locker room."

"She's not a girl, Coach," Randall said quickly. "She's a gifted journalist who already runs circles around me. I doubt she'll be here long before she gets an offer from one of the big city dailies. I wouldn't be surprised to see Heaven Knight on ESPN or walking the sideline of an NFL team within a decade. She's that kind of talent."

"Hold on, Randall. What did you say her name was?"

"Heaven Knight."

Dale chose his words carefully, chewing on the ones that he knew might be perceived as inappropriate. He had never been a person to make crass statements, but seriously? *Heaven Knight?* In the end, he nodded his head, but said nothing.

"Set up a meeting and get to know her," Randall said as he moved away. "She probably won't go as easy on you as I did, but I think the paper will be better for it."

Dale had more questions, but Randall stepped aside to allow those waiting behind him to approach. His conversations with Susan over the next hour took a jagged course, alternating between personal discussions and acknowledging visitors.

"Sorry to spring it on you that I'm moving back," Susan whispered between mourners. "Mom and I had been talking about it for several months. She wanted me to come work with her in the office."

"Selling real estate?" Coach asked.

Susan nodded.

"But what about your degrees? You put so much work into them." *And I put so much money into them*, he considered adding.

"Perhaps I'll return to teaching someday, but for now I want to work at something familiar, something I choose to do because I enjoy it. I grew so tired of all the part-time jobs I had to take on to support us while Evan was unemployed. If I never have to wait another table, it will be just fine with me."

Dale found himself warming to the idea of Susan being back in town. He felt that she sacrificed too much of herself when she married Evan Sturdivant. It was obvious that she was the stronger and smarter half of the relationship, and Evan had repeatedly proven it by flunking out of two grad programs in international relations before finally completing a degree at a college that Dale's lawyer friend, Larry Bob Billingsley, described as a diploma mill. Through all the schools and all the moves, Susan had kept the plates spinning, grabbing jobs whenever and wherever she could, even while pregnant with Max. It was good for her to finally be standing on her own. But divorce?

"You know my feelings about divorce."

"I do. Are you going to disown me?"

Dale took a deep breath, said a few words to Dallas Murray from Mozarkite Hardware, then whispered to Susan, "There's no way around it?"

"Sure, be miserable the rest of my life. Never realize my potential. Raise Max in a home with a father who is focused only on himself. Sound good to you, Dad?"

"There will be questions at church."

"Not for me. I'm not going."

"You were raised in Third Baptist Church, Susan. You have to go. It's expected."

"I'm thirty-five years old, Dad. I go where I want. I've never forgotten how some of those people treated Lacy Hollowell when she came back."

"What else could they do? Lacy Hollowell was a stripteaser at some roadside place down near Hayti. Donald Green saw her himself."

"But she eventually came back, Dad. Just like the prodigal son in the Bible. And what happened? She was ostracized by a church that included three men who were regulars at the club where she performed. And another thing. They're called exotic dancers. Nobody says striptease anymore."

Dale didn't want to go any further down that path, so he changed the subject.

"But real estate, Susan? You saw how hard your mother worked. The late hours. Showing homes to people she knew couldn't afford them. That's something you think you want to do?"

"I loved going to work with her when I was a little girl. Remember how I used to help her stage homes for open houses? I think I'll like it. More importantly, I think I'll be good at it."

Any response Dale might have had was put on hold when Mozarkite's lone florist, Leah Wagner, approached with a large spray of white carnations.

"Mom's favorite," Susan gushed as she bent close to breathe in their fragrance. "Put them in the middle behind the casket where Mom can see them, Leah."

Leah did as she was told, moving a few other arrangements to make room. Susan turned to her father. "Your idea?"

Dale shook his head. Leah pulled a card from the arrangement, handed it to Susan, and was on her way.

"'In loving memory of a favorite guest and friend, from everyone at Katie's Sweet Breeze Inn.'" Susan looked up from the card. "Gulfport, Mississippi. Dad, do you know the Sweet Breeze Inn?"

"Never heard of it. Mom probably had meetings there over the years. She was always trying to find new places to pick up those continuing education classes she had to take."

"She must have really made an impression on them," Susan said as she gazed at the spray. "Evan spends more nights in hotels than at home, and all he ever gets is an occasional free breakfast."

"Never underestimate Linda Fox," a kindly old man named Emerson said as he stepped up to offer his condolences. There was something in the way that he said it that left Dale feeling off-kilter, but whatever it was would have to wait until another day.

◊ ◊ ◊

THE LAST MOURNER passed by at nine-forty, nearly five hours after Albert Robinson had opened the doors.

"I'll give you two a few moments alone with her," Albert intoned before bowing out like a butler in a TV show.

Dale glanced at Susan uncertainly, put his arm around her waist, and pulled her close. Her eyes grew teary as they gazed down at Linda. They were silent for several moments before Susan spoke.

"Remind me to never go to Darcy Fannon's shop," she said, smiling through the tears. "I could have applied Mom's makeup with a spray gun and done better."

"She did the best she could," Dale responded, agreeing with Susan's criticism but for some reason feeling the need to defend Darcy Fannon.

"At least you and I know that Mom's under there somewhere." She looked into Dale's eyes before gently brushing at a stray hair that had escaped its daily dose of Brylcreem. "How are you doing, Daddy?"

It had been a long time since she last called him that, and hearing her say it – Daddy – tugged at something deep inside. How was he doing? Sad? Some, maybe. He expected an outpouring of personal grief, but maybe that came later. Lonely? Not yet, but again, after everything was over, maybe then.

"I'm okay. Standing here making small talk all night was hard. Making arrangements was tough, too, especially with Albert pushing caskets like Chevys on a used car lot. He's still agitated that I settled for this one."

Susan laughed. "He took a run at me, too. He even offered to," she made air quotes with her fingers, 'upgrade Mom before the burial.' He really thinks she should be in a model called *The Corinthian*."

"Nobody can accuse Albert of not hustling," Dale said. "What do you think?"

"About Albert?"

"No, about me choosing the lesser-priced model. Is it an insult to your mother's memory?"

"That's not something I want to think about, Dad. I don't like caskets at all. I'm going to be cremated."

"You can't, Susan. We have a family plot at the church cemetery. There's room for Mom, you, me, and up to three more family members."

"Maybe we can sell a space to Lacy Hollowell," Susan said sarcastically. "Can you imagine the uproar if that *stripteaser* was buried in the church cemetery?"

"That wouldn't be allowed. Church members and family only."

Dale could sense that Susan was ready to debate the topic. He also felt the approach of someone from behind them. He turned, expecting to find Albert. It was that priest, instead.

"Father Clark? I'm surprised you're still here."

Dale had forgotten the priest completely, given how many people had passed by over the past several hours.

"I hope you don't mind, Dale. I hung back until everyone was gone." His eyes shifted to Susan. "Hi, I'm Clark Smith. I was a friend of your mother's many years ago. I came to pay my respects, but I suppose I'm interrupting your family time, so I'll..."

"Nonsense, Father," Susan said, offering her hand. "I'm Susan."

His eyes lingered on Susan's face for several moments. "You have her eyes. And her blonde hair. In fact, you favor her very much."

"People always say that. My mother told me about you, Father Clark."

He became flustered. The brashness from earlier was gone. "Oh, you're just being nice to an old man," he demurred. "I wasn't much more than a speck on the highway that was Linda Purcell's life."

Dale overlooked the priest's use of Linda's maiden name. He seemed older than he had earlier in the evening and had a limp Dale hadn't noticed. He wore a brace on his left leg. Basketball injury, perhaps? Any ill feelings he had toward the visitor were lessened by the reality of the moment.

"Father, feel free to come closer," Dale said, motioning toward the casket.

"Excuse me," Susan interrupted softly. "I'm going to call Evan and see what time he's bringing Max tomorrow."

Father Clark's face clouded with emotion as he moved to within a few inches of Linda's body. Dale flinched when the priest reached out and gently stroked her hand, the left one, over her wedding ring. He could never bring himself to touch a dead body, including his wife's, and was bewildered as to how anyone else could. He shuffled his weight from one foot to another as Father Clark gazed at her for what seemed an interminable amount of time. Then, having witnessed enough, Dale asked, "Father, why did you come?"

Father Clark stopped stroking Linda's hand. He turned to Dale. "Excuse me?"

"You drove hours to pay your respects. I understand and appreciate that, but I'm at a loss as to why."

"I told you why, Dale. Remember? From earlier?"

"You talked a lot about New Jersey and Bruce Springsteen and hamburgers in Columbia. To be honest, you talked a lot about everything. What I don't understand is why you showed up after all these years. You last saw Linda when? Thirty-five years ago? Forty?"

Father Clark nodded. "That's about right. I've kept up with her, though. I knew she was a realtor. I knew she married you and had a daughter."

"But the two of you haven't spoken?"

"I would never do that, Dale. Her life was complete. She didn't need me popping out of her past."

"Okay, Father. So, you've not reached out, but here you are after all these years. You show up, make yourself at home, eat our food, and walk in during a private time between my daughter and me. Why?"

Father Clark fumbled to adjust his collar. There was perspiration on his forehead and upper lip. His eyes reddened. Dale feared that he might burst out crying. A crying priest was the last thing he needed after a long day. He wished that Susan had stuck around, just in case. She would know what to do.

"You're right, Dale. I shouldn't have come. I'll grab my coat and be on my way."

Father Clark took a final lingering glance at Linda before turning and heading down the aisle to the rear of the chapel. A side door opened, and Albert Robinson poked his fat bald head in for a look. Dale motioned him away.

"Father Clark, you still haven't answered my question. Why did you come?"

When he turned to face Dale, Father Clark appeared haggard. There was a defeated look on his face. The priest took a deep breath, then another.

"I never loved a woman before Linda," he said softly. "And I've never loved another since."

Dale had never been one to talk about feelings. Linda used to kid him about it, before the kidding had stopped. Then she just said nothing. Feelings had little place in the life of a football coach, at least a coach from Dale's era. Maybe he took it too far at times. Maybe he should have shown more emotion with Linda and Susan. Maybe he should have been more aware of their feelings. Perhaps he would change for his grandson, Max, after he and Susan moved back to Mozarkite. But starting that change with a priest he had never met before was the last thing he wanted.

Still, he had to say something.

"It was a long time ago."

"No one in the world today knows me as Clark Smith," he said as he leaned his weight on the back of a pew. "My only brother passed away ten years ago, my parents ten years before that. To the rest of the world I'm Father Clark." He paused and offered a weak smile. "It's a damn hard way to live, Dale. It's like I'm no longer a real man."

"I understand." Dale said the words but didn't feel them. To everyone in Mozarkite Dale was Coach. That was his identity. Just like Albert Robinson was the undertaker and Darcy Fannon was the hairdresser nobody went to anymore. The man had chosen to be a priest, hadn't he? Nobody forced a person into the field, as far as Dale knew. So, he was unhappy that people knew him as the priest? If things were so bad, maybe he needed to see someone for help. Like a priest? Inwardly Dale laughed at the irony. Outwardly he remained stoic as Father Clark continued.

"Anyway, I thought that by coming to pay my respects, I might find some part of myself that I've lost. Does this make any sense, Dale?"

"I think so." Another lie. Dale was starting to think Father Clark had a screw loose.

"Linda Purcell was the first girl I ever asked out on a date. We went to see *Star Wars* at the dollar theater in Columbia."

Probably a lie, Dale thought. He and Linda never went to the movies. Linda didn't care for them.

"She loved the movies. We went almost every week. *Chariots of Fire*, *Terms of Endearment*, *An Officer and a Gentleman*. Tell me, Dale, was *On Golden Pond* still her favorite movie?"

"It ranked way up there," Dale said, but he really had no idea. The only one of those movies he had heard of was *An Officer and a Gentleman*. He admired the drill sergeant in that one.

"She loved the interaction between Henry and Jane Fonda. I remember her saying how their real-life relationship spilled over onto the screen. Anyway, the movies were cheap, and she loved them, so we went whenever I could get away."

"Nice memories," Dale said, glancing toward the exit.

"I was going to ask her to marry me, Dale."

Dale stopped looking toward the exit.

"What?"

"I had the ring bought and everything. I planned to do it the weekend after we... the next weekend I saw her, but she called and broke up with me."

"Wait a minute, Father. The weekend after you *what*?"

Again with the blushing. Deeper than before.

"It was a different time, Dale. And you weren't in the picture yet. I was so smitten with Linda. Though we'd only known each other a few weeks, I was certain she was the one. I even told my parents."

"The weekend after you *what*?"

Father Clark raised his hands as if the *what* should be clear.

"We spent the weekend together at the Tiger Hotel. It was both our first times. In my case, it was also my last. I have never been happier than I was that weekend." He choked back a sob, turned away, and said, "and just like that, it was over."

Nothing else was said. Father Clark limped toward the back of the chapel. Dale was lost in his thoughts. Troubling thoughts.

Linda had also been his first. It was also a beautiful experience.

It was their wedding night.

And it was, she had shyly admitted, her first time, too.

2

*T*hey arrived home from the graveside service to a kitchen overflowing with covered dishes and the aromas of casseroles, salads, and desserts.

"I see Dorothy still has a key," Susan said, referring to their long-time neighbor as she pulled back the aluminum foil on a chocolate cake and sampled the icing with her finger.

"And the Woodersons and the Shipleys," Dale replied as he moved through the room. "Help yourself. I'm getting out of this suit."

"Hold on a second, Dad. Let's talk."

Dale had noticed how Susan kept glancing his way during the morning service. He had a hunch as to what was on her mind and didn't want to have that discussion. He continued toward the stairs.

"I'll change and we can talk later. You're moving back, so there will be plenty of time."

"Dad, please."

She sounded like Linda when she spoke. He paused on the first step. When he turned around, he saw she had followed him through the house.

"I asked you yesterday, and I'm asking again. How are you doing?"

"I'm okay."

"I've not seen you shed a tear since I got to town. I'm worried that you've got it all bottled up inside."

"I'm coping with it, Susan. Just because I don't burst into tears every five minutes doesn't mean I'm not mourning." His tone was sharper than intended. He saw hurt in his daughter's face, and that made him hurt, too. He considered apologizing, but that had never been his way. Besides, why was she so worried about his feelings?

Susan remained rooted in place for several moments, her lips pressed tightly together. She offered him a fleeting smile, started to say something, stopped, then said, "I'm going down to Mom's office for a few minutes. Mary Jo has some paperwork I need to sign. Evan and Max are supposed to be here by five. If I'm not back will you call and let me know?"

Susan turned away, grabbed her coat from the back of a chair, and headed for the door. Dale wanted to stop her and thank her for her concern. He wanted her to know how he admired her strength and intelligence, and how happy he was that she would be nearby. He wanted her to know how proud he was that she was his daughter.

He called out to her.

"Susan."

But she was already out the door.

● ● ●

THE HOUSE WAS EMPTY, typical for late afternoons when Linda was working, but it felt different. After waking from a nap, Dale entered the kitchen and glanced around. Susan had returned home at some point during his slumber. She had cleaned up the kitchen, refrigerated the food that needed to be refrigerated, and thrown away a few things, like the two plates of deviled eggs that she knew he detested. The house looked pretty much as it had for the last thirty years.

But it was different. It was four-fifteen, about the time Dale typically arrived home to an empty house. Linda usually got home at six, and he filled those ninety minutes with ESPN and the five o'clock local news out of Cape Girardeau or Poplar Bluff. Longing for routine, Dale returned to the living room and was getting settled in his tan La-Z-Boy when a sudden pain ripped through his gut. He dashed for the first-floor bathroom and barely made it. After ten minutes and a torrent of diarrhea, he struggled to his feet.

And then he flushed.

Nothing happened.

So, he flushed again.

This time the water and everything else started rising, barely stopping before cresting the rim of the bowl. He stared at the situation for a few moments. Plumbing had never been his thing. Linda always knew what to do.

He realized that he needed a plunger, but where did Linda keep it? He nearly called out her name to ask, then remembered. It took fifteen minutes of searching the house before he found it in the back of the linen closet six feet from the wayward toilet. With plunger in hand, he returned to the scene of the crime. Fortunately, the water level had gone down by half.

He flushed again and all hell broke loose.

◊ ◊ ◊

A LITTLE PAST five Dale heard the sounds of car doors slamming in the driveway. He pushed back the living room blinds and saw that Susan and Evan had arrived at the same time. He watched them emerge from their SUVs. Their faces were grim, their movements stiff. Evan opened the back door of his Lexus and went to work on what Dale assumed were the straps of Max's booster seat. After a few minutes of labor, he stepped back to give the little boy space to scramble out.

Dale hadn't seen his grandson since Fourth of July weekend five months earlier when Susan brought him for a visit. She was already separated from Evan by then, but Dale had no idea. Evan missed a lot of family gatherings through the years, so they went on as they usually did.

Max had hit a growth spurt since last summer, that much was

evident from the window. He would be five years old in the spring. Linda had recently reminded Dale that he would start kindergarten next fall. Had she been there, she would have rushed out, scooped the boy into her arms, and covered him with hugs and kisses. But Linda was gone. Dale was on his own and unsure if he should go outside or wait for them to come in. Would Evan stay for a bit or leave? If he stayed would it be awkward? Dale considered going out and striking up a conversation, perhaps trying to get Evan's side of the story. It seemed the fair thing to do. He was headed for the coat closet when common sense prevailed.

Screw the fair thing to do. Susan was his daughter and, by gosh, she would have his complete support.

By the time he returned to the window, Evan was getting into his SUV. Max stood next to Susan, waving as his father backed out of the driveway. They watched him drive away, then turned toward the house. When they opened the front door, Dale was waiting.

"Pop-Pop!" Max exclaimed as he threw himself against Dale's legs. He had indeed grown. His movements were steadier, and his arms and legs were beginning to work in unison instead of flying around like a ragdoll in the wind. Dale bent down and pulled him into an embrace, taking in the sweet outdoorsy smell of an active little boy.

"How are you, Max?" Dale tousled the boy's jet-black hair, then pulled back far enough to get a good look. He had his father's dark eyes and olive skin, but there was a bit of the Fox family there, too. He had Susan's nose and Linda's mouth. Linda used to say he had Dale's cheekbones, but Dale couldn't see it.

"Mimi's not here anymore," Max said as he checked out the room. "She got sick and died." The way the little boy said it, as much question as statement, brought tears to Susan's eyes. Dale, still on his knees, said, "Mimi is gone, Max, but we can still think about her and talk about her. I have some pictures, too. Want to see them?"

"Is she dead in the pictures?"

"Oh, no. She's alive and happy. You're in some of them. Want to get them out and look at them with Pop-Pop?"

He did, so Dale retrieved two of Linda's most recent photo

albums. He and Max sat together on the sofa where they chatted and laughed about fun times. When he looked up, an hour had passed, and Max was starting to grow tired of the pictures.

"The Homecoming bonfire starts in forty-five minutes," he said to Susan, who had silently watched them from across the living room. "Want to go?"

Susan registered a look of surprise. "Really? The bonfire?"

"You remember how much fun those were."

"With the week we've had, I don't think I can get excited about a bonfire."

"Think about Max. He's probably never been to one."

Susan shifted in her chair. "I'm not ready, Dad. I went to so many of those with Mom. It's just not... do you feel like going?"

"Why wouldn't I?"

"I just... I thought that... Mom was buried less than six hours ago. Don't you need time to..."

"I'm paid to coach football. That includes going to Homecoming activities. They'll be expecting me."

Dale was on his way upstairs to change when he thought of something. He leaned back so he could see Susan still seated in the living room.

"Don't use the downstairs bathroom. We've got a mess in there."

❂ ❂ ❂

THE BONFIRE WAS RAGING when Dale drove onto campus. For the past twenty-six years Mozarkite Junior College had signed his twice-monthly checks, and he never grew tired of the place. Twenty-six years and twenty-five Homecoming pep rallies interrupted just once, by 9/11. He steered his six-month old blue F-150, a free lease compliments of Stubby Proctor Ford, toward the open field that separated the college campus from Levin Bennett's dairy farm. Everyone he passed waved, and Dale waved back. That was expected in Mozarkite. He also noticed some curious looks. They hadn't expected him to come, but where else would he be?

He walked through the crisp night air toward the bonfire site as the Polled Hereford Marching Band struck up the school fight song, shamelessly ripped off from Mizzou decades before. The crowd was small, probably about four-hundred, typical for a season when the team was struggling. They were enthusiastic, though, patting Dale on the back as he passed and intermingling words of condolence with encouragement for the next day's game. Dale spotted his friends from the Goldrush Diner seated in their camp chairs emblazoned with the Polled Hereford logo. He changed course to stop by and say hello. Of the four, only the eldest, Homer Bennett, known to everyone as Uncle Homer, got out of his chair.

"Damned if I expected to see you here, Coach." The way Uncle Homer came toward him made Dale think he might try to give him a hug, something that would have been as out of place as a cat in a swimming pool. Fortunately, all Uncle Homer had in mind was to offer Dale the can of Pabst Blue Ribbon that was concealed in his pocket.

"You know I don't drink in front of the boys, Homer."

"Given all you're going through, nobody's going to begrudge you a beer."

Dale looked past Uncle Homer at the other three in the group. "I'll pass, but thanks anyway. Tommy looks like he might need it."

Uncle Homer considered this for a moment, then stuck the PBR back in his pocket. "That boy has enough money to buy his own damn beer."

There were four of them, five if you counted Dale. Three were Bennetts, though Uncle Homer was the only one of the three whose actual last name was Bennett. Homer's sister, Lucretia Bennett, had married a man from Gasconade County named Schaefferkoetter. They had two sons they left with Uncle Homer while they went out West to pan for gold. That was nearly sixty years ago. Lucretia and her husband had neglected to return. Few people could pronounce Schaefferkoetter. Even fewer could spell it, so out of necessity, Uncle Homer's nephews were referred to by everyone in Mozarkite as the Bennett Boys, Plumber Dick and Welder Tommy. Tommy still signed checks with his last name. Dick's checks were embossed with *Plumber Dick*. He was listed in the Mozarkite phone directory that way, too.

Attorney Larry Bob Billingsley rounded out the crew. Uncle Homer was eighty-three, his nephews were in their sixties. Larry Bob, the baby of the group, was in his forties. The Bennetts had welcomed Dale to their table at the Goldrush a few weeks after his arrival in town a quarter century before. They had remained together ever since.

"Dick," Dale said, moving closer to compensate for his friend's lack of hearing in his left ear, "can you run by the house tomorrow? I've got a stopped-up toilet."

"Maybe, but it will be late in the day. Did you try plunging it? Linda keeps the plunger in the bathroom closet behind the toilet paper."

There was a silent moment as all eyes focused on Dick. No one called out his use of present tense. Realizing his mistake, Dick coughed and said, "I'll stop by first thing after I leave the Goldrush."

"Speaking of the Goldrush, are you coming by in the morning?" Larry Bob asked.

"Probably. I have a lot of food at the house, but none of it is break-fast stuff, so—"

As Dale was speaking, the band finished its set, and people turned toward the stage where Dr. Margaret Fuller, Mozarkite Junior College President, was raising her hand for attention. Rather than her usual conservative business outfits, she was dressed in jeans and an MJC sweatshirt that made her look more like a coed than a woman in her mid-thirties.

"I'd let that one teach me a thing or two between the sheets." Uncle Homer wrongly assumed that he spoke just loud enough for his buddies to hear, but as Dale glanced around, he saw the disapproving stares of a few others.

"Dammit, you old bastard, am I going to have to defend your ass in a sexual harassment case?" Larry Bob said between sips from his flask.

Dale ignored the back and forth, concentrating instead on his new boss. President Margaret Fuller had arrived July 1, replacing the irreplaceable Dr. Daniel Trebelhorn Parker, who had ruled as MJC President for forty years. At thirty-five, Dr. Fuller was a stark contrast to the septuagenarian Professor Parker. The fact that she was unattached, blonde, and drop-dead gorgeous had led a handful of unattached Mozarkite men to inquire as to her availability. They got nowhere. Dale had heard through the grapevine that she was seeing a community college dean from her old school in St. Louis. He never asked, and she never volunteered the information. What was certain was that Dr. Fuller worked the longest hours of anyone at school.

"Welcome to our annual Homecoming bonfire and pep rally!" Dr. Fuller effused. "I'm pleased to be a part of the festivities and hope we'll see all of you tomorrow afternoon as our Herefords take on Iowa Western."

The crowd cheered its approval as the band kicked into high gear, and the cheerleaders flipped and danced their way across a makeshift stage. After a few minutes of celebration, Dr. Fuller returned to the microphone.

"Sadly, Coach Fox isn't with us tonight. As you know, his wife, Linda, passed away this week."

Heads turned toward Dale as he stood among his friends off to one side. He knew he should step forward but did not want to embarrass his boss, so he remained where he was as she continued.

"If you will, please join me in a moment of silence in memory of Linda Fox."

Heads bowed, eyes closed, except the eyes of those who glanced at Dale during the extended moment of silence.

"Thank you. Now without further ado, it's my pleasure to introduce your team—"

"Coach Fox is right over here!" Uncle Homer yelled out.

Dr. Fuller searched the crowd until she spotted him, then smiled and said, "I was mistaken. Ladies and Gentlemen, it is my pleasure to introduce Coach Dale Fox and your Mozarkite Junior College Polled Herefords!"

❖ ❖ ❖

THE HOUSE WAS quiet when Dale returned home. Susan's car was in the driveway, which likely meant she and Max were already asleep. Weary, yet still stoked from the bonfire, he rummaged through the array of food containers in the fridge until he had a full plate, took it to the La-Z-Boy, and turned on the TV. ESPN was highlighting the next day's college games, a rundown that never included junior colleges. After hearing more than he cared to about big-time programs with their big-time coaches and players, Dale channel surfed until he came to a movie network playing a title that caught his attention.

On Golden Pond.

He recognized Henry Fonda from *Mister Roberts* and *Midway*, two movies about war and military life Dale had seen numerous times as a kid. The character he was playing in *On Golden Pond* was a much older man struggling with memory loss. As he watched the story unfold, the previous evening's conversation with Father Clark ran through his mind.

She loved the movies. We went almost every week. Chariots of Fire, Terms of Endearment, An Officer and a Gentleman.

Dale, was On Golden Pond *still her favorite movie?*

Dale couldn't remember the last time they went to the movies together. He had read in the *Messenger* that Mozarkite's downtown cinema, the once-palatial *Mercury*, had been chopped up to allow more movies to be shown, but never saw it in person. He vaguely remembered some of the movie titles that Linda and Susan had seen years before. *The Lion King* was one. There was also one about a mermaid and another about a kid whose family left him home by himself. But as far as the last movie he and Linda had seen, just the two of them? He had no idea. Despite what Father Clark said, Linda never cared about movies. What other misinformation was the priest peddling?

Linda was very special to me.

Every guy in my fraternity had a crush on her.

They couldn't believe it was me who caught her.

Caught her!

I never loved a woman before Linda, and I never loved another after.

I was going to ask her to marry me.

We spent the weekend together at the Tiger Hotel. It was both our first times.

The more he thought about it the more certain Dale was. Father Clark was a nutjob. He had probably known Linda, but the other stuff? Likely all made up. Creations of the overactive, undersexed mind of a depressed clergyman in a midlife crisis.

But if that were the case, why had their conversation felt so personal? So intimate?

The staircase creaked. Susan appeared. "Care for company?" she asked softly.

Dale reached for the remote. "Sure. I was just looking for something good to watch. There's a Friday night game on, Western Kentucky and Furman. You want to watch?"

"I'd rather watch this," Susan said, pointing at the TV.

Dale glanced at the screen. Henry Fonda was grumbling at the actress playing his wife, the one who kept calling him an old poop.

"You know this movie?"

Susan laughed. "Dad, what cave have you been living in? Henry Fonda and Katharine Hepburn won Oscars for this movie."

Dale shrugged.

"It was Mom's favorite. I figured that was why you were watching it."

Dale shrugged again. "I thought she liked *Officer and a Gentleman* more."

"Nope. This was her favorite. We watched it again last Christmas, while you and Evan were putting together Max's tricycle. Mom said she actually saw it the week it came out. I assumed that was with you."

Dale, was On Golden Pond *still her favorite movie?*

"Not me, honey."

"Look, there's Jane Fonda," Susan said, her eyes glued to the screen. "She's so beautiful and a really good actress. And did you catch her name, Dad?"

"Yeah. Jane Fonda. I know who she is."

"No, silly, her name in the movie?"

"I missed it."

"Listen for a minute."

It was several scenes before the actress playing Henry Fonda's wife finally spoke the name of Jane Fonda's character. As soon as she did, Susan turned to Dale.

"Chelsea."

"Okay," Dale replied. "And this is important, why?"

"*Chelsea*, Dad? Doesn't it ring a bell?"

And then, the bell was rung.

Linda's black and white border collie. He never understood where the name came from.

Chelsea.

He asked Linda once, soon after they purchased Chelsea from the breeder.

"Why Chelsea?"

"I just like the name."

"For Chelsea Clinton?"

Linda had laughed at that. She was a Republican back then and had little use for the Clintons. Her politics had later taken a hard turn to the left, but that was after she named the dog.

"Mom named Chelsea for her." Susan pointed at the screen. "And speaking of Chelsea, where is she?"

"Out back, I imagine. She stays out there during the day."

There were several beats of silence before Dale stood and stretched. "I'll go get her and bring her in for the night."

◉ ◉ ◉

AT THE CORNER of Main and Cypress, Dale came upon a Mozarkite police cruiser parked in the First Baptist Church lot. An unexpected, yet familiar face was behind the wheel. Wade Ricketts, proud member of the redneck Ricketts clan and all-around pain in the ass.

"Evening, Wade," Dale said to the scruffy cop. "How long have you been on the force?"

"Two weeks, Coach. I've already nailed forty-six speeders, so watch yourself."

"Not going to find many speeders here," Dale said, nodding toward the dark church.

"The Chief wants me to keep an eye on the Tip Top across the street," Ricketts replied with a grin. "Since them towelheads took over, word around town is that they're selling booze to minors."

Dale never considered himself a particularly enlightened man but was stung and offended by Wade Ricketts's slur. The Ricketts were the whitest and trashiest of any white trash in the county, and the fact that Chief Mike Mayberry had deemed Wade worthy of a job on the police force meant that Dale would be voting for whoever ran against him in the next election. Linda had sold the Naser family, the Tip Top's owners for the past seven months, their home on Rolfe Street. They had already put more money into renovating the Tip Top than the previous owners had in twenty years, and to think they would jeopardize that by selling liquor to kids was ridiculous.

"What are you doing out so late, Coach?" Wade asked. "You got a big game tomorrow."

"Linda's dog ran off, and I was wondering if you might have seen it? Border Collie, black and white."

"Tagged?"

Dale said it was.

"Papers?"

Dale nodded.

"Nice dog like that might have been kidnapped right out of your yard, Coach. I mean, everybody in town knows you've been up at the funeral home all week."

Dale chose his words carefully. If Chelsea had been kidnapped it would have been just as likely that a member of Wade Ricketts's family was involved as anyone else.

"She dug out. She's done it a few times before."

"You check the city pound?"

Dale sighed. It was just like a Ricketts to make a simple thing difficult.

"Wade, you know as well as I do that the pound is closed at this time of night. I was hoping you might know if there were any dogs being kept there."

Wade had to know. The city pound was in the basement of the jail. The kid was being an ass, and the longer he kept Dale waiting, the more likely Dale was to have a frank discussion with Chief Mayberry in the morning.

Wade chuckled and sounded like a bully when he did it. "Nah, Coach, there ain't no dogs in the city pound. How about I keep an eye out for your collie? Officer Murray is on patrol tonight, too. I'll alert her so she can be on the lookout."

"That'll work, Wade. Thanks." Dale rolled up his window and continued down Cypress. His phone buzzed. Susan.

"I got Max up so we can look, too. Where do you want us to begin?"

"Try the south side. Lisa Murray is probably patrolling out that way. If you see her, let her know."

"Did she used to be Lisa Sprecher?"

"She married the Murray boy two years ago, the one whose family runs the grain elevator."

"I'll get on it, Dad. We'll find Chelsea. We'll find her for Mom."

3

"*D*id you try the city pound, Coach?" Larry Bob asked over the hubbub of the diner.

"She's not there, Larry Bob. I went by again this morning and checked. Did you boys know that Wade Ricketts is working nights for the town police?"

"Best way to stop crime is to hire the sons of bitches who commit 'em, I reckon." Uncle Homer's observation was met with nods of agreement from the others seated around the table at the Goldrush Diner. Dale had not planned to stop by, but after striking out at finding Chelsea the night before, he was hopeful that someone among the two dozen regulars might have spotted her. No one had. He took a seat, planning to stay just long enough for a cup of coffee, but dug in when Patsy placed his usual breakfast plate in front of him.

"I can't believe Mike Mayberry hired one of the Ricketts," Welder Tommy said.

"Especially Wade," Plumber Dick added. "He's mean and dumb. That's a bad combination for anybody, let alone somebody who's toting a gun for the town."

"Mayberry wanted at least one man on his force who's dumber

than him," Uncle Homer said, drawing guffaws from several of the regulars. Dale sipped his coffee as he surveyed the group of men who had become his closest and most unlikely friends. They were not much to look at. Uncle Homer was as foul-mouthed as any sailor. Rumor was that he had been asked in the 1960's by the Deacons at Mozarkite Lutheran Church never to set foot in their sanctuary again, a claim that Uncle Homer would neither confirm nor deny. His nephews, Dick and Tommy, were identical twins, though no one would ever guess it. Plumber Dick was tall and rangy, thin enough to thaw out frozen pipes in even the narrowest crawlspaces. Welder Tommy, a lifelong bachelor, was squat and bald and smoked two packs of Parliaments a day while he worked at his craft, often without the required eye protection. One of the two had suffered a traumatic head injury as a teen, rendering him in Uncle Homer's words, 'half-retarded,' but after knowing them for a quarter century, Dale couldn't recall which brother it was.

"I'm headed over to your place to fix that toilet," Plumber Dick said as he stood up. "Should I ring the bell, so I don't scare Susan?"

"She's out looking for Linda's dog. The back door is open, so go on in, Dick. I'm sorry for the mess you're going to find."

Larry Bob also got up. "I gotta head out, too. Wilma's getting her hair done first thing, so I'm opening the office."

"You let your secretary come in any time she wants?" Uncle Homer said. "Who exactly runs that office?"

"I've never denied the fact that Wilma Claxton is the glue that keeps the Law Offices of Larry Bob Billingsley humming along," Larry Bob deadpanned. "She always gets her hair done first thing Saturday morning."

Does Wilma go to Darcy Fannon's shop?" Dale asked.

"Not since about fifteen years ago. She went to get her roots colored, whatever that means, and came back to the office with her hair whiter than a polar bear in a snowstorm."

"I remember that," Uncle Homer laughed. "Wilma looked like a big old Q-tip."

"Watch who you're calling big, Uncle Homer," Larry Bob snapped. "I can't guarantee your safety if word gets back to Wilma."

"She'd kick your ass for sure, Uncle Homer," Welder Tommy laughed.

Larry Bob nodded. "And there'd be no way I could defend you in court, because I was here when you said it."

"When are you going to give up those Saturday morning hours at the office, Larry Bob?" Uncle Homer asked. "Does anyone even come in?"

"You'd be surprised," Larry Bob said as he tossed a quarter tip on the table. "Between Friday bar fights and lovers' spats over who controls the TV remote, I get plenty of visitors. See you gentlemen at the game later."

"I guess I'll go, too," Dale said. He slid a twenty-dollar bill under his plate, part for his check and the rest to make up for Larry Bob's lousy tip. "I've got a ballgame this afternoon, so if anybody sees Linda's dog, grab her and leave me a message."

◊ ◊ ◊

"HEY EVERYBODY, this is Coach Fox. Your Mozarkite Junior College Polled Herefords give everything they've got to win each game. The same is true for the boys down at Stubby Proctor Ford. Their selection of cars and trucks is the largest between Poplar Bluff and Cape Girardeau, and their service is championship quality. Best of all, they put you, the customer, at the front of the line. Stubby, Craig, and Topper give everything they've got to get you behind the wheel of a new Ford car or truck. You've seen the sporty F-150 I drive. They have plenty more like it, so if you're in the market for a new vehicle, head out to Stubby Proctor Ford. They're right there where they've been for forty years, on the main highway south of town. Tell them Coach sent you and get a free case of Turtle Wax with your purchase."

After getting a thumbs up from the dope-smoking kid who ran the radio station on weekends, Dale removed the headset and placed it on the control board. Another commercial spot done. Conway Twitty was singing about tight fittin' jeans as Dale exited the cramped studio on the south end of Main Street. The driver of a passing Chevy truck blew his horn and waved. From across the street, Miriam Keplinger wished him and the team good luck as she unlocked the public library. The morning was sunny; temperatures were in the upper forties.

It was football weather.

And that made Coach Dale Fox a very happy man.

◊ ◊ ◊

"HEY EVERYBODY! From Crowley Field in Mozarkite, this is Wally Westmoreland, the voice of your MJC Polled Herefords who will be taking on the always tough Iowa Western Panthers in just a few minutes. Iowa Western comes into the game seven and three and in second place in the conference standings. Your Herefords are three and seven and in eighth place. But, folks, after an emotional week here in Mozarkite, win-loss records don't mean a thing. I've been watching this Hereford team practice and can tell you they've come to play.

More on that in a minute, but first I need to tell you that this week's game is brought to you by your good friends at Clapp Feed Store, where you can stock up this week on Purina Goat Chow at twenty percent off the regular price, and by the folks at Stubby Proctor Ford, the official Ford dealer of the Polled Herefords. Other sponsors include Roland's Barbershop, Wheedleton Grocery, and Wheatley Farms. Your patronage of these businesses is the best way to show how much you appreciate them bringing you Polled Hereford football right here on Country 104.

◊ ◊ ◊

DALE KEPT his pregame remarks short and to the point. Final game of the season. Homecoming. Big crowd. Lots of out-of-towners. Play hard. End the year on a high note. He was about to send the team out to the field when Jeff Devereux asked to speak. Dale remembered their conversation in the condolence line and motioned his quarterback to come to the front. Dale noticed his three assistant coaches casting nervous glances at one another. They knew what he knew. Jeff Devereux might say just about anything.

Jeff silently peered about the room, making eye contact with the fifty-four young men seated in front of him. He adjusted his crotch, sniffed his fingers, and spoke.

"It's not been a great season; I know that. We started out okay, but things went into the shitter pretty quick after that loss at Northeast Kentucky."

Coach considered telling Jeff to tone down the language, but when he looked into the faces of his players, he knew they were hanging on every word. For better or worse, Jeff was their leader. Perhaps his words could break through the funk that had descended on the Polled Herefords over the second half of the season. He allowed Jeff to continue.

"We lost our focus after that game, and as hard as Coach Fox and our other coaches pushed us, we never got it back. Danbury, we should have won. Our defense spotted South Tennessee fifteen they should never have gotten, but we damn near came back and won."

Dale worried how the defense might take the criticism but judging by the nods of agreement he saw around the room, he let it go.

"McCrackenville and Granger, now they just flat kicked our asses, but we kinda expected that."

More nods of agreement.

"But this past week, after Miss Linda died, I felt a change. Did anybody else feel it?"

Hands went up. A few players spoke out.

"Monday practice was the most intense of the season. I know you felt it, too, because I looked across the field at the defense. Am I right?"

Several players responded.

"For sure!"

"You know it!"

"Freaking savage!"

"I decided right then and there that today's game would be dedicated to Miss Linda and Coach. And when I talked to you guys, what did you say?"

The shouted responses were varied, loud, and emotional. There were tears from a few.

"And it doesn't matter that Iowa Western has won seven games, and we've won just three, does it?"

"No!" the team shouted in unison.

"And it doesn't matter that they beat Granger and Danbury, does it?"

"No!"

"It wouldn't matter if they'd just kicked the Green Bay Packers' asses, would it?"

"No!"

"Because this is our field and those people out there are our fans, am I right?"

"Yeah!"

"And most important, it's our time to win, am I right?"

Players stood up as they yelled their responses. It was as emotionally charged as Dale had seen this group of young men. Their eyes were on fire; their faces determined.

"So, let's go out there and knock Iowa Western's asses back to whatever state they came from," Jeff exclaimed, nearly breathless with excitement. "Let's hit them like they've never been hit. Let's block and tackle and run and throw like the team we know we are. Can we do that?"

"Yes!"

"And when it's done, we'll hand the game ball to Coach Fox so he can put it in his trophy case and always remember the way we won for Miss Linda. Are you ready?"

They were.

◊ ◊ ◊

"YOUR POLLED HEREFORDS HAVE JUST TAKEN the field and, folks, from up here in the press box, I can tell you they look excited. Hereford Quarterback

Jeff Devereux announced that the team has dedicated today's game to the memory of Miss Linda Fox, beloved wife of the team's longtime coach. Miss Linda passed away suddenly earlier this week. She was a fine lady who was beloved by Mozarkite residents past and present. In an exclusive interview here on Country 104 this past Friday afternoon, Devereux said that the team has been practicing with an intensity that he hasn't seen in his two years on the Mozarkite campus. We should expect a hard-fought game on both sides. And we'll be back for the opening kickoff right after this message from Stubby Proctor Ford.

● ● ●

DALE SURVEYED the crowd as he followed the team across the field to the sideline. At least a thousand, he estimated, and while they filled just half the Crowley Field bleachers, their number was nearly double the attendance at the past few home games. It was a far cry from the glory days of fifteen and twenty years ago, when the stands were full every week, but times had changed. Regardless of the size of the crowd, it was football. The players were charged up and Dale was where he felt most at home.

It was time to go to work.

4

─────────

"*Hey, everybody, we're back at Crowley Field, where your Mozarkite Junior College Polled Herefords have just suffered a tough 41-7 loss to the Iowa Western Panthers. This is Wally Westmoreland, and we're waiting for a few words about today's game from Coach Dale Fox down in the Hereford locker room on what has been a bittersweet afternoon. Mozarkite got off to a quick start with a kickoff return for a touchdown, followed by an interception of the Iowa Western quarterback. That was all the excitement they could muster, however, as Iowa Western demonstrated why they are now eight and three and close to the top of the conference standings. Remember, folks, Coach Fox's interview is sponsored by Stubby Proctor Ford. Coach Fox drives a Stubby Proctor Ford, and so should you.*"

◊ ◊ ◊

THE KID, a communications major named Corey, entered Dale's office, handed him a headset and took a seat across the desk.

"Thirty seconds," he said before burying his face in his cellphone. Dale listened and waited his turn as Wally Westmoreland extolled the benefits of a Stubby Proctor Ford. He heard a click as his microphone was opened.

"Hereford Coach Dale Fox joins us now. Tough one, Coach. Expectations were very high going into today's game, but the Panthers proved to be too much."

For the next five minutes Dale provided the usual bland responses about how the team played hard and how good the opponent was. Between his canned answers and Wally's repetitive shilling of Stubby Proctor Ford, little of consequence was discussed. That was as it always was.

Until Wally took a left turn into uncharted territory.

"Coach, the Herefords finished the season with just three wins. That's one less than last year and the year before. Are you seeing signs that things will begin to turn around next year?"

What kind of question was that? And how was Dale supposed to answer? He felt a fluttering in his stomach and hoped it wasn't a recurrence of yesterday's diarrhea.

"We'll continue to recruit the same type of players we've always gone after, Wally. Young men who want to play football and achieve in the classroom. That kind of man may not always be the best football player, but that's not what's important to us. We expect our players to represent our college and community in a way that puts us in the very best light. Whether we win three games or a national championship, we do it with the right kind of players."

"Understood, Coach. Thanks for your time. Enjoy the offseason and good luck on the recruiting trail. That's Coach Dale Fox, whose words were brought to you by—"

Dale pulled the headset off, tossed it to the kid, and headed for the shower. When he returned a few minutes later, one of his assistants said that a reporter from the *Mozarkite Messenger* was looking for him.

"A girl," the coach cautioned. "She's in the hallway. She said she would come in, but I told her no way."

"Are the players gone?"

"They were out of here before the fans. It's just you and me, Coach."

"Give me ten minutes and send her in."

◊ ◊ ◊

HER HAIR WAS CUT SHORT. She had bangs and wore large glasses that made her eyes appear huge. Had Dale not known better, he would have figured her for a Chemistry major.

"Coach Fox, I'm Heaven Knight, the *Messenger's* new sportswriter." She confidently offered her hand. "I apologize for not having introduced myself before. I'd like to ask you a few questions."

"I'm short for time... do you go by Heaven?"

She looked at Dale curiously. "What else would I go by?"

Her abruptness caught him off guard. "I don't know. I guess maybe a nickname or something."

"Heaven is fine, Coach Fox." Without being asked, she took a seat. Dale did the same behind his desk. "Coach Fox, your teams are known for excelling in the classroom. To what do you attribute that?"

"I figured you wanted to talk about today's game." Dale grimaced as he sat back in his chair. "Of course, given the outcome, it's probably better that we talk about something else."

"Can I quote you on that, Coach Fox?"

"On what? I haven't said anything yet."

"That you would prefer to talk about something besides today's game."

Dale stared at her for a few moments. It was a ploy he sometimes used to send a message to players who were too brash for their own good or were sticking their noses into things that were none of their business. It worked with the players. Heaven Knight just stared back, waiting for an answer.

"No, I'd prefer you not. I'm used to working with Randall Shockley. He knew what to print and what to leave out."

"We will always be on the record, Coach Fox, unless you expressly tell me otherwise. Now, back to the question. Your teams are typically at the top of the conference academically, correct?"

Dale nodded. "Eleven of the last thirteen years, to be exact. It's important to us that Mozarkite football players hold their own in the classroom. Regardless of whether they go on to play Division I football or not, they need to earn a college diploma and be ready for whatever life brings next."

"Do those standards hurt your teams' performance on the field?"

"We get the best players we can and coach them up. That's what we've always done, and quite frankly we've been very successful at it."

Heaven Knight glanced at a page in the skinny media guide the college put out, then said, "Mozarkite football teams have had four losing seasons in the last five, Coach Fox. And seven of the last ten. At what point do you worry more about the quality of players and less about the academics?"

"Never. That's not the kind of coach I am, Miss Knight. And it's not the kind of institution this is. We value academics above everything else."

"Coach Fox, you haven't had a recruiting coordinator for two years. Does that limit your chances at getting the best athletes?"

"All of my assistants recruit. I do, too."

"But the position of recruiting coordinator, it's been vacant since..." Heaven Knight paused to check her notes. "...since Coach Willis Tompkins stepped aside due to illness."

"We expect Coach Tompkins to return." Dale's tone was pointed, but he didn't care.

"But, Coach Fox, Mr. Tompkins is—"

"I won't discuss an employee of the college with you, young lady. And I'm going to cut this interview short. I have other obligations."

Heaven Knight jotted something down before looking at Dale. "Thank you, Coach Fox." She stood and headed for the door. "Coach Fox, two more things." She said as she stood in the doorway.

"Yes?"

"First, I haven't pushed the locker room issue, but next season I will expect full and complete access to players after the game, just as you allowed my predecessor."

"I cannot agree to that."

"Then I suggest you read up on the subject, Coach Fox. The world moved past this issue decades ago."

"What else was there you wanted to say, young lady?"

"Heaven, Coach Fox. Heaven or Miss Knight. Not 'young lady.' And the second thing is to express my condolences for the loss of Mrs. Fox."

"Thank you."

"I lost my mother seven months ago this week. It hurts like hell. Every day."

And with that, Heaven Knight took her leave. Dale gave her a few minutes head start to avoid crossing paths in the parking lot. He was just getting in his truck when he felt his phone vibrate in his coat pocket. Susan's name appeared.

"Dad, she's back."

For some ridiculous reason, he thought for a split second that his daughter was referring to Linda.

"Who's back?"

"Chelsea. When Max and I got home from the game she was tied to the front porch. She's fine."

"That's good news. We certainly could use a little of it, couldn't we?"

"Yeah... sorry about the game, Dad. But come on home and have a plate of leftovers with Max and me. That'll make you feel better."

Dale doubted it would, but it sounded better than an empty house.

"See you in a few."

5

MOZARKITE MESSENGER
Sunday Sports Edition
Time for a Change?
By Heaven Knight

*T*he words you are about to read might not be popular with many in the community, but that's all right.

Mozarkite Junior College entered yesterday's football game against Iowa Western a heavy underdog. Still, the atmosphere in the stands at Crowley Field was charged with excitement. Some of it carried over from the Homecoming festivities that began with Friday night's bonfire, but mostly it was a feeling that the Polled Herefords were ready to pull off the upset of what had become a lost season, a game that had been dedicated to the memory of Linda Fox, wife of Coach Dale Fox, who passed away earlier in the week.

Second-year Quarterback and team captain Jeff Devereux boldly predicted that the Herefords would beat Iowa Western. He spoke of the hard work that had gone into the week's practices, and how the players were confident they would find a way to beat a Panther team that had bested MJC five of the past six years.

The final score was 41-7. The other guys won.

And, other than a few plays at the beginning of the game, the Polled Herefords were outsized, outmanned, and out hustled. All the practices and all the emotion in the world would not have been enough for this group of players to win.

MJC's football team is not very good.

In fact, they are terrible.

Sure, they get the basics. Even a casual football fan can see that MJC players know how to tackle, block, and do the little things. So do many junior high teams, but you will not find them matching up against Iowa Western, either.

The loss brought an end to another losing season for MJC, their fourth in the last five years and seventh in the last ten. Talk to Coach Dale Fox, though, and you get a feeling that wins are secondary.

"It's important to us that Mozarkite football players hold their own in the classroom. Regardless of whether they go on to play Division I football or not," the veteran coach said in a postgame interview. "That's what we've always done, and quite frankly we've been very successful at it."

Successful?

Coach Fox's won-lost record as MJC's head coach is a lackluster 124-147. Over the past five years that record is just 18-37. While teams from smaller schools, such as Danbury Community College and Northeast Kentucky have adapted with the times, the MJC football team has struggled to find its way over the past decade. Recruiting in particular seems to have taken a back seat, and Coach Fox admits that he has worked without a recruiting coordinator for the past two seasons. Could that be why the Polled Herefords are getting routed on the field? Many players, including Devereux, while obviously talented, do not possess the skills needed to start at the junior college level. An opposing coach who requested anonymity, summed it up this way:

"If the teams are evenly matched, Dale Fox's teams will beat their opponents most of the time. The problem for MJC is that they don't attract big-name players. Coach Fox doesn't take the risks needed to win at this level today."

The question remains, can Coach Dale Fox still provide the type of leadership that wins games? If so, prove it, Coach Fox. If not, it's time for a change.

❢ ❢ ❢

IT WAS easy to guess which of the Third Baptist Church faithful had read the Sunday paper. As soon as they spotted Dale handing out bulletins at his usual post at the side entrance, they made a beeline for him.

"I'm cancelling my *Messenger* subscription first thing Monday morning."

"That hussy doesn't know the first thing about what's important to us."

"I'm going down to the paper and demand they fire her."

"We support you, Coach. Winning isn't the most important thing."

The supporters were fired up, vociferous, and sincere. They were also overwhelmingly women. A few men let Dale know they were supportive, but many others hung back. Was there anything to that? Nah, Dale decided. Typical guys. Just as well, because all the attention was embarrassing. It was nothing, though, compared to what happened when Pastor Mark took his place behind the pulpit.

"I had a sermon prepared today about what we can learn from David and the Philistines, a quite good sermon, if I do say so myself." Pastor Mark's awkward attempt at humor brought muted smiles to the faces of a few of the seventy-five or so in attendance. Others remained somber, as was the way of Third Baptist Church. Dale had always appreciated how they left the jokes, hand-raising, and drum playing to Pentecostals and the liberals around the corner at Second Baptist. Linda felt they took it too far and had started finding reasons not to attend. He remembered the argument they had last spring when she announced her intention to attend some non-denominational bunch that were meeting in the high school band room. Dale refused to go with her. Deacons do not just up and leave their churches. Linda had acquiesced, but he sensed a change in her after that. She was less willing to jump in and help with the things that needed to be done at Third Baptist. Work was keeping her busy, she said. He also noticed that she was listening to that rock-and-roll Christian station out of Memphis.

"But," the Pastor continued, "God gave me a new message this morning."

Had Dale been given a say in the matter he would have insisted that Pastor Mark stick with David and the Philistines. The new message was all about how Job remained faithful during hard times, and while Pastor Mark did his best to make his sermon applicable to everyone, it was painfully obvious that it had been written for Coach Dale Fox, especially when he tried to work in a few football references. Pastor Mark knew nothing about football, and before the sermon reached its merciful conclusion, Job was throwing Hail Mary passes to his linebackers, and God had assumed the position of tight end. Congregants streamed toward the exits as if they were being timed in the hundred-meter dash. Dale was among the first out.

❦ ❦ ❦

"Mom would've kicked Heaven Knight's ass."

Susan was right. Dale knew it. He still remembered how fired up she became when the conference passed him over for Coach of the Year fifteen years earlier after he won eight games and finished second in the standings. The fifteen members of the selection committee, mostly small-town sports reporters, probably remembered, too, given the scathing letters they received from Linda Fox.

"She's a young reporter who's trying to make a name for herself," Dale said between bites from another plate of leftovers.

"At your expense," Susan retorted as she cleaned up the kitchen. "You should write a letter to the editor. Better yet, you should go down and see Scott Pirtle in person. That girl needs to learn what's acceptable in Mozarkite."

"Haven't you heard the expression, 'never argue with someone who buys ink by the barrel?'"

Susan came up behind Dale and planted a kiss on the top of his head. "Dad, you were here before Heaven Knight was born, and you'll be here long after she moves on. This is your home, not hers. If I see her in town, I swear I'll..."

"You'll what, Mama?"

Dale marveled at how her son's three words diffused his daughter's anger. She glanced at Max, smiled, and said, "I'll help carry her groceries."

"Does the lady have trouble carrying her groceries?"

"She would if her arms were broken." Susan winked at Dale. "Want to go apartment shopping with Max and me?"

"What? I assumed you would just live here."

"This is your house. The last thing you need is a five-year-old running around."

"Seriously, Susan, you know there's plenty of space."

Susan took a seat at the table, reached across, and squeezed her father's hand. "Dad, no offense, but we need our space. And so do you. You and I both need to learn to be self-sufficient."

"I'm perfectly capable of being self-sufficient."

This made Susan laugh. "Seriously? What did you have for breakfast this morning?"

"Cereal. Some of those marshmallow charms you picked up."

"You ate cereal. What do you usually have on Sunday mornings?"

She had a point. Linda had always made a big Sunday breakfast, even if she wasn't going to church.

"Do you even know how to cook an egg, Dad?"

Dale scoffed. "Anybody can break open an egg."

Susan got up and went to the refrigerator. She returned with a raw egg that she handed to Dale. "Show me. Break it open on the edge of your plate."

Dale tapped the egg softly against the plate, but nothing happened. He tried again, same result.

An amused expression came to Susan's face as she watched. "You're a big strong football coach. You've got to try harder than that."

The egg nearly exploded with Dale's next effort. Yolk, whites, and shell fell onto the plate. And the table. And the floor.

"I figured," Susan said, grabbing a wet cloth and tossing it across the table. "You're helpless, and the sooner you're forced to fend for yourself, the better we'll all be."

"I'll be fine. I just wish you and Max would stay here."

Susan shook her head. "So, do you want to go apartment hunting with us or not?"

Dale wiped his hands on a napkin, stood up, and took his plate to the sink. "Let me put Chelsea outside, then I'll be ready."

"Any idea who tied her up on the porch?"

"Probably someone who heard me talking about her at the Goldrush." Dale picked up Max, cleaned his hands and face, then put him down. "Tell Mama you want to live here with Pop-Pop," he said, catching a stink-eye from Susan.

"We have our first appointment at two," she responded. "And don't be saying stuff like that."

6

"*And* I'll tell you another thing. If those damned Democrats don't get off their asses and start—"

Dale looked up from his breakfast plate when Uncle Homer unexpectedly shut up. The old man's eyes were locked on the Goldrush's front door where a bell had just announced the arrival of another customer. Judging by the look on Uncle Homer's face, this one might have been better off eating breakfast at home. The fallout from Heaven Knight's story in the *Messenger* had subsided somewhat over the past three days but was far from dead and buried.

"Scott Pirtle, get your ass over here!"

Pirtle, the second-generation owner and publisher of the *Mozarkite Messenger*, was not a man used to being addressed in such a way, and while he was too scrawny to get physical about it, even with an old man, Dale would have understood if he told Uncle Homer to go to hell.

"Give him what-for, Uncle Homer," Welder Tommy encouraged.

"He's too chickenshit to get in your face," Plumber Dick teased. The brothers sounded like schoolyard kids instead of senior citizens.

"Uncle Homer," Dale said quietly. "I know what you're thinking about doing, and I'm asking you to leave it alone."

Pirtle remained just inside the door, absorbing the onslaught directed his way. Uncle Homer pulled himself to his feet, a process that seemed to take forever, leaned on the table, and spoke over the hubbub of the diner, "You heard me Pirtle. Get over here. Now."

That quieted the hubbub. All eyes were on Uncle Homer, except for the eyes that were on Scott Pirtle. Pirtle considered his options for a few moments, then said, "If you need to talk to me, Mr. Bennett, you can come by the newspaper office. I'm here to eat breakfast, and I would prefer to eat it in peace."

Like spectators at a tennis match, heads turned back and forth between Scott Pirtle and Uncle Homer. People in Mozarkite liked a good scrap, and this time they would not be disappointed.

"Peace? If you're so keen on peace, you son-of-a-bitch, how about starting with this man's?" He pointed to Dale.

"Uncle Homer, sit down." Dale's tone left no room for argument, but Uncle Homer was too riled to notice.

"That girl sportswriter of yours kicked Coach when he was down, and by God, I want her fired."

"Me too," Tommy and Dick echoed in unison.

"Why the hell are you doing this here, Uncle Homer?" Larry Bob's lawyerly attempt at encouraging restraint came too late. Sweat broke out on Uncle Homer's forehead and neck. He would either say what he needed to say or have a heart attack. Dale almost hoped it was the latter.

"That article was a low blow," a Goldrush regular said from a nearby table.

"Coach just lost his wife," another regular chimed in, stating the obvious.

While a half-dozen others shared their disapproval, Scott Pirtle remained calm. If Dale had to guess, he would have speculated that Pirtle might be trying to conceal his pleasure with the fracas. Then the newspaperman spoke, and Dale knew he was right.

"I don't tell my staff what to write or not write." Pirtle parsed his words while speaking in a level tone of voice. "Miss Knight researched her story, chased down sources, and reported what she came up with." He paused, looked toward Dale and said, "Coach, I respect you, but I won't have you trying to dictate what goes in my paper."

"I haven't said a thing, Scott." Dale said.

"That's because he's too good a man for that." Patsy Werner had emerged from her kitchen and was more than happy to pile on. "Randall Shockley worked at your paper for years, and he never wrote garbage like that."

"Miss Knight isn't Randall Shockley," Pirtle said calmly. "She's her own person. She has excellent investigative and reporting skills. She won't always write things we can all agree with, but don't we want differing opinions to be presented in our local paper?"

It quickly became obvious that most people in the Goldrush Diner did not want differing opinions, at least when it came to Dale. Three minutes after he entered the Goldrush, Scott Pirtle was back out on the sidewalk.

"You shouldn't have banned him for life," Dale said to Patsy as she refilled his coffee cup.

"I'm pulling my advertising from his paper, too."

"How will people find out the weekly specials?"

"Jumping Jesus, Coach," Plumber Dick said testily. "Them specials ain't changed in ten years. Even with my messed-up brain I can remember that Monday is always Salisbury steak."

So, it was Dick who had suffered the head injury. Dale would have bet it was Tommy.

When the Goldrush had returned to some semblance of normalcy, Larry Bob, seated next to Dale, leaned over and said softly, "Know what I think?"

"What?"

"That Scott Pirtle is happier than a pig in slop that everybody's pissed. He thinks it'll sell some papers."

"Know what, Larry Bob?"

"What?"

"I think you're right."

◊ ◊ ◊

SUSAN WAS SEATED at the kitchen table when Dale returned home. Max was in front of the TV.

"Does he watch a lot of television?" Dale asked.

"Probably too much, but I have to study. I'm taking my final realtor tests tomorrow morning in Springfield."

"Are you taking Max with you?"

Susan looked up distractedly. "Yeah, Dad, he's going to help me with the math section. What do you think?"

"I didn't know. That's why I asked."

"He's staying with Aunt Fran and Uncle Willis."

"What if Willis needs all of Fran's attention?"

"She practically begged me to let Max stay. She said Uncle Willis sleeps through the morning, then watches TV." Susan paused, then said, "What are you doing home on a Wednesday?"

"Bereavement leave. The new college president mandates that we take our full leave period. I have three days of bereavement, so I'm using them."

"You weren't here yesterday or the day before."

"I had one of the maintenance men sneak me into my office. He's at the dentist today, though, so I'm stuck here."

"Gee, Dad, sorry you're stuck with your daughter and grandson."

Dale started to apologize, but saw that she was teasing.

"Dad, I have a favor to ask you."

"Sure."

"Max and I will be moving to our new place in a few days, and I was hoping you might go through Mom's jewelry box and find something of hers that you want me to have." She paused and took a deep breath to push away the tears. "Whatever you pick is fine. I just want something."

"Just take the entire jewelry box, Susan. I have no use for it. You can have it all."

Susan shook her head. "I'm not ready to go through Mom's things yet. I like knowing that everything is right where she left it, but I was hoping you would just pick me something, maybe some piece that had special meaning to you and Mom."

"Well... okay, honey. I guess I can do that. When do you want it?"

"Whenever you're up to it. And, Dad, one more thing?"

"What?"

"Is that old tree swing still in the shed out back?"

"The one from when you were little? Yes, I believe so."

"Could you hang it up for Max? I think he would love it. I know I would love seeing him use it."

"I'll go look right away. Just let me use the bathroom first."

◦ ◦ ◦

ON THE THIRD flush it happened again. Dale turned off the water like Plumber Dick had shown him, cleaned up the worst of the mess, and exited the bathroom, closing the door behind him.

"Don't use the downstairs bathroom," he called out before placing a call to Plumber Dick.

"Coach, have you ever considered a high fiber diet?"

"When can you come over, Dick?"

"I'm installing a toilet in that pretty college president's house this afternoon. A Toto Supreme Two, Coach, if you can believe that."

"Great, Dick. I'm sure you'll do a good job."

"I'm pretty nervous, to tell you the truth. I've never put in a Toto Supreme Two. About the best toilet I've ever installed was one of the high-end Kohler models. This Toto Supreme Two is something special."

"Can you come to my place after you leave President Fuller's house?"

"It depends how long it takes me to install that Toto Supreme Two. Do you want to take a guess how much one of those costs to get installed, Coach?"

"No thanks. I'm kind of busy."

"Seriously, take a guess."

Dale shook his head and tried to keep his irritation from showing in his voice.

"Five hundred?"

"What?"

"Five-hundred dollars."

Plumber Dick cackled. "Damn, Coach, you're way off. Guess again."

"Dick, I don't—"

"C'mon. Guess."

"Eight-hundred?"

"Coach," Dick said, lowering his voice as if he was sharing government secrets. "A thousand."

"Seriously? A thousand dollars for a toilet?"

"Not just a toilet, Coach. The Toto Supreme Two. Did I tell you about the Tornado Flush?"

"Who makes that one?"

"You don't understand, Coach." Plumber Dick's giggling made Dale wonder how he could have ever forgotten which Bennett had the brain injury. "The Toto Supreme Two comes with Tornado Flush. I can't wait to try it out."

"You do that, Dick. Try it out and then come by my place and tell me how it was."

"Will do, Coach. See you later."

Dale checked his watch as he headed out into the yard. The season's final installment of *The Coach Dale Fox Show* aired on Country 104 at seven, and Wally Westmoreland usually liked him to show up fifteen minutes early to check the equipment. He would try to get the swing hung for Max before having to clean up.

Chelsea was gone again.

She usually bounded up the stairs onto the deck as soon as anyone came outside. Dale had become accustomed to turning to the side to avoid the worst of her enthused frontal attacks. It was second nature. But there was no attack and no Chelsea. He called her name, just in case she was behind the shed, but there was no response. He scanned the backyard until he spotted the dog's escape route, a small hole dug in the far corner of the yard under the fence.

How much more could go wrong?

Dale returned to the house and found that Susan had retreated to her bedroom, probably to study. Max was still watching TV.

"Chelsea's gone again," he called up the stairs.

He heard the sounds of creaking bedsprings above him, then a door opening. Susan appeared at the top of the stairs.

"I'm on my way. Where do you want me to look?"

"Same as last time."

● ● ●

No Chelsea.

No swing.

No toilet.

They spent two hours covering every street in Mozarkite. The search took so long that Dale had no time to hang the old swing. Then, Plumber Dick called to apologize for not being able to come over. President Fuller's Toto Supreme Two with Tornado Flush had proven to be more of a challenge than expected. Dale would have to wait.

Now, he thought, as he dressed in khakis and a blue shirt, if only *The Coach Dale Fox Show* somehow got cancelled. That he would not mind. He earned twenty-five dollars and a medium two-topping pizza for each hour-long show. The money was direct deposited into the family vacation account. Most of the pizza went into Wally West-moreland's mouth.

But there would be no cancellation. Country 104 had carried *The Coach Dale Fox Show* for twenty-four years. Wally sold the spots himself. Even in the lean seasons, listenership numbered in the upper hundreds, considerably better than the dozens who tuned in for regularly scheduled old-school country twang. "If you're not on, all we got listening that time of night is drunks," Station Manager Elmo Donnelly had confided to Dale years ago.

◉ ◉ ◉

"From downtown Mozarkite, it's The Coach Dale Fox Show. *I'm your host, the voice of the Mozarkite Junior College Polled Herefords, Wally Westmoreland. We're live at Pizza Lube where a few tables are still available, if you want to come down and watch the show in person."*

Dale glanced around the restaurant as Wally cajoled listeners to leave their warm homes to traipse down to the former location of a failed Quick Lube place that had been transformed into an automotive-themed pizza joint. He'd given the place a year to make a go of it, but they'd surprised him by making five with no sign of letting down.

"Remember, at any time during the show, you can come in and order any medium pizza for just $12.99. That includes the all-new whitewall, which if you're not familiar, is a pizza with white sauce instead of red. They've also got wings, salads, and my personal favorite, Pizza Lube dipsticks – that's cheese sticks with marinara and cinnamon sticks with chocolate. They come in orders of six, twelve, and twenty-four."

Kevin Crowder, his wife Amber, and their four kids were chowing down at one table. The older ones had their faces lowered to their cellphones while the younger ones whined about the jukebox being turned off because of 'that old guy's radio show.' Kevin and Amber ignored the kids and each other as they chomped on pizza and gazed vacantly at the walls. Three strangers, auditors in town to do their annual review of the city's books, were downing wings and pitchers of beer, likely at taxpayer expense. The other tables were open, but the bar in back was two-thirds full of regulars, mostly men who stopped in after work and never bothered to leave. Wally was gnawing through his fourth slice of Dale's ham and pineapple pizza, a combination Dale never would order for himself, but Wally had taken the liberty to order for them.

"Another season is in the books for the Polled Herefords. It was a season that started with much promise but ended on a losing note. Coach, the team was three and three after six games. What changed?"

Dale launched into a lengthy explanation of why the team lost its last five games, saying much while saying little. Sure, there were injuries, but no more than other teams. Most of all, he explained, it was the changing face of competition in the conference. That girl reporter from the *Messenger* had astutely picked up on that. Back during Dale's early years as coach, the conference schools had a gentleman's agreement that they would avoid recruiting players who were of questionable character. It had been a mark of pride, one that Dale had maintained even after the other schools bailed on the agreement. Over time wins and losses had trumped character and integrity, to the point where the other conference schools circled the periphery of the big football programs like hungry sharks surrounding a school of seals, just waiting for some kid to flunk out or get busted for dope or assault.

But not Mozarkite.

"We expect our players to represent the community and the school," Dale explained for the umpteenth time. "That might cost us a win or two along the way, but it'll also keep the school name from being dragged down by ungrateful kids who can suck a small town like ours dry before leaving with nary a word of appreciation."

Confident that he made his point, Dale nibbled on a pizza slice while Wally sang the praises of their sponsors. He was just wrapping up when Heaven Knight walked through the door. She surveyed the room before taking a seat at the end of the bar. Their eyes met and locked, until Dale had to look away to address Wally's next question.

"Coach, they're telling me back in the Country 104 studios that we have a caller with a question. Are you okay with that?"

Call-in questions had once been a staple of the show, but they dried up over the past decade. Dale couldn't remember when they last received one, and Wally had stopped bringing the equipment that patched the calls directly to their table at the restaurant.

Wally placed his cellphone near their speaker and turned up the volume. *"Caller, you're on with Coach Dale Fox. What's your name?"*

"Yeah... uh, my name is Richie. I'm in my truck out on the interstate, hauling a little dirt for Grover Palmer. I live up in Camdenton and wanted to know if Coach Fox has any interest in Tyler Patton."

"Patton was the running back on your state championship team year before last, wasn't he, Richie?" Wally asked.

"He sure was. The boy set school records for touchdowns and yards gained. We all hoped he would go to Mizzou, but his Daddy was from Texas, so he went down there."

"Got in a bit of a dustup a few weeks ago, didn't he Richie?"

"They said he had someone take his math final for him. Truth is, he probably did. Tyler was never any good at math. Everybody around the Lake knew that. Anyway, he's been cut loose by the Longhorns and plans to go to juco next year."

Dale knew all about Tyler Patton. The boy's parents had called him just before Linda passed, interested in him playing a year in Mozarkite before returning to a big school. They were disappointed when he turned them down, but the risk was not one Dale wanted to take.

"From what I've heard, Tyler is looking at schools in Mississippi and Oklahoma," Dale said. "He'll be a good addition to whatever team gets him."

"Why not Mozarkite, Coach," Richie the caller asked. *"You're the closest juco football school to the Lake of the Ozarks. I bet a bunch of people would make the trip every weekend to see Tyler play."*

"He certainly would be a good fit, that's for sure," Wally interjected.

"Like I said, Tyler will be a fine player. I expect to see him back at a big school after next season. Unfortunately, he won't be joining us."

"Thanks for calling in, Richie. Mozarkite has always run a clean program," Wally said quickly after catching Dale's scowl. *"Coach Fox does things like the coaches at Duke and Northwestern, programs where academics and sports are on equal footing. Coach, I would be remiss if I didn't bring up something that everyone in town is talking about. Do you want to comment on the article that was in last Sunday's* Mozarkite Messenger?*"*

Dale looked toward the back of the restaurant where Heaven Knight was watching closely. "Which article is that, Wally?"

"The one by the new sportswriter. She brought up the fact that the Polled Herefords have had a rough stretch the past few years."

"There's no doubt I would have liked for our boys to win more games, Wally. What coach wouldn't? Still, as you were just saying, we have standards at Mozarkite that other schools either don't have or don't care to have."

"But her questioning whether or not you should be coaching, now that's out of line."

"People are entitled to their opinions, Wally. Tell the truth, weren't there some years when you thought the St. Louis Cardinals needed to fire their manager?"

Wally laughed. *"There sure were. Several times."*

"When people share their opinions that means they care. Our fans here in Mozarkite care about their football team." Dale fixed his gaze on Heaven Knight. "The *Messenger's* new reporter cares about sports. Her opinions might differ from ours, but she cares."

Their eyes locked. Heaven Knight acknowledged his compliment with a slight nod.

"Coach, we have another caller. Hello there. Who am I speaking to?"

"It don't matter who you're speaking to, Wally. I just need a minute to say what I need to say. That new reporter—Heaven on Earth—or whatever the hell her stripper name is—is more full of shit than a Christmas goose. That ugly bitch needs to—"

All the color drained from Wally's face as he yanked his cellphone away from the microphone. Dale worried for a moment that Wally might have an on-air stroke. He recovered, however, leaned close to the microphone and said, *"Folks, I'm so sorry about that. We usually operate with a three-second kill switch that lets me edit out profanity, but we didn't have that with us today, so some language made it on the air that was unacceptable. Please accept my apology and the apologies of Country 104. I don't know who that caller was, but if we find out you better believe that he'll be banned from ever calling again."*

The caller might have been unknown to Wally Westmoreland, but the voice was immediately recognizable to Dale and most likely two-thirds of the listeners. Dale appreciated Uncle Homer's sentiment, but his execution was less than stellar. In all, it was the perfect end to an otherwise lackluster day, but there was still one thing left to do.

It was nine-fifteen when Dale arrived home. Max was in bed; Susan was working at the kitchen table.

"No sign of Chelsea?" Dale asked.

"No. I checked the city pound again just before they closed. They know she's missing, but no one has seen her."

Dale sighed deeply and felt the full weight of his weariness settle upon his shoulders. He wanted the day to end, but not before he filled in the holes under the fence. When... if Chelsea was returned, she would not have such an easy time escaping again.

"I'll be in the back yard," he said to Susan.

"It's dark, Dad. What can you possibly have to do out there now?"

"Just a little something for your mother."

7

"Where are you going today, Pop-Pop?"

Dale checked the rearview mirror to make sure that Max was still strapped into the booster seat it had taken a half-hour to figure out. Back when Susan was that age, five-year-olds didn't need booster seats. When Dale was Max's age, he perched on the seat between his parents. The only protection from becoming a human projectile in those days was his mother's arm.

"It's a workday for me, buddy. Have you had a good time at Aunt Fran's house?"

"We made chocolate cake yesterday. We might go to the movies today if Uncle Willis is okay to stay by himself."

The conversation meandered from airplanes to cows and finally on to Santa Claus's visit in a few weeks. Max named off several toys he was hoping for. Dale had heard of none of them. They arrived at the Tompkins's tidy brick ranch home a few minutes before eight. Fran opened the door to wave them in, then retreated back inside to wait. Temperatures had plummeted over the past few days and Dale's aching jaw told him they might go even lower. Some long-range forecasts were teasing about a white Christmas in South Missouri, the first in over a decade.

After laboring unsuccessfully to extricate Max from his cage of a booster seat, Dale finally stepped back to let the boy do it himself. It took him three seconds.

"Booster seats must be hard for old people," Max remarked as he crawled out.

"A lot of things are hard for old people," Dale said.

Fran and Willis Tompkins's place was warm and cozy and smelled of cinnamon. They never had children of their own. Fran had miscarried several times before they gave up. Sad, Dale thought, because they would have been wonderful parents. Fran babysat Susan when she was Max's age, and those memories made it an easy decision when she needed an emergency sitter for a few days.

Fran kneeled to accept a hug and kiss from Max, who appeared delighted to spend this third day in a row with the Tompkins.

"There's a doughnut waiting for you," Fran said, patting Max on the back as he hightailed it to the kitchen. She winced as she straightened up, smiled, and said, "Coffee, Coach? I've got a pot brewing."

"Don't put yourself out, Fran. I'll have a cup at the Goldrush. I heard you might be going to the movies."

"Maybe. It depends on Willis. If he's good enough to be alone for a couple hours we'll go. There's a Christmas movie out that I think Max will love. How is work going for Susan?"

"She got her results from the real estate test yesterday. Can you believe they get them back so fast? Linda had to wait three weeks to find out."

"Times are changing. Technology is a glorious thing, isn't it?"

Dale shrugged. "I'm not so sure about that. My office computer spends more time spinning and grinding than working."

"Don't tell me you're still using that old Dell, Coach?"

Dale said he was.

"Those things were out of date three years ago. You need to update. What kind do you use at home?"

"Linda had a laptop, but I don't mess with it much."

Fran tsk'ed several times. "Don't get left behind. You need to stay current. It'll keep you young. Can I assume that Susan passed?"

"Passed what?"

"The real estate exam." Fran cast her eyes skyward.

"Of course. She's her mother's daughter through and through."

"Oh," Fran smiled, "there's a lot of you in her, too, Coach."

Dale was about to demur when they heard heavy footfalls from the hallway. Fran appeared momentarily alarmed but smiled when Willis came into the living room.

"Hey, Coach!" he said cheerily. "What brings you by?"

Dale glanced at Fran and caught her look of encouragement. Willis was dressed in sweatpants and a Polled Herefords sweatshirt. His eyes were clear, and his face was devoid of confusion. It was as if the past months had been washed away.

Dale approached his friend and offered his hand.

"What are you doing?" Willis asked, grinning uncertainly. "Practicing for a job interview or something?"

"I just thought that... it's been awhile since we..." Dale sensed that the weeks without seeing one another meant nothing to Willis. "Sometimes old friends just need to shake hands."

"Baloney," Willis teased. "Are you on your way to the Goldrush?"

"As a matter of fact..." When Dale glanced at Fran. She shrugged. Her message was clear. Dale was on his own. "Yeah, Willis, I'm going for breakfast."

"Should I ride with you or drive myself?"

"You should ride with me. It's pretty cold out there, and my truck's already warmed up."

"Okeydokey then. I'll grab my coat."

"Your winter coat is in the back of the bedroom closet," Fran called out to her husband as he retreated down the hall. When he was out of earshot, she said, "We get clear moments like this, but they disappear as quick as they come. Are you sure you want to take him to the Goldrush?"

"Absolutely. It'll be fun. I can't wait to see Uncle Homer's face when Willis walks in."

The conversation in the truck was disjointed and awkward, but Dale rolled with it. Willis did most of the talking, and not unlike Dale's earlier conversation with Max, it rambled from one topic to another. When they got to football, Willis discussed two plays he was thinking of implementing with the offense. One, a strongside sweep, they unveiled six years earlier. The second, a pass route with the fullback crossing paths with the tight end, was new and, Dale felt, very innovative.

"I think we can put both those into the playbook next season," he said as they pulled into the Goldrush parking lot. Because of the difficulty Dale had had with Max's booster seat, they arrived at the diner a half-hour later than usual. About half the tables were open, but Uncle Homer and Welder Tommy were still holding court in their usual spot. Uncle Homer's face froze in mid-sentence when he spotted them.

"Well, I'll be a son-of-a-butcher," he exclaimed. He and Tommy gawked as Dale and Willis weaved their way past tables in their direction.

"Willis Tompkins, you old boy!" Welder Tommy called as he pulled out the chair next to him. "Sit yourself down here and tell us what's going on."

Willis slid into the seat as if he left it just the day before, rather than the months it had been since his last appearance at the Goldrush. "Coach and I are working up some new plays," he said proudly. "Can't tell you though." He leveled Uncle Homer with a stern gaze. "Especially you, Uncle Homer. Last time I diagrammed a new play at this table you hightailed it out to the high school to show Coach Farmer. Took credit for it, too, as I recall."

That had indeed happened. As best as Dale could remember it was fifteen years before. Uncle Homer seemed confused for a moment, but he quickly recovered.

"Coach Farmer thought I made up that play by myself. From then on, every time I saw him, he was like, 'Homer, you got any more plays for me? That one you gave me last time won the Eldon game for us.'"

The others laughed loud and long at the story. Dale sensed that they intuited Willis's current condition. They were content to enjoy the clear moments regardless of where they led.

"Any sign of Linda's dog?" Welder Tommy asked after Dale and Willis had ordered breakfast.

"Nothing. It's been three days now, and with the temperatures dropping I'm getting worried."

"What's wrong with Chelsea?" Willis asked.

"She's run away twice."

"I'll bet Linda's worried to death." Willis's comment, innocent as it was, brought silence to the table. Welder Tommy was the first to recover.

"Willis, in case you ain't heard, Miss Linda is—"

"Don't you have work to do, dumb ass?" Uncle Homer said sharply.

"Linda is what?" Willis said, looking from Tommy to Dale.

"Out of town for a few days," Dale said quickly. "I hope I can find the dog before she gets back."

"Well let's finish breakfast and look for her on our way to work," Willis said between bites of sausage.

Despite the trials of the past week, Dale felt good as he joked with his friends over breakfast. Willis had always brought something unique to their group, an easy-going wit and the ability to share stories that often cast himself in a less than flattering light, that endeared him to the others. It was Willis whom Larry Bob had confided in several years before when his wife left him and his law practice was in trouble. Dale knew that Willis had loaned money to Plumber Dick after he'd overstayed his welcome at the riverboat casino in Caruthersville. And after Patsy stepped away from the kitchen to phone Larry Bob and Dick, both dropped what they were doing to come see him. The entire gang was together again.

It lasted about twenty minutes.

Dale was keeping a close eye on his longtime best friend. Willis had them in stitches as he recalled Plumber Dick's encounter with an exploding toilet at the First Methodist Church fellowship hall. He turned the laughter on himself as he recounted his thirty-pound weight loss and how his unwillingness to invest in new pants had resulted in him inadvertently mooning the home crowd during the second half of a Polled Hereford game in Mississippi.

"Those Mississippi boys up in the stands were yelling, 'sooie! sooie!' and I had to check to make sure I wasn't in a canoe with Burt Reynolds." The others immediately picked up on the reference to the movie, *Deliverance*. Even Welder Tommy, who claimed to only have been to three movies in his life, had seen that one.

The light went out just as Willis started spinning a story about Uncle Homer buying condoms for a date twenty years earlier with old Hilda Sturtz. Dale saw the way his face suddenly became like a mask.

"Old Hilda wasn't having any of it though," he said. "She... she..." Willis stopped, looked skyward, then said, "Damn it, Tommy, you've had my chainsaw for six months at least. When the hell are you bringing it back?"

Everyone realized that Willis's lucidity had passed. He almost never cussed, and if he did it would never be at a friend.

"I brought it back, Willis," Welder Tommy said softly. "You used it to cut back those trees between your place and Buster Terry's."

"You're lying! I was just telling Fran night before last, that lying Tommy Schaefferkoetter still has my chainsaw."

Welder Tommy was about to raise a protest, but Dale motioned for him to leave it alone.

"I'll go home and get it right away, Willis." Tommy said as he got up. "I'll drop it by your place."

"About damn time." Willis replied.

Things spiraled downward from there, and by the time Dale got his friend home, he had stopped communicating altogether. They were approaching the front door when Willis said, "I've wanted to see this place since they put it on the market. I promised Fran that after three years in Mozarkite we would get out of that rental house and get a place of our own."

Fran met them just inside the door. Willis looked at her, but there was no recognition. Max was engrossed in a coloring book and paying no attention.

"I guess we're not going to make it to the movies today," Fran said over her shoulder as she led Willis down the hall to their bedroom. "Thanks for giving him an enjoyable morning, Coach. You're a good friend."

Dale was getting back in his truck when he reconsidered. Fran sounded so weary. So sad. The least he could do was hang around so she could enjoy a matinee with Max. He entered the house just as Fran was returning to the living room. When he told her of his plan, she turned him down. Dale insisted, and ten minutes later one very happy woman and one excited little boy were on their way to the movies. Dale settled onto the sofa, pulled out his cellphone, and punched in a number he had called thousands of times before.

"Polled Hereford Athletic Department. Rosie Halliburton speaking."

Dale always smiled when he heard Rosie's salutation. Anyone who didn't know better might think the MJC athletic department was home to dozens of employees. Nope. There was Dale, who did double duty as football coach and athletic director, Bobby Warehime and Daphne Stott, the men's and women's basketball coaches, and an everchanging array of adjunct physical education teachers who had neither offices nor telephone extensions. And of course, there was Rosie, who had been in her position two years longer than Dale, yet whom he felt he barely knew. Rosie was the master of keeping her personal life personal. That was fine with Dale, who appeared as her supervisor on the college organizational chart but considered her his equal in every area.

"Rosie, I'm taking a sick day to be with Willis."

"Oh, dear. I heard he was at the Goldrush this morning. Did he have a relapse?"

"You could call it that. I'll stay here at his place today so Fran can have a break."

"See you next Monday then, Coach. Oh, by the way, President Fuller called wanting to get on your calendar sometime next week. Do you want me to schedule her or let you?"

"Any idea what she wanted?"

"Yes. She wants to review the football season."

Dale felt a hollowness in the pit of his stomach.

"That's strange. Professor Parker never did that."

It was apparent that Rosie was through with small talk. "What do you want me to tell her, Coach? She wanted to know if next Wednesday or Thursday work for you."

"I'm speaking at the Rotary Club on Wednesday, so tell her Thursday."

● ● ●

IT WAS late afternoon when Dale pulled into his driveway. He had spent much of the time at Fran and Willis's thinking about his meeting with Dr. Fuller. Was she going to be more involved in the athletics program than Professor Parker? If so, how would he handle that? Their interactions during her first months had been cordial. He admired her visibility on campus and in town. Margaret Fuller made a point to get out and be in places where students congregated between classes. She knew them, and they were starting to become acquainted with her. Dale's concerns about her youth – he figured her to be close to Susan's age or even younger – didn't seem to be a problem. All he could do was trust her.

"Pop-Pop, look!"

Max was pointing at the front of the house where Chelsea was, for the second time in five days, tied to the porch.

8

"Dad, Aunt Fran just called. Uncle Willis is having a bad day, and she can't take care of Max."

Dale heard what Susan said and realized what it meant. She had been pouring herself into work at Linda's office over the past week, hustling listings, showing homes, and developing new advertising campaigns. She was working from early in the morning until well into the evening, even bringing work home for after Max went to bed. Despite the long hours, Dale picked up on her enthusiasm. She was becoming the Susan who used to come home from college fired up about her courses. He liked the change and wanted nothing to get in her way.

Which meant that he would have to take care of Max.

"I'm speaking at Rotary today. That's not a good atmosphere for a little boy, but—"

"Seriously, Dad? Those guys will love having Max at the meeting."

"I don't know. It's not something that's usually done, so—"

"Do they still meet at the Sirloin Chalet?"

"Of course, just like they have for thirty years."

"Does Chuck Smith still bring Rottie to the meetings?"

Dale knew Susan had him.

"As far as I know, but remember I only go once or twice a year. I'm not a member so—"

"If they can tolerate Rottie the Rottweiler snoring at Chuck's feet, Max won't be an issue."

◊ ◊ ◊

"So, she was back on the porch, just like last time?"

Larry Bob's attention was focused on Max, who was eagerly recounting the story of how he found Chelsea the night before. Dale's friends were a grizzled bunch, except for Larry Bob who maintained a nominal level of professionalism for the sake of his law practice. They cussed more than they should and drank more than they should. They sometimes blew their paychecks on the wrong things and then lied about it if they were caught. They were far removed from Max's life in Chicago and Africa, but as he shared the story of Chelsea's return, they showered him with the kind of attention a little boy craved. They leaned in close. They asked questions. They acted as if it was the most exciting story they had ever heard.

Dale remembered again why he liked them so much.

And when Uncle Homer asked Dale if he wanted him to watch Max while Dale spoke to the Rotary Club, the decision was an easy one.

◊ ◊ ◊

"How's recruiting going, Coach?"

"Does Jeff Devereaux have a chance to catch on with a big school?"

"Which teams will be strong in conference next year?"

The questions were familiar. Things never changed much with the Mozarkite Noon Rotary Club. Thirty-five men. No women. It didn't matter that the national organization had started accepting women three decades earlier. In Mozarkite women had their clubs, men had theirs. Dale vividly remembered showing up to speak at an

August meeting ten years back and being surprised to see one of his colleagues, a first-year liberal economics professor from New Orleans by the name of Phyllis Dixon-Kent, enter the meeting moments before it was called to order. Chaos ensued, and Dale and Dr. Dixon-Kent were politely asked to get the hell out of the Sirloin Chalet's banquet room so the boys could discuss things. By the time the smoke cleared, the national organization had threatened to pull Mozarkite's charter unless they admitted the female applicant. She was unanimously accepted at the September meeting, just before everyone else resigned. Two months later, a new group, the Mozarkite Rotos, began meeting at the Sirloin Chalet. They had no association with Rotary or any other organization and could do damn well as they pleased. Phyllis Dixon-Kent did her best to keep the real Rotary afloat, but after nine months and five members, they folded. Dr. Dixon-Kent left Mozarkite for the University of Minnesota after two tumultuous years. Over time the Rotos started calling themselves the Rotary Club again. If the national organization got wind of it, they might object, but so far, so good.

Dale could answer their questions with ease. He tossed out a few inside anecdotes, stuff he embellished just enough to impress a bunch of good old boys who thought they knew more about football than they did. The hour was nearing an end when an accountant named Bernie Walton asked if Dale ever spoke to Andre Jameson. Just hearing his name brought a reverent silence to the room.

"I haven't spoken to Andre in a couple years, since just after he was inducted in the Hall of Fame," Dale answered. "He asked why I hadn't come up for the ceremony, but we were so busy getting ready for the season that I couldn't break away."

"It was an amazing day," a Rotarian in the back said reverently. "I recorded it and watched it a half-dozen times."

"I watched it more than that," another said.

"Remember when he used to come into the Mozar-Mart?" the Mozar-Mart owner asked, more to let the others know that he had a connection to Andre Jameson than anything else.

"He came to the Methodist Church once," a portly codger named Buster said proudly. "He even took communion."

"You should've kept the cup," someone chimed in. "It might be worth a lot of money."

It had been over twenty years since Andre Jameson last took the field for the Polled Herefords. He played wide-receiver and safety, excelling at both positions. The University of Florida made him a full-time wide receiver. The NFL made him a millionaire many times over. And a Hall of Famer.

"How was he to coach, Coach?"

"Easy. The best usually are," Dale said. "Andre practiced harder than anyone else. He learned his assignments and the assignments of everyone else on the field."

"Did you know he would be as good as he was?"

Dale shrugged. "I knew he was fast. The thing was, Andre had only played two years of junior varsity football. His parents preferred that he concentrate on track, so he gave up football after sophomore year. It was only after he showed up here to run track that he decided to try football again."

"Great decision for Andre," a Rotarian said.

"And Mozarkite," someone added.

"I was too young to appreciate that team," Darryl Lister, the junior high assistant principal said. "How good were they?"

"Twelve wins, two losses," Dale said. "We lost the second game of the season to Harridge Community College on a field goal with no time left on the clock, then lost to Central Louisiana in the national championship game."

"Central Louisiana had four boys who went on to play in the NFL," a Rotarian pointed out.

"Andre set records for receiving that will never be broken," Dale said. "There was nobody in the conference who could catch him if he got a step on them. He was one of the most amazing athletes I've ever seen."

"What's he doing now, Coach?"

"Andre still lives in Houston. He operates several businesses. He does a lot of investing. He's a TV analyst on a few college and pro games. Some public speaking. He's done well for himself."

"What would it take to get another Andre?"

"That's a tough question. Andre fell into our laps. Other schools never figured that his parents would allow him to play football."

"It sure would be fun to experience a season like that again." The Rotarian's softly-spoken words brought dreamy looks to the faces of his friends.

The Rotarian President stood and took his place behind the podium. "If there's nothing else, then I want to thank Coach Fox for—"

"I have a question."

The speaker was a third-generation Mozarkite shoe store owner named Grayson Pack. Dale had known his father and grandfather, but he only knew Grayson to say hello.

"The *Messenger* reporter asked some tough questions the other day. Perhaps the timing was bad, but Coach, can we catch up with the rest of the conference?"

Dale took a sip of water and cleared his throat. "We're not behind the rest of the conference."

The way the young man waved him off was disrespectful, but Dale remained outwardly unperturbed. He said nothing while he waited for Grayson Pack to continue.

"As far as wins and losses, we're falling way behind. Mozarkite's record the last five years is the worst in the conference. There are plenty of good players out there, but it doesn't seem like we're getting any of them."

Grayson Pack was showing off, and Dale considered putting him in his place, but chose a different approach.

"Let me ask you a question, Grayson. Let's say someone applies for a job in your shoe store. They have previous experience selling shoes, and you hear that they're one of the best shoe salesmen in the area. They sell more shoes than any two of your current employees. Do you hire them?"

Young Grayson Pack looked at Dale as if he were nuts. "Well, yeah. Damn right."

Other Rotarians offered nodding agreements. Dale continued. "Okay, now suppose that, in the process of screening the person, you find out that he might have had issues at his previous job. Maybe he didn't get along with the other salespeople, or maybe he was often late for work. Do you still hire him?"

"I see what you're doing, Coach, but it's not the same."

"It's exactly the same."

"No, it's not. I run a business. We have to make money to survive. You're a junior college football coach. Unless I'm mistaken, junior college is the place where students go when they're not ready for the big time, right?"

Dale considered the question for a moment, then said, "Technically, you're right. Community college is a way for students to save money or get their grades up, but it's a lot more than that."

"I guess I wouldn't know about that," Grayson said in a haughty tone. "I got into the University of Arkansas."

"And you're proud of that?" The guys roared at their fellow Rotarian's jibe at Arkansas. Though the state line was less than twenty miles away, Mozarkiters were Missourians to the core.

"We made a decision years ago that our football team would maintain player standards that exceeded the minimum. We attract young men who want to play football, but also have their heads on straight. They aren't in trouble with the law or taking drugs. They're good kids."

"But bad football players."

Grayson Pack's observation brought a round of boos from the others. The President quickly returned to his feet and thanked Dale for coming. A dozen or so Rotary members came up after the meeting to apologize for their fellow member's remarks. Grayson Pack made a beeline for the door.

● ● ●

LINDA KEPT her jewelry box in the closet. It sat on the floor and was about four feet tall. Walnut. Dale had gotten it for her on their tenth wedding anniversary. Or rather, he told her to pick the one she wanted, as he knew nothing about jewelry boxes. She protested, telling him she didn't care if it was perfect, as long as he picked it out, but there hadn't been time. In the end she went to a furniture store in downtown Mozarkite, located in a space that eventually became a consignment shop. She burst into tears when Dale complained about the price. One hundred and seventeen dollars. And forty-seven cents. Three weeks later, decked out in some of her best jewelry, Linda walked in and quit her job as receptionist at the Farm Credit Union to open her own real estate office. Boy, they had a row about that, he and Linda. Selling real estate part-time, like she had done for the previous four years, was one thing. Giving up her salary at Farm Credit was another. They made an agreement. If after two years she wasn't covering her previous salary, she would go back to a regular job. Linda had made it in one year. After three she was making more than Dale. After ten she was making twice his salary. Dale had grown to appreciate Linda's real estate career.

He pulled open the top drawer and peered inside. Bracelets. Lots of them. A couple he recognized, many more he didn't. The drawers below contained necklaces hanging on tiny hooks that reminded Dale of the old stalls they'd replaced in the football locker room a decade before. He glanced through them for a few moments, then opened another drawer. Rings. He counted forty of them, with colors and stones of all shapes and sizes. One he recognized. Linda's original wedding set. He remembered the cost of that, too. Three-hundred and fifty dollars. Even thirty-five years ago, that kind of money didn't buy much jewelry. After she started doing well with the real estate office, Linda had asked if he would mind if she 'upgraded' her wedding set. Dale supposed that he should be offended that she no longer wished to wear the set he had selected, but as he hadn't worn his wedding ring since the year after they'd married, he knew the argument would never hold water. Three weeks later Linda was wearing what could best be described as a rock. Two older men from church had pulled Dale aside to advise him that some people might think Linda was getting too showy. That bothered him at first, until he started getting compliments from Linda's friends who had seen the new ring and told him he had great taste in women and jewelry. Over time the concern at church had diminished. Still later Linda stopped going.

Dale picked up the wedding set, examined it closely, and replaced it. Susan probably would not want another wedding set, even her Mom's. She already had one. He returned to the necklaces, pulled out the little locker-room hooks, and searched until he found one that he remembered her wearing the year before at the South Missouri Realtors' Ball. It was green, like her eyes, and he remembered two of Linda's friends complimenting her on it while they waited for drinks at the cash bar. Dale had no clue when she purchased it or much of anything else in the full case. He had chosen a few pieces through the years, hurriedly purchased bracelets and necklaces he picked up the day before her birthday or two days before Christmas. Try as he might, he couldn't recall which pieces they were, so he settled on the green necklace from the Realtors' Ball. He removed it delicately, but not delicately enough to keep from pulling out two other necklaces with it. One was a flat gold necklace with a tiny heart dangling from it. The other necklace was pearl. It looked expensive to Dale's untrained eye. For some reason there was a piece of clear tape that connected the necklace to a small envelope. Dale opened it and found a handwritten card.

"Pearls are always appropriate."
Jackie Kennedy.
You are my pearl. W.
W.
W?

The handwriting was perfect. Whoever had penned it paid attention during penmanship class in elementary school. There were flourishes on the *P* in *Pearls* and the *K* in *Kennedy*. The W at the end looked like something from a wedding invitation.

W?

"Dad? Are you up there?"

Dale tucked the card and pearl necklace back into Linda' jewelry box. He pocketed the green necklace, closed the box, and went into the hallway. Susan was standing at the bottom of the stairs.

"Susan, I picked out something of your mother's that you can have. By the way, do you know anyone who would've given Mom a—"

Susan cut him off. "Do you know where Max is?"

Dale's breath caught. Then he remembered. He checked his watch and felt a wave of concern. Five-twenty. Eight hours since he left the Goldrush.

"Sure. He's with Uncle Homer. We were at the Goldrush this morning, and he offered to keep Max while I went to—"

"He was thrown off a horse, Dad!"

Dale's chest tightened. "Uncle Homer's horse? Old Betty? She's so gentle that—"

"I've been trying to call you for the past two hours. We've been at the Emergency Room at Mozarkite Memorial."

"Oh my God, Susan. I want to go see Max right now." The trembling started at Dale's core and quickly moved to his extremities. Sweat broke out on his face and under his arms. He thought he might need to sit down for a moment to get himself under control, but there was no time for that. "I'll grab my coat and—"

"Hey, Pop-Pop!"

Max came out of the kitchen just as Dale reached the bottom of the stairs.

"Max?" Dale looked the boy over carefully. No bandages, no broken bones. Then he looked at his daughter. No bandages or broken bones there, either. Just a look of utter disappointment.

"He's fine. He hit the ground pretty hard, but it was soft and little boys tend to bounce. But Dad, how could you *forget your grandson*?"

◊ ◊ ◊

DALE REMAINED in his La-Z-Boy until eleven-thirty. Ninety minutes beyond his usual bedtime. Max had been none the worse for wear, and he blabbered on through supper about how much fun he had at Uncle Homer's house.

Susan had said little.

After supper, she and Max went upstairs for his bath and bedtime stories. That was before eight. Dale heard nothing else from Susan and assumed she had gone to bed, so he turned on the TV, but found it difficult to concentrate on whatever basketball game was on.

He had forgotten Max.

Completely.

What would Linda say?

"Dad?"

Susan had entered the room and taken a seat on the sofa. Dale barely noticed.

"Susan?"

"Are you okay, Dad? You looked as if you were a million miles away."

Dale tried to speak, but the words wouldn't come. A hollowness seemed to consume him. Then, he felt something he had not felt in years.

He took a deep breath. It caught in his throat.

He had forgotten Max.

"It's probably just as well that you're getting your own place, seeing how I—"

Dale knew that if he tried to say one more word, he was going to...

Throw up? Maybe.

Cry? Yep. He was going to cry.

He hadn't cried when his parents died.

He hadn't cried when Linda died.

But the thought of Max being thrown from Old Betty?

Max, lying on the ground, the wind knocked out of his lungs.

Probably trying his best to be a big boy.

And wondering where his Pop-Pop was.

And why he left him with Uncle Homer.

That was enough to make him cry.

So, he stopped speaking and just sat there, staring at his lap. Hoping Susan would get the hint and go back upstairs.

"He's okay. You know that, right?"

Susan's words only made it harder to keep from crying. Still, Dale fought it off.

"And I know that Uncle Homer would never hurt a fly."

Dale took a deep breath. "He might... if the fly is Scott Pirtle at the *Messenger*."

He thought that humor might head off the tears, but a few came anyway.

Susan laughed. "I heard how Uncle Homer gave him hell at the Goldrush."

Dale did not answer. He couldn't. He kept his head down, so Susan got off the couch and kneeled at the side of his La-Z-Boy. That made it harder. More tears. He rubbed at them with his sleeve. Susan stroked his arm.

"I'm glad to see you're human after all," she said gently.

Dale said nothing.

"It was asking a lot to saddle you with Max at the last minute. I should've been more considerate. I'm sorry, Daddy."

There she was calling him *Daddy* again. Just like at the funeral. Twenty-five years of *Dad*, and now she was back to *Daddy*.

Dale shook his head and wondered if he looked as bad as he felt.

"You look so sad, Daddy."

Obviously, he did.

"Max is fine. I overreacted. If I'd been thinking more clearly, I would've remembered how much fun I used to have at Uncle Homer's farm when we went there." She laughed, then said, "Do you know what he used to tell me when I was a kid?"

"It's hard to tell, knowing Homer."

"I was at his house one day. Aunt Donna was still living, so I would've been nine or ten years old. Anyway, we were eating lunch. Aunt Donna always made fried bologna sandwiches. I loved those and Mom never made them."

"Mom had a thing about bologna," Dale said weakly. "She read someplace where bologna caused cancer."

"Whatever, but anyway, Uncle Homer always had a drink with lunch. Something in a tall glass, but I never knew what."

"Vodka and tonic."

"Well, there you go," Susan said with a grin. "Vodka and tonic for lunch. Anyway, he had several that day, and he seemed really happy."

"Drunk. He gets happy when he's drunk," Dale said. "And sleepy. He gets sleepy, too... and sometimes belligerent."

"Good for Uncle Homer. Now, will you let me finish my story?" Susan pinched his arm playfully. "Anyway, after his third or fourth vodka and tonic, Aunt Donna cut him off. He called her some dirty name I don't remember, then she slapped him on the back of the head. I knew they were playing, but he looked at me, raised his glass, and said, 'Susie, Susie, never drink the boozy.'" Susan paused to laugh at the memory. "I thought that was the funniest thing I'd ever heard. The next day, at school, I shared it with my class during show-and-tell. Daddy, you should have seen Mrs. Gladding's face!"

Susan's laughter grew louder. She smacked the arm of Dale's chair. "Susie, Susie, never drink the boozy." Today at the hospital I reminded him of that.

"Did he remember?"

"Oh, hell yes. Then he said, 'But you didn't listen to me, did you?'"

The laughter continued for a few moments, before fading to silence.

"I'm so sorry," Dale said.

Susan hugged him, "I know. Me too."

More silence.

"I guess I'll go on to bed." Dale stretched but made no effort to get up. He liked having his daughter at his side.

"Can I ask you another question?" she asked gently.

Dale said she could.

"Are you okay?" Before he could tell her that he was, Susan cut him off. "I know you hate being asked, but I see changes in you."

"What do you mean? I'm still me."

"No, you're not. One example, you don't work as hard as you used to."

"Sure, I do, Susan. I put in the hours and then some."

Susan shook her head, then looked him in the eyes. "You spend more time at the Goldrush than you used to. And your teams, Dad. Does it bother you that you don't win much anymore?"

Dale sat up straighter, the fatigue suddenly retreating. "You don't understand, honey. We have a way we do things here. That new girl at the newspaper doesn't understand either. Same with Owen Pack's boy."

"Grayson?"

"Yeah, he runs the shoe store now."

"I went to school with him. He's a dick."

Dale was now fully awake. "Susan!"

Susan giggled at his reaction to her choice of words. "Sometimes the shoe fits. But, back to football, I know you have a way you do things, but I also remember how adaptable you used to be. Remember when you dropped the Wing T formation?"

Dale did. "People were mad for weeks. They loved that Wing T."

"But that team went eight and three," Susan said. "That shut them up real fast." She paused, then said, "so what happened?"

"The game's changing, and not for the better. Juco used to be the place where kids who weren't quite good enough for the big schools got to go and play. We built players, Susan. Like Andre Jameson. He came here and flourished. Now we're the dumping ground for players who get bounced from the big programs. Criminals, druggies, kids who don't care about school and grades." Dale squeezed his daughter's arm. "Did you hear about that college in Kansas that let a kid get a whole year's worth of credit in a summer?"

"You don't have to be that school, Dad."

"That's what it's coming to. Kids are going to places like Mozarkite, small junior college towns, they come from busted homes and crime-ridden cities. Some have parents who are meth heads. They don't want to work in class. They think they're better than everyone else because they came from Division I. I don't want that for our school. Or for our town. Does that make sense?"

Susan shrugged. "Can you have some of it without having all of it?"

"What do you mean?"

"I'm not sure what I mean." Susan got to her feet and stifled a yawn. "I just don't like reading criticism of my Daddy in the paper or hearing you have to defend yourself on the radio."

"Don't worry about me, honey. I'll be fine. Oh, by the way," Dale reached into his pocket, retrieved the green necklace, and held it up "I got this from your Mom's jewelry box. She wore it to the Realtors' Ball."

Susan gasped as she gingerly handled the necklace. She turned it over several times, then remarked. "This is beautiful. I'll wear it tomorrow." She bent over and kissed Dale on the cheek, a big sloppy kiss like when she was a kid. "Thanks, Daddy. I love it!"

He looked up at her and said, "Susan, who do we know with the initial *W* in their name?"

"Lots of people, probably. Why?"

Dale considered telling her about the card but stopped. "I found a note in your Mom's stuff, signed by someone with a *W*."

"A personal note?"

"A thank you note of some kind. Nothing big, but I couldn't place it."

Susan thought for a moment. "Uncle Willis? Wally Westmoreland? Wanda Hennecke? Rachel Wilcox at City Hall? Lots of W's, Dad."

"I guess I'll probably never figure it out, then. I'm going to bed."

"Want me to let Chelsea in?" Susan asked.

"I'll get her."

Dale opened the back door and called her name, but there was no response. He turned on the outside light and scanned the yard, but she was gone again.

9

"Ladies, are you still searching for that perfect Christmas gift for the man in your life? Here's an idea that'll make him happy. A new Ford truck from Stubby Proctor Ford is—"

Dale pulled off the headset and whistled to get Clint Townlain's attention on the other side of the window. "Clint, this seems sexist. There are plenty of women in Mozarkite who drive trucks. Why are we telling them to buy one for their husbands?"

Clint, Country 104's longtime advertising manager, bristled at the interruption. "If this is what Stubby wants, it's what Stubby gets."

"How about if I say something like, 'Folks, are you still searching for that perfect Christmas gift for that special person in your life?'"

"Coach, since when have we questioned what Stubby wants in his ads?"

"I just thought that he might—"

"If Stubby was giving me the use of a free truck in return for these ads, I'd say about anything he wanted me to say." Clint lit a Pall Mall and blew smoke toward the glass.

Dale shrugged, checked the copy, and read the ad as written. When he was finished, Clint turned off the *On Air* light, pushed open the door, and said, "I heard you left your grandson with Uncle Homer yesterday and forgot about him."

Mozarkite. Where gossip traveled at the speed of light.

"The guys at the Goldrush already let me have it with both barrels this morning. But if you need to add to the misery, go ahead."

Clint took a drag from the cigarette and shook his head. "I got two grandkids I've never even met, so far be it for me to say anything. This is the last ad of the year, Coach, so have a good Christmas."

◊ ◊ ◊

DALE NEVER ENTERED the office of President Margaret Fuller without recalling the first time he met her predecessor, Dr. Daniel Trebelhorn Parker, a quarter century before. Professor Parker was a diminutive man who seemed ancient, but probably was not more than fifty at the time. Despite his slight physique, the man was a legend in Mozarkite, acknowledged and revered by everyone as the force behind the state's decision to put a junior college in their tiny backwater town. In their initial meeting, he told Dale what he expected from his football coach, then asked if he could meet those expectations. When Dale said he could, Professor Parker slid a contract across the desk for him to sign. After Dale asked for twenty-four hours to think about it Professor Parker silently returned the contract to his desk, picked up his phone, and asked his secretary to contact the next applicant. Dale practically had to beg to get the contract back. He was glad he had.

Whereas Professor Parker ruled like a despot, albeit a kindly one, at least some of the time, Margaret Fuller was the product of a different time and place. She was young, self-assured, and as smart as anyone Dale had ever met. She was cordial but made a point to keep a friendly distance. She was, first and foremost many suspected, a player of the game. In this case the game was to stay in Mozarkite just long enough to earn the next big promotion. Some were saying President Fuller would be long gone in five years. Dale was not sure about that, but he was sure that she was his boss. And she wanted a meeting, so he went. He even put on a dress shirt instead of his usual Polled Hereford polo.

"It's good to see you, Coach Fox. I heard you've been grandson-sitting the past couple days."

Dale stood in the door, unsure how to answer. Had she also heard that he left Max with Uncle Homer? And how Max had fallen from Old Betty? If so, she probably had doubts as to his suitability as a grandfather.

"My daughter is moving back to Mozarkite. She's been staying with me. I'm out of practice when it comes to kids, but I'll get the hang of it eventually."

"I'm certain you will. Come in and have a seat."

The office was Professor Parker's. The walls were the same. The light fixtures, too. Everything else, though, had been transformed. The Professor's old oak desk had been replaced by a dainty model with no drawers where a person could hide stuff. Dale had no idea why someone would want a desk without drawers, but it appeared to work well for Dr. Fuller. Her chair was white, as were the two chairs across from it. Sedate floor lamps gave the room a warm glow. Professor Parker's family pictures had been replaced by diplomas. Three of them. Bachelors from Southern Illinois University, Masters from Mizzou, Ph.D. from Northwestern. Impressive credentials.

"How's your new toilet?"

Dale regretted asking as soon as the question was out of his mouth. President Fuller appeared flummoxed.

"How did you know that little tidbit?"

"Plumber Dick—Dick Schaefferkoetter. Some people call him Dick Bennett, too. You had him install it. He was pretty excited about it."

"Excited? Does he not install toilets very often?"

The conversation was not going where Dale had expected.

"Oh, he installs plenty of toilets, but... yours was the first..." Dale couldn't recall the name of the toilet. He considered calling Plumber Dick but realized that would be ludicrous. "You need to understand, Dr. Fuller, Mozarkite is the kind of town where people... uh... talk.

Plumber Dick knows plumbing, so he talks plumbing. If you're visiting with his brother, Welder Tommy, well... uh... he'll talk about welding."

President Fuller nodded slowly, probably coming to grips with the fact that she had landed in the most backward slice of America this side of the Dukes of Hazzard. Dale plowed ahead despite the signals he was getting from his boss.

"Of course, Welder Tommy can also talk about fishing. Fly fishing. He's darn near an expert on that."

Dale considered asking his boss if she had a gun he could borrow to put himself out of his misery. Why on God's green earth was he acting so strange? Was he nervous about what they were about to discuss? Thankfully, Dr. Fuller steered the conversation to the purpose of their meeting.

"I only have forty minutes, Coach Fox, and I want to make sure we have plenty of time to talk. Tell me your thoughts on this past football season."

Dale spent the next fifteen minutes walking game by game through the season. He shared statistics, told inside stories, and the occasional anecdote. What he said was not much different from his Rotary speech the day before. Dr. Fuller listened intently and even took notes. There was silence for a few moments after he finished. Then it was her turn.

"Coach Fox, three wins isn't very many."

"I agree. I start every season aiming for a championship, Dr. Fuller. We get the best young men we can, prepare them as best we can, and play hard every game. Some seasons are better than others, unfortunately."

"You currently don't have an assistant coach who is responsible for recruitment."

"We do, but he's ill. We've left the spot open for him. The last thing we want to do is give him the idea that he's being cast aside."

"Willis Tompkins?"

"Yes, ma'am."

"Coach Tompkins has been on medical leave for two years, Coach

Fox. And while I commend your commitment to your friend, it's time to put the needs of the team ahead of the individual, don't you think?"

"I'm not comfortable with that, Dr. Fuller."

Dale could tell by the look on her face that President Fuller wanted to push the issue.

"There are some who question the quality of athletes we attract to Mozarkite, Coach Fox. Do you have any thoughts on that?"

"You must have been listening to my radio show after the last game."

Dr. Fuller blinked several times. "You have a radio show?"

"Every week during season."

"What station is it on?"

"The only station in Mozarkite. Country 104."

"Ahh. I listen to satellite radio."

"I don't think my show's on there."

Dr. Fuller laughed. "I'm going to venture a guess that technology isn't your big thing, Coach."

She had a nice laugh. It made her seem much more down-to-earth.

"I get by, but my wife keeps telling me I need to be able to do more than email."

There it was again. Another reference to Linda in present tense. Dr. Fuller's smile remained, but Dale saw how she leaned in. "Again, Coach, I'm sorry about your wife. How are you getting by?"

Why was everyone so concerned about his well-being? Couldn't a person keep personal things personal anymore? When Dale didn't respond, Dr. Fuller forged ahead. "Our football players aren't as good as everybody else's."

"We strive to get good young men who we are confident can succeed, then we coach them up to the level of competition." Dale gazed through a large window to the President's right, then said, "Things might not have gone as well as I hoped the last couple years, but I'm confident we'll be back at the top of the standings before long."

"Good young men who can succeed?"

"That's always been our approach."

"But we're a junior college, Coach."

"I am aware of that."

"Do you know the percentage of juco students who drop out?"

"Athletes?"

"Students. All students."

Dale shrugged. "Twenty percent?"

Dr. Fuller shook her head. "Try again."

"A third?"

The thumbs-up sign she gave Dale didn't mean he'd guessed correctly. Higher.

"Forty?"

"Try seventy-five."

"No way."

"Way. Seventy-five percent of students who start at junior college never finish. Want to see the numbers, Coach?"

"Then you should be especially proud of our football program, President Fuller. Eighty percent of our players earn their two-year degrees. Nearly all of those go on to four-year schools."

"How many continue to play football at four-year schools?"

"A third."

"How many of them start at the next level, or even make an impact?"

Dale shifted in his chair. "Look, Dr. Fuller, college coaches know the kind of player they can expect from Mozarkite. Well-coached, good in the classroom, good teammates, good men."

"The kind of kids four-year schools don't have to worry about?"

"Exactly."

"The kind of students who raise their team's cumulative grade point average?"

"Correct."

"The kind of players who ride the bench and rarely see the playing field?"

Dale's mouth went dry. He wished he had a bottle of water. "Dr.

Fuller, I'm not sure if you're trying to insult me or make a point."

Margaret Fuller did not back down. She placed her arms on her desk. Her eyes bored into Dale's. "Coach, we're not Harvard."

"Excuse me?"

"We're not Harvard or Stanford. We're not Duke or Northwestern or MIT. We're not Mizzou. We're not Missouri State or Missouri Western or SEMO. We're Mozarkite Junior College."

"Respectfully, Dr. Fuller, I've been here for over twenty-five years. I know who we are."

"Do you? Really, Coach Fox? Don't misunderstand, there's nothing wrong with who we are. We're a community college. Our job is to help kids who can't access a four-year school for one reason or another. If it's finances or grades or home life, whatever. It doesn't matter. They can enroll here and find out if college is for them." Dr. Fuller sat back, picked up a pencil, and absently began to tap it on her desk. "Sadly, most find out that college isn't for them. At least they didn't have to go thousands of dollars into debt to discover that."

"I understand that, but that doesn't mean our football program has to adopt those same standards."

"So, you think your program is better or more important than the rest of our school? Is that what you're saying, Coach?"

"No!"

Dr. Fuller's eyes widened. Dale realized he had spoken more directly than the situation dictated. They sat for a moment, each considering the other. Dale thought about apologizing, but what was there to apologize for? Were they not two educated people having a frank discussion?

"Because if you are saying that, Coach. If you think your program is more important than everything else, I'll let you in on a little secret."

Dr. Fuller allowed the moment to draw out. His curiosity piqued, Dale leaned in and waited.

"For a small-town college like Mozarkite, a football program can be one of the biggest draws we have. When our team is winning, the community is more engaged with the school. When the community is proud of their school, they encourage their kids to go there. The stands were half-full for Homecoming. It was the biggest crowd all season. But I'll bet it's nothing compared to the number of people who turned out when you were competing for conference titles. Would I be correct?"

She was. Dale smiled at the memory. "There were games when the stands were full to capacity and people rimmed the field in their lawn chairs."

"You had Andre Jameson on your team for two years."

"We sure did. People came from all over South Missouri to watch him."

"I've heard. Wouldn't it be great to return to big crowds and winning football?"

There was something in the way she said it. *Wouldn't it be great?* Dale felt as if he had fallen into a trap, with the door closing behind him. She wanted him to sell his soul for a few more wins. She wanted him to sacrifice everything that was good and right about the Mozarkite football program to help bolster the college's image. Enhancing the image of the college was her job.

She continued. "I was at a convention a few years ago where someone described a small college football program as the school's front porch. If your front porch looks good it encourages visitors to see the rest of the house. Would you agree?"

"I don't agree, Dr. Fuller. But even if it is the case, you can rest assured that your front porch is as clean as any in America. No scandal. No corruption. We don't have athletes earning a year's worth of credit in a couple months. Our players are here to play and here to learn. It's the way I choose to build my program, and it's worked for me for a quarter century."

If she argued the point, Dale would give as good as he received. Margaret Fuller may know academics. She may like to spin stories about football being the front porch, but in the end, the football program was his.

She sidestepped an argument.

"Let's pick this up in a couple days," she said after checking her watch. "In the meantime, I would like you to consider hiring a full-time assistant coach to fill the open spot on your staff."

"It's not an open spot, Dr. Fuller. Willis Tompkins might be—"

"Then we'll create another staff position for Coach Tompkins when he returns. But until then, you shouldn't be understaffed. Your competition isn't, and right now they're kicking our butts."

Dale considered objecting further, but knew their time was short. He gathered his notes and headed for the door.

"Coach Fox?"

What now? He turned back. Dr. Fuller was still seated. Standing over her, Dale noticed how petite she was. Her appearance seemed incongruent with her position. But then so had Professor Parker's. And he had done just fine.

"Yes, ma'am?"

"Dale... Coach Fox, my father passed away a couple years ago. He was fifty-five when he died."

"I'm sorry."

"He was the head basketball coach at a little private school in Minnesota. Four hundred students, no scholarships. They didn't even have a team bus until his last few years as coach. They would travel to games in station wagons."

Dale knew of such programs.

"He never complained, Coach. In fact, he loved it. He could never imagine doing anything else. He was a coach. That was what he did... until he had a heart attack that killed him."

Dale was dumbstruck.

"Seriously, Dr. Fuller, that's a terrible way to go. I'm really sorry for what your family went through."

Her smile was sad, and Dale could tell that at that very moment she was visualizing her father doing what he loved. "My point is this," she continued, "at the end of the day, sports aren't life. Especially at this level. We just do what we can and hope for the best."

Dr. Fuller rose from her desk, smoothed her dress, and came around to where Dale was standing. "Don't let a game do to you what it did to my Dad."

10

$\mathcal{D}$ale rang the doorbell and waited several moments before he heard approaching footsteps on the other side. Fran Tompkins opened the door and smiled when she saw who it was. Despite her attempt to conceal it, Dale could see she was run down.

"Bad time?"

"Most are these days, but I'm glad to see you, Coach."

Dale followed Fran to the kitchen. The cinnamon smell that had welcomed him the previous week was gone. The air had a sour tinge to it.

"I was hoping that Willis might be having a good day. They enjoyed seeing him at the Goldrush last week."

Fran shook her head sadly as she poured him a cup of coffee. "What day is it, Coach? Sunday?"

"Monday."

"Was it last week when you took Willis to the diner?" Fran leaned against the counter and pushed a tuft of gray hair away from her forehead. Dale noticed two large stains on the front of her yellow t-shirt that appeared to be fresh. She blinked a few times before saying, "I've lost all track of what day it is. The morning Willis spent with you was the last good spell we had. This weekend was especially hard."

"I'm sorry, Fran. Want me to stay with him today? You deserve some time away."

"I would love nothing more, Coach, but you're expected at work. You can't keep using your sick days to fill in here." Fran sighed. "We'll be fine. He's been sleeping until ten. That's good because it gives me a couple hours to pull myself together."

Dale took that as an invitation to leave. "I'll get out of your hair so you can have some quiet time."

"Please don't, Coach. To be honest, my friends don't come around much these days. I understand why. Some don't want to see Willis in his condition. Others are just more into themselves." She smiled sadly, then said, "I miss Linda. She made a point to stop by a couple times a week. She would ask about Willis, but I always knew she came to see me. That made me feel good. If you have a few minutes, come in the living room and enjoy your coffee."

Once they were seated, Fran said, "I know you want to ask about Willis, but that's a downer. Let me ask how you're doing instead."

Dale was prepared to deliver one of his usual guarded responses. *I'm fine, work is fine, Susan and Max are fine. Everything's fine.*

But something told him not to. Maybe some inner voice. Maybe a desire to share what had been on his mind since the previous week's meeting with Dr. Fuller. Maybe the need to ask someone his nagging questions about Linda. Since Linda and Fran had known each other for years, he chose to start there.

"I found a pearl necklace in Linda's jewelry box that was sent to her from somebody with the initial, *W*. There was a card with it that had a Jackie Kennedy quote written inside."

"Pearls are always appropriate." Fran said quickly.

"How did you know that?"

"Every girl listened when Jackie spoke," Fran said. "I was only ten or eleven at the time, but I remember how women started going crazy over pearl necklaces. Those who could afford them purchased the real thing. The rest of us bought dime-store imitations."

"I think these are real."

Fran laughed. She sounded like the old Fran, before Willis's problems began. "How would you know, Coach? Are you suddenly a jewelry expert?"

Dale felt his face flush. "I don't know, really." He grinned. "Linda could tell from the few times that I bought her jewelry that I was lost."

Fran reached across and squeezed his hand. "Linda knew what she was getting with you, Coach. And as far as the mystery person who gave her the necklace, are you worried it was a man?"

More blushing. "I don't know, Fran, I mean—it just seemed..."

"What man in Mozarkite could quote Jackie Kennedy? Can you name one?"

Dale couldn't.

"Did you consider the pearls might be from a client?"

Dale hadn't.

"Linda had so many people she worked with, and everybody loved her. Perhaps someone gifted her the pearls for her work."

It was that easy for Fran to allay his concerns.

At least when it came to his worries about Linda.

"Now what else is on your mind?"

How did she know there was something else? Was dowdy old Fran Tompkins a mind reader, or one of the most perceptive people on earth?

"I'm getting pushback about our team's performance."

"That new sportswriter at the *Messenger* certainly gave you what-for."

"I was hoping you didn't see that."

"It's the local paper, Coach. People read every page." She chuckled and said, "Obituaries first, though. Always the obituaries first."

Dale nodded. "Me, too. What's that say about us, Fran?"

"We're human. We read the obituaries, and some small part of us thinks, 'well, life might not be perfect, but at least we're still here.'"

"Linda was probably saying that a couple weeks ago." Dale stared at a photo on the wall across from the sofa; Fran and Willis on an Alaskan cruise ten years ago. Willis would have been in his early fifties then, but he looked closer to thirty. Other than her hair gray-ing, Fran had changed little.

"Linda's life was short, but she certainly squeezed the most out of it." Fran said reassuringly. "I wish I had her spirit. Did she ever tell you about the time we went on that bus trip to St. Louis?"

Dale had no recollection of any bus trip.

"Maybe. Tell me again."

"It was the Mozarkite-ettes, back when the club was still fun." Fran's face scrunched up. "After Sue Lansing and her Bible-thumpers got control, they put an end to the really fun trips. Anyway, we left at noon and, as always, a few of the girls brought wine for the trip. It was the cheap stuff, but sometimes that's just what you need. We went to that shopping mall in St. Louis. You know the one, Coach, with the big dove sculpture out front?"

"I'm afraid not."

"They have one of those craft stores all the girls like. I don't care much for that kind of stuff. Linda didn't either, but a lot of the girls do. While they shopped for crafts, Linda and I went to the food court. They have a California Pizza Kitchen, so we split a shrimp scampi pizza, if you can believe that. I mean, who in the world thought of putting shrimp on pizza?"

It was the kind of story that Dale would have usually pushed toward a quick end, but the thought of Linda and Fran palling around the shopping mall made him long for the past. He could see them in his mind. Young and active, laughing about pizza topped with shrimp. Fran considered Linda to be her best friend. That had been Linda's way. There were likely a half-dozen women in Mozarkite who counted Linda Fox as their best friend.

"By the time we finished the pizza it was time to get back on the bus. When we got there, it turned out that the bus driver had gotten into our wine stash."

"Seriously?" Dale had never heard the story.

"Um-hmm. He was from that charter company that runs out of Piggott. I didn't even notice, but Linda did. She picked up on how much happier he seemed than on the ride up. She had him pinned up against the side of the bus with her finger in his face, talking to him like he was a schoolboy. He finally confessed, so Linda marched him to the back of the bus and made him lie down. The back seat was one of those long kind that stretches all the way across. Next thing you know, the bus driver is snoring away, and Linda's driving the bus back to Mozarkite."

"Linda has never driven a bus in her life," Dale said, laughing at the story.

"We figured that out after she started grinding the gears, but by the time we reached Eureka, she was doing pretty good."

Dale laughed harder at the thought of Linda driving a massive charter bus. "And to think she never mentioned it."

"Oh, she probably did," Fran said. "You just weren't listening."

Dale stopped laughing. "Why would you say something like that, Fran?"

"Woman's intuition." Dale was surprised by the certainty with which Fran answered. He considered objecting, but she changed the subject.

"You need to fill Willis's spot on your coaching staff."

"No. I already told Dr. Fuller that I'm keeping that spot open. It's not fair to Willis after all the years that he—"

"Willis will never know, Coach."

"What if the experimental medications work? What if he gets to where he can come back? What kind of friend would I be to just—"

"We stopped the experimental meds last month. Nothing is going to bring back the Willis we knew."

Dale shook his head. "We saw the old Willis just last week, Fran. He's still in there someplace. Everyone in church is praying for him to recover. I can't desert him."

Tears rimmed Fran's eyes. "There's no hope. The doctors said we were wasting our money. I've accepted that and you need to as well. Fill Willis's position, Coach. Get yourself someone to make the recruiting trips. Pick someone good, so the team can get back to how it used to be."

They grew silent. Fran had made her point. She made several points, and Dale knew he had some serious thinking to do.

But still, there was one more thing. Dale didn't address it until he was leaving.

"Fran, can I ask a favor?"

"Of course."

"Susan brought up something at Linda's funeral that had never occurred to me. It didn't bother me then, but it started to later on."

"What's that."

"Nobody calls me Dale anymore, Fran. I'm Coach. Even our new President calls me Coach Fox."

Fran laughed. "It's who you are. You worked hard to earn that title."

"I know, and I enjoy hearing it. But, Fran, I need someone in the world who still calls me Dale." He paused and took her hand in his. "Will you please be that person?"

● ● ●

FREED from the pledge he made to himself regarding Willis Tompkins's position on his coaching staff, Dale decided to begin his search for a replacement. After Max was in bed, and Susan had settled down in what had become her usual spot, working on real estate business at the kitchen table, he pulled out a legal pad and started putting together a list of qualifications for the job. The Mozarkite football staff was small, Dale and four assistants. Willis's was the only full-time position. The other three, good veteran coaches, were part-timers who worked at other jobs that allowed them to be involved with the Mozarkite football program. None had aspirations to become full-time assistants. That meant he would need to bring someone in from outside. What kind of person did he want? He went to work on answering that question, jotting notes as he went along.

Mature – Forty or older, fifty would be preferable. Someone who could relate to the players as an authority figure.

Family Man – No divorces or scandal. Married men take the job more seriously.

Christian – A churchgoer is essential in Mozarkite.

Understanding and Accepting of Program Standards – We recruit young men who will succeed in football, the classroom, and life. We don't take chances on players with questionable backgrounds.

Satisfied, Dale decided to start an online search of prospective coaches who might fit his requirements. It would have to wait until tomorrow, however, unless...

"Susan?" he called out from the living room. "Do you ever use your Mom's laptop?"

"I use my own. Mom's is still plugged in on her desk."

Dale got up and walked to the room off the kitchen that had been designed as a pantry, but Linda had long ago appropriated for a home office. The space was tight, with barely enough room for a small desk. Dale had always felt claustrophobic when he stepped in, but he figured he could hold that off for a few minutes. After pushing several buttons on the side, the laptop came to life. The first thing he encountered was a password request.

"Susan, any idea what your mom's password might be?"

"Try *Linda Fox Realty*, all one word."

He tried.

"That didn't work."

"Try *We Sell Homes*, all one word."

He tried.

"That didn't work, either."

"Try *Mimi Loves Max*, all one word."

He tried.

"That did it. Thanks."

Dale's experience with computers was limited to the large desktop model in his office, but he found himself adapting as he worked. After searches on several coaching websites he was familiar with, he gave up. Every prospective coach listed his life goal as being the head coach of a major college program. That was the last kind of person he needed in Mozarkite. After reaching several dead ends, he closed the web browser. All that remained on the screen were a half-dozen file icons.

Prospective Sales.

Prospective Clients.

Business Expenses.

Personal Expenses.

Income Statements.

And one more, simply titled, *W.*

He clicked on *W.* It opened.

Inside were several more folders, arranged by years, beginning with the current one and going back for seven previous. Dale clicked on one, but it was password protected.

MimiLovesMax

Nothing.

LindaFoxRealty

Nothing.

WeSellHomes

Strike Three. A warning appeared on the screen telling him he had exhausted his guesses. He considered trying the other files, but focused instead on a single photograph. The thumbnail was too small to make out details, but when Dale clicked on it, it expanded to reveal Linda standing in the middle of a group of women he didn't recognize. She appeared ebullient, even giddy, and dressed in a nice-fitting yellow blouse. Over her head she hoisted a trophy, maybe a foot in height. Dale leaned in close to the screen to try to read the inscription.

Karaoke Champion!

The date on the trophy was from September of the previous year.

"Who are those women?"

Dale jumped and nearly turned over the desk chair.

"Sorry, Dad. I thought you heard me come in. Who are they?"

Dale straightened up and backed away from the screen. "I don't know. Probably at a convention someplace. It was in September, so I was busy with the team."

"Man," Susan giggled. "Mom really got around. I think she's drunk."

"Why would you say something like that? Your mother never drank enough to get drunk."

"C'mon Dad. Look at her eyes. And that silly grin. She's hammered."

Dale didn't have a response, so he closed the picture.

"What's the *W* file?"

"I don't know. I'm going to bed."

"Well open it, silly. My curiosity is piqued. Wasn't the note you found in Mom's jewelry box signed by *W*?"

"I don't remember."

"You do, too. Don't you want to find out who the mysterious *W* is, Dad?" Susan reached past Dale, clicked on the file, and was greeted by the same warning screen.

"You already tried?"

Dale said nothing.

"Would you mind if I try to backdoor it? I'm sure I can figure out the password. Mom wasn't very creative."

Dale closed the laptop, unplugged it, and placed it under his arm.

"I would rather leave it alone. It's none of our business."

He felt Susan's eyes following him as he left the kitchen and headed for the stairs. She likely perceived how he really felt, how he wanted to know for certain that Fran had been right about *W* just being another satisfied client. Yes, he wanted to know the contents of the *W* file, and he would find out soon enough.

Around one-thirty, Dale awoke for his usual trip to the bathroom. After taking care of business, he was returning to his bedroom when he noticed that Susan had left a light on downstairs. It was in the kitchen, and as he went down to turn it off, he smiled at the memory of his frequent rebukes of a preteen Susan to *'Turn the lights off when you leave a room.'* A lot of good that had done.

Then, a sound from outside, like a tree limb scraping against the side of the front porch. It was cold and dark, but Dale decided to check anyway. Mozarkite was the kind of place where people could step onto their front porch in the middle of the night without fear. The few incidents of overnight gunfire over the past decade were usually traced back to the Ricketts' place on the edge of town. Of course, with Wade Ricketts policing the night shift, any calls to complain would likely be soft-peddled. Still, there was no hesitation on Dale's part to step out onto the cold porch in his flannel pajamas.

A stiff northerly wind had kicked up. It created a stir as it blew through the bare branches of the oak and birch trees along the street.

But that wasn't the source of the noise.

Chelsea was back.

Just as before, and the time before that, she was tied to the porch rail with baling twine. She wagged her tail and licked Dale's hand as he untied her.

"You've become quite the wanderer, girl," he said gently. The collie showed no signs of wanting to run at the moment, however. She shuddered as Dale rubbed her neck. A reaction to the cold, he thought.

"Want to sleep in your Mama's bed tonight, girl?"

She thumped her tail in enthused acceptance, then followed Dale inside.

11

*D*ale arose earlier than usual. It was his way of acknowledging that perhaps Susan was right. He had started sleeping in and showing up to work later. It wasn't a big thing. Locals knew the kind of hours Dale put in during football season. But still she had a point.

His musings were interrupted by Chelsea belly flopping onto the bed with the finesse of a whale. She licked at his face and neck, then went still when she looked at the empty side of the bed. She whimpered, then slowly jumped back to the floor and lowered herself to a spot next to the bed. Dale reached over and stroked her head.

"I know, girl. You miss your Mama, don't you?"

The collie raised her head and gazed at him with sad eyes. Somehow she knew that this wasn't just another of Linda's work trips. She'd started the night eagerly taking Linda's place on the bed, before growing restless and relocating to the floor. Yes indeed. Chelsea knew.

"Is that why you keep running away? Where do you go? You're not getting into trouble, are you?"

Chelsea had started to snore. Dale rubbed her head one more

time, then headed for the shower. His follow-up meeting with Dr. Fuller was at eleven, and he wanted to be on top of his game.

● ● ●

"WHAT ARE you doing over Christmas break, Coach?"

The sight of Uncle Homer talking and gesticulating with his fork while chewing with his mouth open might have made lesser people nauseous. The guys at his table had long grown accustomed to his peculiarities, though, and Dale didn't bat an eye.

"It's not Christmas break anymore." Larry Bob spoke to Homer from behind the pages of the *St. Louis Post-Dispatch*. "It's Winter Break, you old narrow-minded bumpkin."

Larry Bob was prodding the bear. The twins turned to watch their uncle's reaction.

"Damned if I'll ever call it *Winter Break*," Uncle Homer replied sarcastically. "If it weren't for the Pilgrims and Christopher Columbus and those other boys seeking freedom from those sons-of-bitches in England, we'd still be wearing short britches and talking like fancy boys."

Dale had learned years ago that Uncle Homer's bluster was about twenty percent sincere and eighty percent hot air. He loved spouting outrageous claims that he knew to be false, hoping to get a rise from the others. Sadly, what Uncle Homer had yet to figure out was that Plumber Dick and Welder Tommy took what he said as gospel. Later in the day there would undoubtedly be some poor farmer needing a seam welded or a stay-at-home mom needing a leaky pipe repaired who would be subjected to stories about Christopher Columbus's need to be free of the English monarchy and Americans wearing short pants.

"Like I was asking, Coach, before I was *rudely* interrupted," Uncle Homer shot a withering glare at Larry Bob, still hiding behind his *Post-Dispatch*, "what are you doing over your *Christmas* Break?"

"Susan thinks I should start going through Linda's stuff. Besides that, not much of anything. Between football season and Linda's passing, it seems like years since I've had any time to relax."

"Gonna give that recliner a workout, eh, Coach?" Welder Tommy said with a wink.

"I plan to. There will be bowl games to watch and some college basketball. I may even try delivery pizza."

"You do that, old boy," Uncle Homer said.

"You'll gain twenty pounds in a month," Larry Bob chimed in.

"If anybody knows about gaining weight, it's you, Larry Bob," Plumber Dick teased. Welder Tommy and Uncle Homer, burly men with a nice layer of fat around their midsections, were noticeably quiet.

◐ ◐ ◐

"What's the problem with it, Coach?"

Hurley turned the laptop over several times, as if he were looking for a secret door. The MJC tech guy was a peculiar one. Dale didn't know what he did other than work on computers. Of course, given the student body's proclivity for knocking the school computer labs' equipment offline, Hurley probably had more work than he could handle. But as to whether or not he was married, enjoyed travel or hobbies, or still lived in his parents' basement, Dale had no idea. In fact, he was unsure if Hurley was his first name or last. That's just what everyone had called him during the decade he had been at the college.

"I can't get beyond the passwords."

Hurley turned it upside down, read something on the bottom, then said, "It's not college property. I can't work on it." He handed the laptop back to Dale. "Did you get it from a pawn shop or something?"

"It belonged to my late wife. It's only a year old, and I was hoping to use it at home."

Dale sensed a change come over Hurley when he mentioned Linda.

"You going to use it for college related stuff, Coach?"

"If I can make it work."

Hurley held out his hands. "Give it here. Dr. Fuller might have a cow if she finds out, but I don't mind helping you. Can I keep it over the Winter Break? I'll probably take it home and try to figure it out there."

"I appreciate that, Hurley. Any big plans for the break?"

"I'm headed to Jamaica with my wife and kids. Only for a week, though. I'll still have time to get past those passwords. I'll call you when I'm done."

● ● ●

"I'm glad you reconsidered, Coach Fox."

"It's time, Dr. Fuller. I suppose I've known that for a while, it's just... I didn't want to turn my back on Willis Tompkins. He was so loyal over the years."

"Everyone needs a good and faithful friend." Dr. Fuller returned to her desk, motioning for Dale to follow. He placed his scuffed briefcase, a long-ago gift from Linda and Susan, on the chair next to him and pulled out the legal pad he had been using for several days.

"I've put together a list of potential candidates. I'll make contact over Winter Break and set some interviews up for the first of the year."

President Fuller's face lit up. "Fantastic, Coach. You've really put some work into this, haven't you?"

Dale admitted that he had.

"What criteria did you use?"

"I went with people I'm familiar with, and who know the kind of program we run. There are seven names. Three are high school coaches from the area, two are longtime assistant coaches. The other two are former coaches who have moved on to other jobs."

President Fuller's face wasn't lit up anymore. "I see. So, how many of the names on your list have state championships to their credit?"

"There's more to football than championships." Dale said crisply. "These are the kind of men that parents want their sons to play for."

"Why?"

"Why what?"

"Why would parents want their sons to play for these men?"

Dale shifted in his seat, trying to remain comfortable in a situation that was becoming increasingly uncomfortable.

"First, they care about their players. They're family men who have kids of their own. Second, they know football. They understand the intricacies of the game and are good strategists. Third, they—"

"They know football?"

"Very much."

"And they've won?"

"All have had good teams over the years, Dr. Fuller. But like I was saying, they don't look only at the scoreboard. They—"

"How many have won a state championship?"

Dale glanced at the list, but he already knew the answer. "Coach Lavery over at Monett. He won a championship back in..." Dale tried to remember the year, but couldn't. "It was back when they had that linebacker who went to Oklahoma, so that was... fifteen years ago? Twenty?"

What Dale left out was that Coach Lavery was an assistant on that Monett team, not the head coach. Dr. Fuller appeared unimpressed. She jotted some notes on her own legal pad, then stared at the wall to the right of her desk while she chewed on the tip of her pen. She was building up to say something, Dale was sure of it.

"Coach, you're a baseball fan, aren't you? I've seen the St. Louis Cardinals jacket you wear sometimes."

"I sure am. I'm like a lot of men my age. I grew up listening to Jack Buck and Harry Caray on the radio. I used to be able to name every player on the team. Can't anymore, though, given how they come and go, but I still watch the games."

"How much of their success is attributable to the people who run the organization? The general manager, the coaches, the manager?"

"We're not the Cardinals, Dr. Fuller. We're Mozarkite Junior College. We play junior college football."

"But why can't we be the Cardinals of junior college football?"

"The St. Louis Cardinals have a tradition that goes back long before you and I were born. They have a following that includes millions of people across the Midwest. I don't think it's reasonable to expect any team to live up to that."

"What's your legacy, Coach Fox? What will people remember about the Polled Hereford football team after you're gone?"

"After I'm gone?" Dale felt his heartbeat begin to race. "What is this about? Are you threatening to get rid of me? If you are, you better think twice."

"Coach Fox, it's nothing like that at all. I was only—"

"Because I have four years left on a five-year contract that I signed before Professor Parker retired. He wanted to make sure that—"

"Don't get me started on that, Coach." Dr. Fuller placed her arms on her desk and leaned in. "With all due respect, Professor Parker should never have done that. No one at this level gets a five-year contract."

Dale knew she was right. He had even questioned Professor Parker before signing the contract. "It'll keep you safe regardless of what happens after I leave," the old man had said. As he faced off with the Professor's successor, Dale was glad he'd had such foresight.

"It is what it is," Dale snapped. "I've given my life to this school, and Professor Parker saw fit to reward me for that. You weren't here, so it's not your place to second guess what he did."

Dr. Fuller winced at his directness. She squeezed her eyes shut, opened them, and shook her head. When she spoke again her voice was softer. "I apologize, Coach Fox. It was out of line to mention your contract. Will you forgive me?"

The tension between them eased as soon as she finished speaking. The defensiveness Dale had felt just a few moments earlier ebbed. There was more to Dr. Margaret Fuller than the hard-charging young administrator persona. Of course he forgave her. She was his boss, and while he knew he could count on some members of the college's Board of Trustees to be in his corner if it ever came to a showdown, he wanted theirs to be an open and amiable relationship.

"I want everything about MJC to be the best," Dr. Fuller continued. "No student should be ashamed to list Mozarkite Junior College on their resume."

She had a point. Dale had heard others mention friends or family who listed only their four-year colleges, conveniently leaving off MJC. It was an image problem faced by many community colleges, and it pained him to know some felt that way about his school.

There was fire in her eyes as Dr. Fuller continued. "We have some staff here, Coach, some newer, but also some who have been around for years, who don't care. Some will give passing grades to anyone who enrolls; others delight in seeing half their class drop after the first exam. There are a few who post office hours but never show up." She emitted a long, slow sigh before continuing. "And the worst are the ones who just don't like students."

"My players know which teachers to take and which to avoid," Dale admitted. "A couple have it in for football players in general. If one of our boys gets in their classes, we have to monitor every assignment to make sure they're getting a fair shake." What he did not say was that, on a number of occasions, he had intervened with those instructors on his players' behalf. One in particular, a biology instructor with a chip on his shoulder, attempted to stonewall Dale two years earlier, until Dale had enlisted the help of a former player, now a professor of Life Science at Vanderbilt, to refute the teacher's claims about the quality of the player's work. The teacher avoided him at faculty meetings, but he stopped blackballing the few football players who dared take his class.

Dr. Fuller acknowledged his observation. "Most students know who to take and who to avoid." She stuck her chin out, reminding Dale of the look of determination he saw on Susan's face, back when she was mastering a new skill. "Instructors don't have five-year contracts, Coach. And you can take it to the bank that I'm going to do everything I can to weed out those who aren't doing right by our students. MJC should be synonymous with academics."

"I agree, and that's why I run my program the way I do."

Dr. Fuller shook her head. "But it's different for football, Coach. We need to build a winning tradition *and* attract the best players.

Having one without the other leaves us with an incomplete program. And frankly, I don't think some former high school coach with middling results is going to help us get there."

"I can help them become the kind of assistant coach our program needs."

"Your job is to be our head coach. Why should you have to do that *and* train some new assistant, especially when there are people out there who can do the job?"

"It sounds like you have someone already in mind, Dr. Fuller."

Dr. Fuller raised her hands. "No. I don't know anyone, but you do."

Now she had Dale's interest piqued. He gazed at her, waiting.

"Andre Jameson."

Dale laughed. He didn't mean to, and certainly did not intend to disrespect his boss, but he laughed. Dr. Fuller appeared to be confused by his response, but quickly began laughing, too.

"I didn't mean that he would come here to be your assistant coach," she said, her eyes twinkling. "We could never afford him, even if our head coach hadn't received a five-year contract."

This time her reference to his contract made Dale chuckle. Dr. Fuller was quick, and good at her job.

"But he knows people. Lots of people."

She was right. Andre knew people at every level of football. He rubbed shoulders with the biggest names in the game. But...

"I don't want to put Andre in a position like that. He's a busy man. Between his businesses and the work he does in radio... it's just asking too much."

"Try."

"No, really, that's not the way I—"

"Try. Call him and ask. What's the worst thing that can happen?"

Dale shrugged.

Dr. Fuller continued. "What's the best thing that can happen?"

Dale shrugged again.

"Well, if the cat's suddenly got your tongue, Coach, I'll tell you what the best thing is. Andre Jameson helps you find a recruiting coordinator that brings players to Mozarkite who win games and do well in class. They go on to star at big colleges and maybe the NFL. Then people start talking about how good the Mozarkite football program is. The next thing you know they're wanting their kids to play here. Even better, they want their non-football kids to come here, too."

"I don't want some flash in the pan to come here only to pad his resume. I prefer coaches who commit."

"Does it really matter? Wouldn't you prefer a superstar assistant who does so well that the big schools want to steal him away?"

"Is that what you are, Dr. Fuller? A superstar who's going to be stolen away?"

She considered his question for several moments.

"If you're asking if my long-term career plans end in Mozarkite, Missouri, the answer is no. I aspire to lead a large university, maybe even an Ivy League school." She grinned. "Will I make it? Who's to say. I'm thirty-six years old. There are college presidents who are five years younger than me, some of them have Ivy League degrees. I can't beat them in terms of diplomas, but I can sure as heck out-hustle them."

Dale admired Margaret Fuller's bluntness. They were following two very different career paths, and he had little doubt that hers would lead to positions and places beyond MJC. His had culminated in their little town where he had the respect and admiration of most anyone with whom he came in contact. That was fine, too.

"I'll get in touch with Andre."

12

"What are you and your Grandpa doing today, Max?"

Max gulped down the last of his chocolate milk before turning to face Welder Tommy.

"Me and Pop-Pop are putting up a swing behind the house."

"Wasn't that job supposed to have been done a few weeks ago?" Larry Bob asked, looking at Max, but speaking just over his head to Dale.

"Things got busy," Dale said. "Between Linda's dog and things at work, time got away from me." He paused and mussed his grandson's hair. "Today's the day, though. We stopped by the hardware store yesterday for rope."

"That grandpa of yours is more fun than a barrel of monkeys, ain't he?" Uncle Homer said, careful not to drop any blue words into the conversation. "How many days has he been taking care of you now?"

Max didn't know. Dale did. So did the others. They were setting him up for some harmless fun.

"Well, it's Wednesday," Plumber Dick said, gazing skyward as he did the computation. "That means this is the... third day."

"And what have you and your Pop-Pop done this week?" Uncle Homer again.

Max was paying scant attention to the conversation. His focus was on the stack of strawberry pancakes that Patsy had whipped up for him. He had already plowed through the mound of whipped cream and was nibbling at the berries. Once they were gone, Dale would drench the cakes in syrup that would wind up on everything within arm's reach.

"Let's see," Larry Bob chimed in. "You and your grandfather have eaten breakfast here at the Goldrush three mornings. You went to the hardware store to buy rope yesterday."

"Don't forget the water bill," Welder Tommy said. The others were cracking up.

"Oh, yes. You went to City Hall to pay Grandpa's water bill." Larry Bob was drawing things out for the benefit of his friends. "That sounds like a great week."

"Maybe better than Disneyland," Uncle Homer snickered.

Dale let them have their fun. Truth was, there was plenty that needed to get done. He still hadn't called Andre Jameson to see if he had ideas for the assistant coach position. The house needed a good cleaning. And then there was Chelsea.

"What's the latest with the dog, Coach?" Plumber Dick asked.

"She's run away five times. She keeps digging out under the fence. She never did this before, and I don't know how to get her to stop."

"You can put her on a leash tied to a tree," Dick suggested.

"I tried that. She just gets all tangled up. Then, when I let her off and leave her alone, she's gone again."

Uncle Homer asked, "Any idea who keeps bringing her back?"

"None. She's always tied to the front porch with baling twine. I've asked the neighbors, but nobody's seen how she gets there. Maxine Shipley, from across the street, saw a white car in the driveway but couldn't remember what day it was."

"What are you going to do?"

"I don't know. I'm worried she's going to get struck by a car. Susan and I go out looking for her but there's never any sign of her in the streets."

The conversation moved on to gas prices, the Kansas City Chiefs, politics, and Larry Bob's detailed account of a meth lab bust in neighboring Parker County before the others returned their attention to Max.

"Is Santa Claus gonna find you this year, Max?"

"I'm going with my Dad at Christmas." Max's face and hands were covered with syrup. Dale handed him a napkin. The others said nothing.

"Evan is coming to get him on Christmas Day," Dale explained. "I think Susan has some plans for him before he leaves."

"You think?" Uncle Homer said quickly. "Today's the twenty-first. Christmas is Sunday. Geesh, Coach, maybe you should find out."

"Probably," Dale shrugged. "Linda always took care of that stuff."

When Dale looked up from his eggs, Homer was watching him from across the table.

"What?"

Uncle Homer shook his head slowly. "You got yourself a little one now, Coach. It might be time to get with the program."

◊ ◊ ◊

IT WAS after nine at night and Walmart was still mobbed. Every square inch of the place was filled with people, carts, or merchandise. For being so close to Christmas, few shoppers appeared to be in festive moods. Even acquaintances that Dale ran into wore grim expressions more appropriate for a call from the IRS.

Getting from the entrance to the toy section took ten minutes. Along the way he witnessed two men nearly come to blows over a fishing rod. A young woman he had seen behind the counter at one of the local convenience stores elbowed a construction worker in the throat to get at something called a mystery egg. He sidestepped a puking toddler whose father was oblivious to his plight and finally reached the toy section. It was picked cleaner than a plate of rib bones from Jessie's Barbeque. A mother who arrived at the same time as Dale spouted a string of profanities as they stood side-by-side, inspecting the slim pickings.

"Braylon wanted a dinosaur," she said angrily.

"Did you try the pet store?"

Dale's attempt at humor made him the target of her next outburst. He stepped away and immediately encountered a store employee he recognized.

"Hattie? I didn't know you worked here."

Hattie Conroy was in her early seventies. Everything about her looked grandmotherly except her scowl.

"I started three weeks ago, but I'm quitting this weekend. Toby said it would be good for me to find a job and get out of the house, so here I am."

"And where's Toby?"

"Sitting at home on his fat ass watching reruns of *Everybody Loves Raymond*." Hattie looked at the chaos all around her and said, "As you can see, everybody's lost their mind all at once. I never waited until the last minute to do my Christmas shopping, and now I know why. Only idiots would be in here this close to Christmas."

She paused, glanced at Dale, and said, "Sorry, Coach. I didn't mean you. Is there anything I can help you with?"

"Well... yes, I need presents for my grandson."

"He's not in school yet, right?"

"Right."

"We got nothing for him, then, Coach. If he was older, or a girl, I might be able to help you. Everything we have left is at the end of the row, and I'm telling you it ain't much."

Dale saw the few scattered items where Hattie was pointing. "Maybe I'll get him a coat or something, then."

Hattie wheeled to look Dale in the eyes, her hands went to her hips. "What kind of man buys his grandson a coat for Christmas?"

"I guess... none," Dale replied. "Thanks anyway, Hattie."

Dale grabbed a few of the remaining items that looked as if they might appeal to Max, then spent ten minutes doing battle with a self-service checkout stand. He was trying to remember where he parked his car, when the lady who had been looking for a dinosaur approached.

"Sorry for the rough language," she said, keeping her gaze focused away. "The dinosaur was the only thing my boy wanted, and I got so pissed when I saw they didn't have it."

Dale looked her over before speaking. "Do you live here? I know most everybody in Mozarkite, but I don't remember you."

"I moved here to live with my boyfriend in September. He's from here." The woman identified a lowlife whose name Dale did recognize, but for all the wrong reasons. Doyle Ricketts. Brother of Wade, Mozarkite's newest cop.

"We met in Springfield. I was cleaning rooms at a motel where he was staying with a construction crew."

"Well, good luck finding the dinosaur."

"Ain't gonna find it now. This was the only place in town that had it. That lady working in toys, the old one you were talking to, she checked and said they have six of the dinosaurs left at the Walmart in Kennett, but I got no way to get there."

"Have your boyfriend take you. I see him ripping around Mozarkite in that Chevy pickup. If he's going to waste gas anyway, why not waste it on his son?"

"He ain't Braylon's dad. I had him before." The woman took a deep breath, and Dale realized she wasn't a woman at all. She was a girl. Early twenties at most, but already looking a decade older. "And we ain't together no more. He took up with a girl he liked in high school. I'm working at the Days Inn, saving money for a car of my own, then I'm going to get the hell out of here. Maybe go back to Springfield where I got family."

Dale knew he should do something. He considered loading her and her son in his truck and returning them to their family in Springfield, but that was three hours each way. Still, it was Christmas.

"I'll tell you what," he said. "I need to buy some toys for my grandson, and you need to find a dinosaur. How about we help each other? I'll drive us to the Walmart in Kennett, and you help me pick some things for my Max."

The girl scrunched her eyes as she considered the proposal.

"How do I know you won't rape me and dump me someplace?"

Dale introduced himself. "I'm the football coach at the college. My wife died a few weeks ago, and this is my first Christmas having to buy gifts for my grandson. I have no idea what I'm doing, and your help would be greatly appreciated. By the way, what's your name?"

"I'm Rowena."

"I'm Coach... but call me Dale. Nobody calls me Dale anymore."

13

"Dad, don't you think maybe you went a little overboard?"

Dale never cared for cussing or salty language, but all he could think of in response to Susan's question was that he really didn't give a shit. Max was ecstatic over the gifts he found under the tree. Nothing else mattered.

"It's been a difficult year for him," Dale said instead. "Let him enjoy."

"Yeah, Dad, but that dinosaur toy?"

"It says on the box that it's for kids aged four to eight."

"You bought two of them!"

Three, actually, but Susan didn't need to know about the one being enjoyed across town by a little boy named Braylon. The Kennett Walmart still had plenty of toys, and with Rowena's help, they had stocked up.

"And to think that Mom didn't believe you had any Christmas spirit."

Dale left the chaos of the living room to check the front porch, hopeful that Chelsea had returned after running off two days before. She had not. It had snowed overnight, not enough to qualify as a white Christmas, but more as a gray, muddy Christmas. A young father down the street was attempting to pull his two little boys on a sled, but they kept getting hung up on patches where the snow and ice had melted away. They turned the corner and nearly collided with an oncoming car going too fast for the conditions.

It was Susan's soon-to-be ex-husband, Evan Sturdivant. And he was early.

Two hours early.

There was something terribly unfair about a little boy having to leave behind his new toys to go spend time with his other parent. Dale knew it happened all the time, but it saddened him, nonetheless. Divorce had never touched his life. Until now.

Evan pulled into the driveway. Dale considered retreating into the house, but didn't like the way it might look, so he remained on the porch. Evan stepped out of his Lexus and waved.

"Merry Christmas, Coach!"

Screw Merry Christmas. Evan was two hours early. He was cutting into Susan's time with Max. Dale's, too.

"Evan." Dale was about to ask him in when Susan came out on the porch behind him.

"You're early."

"I spent last night in St. Louis with my cousins. I left early because I was worried about the roads. If you want, I can go wait at the Waffle House for a couple hours."

Dale wanted him very much to go wait at the Waffle House. Max was having the time of his life, and Dale did not want to see it end so soon.

"Of course not," Susan said brightly. "Not on Christmas Day. Come in."

Max was delighted to see his father. Or perhaps, Dale suspected, Max was excited to show his father the mountain of new toys he had gotten from Santa. Evan was a good sport about it, though he didn't get down on the floor with his boy like fathers usually did with their kids. He remained on the sofa, responding effusively as Max brought each new toy over for his inspection and approval.

Max was growing sleepy. He had awakened at five-thirty, thrilled with the prospect of Santa's visit. It was nine-thirty, and his eyes were heavy.

"Maybe it's a good time to head back to Chicago," Evan said.

True, Dale thought. It probably was. Max would probably sleep for most of the seven-hour drive.

But still, he didn't want to let the boy go.

"I've got his bag packed," Susan said.

When they looked at Max, he was fast asleep, his head resting against one of the dinosaurs.

"Susan," Evan said. "I thought we had an agreement about Christmas."

"What do you mean?"

Yeah, Dale thought, what do you mean?

"In the past we've only gotten Max a couple of things. We didn't want him to become spoiled like..." Evan paused as he glanced at Dale, then back at Susan. It was too late. Dale knew what Evan Sturdivant had been about to say.

Spoiled like your parents used to spoil you at Christmas.

Linda went all out for Christmas. Presents, presents, and more presents. Early on, Dale had complained about the money she spent on Christmas gifts, but there was no stopping her. Susan, as an only child was the main focus of Linda's generosity, but nephews, nieces, and cousins were also included. Susan kidded about it later. She could do that. She was family.

But Evan Sturdivant?

Not family. Not anymore.

"Let's not do this, Evan." Susan quickly got up. "I'll go get Max's backpack."

If Susan was not going to say anything, Dale knew he would. He waited until she was upstairs before inviting Evan to the kitchen for a cup of coffee.

"I gave up coffee. I'm giving up all stimulants. And meat. I'm vegan now, Coach."

"Well, come with me anyway."

Dale made sure that his tone left no room for mistake. Evan lifted his scrawny ass from the sofa and followed him to the kitchen. Dale poured his cup slowly, buying time to allow his temper to simmer. There was not enough time, however. He took a sip, calmly set the cup on the countertop, and turned to face Evan.

"I bought the toys."

"Coach, I didn't know. But just so you understand, Susan and I always agreed that we—"

"Evan, you can do what you want in your house, but when Max is here, I'll buy him what I damn well want to buy him."

"He's not your son, Coach. You don't—"

"And if I get word that you didn't spend plenty of time with him, you'll have me to contend with. Do you understand?"

If Dale expected his mild-mannered, wonky, almost-ex-son-in-law to cower, he was in for a surprise.

Evan smirked.

The son-of-a-bitch smirked.

"You're giving advice on spending time with your children? You, Coach?"

"Don't try to turn this around on—"

"You don't think that I've heard about how you were as a father? About how you were always working? About how disengaged you were from Susan when she was a child? She told me everything, Coach."

Dale was pushing sixty. Evan Sturdivant was thirty-five. A fight between them would still be one-sided. Dale wasn't large in stature, but he was certain he could wipe the floor with jog-running, yoga-posing, tai-chi-practicing Evan. And he was just about ready to when Susan returned.

She sensed the tension.

"What's going on?"

Dale found himself crashing back to reality. He had been just about to whip Evan Sturdivant's ass, right there in the kitchen, with Max sleeping less than thirty feet away.

And for what? For being the same kind of father that Dale had been himself?

"Are you sure you're okay with me taking him early?" Evan asked, wiping a sheen of perspiration from his brow.

"Uh..." Susan was still trying to figure out what she had walked into. "Yeah, it's fine. Just make sure to bring him back two hours early on New Year's Day."

● ● ●

TRY AS SHE MIGHT, Susan was unable to get the real story about what happened between Dale and Evan. They'd exchanged presents, ooh-ing and ahh-ing over trinkets neither of them really needed, then, late in the afternoon, Susan asked if Dale minded if she went to visit her old teacher, Effie Camper. He didn't. He had something he still had to do, anyway. As Susan was leaving the house, she called from outside.

"Chelsea is back."

And she was. Secured to the front porch with the same baling twine as always. None the worse for wear.

"I wish you could tell me where you go," Dale said gently as he poured her a bowl of kibble.

But Chelsea was not giving up her secrets, and Dale had some-where to be.

● ● ●

TWILIGHT WAS DESCENDING on Mozarkite as Dale parked in front of the duplex on Sage Street. When he and Linda moved to Mozarkite thirty years before, the row of apartments was bright and new, with a sign out front proclaiming them the *Joe Eftink Apartment Homes*. Joe Eftink passed away fifteen years ago, and his heirs had neither Joe's concern for nor inclination to maintain the *Joe Eftink Apartment Homes*. They were rundown. The expansive lawns were littered with scrub grass and trash, ranging from empty wine bottles to used Pampers. It was the closest thing Mozarkite had to a slum, and it made Dale sad to think of Joe Eftink and the terrible tribute to his memory.

Dale locked the car and approached unit 102-B. He knocked and waited. Someone from an adjoining unit cracked open a door, looked Dale over from head to toe, then retreated back inside. After several moments Rowena opened the door. Her wary expression morphed into joy when she saw who it was.

"How was your day?" Dale asked.

"The best damn day—sorry, Dale. I've been cussing a lot less, I promise. It was..." she got a dreamy look on her face "...Braylon was the happiest little boy in the world." She reached up and pecked Dale on the cheek. "And it's all because of you."

Dale felt his face begin to burn. Rowena saw it, too. She giggled, then held the door open for him. "He's already down for the night, if you can believe that. He wore himself out on the bicycle."

"How about the dinosaur?"

Tears rimmed Rowena's eyes. "He was... I just can't describe it, Dale. He saw it and started crying."

Rowena invited him to have a seat, but Dale declined. "I need to get home. I just wanted to stop by and give you these."

Her eyes grew large when he held out a set of car keys.

"It's nothing special. Eight years old with a lot of miles on it, but the boys at the auto shop said it would get you by for a couple years. It will allow you to get back to Springfield and on your feet again. The tank is full, too."

If, sometime in the future, Dale were asked to describe what Christmas should really feel like, he would say it was like the next few moments at Rowena's tiny duplex. She was in equal parts speechless, effusive, bubbly, tearful, and most of all, appreciative. They walked around the car, then she started it and drove around the block while Dale stayed back with a sleeping Braylon. When she returned, she made coffee. Dale accepted.

Then, when they were seated on the sofa, Rowena moved closer and placed her hand on Dale's knee. That was where the Christmas feeling stopped. Rowena was younger than his daughter. She was a lost girl with a child trying to make it in a grown-up world, and the last thing Dale wanted was what she saw as the only thing she could give in return. He said his farewells and left the duplex. The walk home, nearly two miles, was unpleasant in the cold and slush, but the feeling of doing good for someone made it easier. He was home before he knew it.

The house was empty.

No Max.

No Susan.

And no Chelsea.

Somehow she had escaped the house. He was checking for open doors when he spotted something on the kitchen counter.

A plate of fudge and cookies.

No note. Just sweets.

Chelsea had probably made a dash for it when the person dropping off the plate had come inside. Once again, he'd forgotten to lock the front door. An unlocked door might result in disaster at the *Joe Eftink Apartment Homes*, but in Dale's neighborhood it resulted in fudge and cookies.

And a missing dog.

Well, if Chelsea felt the need to run off, her wish had once again come true. Dale knew he probably should go look for her, but he was still cold and wet from the walk home.

And the fudge looked delicious.

And the cookies were oatmeal raisin.

And chocolate chip.

So, he sat down in his La-Z-Boy, turned on the TV, and cleaned the plate.

Merry Christmas.

14

"What do you have there, Coach?" Larry Bob was eyeing the scrap of paper Dale pulled from the pocket of his jeans. Plumber Dick was eyeing Larry Bob's last link of sausage.

"If your dirty plumber hand gets within a foot of it, I'll stab it with my fork," Larry Bob said as he waved the utensil around to make his point.

"That boy's got eyes in the back of his head," Welder Tommy observed.

"You got to when you're as bad a lawyer as he is," Patsy interjected as she refilled coffee cups.

"Damndest thing about lawyers is that ninety-nine percent of 'em give all the rest a bad name." Uncle Homer's observation brought hoots of agreement from his nephews. "Will Rogers said that."

"The hell he did," Larry Bob said irritably, helping himself to one of the breakfast biscuits Patsy left on the table. "It was Steven Wright."

"Is he one of your clients?" Plumber Dick deadpanned.

"He's a comedian," Larry Bob said. "And you guys can kid all you want, but at the end of the day I'm the one going home to that big house on Elm Street."

"Know what's a damn shame?" Uncle Homer continued. "A bus load of lawyers going off a cliff with an empty seat."

"That was Will Rogers who said that." Plumber Dick said with conviction.

"You're a dumbass," Welder Tommy said, shaking his head. "Did you ever see any busses in those movies? Will Rogers rode that horse, Trigger."

"I ate at one of his restaurants once," Dick said. "Back in Virginia. It was that time when Margo and me went to see the ocean. You remember when we did that, Coach?"

Dale did not, and since Margo had fled from Dick and Mozarkite two decades earlier, it was not a surprise. Neither was the fact that neither boy could differentiate one Rogers from another. There was no need to try to correct them, so he consulted the list Larry Bob had asked him about instead.

"It's a list of things I have to get done today, Larry Bob. Tommy, what time can I pick up your horse trailer?"

"He still ain't cleaned the hog shit out of it from when he took it to the State Fair," Plumber Dick said.

"I did this morning," Tommy said, slapping his brother on the head for good measure. "I even pulled it into the shed so the water wouldn't freeze on it. You can get it anytime, Coach."

"How much stuff does Susan have?" Larry Bob again, always with the questions.

"My garage is full, but it should just be one load. The big stuff is being delivered." The day after Christmas, Susan and Effie Camper had visited two Mozarkite furniture stores and a consignment shop. The furniture stores offered delivery. The items from the consignment shop were the reason Linda's car had spent the past several nights in the driveway. Two football players who had already returned from break would do the heavy lifting.

"Any big plans for tonight, Coach?" Plumber Dick asked. "I remember how Miss Linda always liked going to the Moose Lodge thing."

Dale shook his head. He hadn't thought of how he would spend

New Year's Eve, other than helping Susan get moved into her new place.

"Linda sure did like that Moose Lodge thing," Larry Bob said. "It was the only time I ever remember seeing her get tipsy."

"Remember when she and Willis did the jitterbug?" Uncle Homer asked, laughing at the decade-old memory. "Who had a clue that Willis could jitterbug?"

Dale smiled at the memory of Linda and Willis cutting the rug. "They both loved to dance. Are you going to the Moose Lodge thing, Homer?"

"Yeah, I got some business up there, so I bought a ticket."

'Business' usually meant that Uncle Homer had been spending time at the still he covertly operated in an area of woods overrun with briar thickets and wild boar. It was said that there was a time, long before Dale arrived in Mozarkite, when the area was teeming with fulltime bootleggers, many of whom lived in homes bought and paid for by their hooch. Uncle Homer was the only one left, and even his operation was part-time.

"I'm going to the roller derby down in Jonesboro." Welder Tommy sounded as delighted with his plans as Max had been Christmas morning. "It's ladies' night, so the women get in for half-price."

"Hoping you'll find yourself a good woman, Tommy?" Larry Bob asked. Dale knew where his friend was headed, but Tommy was a bit too slow to keep up.

"You know," Tommy said, relaxing into his chair in a way that pushed his ample gut out for all to see. "I bought two seats on the third row. Paid top dollar, too. I'll play it cool, but if there's any ladies looking to spend the evening watching derby from the good seats, I'll be ready."

"What happens if two women want good seats?"

"I only got one, so I guess I'll have to pick."

Larry Bob moved in for the kill. "Or, they'll kick your ass and take the seats for themselves."

"Don't be kidding my nephew," Uncle Homer jumped in. "I'm hoping tonight's the night he becomes a man."

The laughter was loud and bawdy. Even Dale couldn't help but laugh at a refrain that had lasted for as long as he'd been coming to the Goldrush.

"I became a man when I was in eleventh grade," Tommy protested. "You guys know all about that. I told you before. Ellen Biggerstaff and me. Out at the lake."

"Pretty damn convenient that the only woman you ever claim to have been with isn't here to defend herself," Larry Bob said.

"How can I help it that she up and died? Weren't none of my doing."

"You sure you didn't crush her, Tommy?" Uncle Homer said, joining in. "Because I don't remember seeing Ellen Biggerstaff after you and her... you know."

"She had cancer, dammit." Tommy's voice was rising, as it always did when the conversation detoured in the direction of his love life. Before they could pile on, he got up, threw a ten on the table, and put on his coat.

"The trailer is ready whenever you want it," he said to Dale as he exited the Goldrush.

"We really need to stop kidding him about Ellen Biggerstaff," Uncle Homer said as he watched his nephew stalk out.

"You're usually the one who starts it," Larry Bob replied. Then, turning to Dale, he said, "Sorry I can't help you move Susan's stuff. I've got court in Laclede County today."

"You have court on New Year's Eve?"

"Yep."

"Lawyer or defendant?" Homer asked.

Larry Bob winked, flipped Uncle Homer the bird, then followed Tommy out the door.

◊ ◊ ◊

DALE'S CELLPHONE was buzzing when he returned to his truck following Susan's move in. An out of state number, probably someone warning him that his social security number had been compromised. Those calls had started coming in several times a week. He ignored it, started the truck, and headed out of town. He was backing the horse trailer into Welder Tommy's barn when the phone rang again. Same number. Since those social security calls never used the same number, he answered.

"Happy New Year, Coach. Are you going to be ringing it in with friends?"

The deep voice was rich and resonant, like you heard on TV or radio. That was because it was a voice from TV and radio, at least occasionally.

"Andre Jameson. I was going to call you next week."

"Great minds, Coach. Great minds. First things first, I'm so sorry about Linda. Did you know she called me the week before she passed?"

Dale hadn't.

"She wanted my recipe for rib rub. I couldn't believe she remembered, but she did. I made ribs for her back when she came to Houston, when was it? Maybe four or five years ago."

Dale did not know Linda had visited Andre.

Nor did he know that Linda had planned to make ribs.

"She called me back the next week to let me know how good they'd turned out. What a woman, Coach. You won the matrimonial lottery, you know that?"

Dale didn't know Linda had actually made ribs.

Or who she made them for.

Because he hadn't had ribs since their last trip to Springfield, at that old place they'd gone to for years, Tiny's Barbeque.

"I sure did, Andre."

"I wanted to be there, but I was obligated to do the local college pregame show that week. There was no way out of it. I'm sorry for that, but I hope you got my flowers."

Dale acknowledged they did, though he didn't know for sure if they had or not. There were so many flowers.

"I appreciate your thoughts, Andre. Linda loved you like a son."

"A son?" Andre laughed. "Coach, Linda wasn't old enough to be my mother. I was totally crushing on her back in college. She knew it, too. I was such a country bumpkin that I didn't know how to hide my feelings. Thankfully, she was sweet about it and never laughed in my face."

This was news to Dale, too. Fortunately, Andre did not have a *W* in his name, so that eliminated him from the list of people who might have sent the necklace.

Yeah, the necklace still nicked at the periphery of his mind.

"How's Susan doing, Coach? I remember how close she and Linda were."

"She's back in Mozarkite. I've spent most of the day getting her moved into her new place. She has a son, Max, who is with his father in Chicago, but gets back tomorrow."

They chatted about old times for a few minutes before Andre got down to the business at hand.

"Look, Coach, I'm going to be in town next week. President Fuller invited me and, since I had some long-overdue meetings in St. Louis, I decided to drive and stop by Mozarkite."

"Really, Andre? Dr. Fuller invited you?" This was news.

"She asked if I was interested in becoming more active as an alumnus. Honestly, I'd never considered it. We're meeting for dinner, and I was hoping you and I might visit at some point that day as well."

"Yes, I would like to visit. Actually, I was wanting to pick your brain. Willis Tompkins is ill and can't coach anymore, and I was wondering if you might have some suggestions as to a replacement."

"I think I can come up with some names for you, Coach. Offense, right?"

"Yes. And recruiting."

"Let me get to work on it. By the way, there's a good-looking boy down here in Houston who plays at one of the inner-city schools that never does well in football. He's raw, but fast as all get out." Andre threw out the player's name. "Have you heard of him?"

Dale had not.

"Neither have a lot of coaches. He's getting some interest from a couple of small colleges, but I believe he would benefit from starting out at junior college. We've visited a few times, and I think he would consider Mozarkite if I talk it up."

"Let me do some checking around and get back to you, Andre. We'll put that on our list for your visit."

◊ ◊ ◊

DALE PULLED into the driveway at half-past eight. The call with Andre was troubling him. Sure, it would be great to sit down with his best player ever, but why had Dr. Fuller invited him? Was she trying to get Andre more involved with the football program? Or was it more than that?

Was she considering him as Dale's replacement?

The thoughts vanished when he saw Chelsea tied to the front porch. He pulled his truck alongside Linda's Escalade, got out, and went to the house. Chelsea wagged her tail in excitement, then jumped up to greet him. But as soon as Dale untied the bailing twine she took off. He called after her, then ran back to his truck, and gave chase. For several blocks he was able to keep visual contact until Chelsea made a quick left turn and disappeared into an alley behind the Bowl-a-Rama. Dale parked, jumped out, and jogged down the alley, but it was too late.

Chelsea was gone again.

Back home, he pulled Linda's SUV back into its space in the now empty garage and glanced around to see what she'd left inside. There were four yard signs that he would get to Susan before deciding what to do with the vehicle. There was a box of business cards, two pairs of reading glasses, and Linda's bulky calendar, stuffed with all matter of paper. Dale held it to his nose and inhaled the scent of Chanel Number Five. Despite being one of the least observant men in the world when it came to such things, he knew the name. Linda had worn it for years. It permeated her clothing, her possessions, their bedding. It was as familiar to Dale as Linda had been, and the scent of Chanel made him feel something deeper than he had felt since she'd passed. He turned on the Caddy's dome light, opened the planner, and looked inside, immediately recognizing Linda's flowing script. There were notes and reminders that no longer mattered, meetings from the past, and a few from the future that would never take place. In between the monthly tabs for June and July of the previous year, he pulled out a photograph.

Linda.

Fishing.

Fly fishing.

Not actually fishing but holding up her catch.

A sign behind her proclaimed the location as Bennett Springs, a popular fishing destination a few hours away.

Linda had a half-dozen good looking trout on a stringer. She was smiling. Radiant, even.

And on the back, in a handwriting he'd seen before, a handwriting that wasn't Linda's, were the words, '*Something's Fishy!*'

It was signed, *W*.

15

*L*arry Bob's butt and gut bumped five diners as he bulldozed his way through the early morning throng to get to his seat. He was either unaware or chose to ignore the contact.

"Guess who I just saw coming out of the Best Western?"

"What were you doing all the way out by the highway?" Plumber Dick asked.

"Gas is cheaper out at the Conoco. But guess who I saw?"

"How much cheaper?" Bits of egg fell from Welder Tommy's mouth as he spoke.

"Four cents."

Just four cents? From the look on Tommy's face, Dale figured he was either trying to do a mathematical calculation or suppress a fart. It turned out to be the former. "It's seven miles out there and seven miles back. That's fifteen miles. What kind of mileage are you getting with that Durango, Larry Bob? Twelve? Fourteen?"

"Would you shut the hell up. I'm trying to tell you who's in town and you're worried about a few pennies worth of gas."

"It sounds like you're the one worried about a few pennies of gas," Uncle Homer quipped. "And I think you're lying anyway. I know for a fact that the Conoco is the only place around that sells those little breakfast sausages that spin around on those rollers. You went out there to feed your face, didn't you, Larry Bob?"

"Did you get one of them little sausages on the rollers?" Plumber Dick's tone was stern, almost accusingly so. He sounded like someone who had just learned that his girlfriend was stepping out on him.

Larry Bob threw his hands up. "What the Hellman's Mayonnaise does it matter what I was doing at Conoco? I was there, and I saw somebody coming out of the Best Western, and you'll never guess who it was."

"Andre Jameson," Uncle Homer said.

The color washing from Larry Bob's face brought uproarious laughter from Uncle Homer.

"How did you know Andre Jameson was at the Best Western?" Larry Bob looked as if he had just lost a big court case. Others seated nearby heard his question and immediately started buzzing about the news.

"Darlene Tildon works as night maid out there, remember?" Uncle Homer asked.

They all knew Darlene Tildon and that she worked at the Best Western.

"Her husband, Ducky, stopped by my place last night. He told me."

"Why was Ducky Tildon out to your place?" Plumber Dick asked.

"I was having an Avon party you numb nuts. Why do you think he was there?"

Dick chewed on the question that everyone else knew the answer to. Ducky Tildon drank like a fish. A fish who had probably gotten behind on paying his credit card bills, which means they were declined at Mozarkite's seven liquor stores. Uncle Homer didn't accept credit cards for his firewater but he did deals better than any used car salesman, and Ducky Tildon owned guns. Lots and lots of guns, but likely one less than he owned two days ago.

So, Andre was already in town.

From what he had told Dale when they last spoke, Andre was stopping through for a couple hours. Instead, he had spent the night at the Best Western. It seemed there was more going on with Andre than Dale had considered.

Or maybe not.

Maybe Andre had gotten an early start and arrived in Mozarkite faster than expected. There could be any number of reasons why he spent the night in town.

"School starts back today, right Coach?" Uncle Homer's question interrupted Dale's thoughts, which was probably a good thing.

"Yeah, Homer, I'd better get going."

"Will you see Andre Jameson today?" Larry Bob asked.

"Yes. We're meeting later."

Larry Bob pulled a napkin from the chrome dispenser on the table and handed it to Dale.

"Would you mind getting his autograph for me? That guy is in the Hall of Fame. It should be worth a few bucks."

◊ ◊ ◊

DALE WAS PREPARING to back out of his usual parking spot in the alley behind the Goldrush when a rusty gray Chevy pickup screeched to a halt behind him. Not sure if the driver realized he was trying to leave, Dale opened his door and got out. The Chevy's driver-side door opened at the same time. Out stepped Doyle Ricketts.

"Keep your nose out of my business, old man," Doyle barked as he came around the front of the truck. The whites of his eyes were huge, and his nostrils flared. He looked like a rabid dog.

The passenger door opened, and Mozarkite Police Officer Wade Ricketts crawled out. He was grinning from ear to ear.

Doyle was ten feet away and approaching. His hands were balled into fists. There was spittle in the corners of his mouth. He was close and he was big, bigger than Dale. And younger. Much younger. Dale didn't take his eyes off Doyle, but he spoke to Wade.

"Wade, your brother needs to step away."

"I ain't never been able to tell Doyle what to do, Coach." Wade was still grinning. "Especially when somebody's been messing with his woman. And do you know what, Coach? It sounds like you messed with his woman."

The winter air was still. The parking lot, other than the three of them, was empty. The four other cars in the tight space belonged to Patsy, her cook, dishwasher, and waitress. Customers, except for Dale, parked out front or on the street.

"We can probably make this all go away," Wade continued. "Coach, how about you apologize to Doyle for messing with his girlfriend."

"There's nothing to apologize for," Dale replied calmly. "He kicked Rowena and her son out of the house. She needed help, so I helped."

"You did a lot more than help, you old bastard," Doyle growled. "You bought her a freaking car. You're screwing her, and I'm gonna mess you up for it."

Doyle Ricketts lunged at Dale. A last minute sidestep kept him from receiving a full-on tackle from a man as large as many of his linemen, but it was not enough to subdue his assailant. After scrabbling on the ground for a moment, Doyle threw himself at Dale's ankles. Dale went down hard on the asphalt. The back of his head made contact, and he saw stars. Anticipating what would likely happen next, he shielded his face and tried to roll away.

Then came the unmistakable explosion of a gunshot. And silence.

Dale assumed he had been shot, probably by Wade Ricketts. It had to be Wade, because Doyle was on the ground three feet away, his mouth gaping open as he looked across the parking lot.

He felt no pain, but didn't they say that gunshots usually killed you before you felt anything? Where had he heard that? At the moment it sounded ridiculous. No, he concluded, he had definitely not been shot.

"Patsy, put it on the ground right now!"

It was Wade Ricketts who shouted the command. There was only one Patsy that Dale knew. He dared glance toward the rear of the Goldrush, and, sure enough, Patsy Werner was holding a pistol.

"Your hand is shaking, Patsy," Wade said. "You're going to shoot somebody. Maybe even yourself. Put it down. *Now.*"

"Go to hell, Wade Ricketts."

Wade blinked several times, then said, "Patsy, you're disobeying an officer of the law. That kind of shit'll get you serious jail time."

"I don't see a badge or uniform." Patsy used the gun to wave toward an open spot in the parking lot. "Now move over there and get face down on the ground."

"Holy Mary, Mother of God!"

Bridgette, Patsy's fifteen-year-old waitress, had stepped out the back door with a bag of trash. When she saw what was happening, she dropped the bag. It split open at her feet. Food, dirty napkins, and empty cans spilled out.

Patsy didn't take her eyes off the Ricketts boys as she spoke. "Bridgette, go back inside right now. Do not tell anyone what's happening out here. Do you understand?"

"Yes, Miss Patsy."

"You're going to do two things. First, call 911 and tell them to get a police car over here, preferably a sheriff's deputy."

"There's no need for that, Patsy. I'm a cop. I can—"

Patsy waved the gun in Wade's direction. That shut him up.

"After you call, go out front and tell Larry Bob Billingsley to come out here. Don't let anyone hear you, understand?"

"Yes."

Dale caught a slight movement as Wade Ricketts turned toward Patsy. They were twenty feet apart, but Wade stealthily had closed three feet of the distance. Patsy saw the motion, too, and fired the pistol a second time. Wade swore as he hit the ground and covered his head.

"Move again and I'll put it right between your eyes."

"It's gonna be a lot of fun getting all dressed up in my uniform to testify against you, Patsy, you stupid bitch," Wade said in a cocky tone that belied his place in the situation.

"You'll never wear a police uniform again," Patsy said quietly.

"What the—Patsy, did you shoot somebody?" Larry Bob was breathing hard from the exertion of the short walk to the parking lot. The color drained from his face when he spotted his friend on the ground.

"Coach, you're bleeding! Did she shoot—?"

"Not her, Larry Bob. And I'm not shot. I got knocked down."

"I figured you would be Coach's lawyer when this all goes to trial," Patsy said. Sirens filled the air as she told Larry Bob what she'd seen.

◆ ◆ ◆

FOLLOWING two hours getting checked out at Mozarkite Memorial Hospital and another two hours answering questions at the Mozarkite police station, Dale had been driven home by Susan. After peppering him with questions, mainly about his condition, she had put him to bed. He slept from one-thirty until three-thirty, when Andre's phone call awakened him. He tried to hide the wooziness and stiffness he still felt but was unsure how good a job he did.

Andre Jameson was one of maybe five people within fifty miles who had not yet heard about Dale's encounter with the Ricketts brothers. He gasped when Dale answered the door with a bandage on his head. He and Dr. Fuller had been in meetings since nine that morning, seven hours earlier.

"Where are they now?" Andre asked after Dale had relayed a condensed version of the encounter.

"County lockup, at least until the judge sets bail. Chief Mayberry already went by and told Wade Ricketts that he's fired from the force."

Andre offered to postpone their meeting, but Dale wouldn't hear of it. He was always happy to see his former player. Any former player, for that matter. More to the point he wanted to know what had kept Andre and Dr. Fuller behind closed doors all day. He turned down Andre's offer to go out for supper, preferring to order a pizza and stay at home, away from prying eyes. Between the assault and

Andre's presence in town for the first time in years, Coach Dale Fox was getting more attention than he wanted.

They spent most of an hour catching up. Dale enjoyed hearing Andre's stories about his life since football. Andre had proven to be one of those few retired players, particularly players of color, who had overcome the undeserved stereotypes and carved out a prosperous post-playing career. He was successful in local media back in Houston. He was successful in business. He was smart, handsome, wealthy, and happily married with five children.

"Did you ever think it might be like this when we first crossed paths?" Andre asked as they relaxed in Dale's living room over pizza and iced tea. "I mean, the way things turned out for me?"

"Not at all," Dale admitted. "I always figured that players at the big schools would catch up to you, but you kept getting faster. The NFL thing blew me away, but you worked so hard. I shouldn't have been surprised."

Andre laughed. "No one was more surprised than me. When I got to Florida, I was fifth on the depth chart at wide receiver during summer workouts. I planned to do what I needed to remain on the team, but mostly keep my focus on getting my degree. Next thing I knew, I was starting against Alabama."

"Academically and professionally, nothing you do surprises me. You brought an intensity to the program here, not just on the field, but in the classroom. Other players saw you and wanted to be like you. You probably impacted players here for six years after you left. They knew how hard you worked to be a good student and a good player."

Dale meant every word, and he could tell that Andre appreciated hearing them. The man was used to being adored. He was complimented and slapped on the back everyplace he went. Still, when someone who had known him, really known him, said those kinds of things, well Dale could see it touched Andre.

"What did you think of that boy from Houston I told you about?"

Dale had expected the question and was ready for it.

"Great talent, Andre. On video he reminds me of you."

"Is he coming?" Andre seemed excited by the prospect. Dale was about to bust his bubble.

"The baggage is too much for Mozarkite. He has a drug possession charge pending, and a D+ grade average. We'll have to pass."

Andre licked his lips, then said, "I knew the grades weren't the best, but, Coach, it's not a drug charge. It was grass, and the boy maintains it was below the level that Texas classifies as illegal marijuana. His lawyer expects the charges to be dropped."

"Maybe, but still, I prefer not to take a chance."

Andre became quiet, Dale felt his disappointment. They remained like that for a few moments, chewing their pizza and not speaking. It was Dale who broke the silence.

"As I mentioned on the phone, I need an assistant coach to work with our offense and take the lead in recruiting."

Andre pulled out his cellphone and started going through his contacts. "I can give you a half-dozen names right now. Guys who want very much to break into coaching at this level."

Dale got up and went to the kitchen. He returned with paper and pen. "Write them down, but just three. The best three."

They were quiet for several moments as Andre transferred names and phone numbers to the pad of paper. When he finished he held it out for Dale. "The first two are working as interns at mid-level schools that have had some success. They are looking for paying positions that will get them in the door. The third was fired as head coach from a Division Three school year before last. He's been working in sales, but wants back in."

Dale scanned the names but did not recognize any of them.

"If you're serious, Coach, you need to move fast. I know for a fact that all three are being considered by other schools. A word from me can help you land them, but don't wait long."

Dale folded the slip of paper and placed it in his pocket. "I'll look into them, Andre. Thank you."

"I'm glad I can help."

"How did you like Dr. Fuller?"

Andre's face brightened. "I like her very much! She seems smart and very competent. Mozarkite is lucky to have her." He laughed as he said, "She's a different direction from old Professor Parker."

"She is indeed. The two of you certainly spent enough time together to get acquainted. What all did you talk about?"

"She was gauging my interest in becoming a more involved alumnus. We talked about the role of community colleges, the types of students who enroll, what the future will look like." Andre paused, then added, "We talked about football."

"Football?"

"Yes, football. We discussed the sport in general and also the Mozarkite football program."

Dale would always remember that as the moment that a small part of his respect for Andre Jameson faded away.

"Don't you believe that if my program is being discussed, it would've been best if I were there?"

"Are your players always there when you discuss their performance?"

That one stung. Dale shook his head. "That's different and you know it, Andre."

The situation was growing more caustic, but Dale wanted his feelings known. He'd sensed since the end of the season that his grasp over some aspects of his life was moving beyond his control. Linda's sudden death disrupted his home. The little things he was finding, like the pearls and the photographs, were disrupting his equilibrium. The scuffle in the Goldrush parking lot had disrupted his confidence. And now Andre and Dr. Fuller were disrupting his livelihood.

Well, he might not be able to wrest control of the other things, at least not immediately, but he could put the brakes on the interference with football.

Andre must have sensed Dale's resistance, because his tone quickly became more conciliatory. "Coach, I don't want to run your football program. My life is full and busy enough as it is. The truth is, Dr. Fuller called me for advice, and I was willing to provide it based upon my experience with the game."

Dale wasn't having any of it. "So, you think your experience and expertise are somehow more valuable than mine?" he snapped.

"Not at all. But my experiences are different, and sometimes it's valuable to get a different perspective. Don't you do that when you go to coaches' clinics? Don't you do that when you pick the brains of your colleagues from other schools?"

The truth, which Dale was loathe to admit, was that he hadn't been to a coaching clinic in over a decade. The way other coaches were bending and genuflecting to the needs and wishes of the big schools had led him to avoid their advice as well.

"Your new college president is not a football coach. She sees that the program isn't winning as much as it used to, and she wants to know why. She's spoken to you about it and now she's—"

"How do you know?" Dale moved to the edge of the sofa and placed his plate on the coffee table.

"How do I know what?"

"That Dr. Fuller has spoken to me?"

Andre hesitated, aware that he might have overstepped.

"Because if she told you that, she's breaking my confidentiality, and I will not accept that."

"Coach, please. We talked football and... where are you going?"

Andre's question was directed at Dale's back as he had already crossed the room to go look for his cellphone.

"To call Dr. Fuller and get to the bottom of this. I'm done talking about this, Andre. Do you need directions back to your hotel?"

Dale paused in the hallway and looked back. Andre was getting to his feet. The usually unflappable man appeared stricken by the turn of the conversation. Well, too bad. That made two of them. Dale found his phone and called the number Dr. Fuller had provided him. It went to voicemail. He was ready to spill out all the emotion he was feeling at the moment, but what good would that do? It never worked when he was coaching a game, and it would likely not work in dealing with his boss, either. By the time he heard the beep, he was ready.

"This is Dale Fox, Dr. Fuller. Andre Jameson just left my house. I would like to visit with you about the football program... *my* football program as soon as possible."

As he was disconnecting, he heard the front door close. Andre had let himself out. A few moments later he was at the window watching his greatest player drive away. Would things ever be the same between them? Would anything ever be the same? Football? Life? They were deep thoughts, deeper than Dale cared to delve, but the recent turn of events had him going deeper in his thoughts. He did not particularly like it. The best thing about Mozarkite was the sameness. He craved routine, always had. It tended to make Linda stir crazy, but Dale reveled in it. Breakfast at the Goldrush, the kibitzing between the regulars, work, coaching, home. His La-Z-Boy. Bed at ten-thirty.

There was a rustling someplace in the house. Dale listened for a few seconds before he realized what it was. He went downstairs and opened the front door.

Chelsea was back. Again.

Tied to the front porch. Again.

"I'm getting tired of this," Coach said irritably as he loosened the string. Chelsea tilted her head as if she could understand, then nuzzled his hand, moved past, and entered the house.

At least the dog was home.

For now.

Dale went to the kitchen and filled her food and water bowls. She ate, but not in that ravished way one would expect from a dog on the run. Several times she paused and glanced at him, checking, it seemed, to be sure he was all right. Dale noticed a stack of mail that hadn't been there earlier. On top was a note from Susan.

This came to the office. I pulled out the stuff related to work. The rest is yours. I hope you're feeling better! Max and I love you, Susan.

Most of the bundle consisted of magazines. He remembered Linda mentioning that she got a discount if she bought them for the office. *Better Homes and Gardens, Southern Living, Missouri Life, Midwest Living*. Dale would not be looking at them, so he placed them on the counter for Susan to take back to the office. That left envelopes, including renewal reminders for two of the four magazines. Those he put with the magazines.

Two envelopes remained. One was a giving statement from that start-up church that Linda had hung out with. Dale nearly passed out when he saw how much she had given. No wonder she had it sent to the office. According to the colorful brochure enclosed with the statement, Linda's money had been pooled with that of other members to support missions in Africa, South America, and Los Angeles. Smiling faces, mostly black and brown, looked up from the slick paper. Unless everyone was a lot more generous next year, some of those faces wouldn't be smiling, because they weren't getting any more money from the Fox household. Dale slid the brochure into the trash but set aside the statement. It would go to the tax man.

A Visa statement remained. Dale could not remember the last time he'd used the card. He wrote checks for anything that cost more than one of the five twenties he carried in his wallet, secure with the knowledge that Ginny Sowers down at the bank would transfer money between savings and checking when needed. Linda preferred the Visa, though, and used it extensively for work. *Easier to reconcile, easier to claim on taxes*, she'd often said.

The envelope was stamped *PAST DUE*, reminding Dale that he hadn't thought of the card since Linda's passing. He opened it and was happy to see that the amount due, even with late fees, was less than five-hundred dollars. But then why wouldn't it be? The last time the card had been used was two days before Linda passed, at the McDonalds in West Plains. Dale glanced down the list of charges, mundane expenses, mainly food, until he came to the next-to-last, a charge for two-hundred and eighty dollars for a hotel in Branson.

Branson?

The expense was labeled, *SPA SERVICES – COUPLES MASSAGE*. Dale did a double-take.

Couples massage?

Branson?

The date of services was a Saturday he remembered very well. The team had gotten trounced down in McCrackenville, then a bus tire had blown out on the trip back to Mozarkite, delaying them three hours. Linda hadn't made the trip, but that wasn't unusual. She did a brisk walk-in trade on Saturdays. He would call the credit card company in the morning and get the mistake straightened out.

It was a mistake.

Right?

ale was sore, and his head hurt from the previous day's encounter with the Ricketts boys.

That was bad.

His dustup with the Ricketts brothers was on the front page of the *Messenger*.

That was worse.

And then his phone rang. Dr. Fuller. He let it go to voicemail while he read the news account. Assault. They were calling it assault.

Old women got assaulted.

Young girls got assaulted.

Football coaches did not get assaulted.

Bear Bryant was never assaulted.

Shula, Osborne, Eddie Robinson. Their names would never appear in a news article next to the word, *assaulted*.

Landry, Lambeau, Halas. Never.

Dale Fox. Assaulted.

Why didn't the *Messenger* say he was *ambushed*? Now that was a good word. Guys could get ambushed. They used the word all the time in the old Westerns Dale had watched as a kid.

Even worse, the story was written by Heaven Knight. She had

already ambushed him once, back in the fall with that hit piece about his coaching record. Why couldn't she have at least used that word to describe what had happened in the Goldrush parking lot?

She had taken the time to contact Larry Bob. And Rowena. Rowena *Locker*. Dale hadn't even known her last name.

'My client was getting in his truck to go to work when the assailants assaulted him.'

'Coach Dale Fox went out of his way to be nice to my son and me after Doyle Ricketts threw us out right before Christmas.'

Heaven Knight described him as *a respected and long-time coach and community leader*. She made note of Linda's recent passing.

And of the recent dip in performance of the Mozarkite football program.

She had to work that in there somehow, didn't she?

Dale reread the story, then checked voicemail. Dr. Fuller began by expressing her sympathy. The *senseless assault*, she called it. Then she asked him to come to her office at nine.

It was eight-fifteen.

Dale had planned to stop by the Goldrush, but after the *Messenger* piece, it was the last place he wanted to be. He didn't want anybody's pity. He didn't want people thinking of him as some old man who can't defend himself. While he showered and dressed, he could hear the constant buzz and beep of his phone. Eleven missed calls. Uncle Homer, both nephews, Larry Bob twice. Patsy. The rest were numbers he didn't recognize, but the messages they left made it clear of their intentions. Two area TV stations and three newspapers, including the big one in Springfield. All requested interviews.

No chance of that.

Dale had a meeting to get to.

And a football program to save.

◊ ◊ ◊

Dr. Fuller caught him completely off guard when she pulled him into a hug. Professor Parker would never have done anything of the sort.

"I've been so worried about you," she said, pulling away to examine his head. "I called your daughter yesterday, and she said that—"

"Why would you call Susan?"

His tone caused her to step back in surprise. When she spoke, her tone was tentative. "I wasn't sure if you were in the hospital or home, so one of the secretaries here suggested I call her. She told me you were sleeping, and I didn't want to bother you."

One minute into their meeting and things were already going off the rails. Dale couldn't read her. Was she sincere? Was her concern a ruse? Stay close to your friends and closer to your enemies? That kind of thing?

"I'm fine. Really. Thank you, though. Andre Jameson came to my house last night."

"He said he was going to."

"You told him about our conversation. About the football team."

Dr Fuller nodded. "We talked about—"

"Our private conversation. About my performance as coach."

It was quiet for several moments as she considered what he'd said. He could see the moment when she realized the gravity of what she'd done. They hadn't even gotten seated yet.

"Sit down, please. Let's talk about this."

"You breached my confidentiality, Dr. Fuller. Let's begin there."

"Coach Fox, I can assure you that—"

"That what? Either you shared private information from our conversation or you didn't."

When it was apparent that he wasn't going to have a seat, Dr. Fuller did. She sat back in her chair and looked at the ceiling, her fingers tented in front of her face. They remained that way for a bit before she spoke.

"I did. And I know better. I'm sorry."

Dale nodded.

"My intent doesn't matter. The fact that I want you to succeed as our coach doesn't matter. I violated your confidentiality."

Dale nodded again. He wasn't going to make this easy.

"Can you forgive me?"

He considered the best way to respond. He could demand that she report her transgression to the Trustees. He could tell the *Messenger*. Heaven Knight would probably give her left arm for a scoop like that. If it went public, her word against his, the people of Mozarkite would see it his way. He could really throw his weight around, make things hard for the new President. Perhaps she would reconsider her decision to leave St. Louis. Life was different in small towns; that was something Dr. Margaret Fuller needed to learn. A lesson she needed to be taught. So what better time was there?

"Of course I forgive you."

So much for taking the tough approach.

Dr. Fuller's face brightened. When she offered Dale a seat the second time, he took it.

"I thought long and hard about having you attend my meeting with Mr. Jameson, Coach. In the end, I needed a perspective that wasn't colored by your presence."

"And?"

"Andre Jameson considers you one of the most influential people in his life."

Dale said nothing.

"He would never have played professional football had you not taken a chance on him."

Dale still said nothing, but the words were having an effect on him. Warming his heart.

"He compared your game day strategy to the coaches he played for in the NFL. He said you never lost your cool, which allowed your players to take chances."

"Andre Jameson made my job easy. He was incredibly coachable."

"He loves you, Coach Fox."

Okay, this was going too far. Love? Dale wished Dr. Fuller would take the conversation in a different direction. Then, she did.

"But he thinks you've allowed yourself to fall behind."

"I disagree."

"Then why aren't we competitive anymore?"

"We are competitive. It just doesn't always show up on the scoreboard."

"If the scoreboard doesn't show a win does it really matter, Coach?"

"It matters to me."

Dr. Fuller stood up. "Would you like a cup of coffee? Water maybe?"

"I'm fine."

"Would you mind if I..." she nodded toward a coffee bar she'd installed in the spot where Professor Parker used to have file cabinets.

"Certainly. What happened to Professor Parker's file cabinets?"

Dr. Fuller laughed. "Do you know what was in those cabinets?"

"Files?"

She shook her head and laughed again, a gesture that always seemed to make her look more like a coed than President.

"Supplies. Chalk, paper clips, light bulbs for projectors that hadn't been used since the seventies. Thumbtacks. Typewriter ribbons for typewriters that were phased out years ago. It was amazing. I considered calling the Smithsonian."

"He was frugal, that's for certain." While Dr. Fuller sipped her coffee, Dale shared a couple stories of exactly how thrifty the former President had been. It was a light-hearted moment, and he wished it could've remained that way, but it wasn't to be.

"Coach," Dr. Fuller said in her President voice, a clear signal that they were returning to the matter at hand. "Again, I'm sorry for how I shared information with Mr. Jameson that I shouldn't have. But the matter remains. Our football program is losing more games than it wins. We're getting beat on recruitment. We don't even have a person responsible for recruiting. You presented several names last week, and I checked them out personally. They're good men."

"I agree."

"But they're old-school, Coach Fox. We need someone who can go toe to toe with the recruiters at our competitor schools. We need someone who talks the talk of today's players. Someone the players can relate to."

"Coaching isn't about relating to players. It's about earning their respect and getting them to give their best effort."

"Andre Jameson says that's not the case anymore, Coach Fox. He was describing the coaches who are most successful with today's players. They relate to their players or surround themselves with assistants who do. They're aggressive in recruiting."

Dale was unsure how to respond, so he didn't.

"We need that kind of person."

"So, are you telling me who I should hire?"

Dr. Fuller raised her hands. "No, Coach. I'm asking you to listen to someone who wants to help."

With that, Margaret Fuller stood and offered her hand. "You're our coach. You have a contract that says so. I only ask that you consider my suggestions."

◊ ◊ ◊

ANDRE WAS LEANING against the wall next to Dale's office when he arrived ten minutes later.

"I thought you had meetings in St. Louis," Dale said, reaching past to unlock his door.

"I love you, Coach. I don't want anything coming between us."

Dale considered Andre for a few moments. He would never have another player of his caliber. His was a once in a lifetime kind of talent.

And it was unlikely he would ever have a young man so dedicated to his studies. Or so revered by his teammates. Or respected by his coaches.

Andre was the total package. And that hadn't changed. Millions of dollars hadn't changed him. The Hall of Fame hadn't changed him. He was still Andre.

"I love you too, Andre. Come in and talk to me."

◍ ◍ ◍

"Country Palace Inn, this is Becky."

"My name is Dale Fox. I have a charge on my credit card for a couple's massage that I need to speak to someone about."

"Certainly, sir. Was the amount wrong?"

"I've never stayed at your hotel. I think it was a mistake."

"Let me transfer you to our spa manager."

◍ ◍ ◍

The date was right.

The billing address was right.

The spa manager even brought the therapist on the phone. She described Linda to a tee. She even remembered that she sold real estate in a small town a couple hours east.

What she couldn't remember was the other participant in the couple's massage.

"I was Mrs. Fox's therapist, someone else did the other person."

Dale asked to speak to that therapist, but the manager balked. He could tell she was starting to become suspicious of his intentions.

He explained that Linda had passed away, and he was closing out her accounts. That softened her up, but she still didn't give him the name of the therapist.

"Our massage therapists are independent contractors," she explained. "They come and go."

And the therapist who had performed the other massage? Was she still there?

Nope. She'd moved to a place called Anna Maria Island. In Florida.

No forwarding address.

No phone number.

And no answers.

Dale hung up and was making his way through the house turning out lights and checking doors. It was only eight-twenty, but it had been a long and difficult day, plus his shoulder and head still ached from the assault that he was calling an ambush. Chelsea followed him around the house, and Dale anticipated her running off when he opened the front door to take a look around, but she remained beside him. When his phone rang, he hoped it might be the spa manager calling back with more information.

It wasn't.

"Coach Fox, this is Heaven Knight. Did I catch you at a bad time?"

"How did you get this number?"

"The Rolodex here at the office."

Dale was in no mood to speak to the press, but not speaking wouldn't make things any better. "What do you need, Miss Knight?"

"Did you see Andre Jameson at any point in the past two days?"

"I saw Andre yesterday and today. We had dinner last night, and he came to my office today for a visit."

"What did you talk about?"

"Football. Life. His career and business interests. Family. Not that it's any business of yours."

The line went still for several beats before Heaven Knight spoke again.

"Are you still the head football coach?"

Dale's hand trembled, and he felt his stomach lurch.

"Of course. Why would you ask?"

"Are you aware that Andre Jameson spent several hours with President Fuller yesterday?"

"Yes."

"Do you know if he was offered the head coach position?"

What?

Was there more to the meeting than he'd suspected?

Was Andre angling to return to Mozarkite as the new head coach?

Dale thought on it for a few moments, then started laughing.

"What? Why are you laughing, Coach Fox?"

Her question only made him laugh harder. She was so young and had no real understanding of life.

"Coach Fox?"

"Heaven... Miss Knight," Dale got the laughter under control. "Have you checked into Andre Jameson's net worth?"

She admitted she had not.

"You really should. And when you find out how much he's worth, remember that only part of that came from playing pro ball."

"I don't understand."

"I know, and that's why I'm trying to explain. Do you know what my salary is?"

Again, she didn't, so Dale told her.

"Now do you understand why I was laughing?"

"Word is that he was offered the job and is considering it."

"You had better check your sources, Miss Knight. They're not in touch with reality. Andre can't afford to give up his business interests to move to Mozarkite, and the college can't afford what it would take to get him here."

"My source is solid, Coach Fox... or so I thought. Perhaps I was wrong."

"Definitely wrong in this case."

"Then what did he and President Fuller talk about for so long?"

Heaven Knight's voice had a sudden edge to it. She'd been duped by someone she trusted. A source who wouldn't be a source much longer.

Dale started to answer, before thoughts of his morning meeting with Dr. Fuller came rushing back.

"I know some of what was discussed, but I can't break the confidence of Andre or Dr. Fuller. I'm sure you understand that."

"Yes, sir, Coach. I do. And I think it's safe to say that there's no story here. I apologize for disturbing you at home."

"Miss Knight?"

"Yes, Coach?"

"After you've been here a while, you'll learn who to trust and who is trying to stir the pot."

"Yes, sir. I hope so."

"I know that you said to always assume we're on the record, but if you want to pretend as if this conversation didn't happen, I'll do the same."

Heaven took a couple deep breaths before replying. "I appreciate that. And Coach Fox, I'm sorry about what happened to you yesterday."

"Thank you. And please, next time I get assaulted, please don't call it an assault."

"Excuse me?"

"Did you ever hear of a football coach being assaulted?"

"I guess not."

"Me neither. Maybe next time you can say 'ambushed.'"

17

$\mathcal{E}$veryone at Third Baptist knew that Coach Fox was responsible for filling the communion cups. It had been that way since Harold Palmer died. Everyone knew it, just like they knew that Billy Massey was responsible for breaking the communion loaf. They also knew that Billy usually had Mildred break the bread before they brought it to the church, because Billy's fingers were still greasy from working with his buddies on the stock car he raced in the summer at the track near Paducah.

So, when Cassie Whitman found Coach in Room 7, the Communion Preparation Room, next to the Senior Citizen's Sunday School room, he was perplexed when she said, "Oh, hi, Coach, I didn't know you were back here."

Perplexed and also suspicious. Cassie had been going to Third Baptist for twenty years. She sang in the choir and was the substitute teacher in the Little Wranglers' Sunday School class. Where else would she expect him to be before church on Communion Sunday?

"Cassie, how are you?" Dale smiled but didn't stop filling the cups. He had learned his lesson the hard way, four years before when Billy got him talking about the previous day's game for so long that the cups weren't ready during the first hymn. Pastor Mark started church at ten-thirty whether the cups were ready or not. It had been a mess.

"I'm well."

Dale glanced up from the communion cups when Cassie didn't say anything else. He expected that she had moved on, but she was still standing in the doorway. Billy, having already broken the loaf at home, was in the sanctuary with Mildred.

"Is there something I can help you with, Cassie?"

"No, I was just... passing by."

Twenty-four more cups to fill. One tray. It was the one for the left side of the sanctuary, and Dale usually poured less grape juice for that side because it was where parents with small children sat. They often grew weary from the struggle of keeping the children under control and used the hymn between Pastor Mark's sermon and Communion as a time to escape. Dale prided himself of minimal waste of grape juice.

"Did you get the cookies and fudge I dropped off?"

Dale stopped pouring. He glanced around the Communion Preparation Room, but didn't see any cookies or fudge. "I guess we didn't, Cassie? Did you leave them on the table? Sometimes the kids from the junior high class come in here. If they found them, you can bet there wouldn't be any left."

Cassie Whitman's laugh was nice. Not one of those restrained laughs that people seemed to use anymore. He looked up and smiled in return.

"No, silly. I left them at your house. Back at Christmas."

Dale stopped pouring again. "That was you?"

Cassie nodded. "Did you like them?"

"I ate the entire plate that night. They were delicious."

A smile lit up Cassie's face. "I'm so glad."

"Why didn't you put your name on them? I've been wondering ever since Christmas where they came from." That wasn't true. There had been so much going on in his life that Dale had forgotten the treats, but Cassie didn't need to know that.

"I assumed you would be home. There were lights on. I knocked, but nobody came, so I opened the door and called out, then I left them on the table. I completely forgot to leave a note."

"Thank you, Cassie. They couldn't have arrived at a better time."

An awkward silence followed. Dale glanced from Cassie to the clock, then to the remaining communion cups.

"I don't have anyone to bake for these days after... I mean with Hayden and Missy living out of state. I was glad to do it."

"I appreciate it, Cassie."

Cassie uttered a clumsy farewell and was on her way. Dale had picked up on the slight pause before she mentioned her adult children living out of state. She had been about to make, he suspected, a reference to her ex-husband, Frank. They'd divorced two years earlier. Frank moved to Jefferson City to work at the prison. Cassie had remained in Mozarkite, which Dale suspected was itself a prison of sorts for her. Why she had continued attending Third Baptist was a mystery, given how some of the old women clucked behind her back about the circumstances surrounding the demise of the Whitman marriage. Their behavior, the old biddies, not Cassie's, had been one more reason that Linda had started going to the new church at the high school.

After placing the communion cups in their stands, Dale took his usual spot in the third row from the rear, right side. Several times during singing and Pastor Mark's sermon, he saw Cassie Whitman glance back at him from across the aisle, three rows ahead. Others must have seen it, too.

"Watch that one, Coach Fox," Bertha Broderson warned as he was returning the communion trays after the service. "You know her past."

Fact was, Dale didn't. No one really knew what had happened other than second-hand tellings of Frank Whitman's version of things. Frank maintained that Cassie had developed a relationship that went beyond friendship. In his version of events, Cassie had claimed that she was going to visit their daughter Missy in Nebraska, but instead spent a few days in Memphis with a secret lover.

Cassie, for her part, had remained silent. She tried to be friendly

and cheerful to everyone, including Bertha Broderson and her gaggle
of bingo-playing buddies. At home Linda had sometimes referred to
them as Bertha Broad Ass and the Bitches of Eastwick. Dale didn't
like the profanity, but he didn't like Bertha and the others any more
than she did. Frank Whitman had never been a favorite either, not
since he'd lied to Dale about what it would cost to have him paint
their house. Nope, if he had to pick a side, he would side with Cassie.

◊ ◊ ◊

FRAN'S CHICKEN tetrazzini was out of this world, and when she
extended an invitation to come over after church, Dale jumped at it.

Willis was in the living room when he arrived. He recognized
Dale for a few minutes, but had no idea what year it was. Then,
when Fran came in to set the dining room table, Willis asked Dale
who she was. He saw the hurt that flashed across Fran's face before
she pulled herself together, put on a smile, and called them to
dinner. Willis said he was not hungry, so Fran helped him back to
their bedroom. When she came back twenty minutes later, she
nearly started crying when she saw that the chicken tetrazzini had
grown cold.

"It's always better warmed up a second time," Dale said, getting
up from the sofa and taking the tetrazzini to the kitchen. "Ten
minutes and it should be as good as new."

Fran objected at first, then sat down at the table when Dale told
her to relax. After setting the oven and placing the dish inside, he sat
across from her. She had worked hard to mask her exhaustion with
make-up and the latest hairstyle, but Dale could see the toll it was
having on her.

"Have you considered a nursing home?"

Fran nearly started to cry again.

"That wouldn't be fair to Willis."

"I watched how you had to almost wrestle him to bed, Fran. It's
not fair to you. Besides, he's no longer the Willis we know."

The conversation seesawed back and forth for several minutes, until the tetrazzini was done, and Fran scooped some out for them. He sensed that she wanted to change the topic, so he let her.

"Why was Andre in town?"

There were several ways to answer her question that would give the impression that Dale was still in charge. It was Fran, though. She deserved the truth.

"President Fuller wanted his opinion about the football program."

"Some blabbermouths in town are claiming he's replacing you as coach."

"Do you believe that?"

Fran smiled. "He couldn't take the pay cut. Have you seen pictures of his house?"

Dale had not.

"They were in one of those lifestyle magazines I read. There's nothing like it in Mozarkite, and he would be a fool to build one here."

"People are still going to talk, though. I met with him while he was here. He's pushing me to consider an outsider to take Willis's place."

Dale had expected Fran to find the notion ridiculous. Her response surprised him.

"Remember when you and Willis were getting started? How you looked at the old coaches in the league and wondered why they never changed?"

Dale chewed slowly, reluctant to admit that he remembered.

"Maybe it's time, Coach. Not time for you to retire, certainly, but time to bring in some new blood."

"Fran, I don't need Andre Jameson's help to find an assistant coach."

"Perhaps not, but why would you not accept it? How many coaches at this level do you know who are friendly with someone with Andre's connections?"

"I like to work with assistants I know and trust."

"Yeah, and how's that working for you these days?"

Dale stared across the table at her. She met his gaze.

"Okay then." Dale flashed a playful grin. "I won't bring up Willis going to a nursing home, and you steer away from who I hire."

"Fine," she countered. "Are you going to ask Cassie Whitman out on a date?"

Dale dropped his fork. "I came straight here from church. How in the world did you hear about that?"

"She's a nice woman, Coach," Fran replied, ignoring his question. "She's pretty, she's sweet. She's also smart."

"She's a lot younger than me," Dale countered. "And how about that mess with Frank?"

"If Frank Whitman were my husband, I would look for any way out I could find."

"Fran, some folks say she cheated on him."

Fran pushed her plate away and sat back. "Some folks say that Andre is replacing you as coach. And as far as Cassie's age, she's in her late forties, maybe fifty. That's not exactly jail bait."

They laughed at Fran's naughty inference. Dale considered asking Fran's opinion on the things he'd discovered over the past few weeks, the things that had made him wonder about Linda. She already knew about the letter from *W*. What she had not heard about were the funeral flowers from the Sweet Breeze Inn in Gulfport and the couples' massage in Branson. Then there was the stuff on Linda's computer, but that would have to wait until Hurley, the tech guy, got back to him. He'd not gotten a chance to work on it over the holidays but promised to be done soon. Bringing it up to Fran could wait until then. Or it could wait forever.

After an hour of post-lunch conversation, Dale said farewell and headed home for an afternoon of rest and TV. His phone buzzed with a message. It was Susan. He called back.

"Dad, do you know that blue winter coat Mom got a couple years ago?"

"Maybe."

"I need one, and it would be perfect. Can I have it?"

● ● ●

IT TURNED out that Linda had three blue winter coats. A red one and white one, too. He took them all downstairs and placed them next to the front door. Chelsea scratched at the door to get out, but Dale didn't open it. She protested, so he took her to the kitchen and opened the back door.

"Five minutes. And don't you try to get out."

Returning to the living room, he picked up one of the coats and looked through the pockets. A box of Tic Tacs, a pen engraved with Linda's name and number, and a ten-dollar bill. He pocketed the ten and moved on to the next coat. More Tic Tacs, Tums, and a five-dollar bill. The next coat contained a packet of mild salsa from Taco Bell and a folded photograph. Four women, one was Linda, seated at a table in a bar. They were drinking fancy drinks with umbrellas in them and had been caught in mid-laugh by the photographer. Dale examined the photograph closely but did not recognize the other women or the bar. He flipped it over and found an inscription.

Things get a little crazy on date night! W.

18

*D*ale was in no mood for the usual shenanigans when he arrived at the Goldrush. The others picked up on it and steered clear.

For a few minutes.

Until Uncle Homer couldn't take it anymore.

"What the hell crawled up your ass this morning?"

"What are you talking about?" Dale snapped.

"You're pissed at the world. It's written all over your face."

Dale shook his head, then shot daggers at Uncle Homer. "Everything's fine, Homer."

"Hell it is," he sassed back. The nephews watched the exchange silently. Larry Bob appeared ready to jump in if needed, but Uncle Homer was doing a fair job on his own.

"I know it ain't that dust-up with the Ricketts boys. They ain't dared show their face in town since they bailed out."

"Thanks to your able attorney getting that restraining order," Larry Bob said, finally jumping in.

Dale was appreciative of the work Larry Bob had done on his behalf in the two weeks since the incident behind the Goldrush, and even more appreciative that he gave him a break on the fee.

"So, if it ain't the Ricketts boys, it must be that smoking hot college president."

"Homer, do you know how ridiculous it sounds for a ninety-year old redneck to call a woman smoking hot?" Patsy had come up behind Uncle Homer with the coffee pot, making sure to hold it within a few inches of his left ear.

"I ain't ninety, you sassy hash-slinger," Uncle Homer snarled. "Won't be for many more years. So you just—"

"Not that many," Plumber Dick jumped in. "That cake we got at the Piggly Wiggly bakery for your birthday last fall said you were eighty-five."

"That's because you and your retarded asshole brother were in charge of getting the cake," Homer spat.

"I'm not the retarded one," Welder Tommy protested. "Wasn't me who got his head busted in."

"You coulda fooled me," Patsy said.

"Me, too." Larry Bob grinned from ear to ear as he spoke. "I think both of you are what they call, *slow*."

"You want to see slow, just wait until you have another pipe bust because your college-educated ass forgot to turn on the heat in the cellar," Dick yapped. "You'll have a damned swimming pool down there before I get around to helping you."

The conversation digressed from there. Still, as the boys and Larry Bob exchanged insults, Dale caught Uncle Homer watching him across the table. Homer Bennett was a foul-mouthed, opinion-ated old cuss, but he was also very perceptive. He knew there was something going on, but with everything else happening, was unable to pull Dale aside to find out if he needed anything. It was just as well. There was nothing Uncle Homer or any of them could do to help. He had run up against the system and the system had won.

At one-fifteen, President Fuller was holding a full-blown press conference to announce that Andre Jameson would be joining Mozarkite Junior College as an unpaid consultant to academics and athletics, reporting to President Fuller. He would do most of his consulting from Houston, but Dale saw it for what it was: an attack on his credibility as head coach. And he didn't like it one bit.

◊ ◊ ◊

DALE CLOSED HIS OFFICE DOOR, picked up the desk phone, and was placing a call when his cellphone buzzed.

Susan.

"Dad, I'm finally getting around to cleaning out Mom's desk, and I'm not sure what to do with everything."

"Use your own judgement, Susan."

"I'd rather box it up and bring it home to you."

"Okay, then."

"There's one thing that has me puzzled. Mom's passport."

"What about it?"

"The places that are stamped. Grand Cayman, Cozumel. And Cuba? Dad, you guys went to Cuba last year and I didn't even know it."

What?

"I've not been to any of those places."

"Well, you sure were kind to let Mom go without you. The Cuba trip really caught me by surprise."

There was no way she was more surprised than Dale. He considered asking dates and specific locations but didn't want her to start worrying. Besides, there was still a call to be made and the press conference in a couple hours.

"Your mom liked to get away sometimes. Put it in the box with the other stuff and drop it by the house. How's Max adapting to his new home?"

"He's made two friends on our street, so he's doing well." Susan tossed out the surnames of Max's new buddies, the offspring of decent hard-working families. Her new neighborhood wasn't as nice and well-kept as some areas of town, but it was safe, and that was most important.

After they were off the phone Dale sat back for several moments and tried to visualize Linda lying in the sun in Grand Cayman or shopping in Cozumel. Who had she sunned with? Who was her shopping partner? There had to be a shopping partner, because Linda never liked shopping alone.

Was it W?

There was too much to consider. The jewelry, the picture, the massages, and now, the trips. What was Linda up to? And who was she up to it with?

Dale retrieved his desk phone and consulted the list of juco coaches that he'd maintained for twenty years. Nearly all of the original names were crossed out, as were many of the replacements, and even some of the replacements' replacements.

One of the original names remained, however. That was the one he was calling. After getting past a receptionist, his call was put through to Jack Morrisey, long-time football coach at North Central Oklahoma.

"I've been expecting to hear from you, boy!" Coach Morrisey still had the vibrant intonation of a thirty-year old.

"How long would you have waited to hear from me before you picked up the phone yourself?" Dale asked good-naturedly.

"It's never necessary. I know that every fourth year our teams are going to play each other. I don't even bother to call anybody else."

He was right. North Central Oklahoma and Mozarkite had squared off every fourth year for the past twenty. It always worked out so that their respective conferences had openings at those intervals. Five games total. Three wins for North Central, two for Mozarkite. North Central had won the last two, however, and Dale knew they would be heavily favored for the upcoming game. It didn't matter. Dale never dodged Morrisey, and Morrisey always re-upped to knock heads with him.

They shot the breeze for a few minutes, gossiping about old coaching acquaintances who had moved onward, downward, or to the great beyond. Both had passed that stage where they were considered contenders for jobs at bigger schools, and while they usually didn't chat more than once every year or so, Dale was certain that

Jack Morrisey was just as happy in his current situation as Dale was in his.

Or as happy as he'd been until a few weeks ago.

"I got a call last month from a reporter at your local paper," Coach Morrisey said during a lull in the conversation.

"Heaven Knight," Dale answered, trying to sound nonchalant. "Quite a name, isn't it?"

Coach Morrisey ignored the dig, which made Dale wish he hadn't made it. "She wanted to pick my brain about our program's success over the last few years. I wasn't sure where she was headed with that, so I told her I preferred not to speak on the subject to the out-of-town press."

It made sense. Coach Morrisey was Dale's contemporary. They were similar in many ways except that Morrisey's North Central team had averaged seven wins over the past five years. Jack's program also had success in sending boys to the big colleges and, more importantly, they had sent three to the NFL over that same period.

"She's new and trying to make a name for herself," Dale said of Heaven Knight. "Aim for the biggest target in town, I guess, right?"

"I guess so. I also heard that Andre Jameson might be taking over as coach, but I knew that was a rumor. I told my buddies, 'Coach Dale Fox will step aside when Coach Dale Fox is good and ready.' I also remembered how you just signed that five-year contract. That job security made you the envy of every juco coach in the region."

"Andre is going to be doing some advising," Dale said. "Mainly academics, but if I can get someone of his caliber to give me his five cents worth on the team, I'll take it."

"Smart move. It can't hurt with recruiting, either."

"You sure don't have any problem with that, Jack." Dale paused, considered what he was about to ask, then almost didn't. "How do you keep your program on top?"

Coach Morrisey demurred, but Dale pushed. "Seriously. You are still a force in your conference. What's made the difference?"

Coach Morrisey chewed on the question for a few beats. "I had to realize about ten years ago that I was no longer able to relate to my players the way I used to. I'm not a young man anymore, so I make sure to surround myself with assistants who the boys can talk to about things."

Dale wasn't sure he agreed, but he didn't push it.

"You know as well as I do, Dale, young people today have more personal issues and problems than we did at their age."

"Maybe, but I think we were better at overcoming our problems without having to whine about them. We didn't put our lives out there on Facebook or Twitter. When we ran into issues, we dealt with them."

"Growing up, how many kids did you know who were homeless?"

Coach Morrisey's question almost seemed ridiculous. Dale had grown up in a Missouri farming town where everyone knew everyone else. No one was homeless. Some had homes that were much nicer than others, but everyone had a home.

"Me neither," Coach Morrisey said when Dale didn't respond. "But right now I have two boys on my team – one from inner-city New Orleans and the other from a little backwater town in Southern Illinois – who don't have homes to go back to. They stayed with families here in town during winter break. I can't imagine how hard that would be."

Dale agreed, though he hadn't had any homeless players, at least none he was aware of.

"And the stuff they go through. There was a boy on our team when I was playing college ball down in Texas," Coach Morrisey took a deep breath, "Brixton Michaud was his name. Our coach caught him with some pills; I can't remember what they were, but boom, Old Brixton was sent packing. Thankfully, today we believe in second chances. And sometimes even third chances."

Not at my school, Dale wanted to interject. The longer they talked the more obvious it became that Jack Morrisey had grown soft in middle age. How could he look at himself in the mirror after bringing back kids who had repeatedly flaunted the rules?

"Well, Jack, I'll get the game set up for our place next fall. I'll let you know when the conference approves it, but I don't see any problems. It's good talking to you." Dale hung up fully expecting it to be the last time he and Jack Morrisey planned a game together. Why bother? Morrisey was just one more of the many who had lost their way.

● ● ●

DR. FULLER WAS IMPECCABLY DRESSED in a blue pants suit. A Mozarkite Junior College pin was affixed to the lapel of her jacket.

Andre Jameson was wearing a gray suit. He wore an MJC pin on his lapel, too.

Dale showed up in sweats. No lapels, no pin.

In addition to the usual attendees, Wally Westmoreland, Heaven Knight, and the weekend sportscaster from the TV station in Cape Girardeau, there were reporters from network television affiliates in St. Louis, Springfield, and Little Rock and a national reporter, Nancy somebody-or-other from ESPN. Andre Jameson was big news.

Dr. Fuller opened the presser with comments about how Mozarkite Junior College was rising to meet the needs of today's students. She highlighted the school's strategic plan, then segued into how Andre's background and experiences would be of benefit. She was eloquent and sophisticated and projected an image of MJC that belied the fact that the school had risen out of a former cow pasture on the edge of a town with two stoplights. Judging by the impressed looks on the faces of the media gathered in the cramped conference room, she was nailing it.

And then Andre ascended to the podium. The clicks and whirring of cameras threatened to drown out his words, but Andre was used to the limelight. He waited until the flurry of photographs abated before beginning his remarks. He was eloquent, erudite, and, despite being over forty, still had the looks of a cover model for a fashion magazine. He spoke of what Mozarkite had meant to him, heaping lavish praise on Dale in the process. He discussed what he hoped to bring to the relationship, about how he wanted students to be successful graduates and citizens, about how he wanted athletes who could follow his path to major college programs and professional football. Dale was impressed with all he had to say, but couldn't help but think that Andre was talking about a place that wasn't Mozarkite. He was lost in his thoughts and missed the first time that Andre called him forward. Red-faced, he moved to the dais and leaned in to the microphone mounted on a podium.

That was when he realized he hadn't given any thought of what he might say.

They stared at him, the press. He saw Heaven Knight and noticed how at home she looked among her more well-known colleagues. Wally Westmoreland was poised on the edge of his chair, his handheld recorder stuck out in front of him, ready. The others stared and waited. He had to say something.

"Andre Jameson is the best player to ever wear the Polled Hereford uniform. What he's achieved on the football field, in the boardroom, and as a husband and father has inspired and motivated men who came after him." Dale paused to give the press time to catch up with his rushed statement. Out of the corner of his eye he could see that Andre had his gaze directed at the floor. Dr. Fuller was looking straight at Dale, hanging on every word.

He was about to give her something she wasn't expecting.

"President Fuller feels that Andre can be a benefit to our college, advising our academic and athletic departments. I don't see anyone here representing academics, so I'll have to assume that I'm speaking for both. If so, this is the first time I've been the spokesman for academics at MJC. I'm sure that my colleagues in History and Science are excited about that."

The press chuckled. Andre had stopped staring at the floor. Dr. Fuller appeared uncertain, on edge about what might come out of Dale's mouth next.

"While I'm happy that Andre is going to be involved with our college, I also want to point out that MJC was a good school long before he came here, and it will continue to be a good school long after he—and all of us—are gone."

There was no question as to who Dale was talking about when he said, 'all of us.' He punctuated the comment by looking directly at Dr. Fuller. Her eyes blazed for a moment before she composed herself, and Dale knew then that she could be a worthy adversary if backed into a corner.

"On another subject, I am pleased to announce that our football program has, over the past couple weeks, signed several new players. My coaches and I are excited to know that they'll be attending MJC in the fall."

As Dale read off the names, positions, and high schools of five new recruits, he saw the eyes of the out-of-town press glaze over. They cared nothing about a tight end from Fredricktown or a defensive lineman from Hillsboro. They showed up to see the legendary Hall-of-Famer Andre Jameson in the flesh, and to find out what problems in backwater Mozarkite had led to his return. If Dale could delay their gratification, all the better.

When Dale paused, Dr. Fuller approached the podium and motioned for him to step back. She turned to the press, smiled, and said she and Andre would now take questions. Her unspoken message was clear. Dale was finished for the day. He was free to go. Dismissed.

That was fine with him. As he was moving away from the dais, Dr. Fuller called on Heaven Knight from the *Messenger*.

"I have a question for you, Dr. Fuller. And one for Coach Fox.

Dale stopped in his tracks.

"Dr. Fuller, how involved were your academic department heads in the decision to have Mr. Jameson consult with the college?"

As prepared as she was, Dale could see that Dr. Fuller had not expected such a pointed question, particularly from a local reporter. He maintained a poker face while he inwardly cheered Heaven Knight for her willingness to ask hard questions.

Then he remembered that Heaven had mentioned that she also had a question for him. It wouldn't be a softball.

Dr. Fuller's response was rambling and circular and said a lot without saying anything. She had little doubt that Andre's input would be welcomed across the campus. He wouldn't be involved in day to day operations or specific issues related to curriculum; he would provide valuable input related to direction and mission. She then went off on a tangent; a story about someone leading a group of workers cutting down trees in a jungle. She compared herself to the leader of the tree cutters, then made some far-reaching analogy about Andre as the leader's eyes in the sky, making sure the tree cutters were cutting down the right trees. The media eyes were glazing over again.

"My next question is for Coach Fox," Heaven said, cutting off Dr. Fuller mid-jungle. "How do you feel about Dr. Fuller and Andre Jameson's involvement with your program?"

Dale thought about his response. He probably should toe the company line and answer the question with more lavish praise of Andre. But then again, he hadn't even been consulted about the decision to invite him back.

And if he had? Would he have agreed that Andre's involvement with the football program could reap dividends? Maybe. Dale didn't consider himself an obstinate person, but there was a certain amount of respect that went with having coached for thirty years. Dr. Fuller, by circumventing him, hadn't given him that respect.

"I'm used to running my football program. I was hired many years ago to run it the way I saw fit. Our former president was hands-off in that respect." Dale looked around at the press, trying to form his thoughts. "I have a lot of respect for Dr. Fuller. I feel she wants MJC to grow and improve. I guess if she feels that having Andre involved will help achieve that, then I can support it."

There you go, Dale thought. He made his point without throwing his boss completely under the bus. If only it was enough for Heaven Knight.

It wasn't. She turned her next question in a different direction, aiming straight at Dale's recruiting.

"You just named five new recruits. Were any of those players being recruited by larger four-year colleges?"

"I can't say for certain. We didn't talk about it."

"Any all-staters in the group, Coach Fox?"

Dale acknowledged there weren't. "Two were all-conference, though."

"Any record holders at their respective schools?"

One of the boys was in the top five at his school for receptions, Dale explained. He knew where Heaven Knight was trying to lead him. So did the others. They had noticeably perked up after being lulled into boredom by Dr. Fuller's tree cutting jungle story.

"Will these young men help return Mozarkite's football team to the top of the conference standings?"

"They'll work hard, that's for certain. They come from good families with good work ethics. Their high school coaches are high on them."

"Coach," Heaven continued, "are you planning to hire someone to recruit and run the offense?"

Dale glanced at Andre and Dr. Fuller. Both appeared ready to cut the press conference short and get the heck out of Dodge. He was ready, too.

"Dr. Fuller has indicated that she wants to fill the position. I've been considering a number of possible candidates."

"Has Mr. Jameson been involved in your search?"

"Yes, I've asked for his input."

Two of the TV reporters were already tearing down their equipment as Dale looked around to see if there were more questions. Seeing none, he stepped off the platform, made his way between the folds of the curtain that served as a backdrop, and exited through a rear door. It was too early to go home, so he headed to his office to wait out the impending storm.

◊ ◊ ◊

THE STORM DID NOT COME.

Dale had expected a phone call or visit from Dr. Fuller. He'd been more forthright than she was probably used to, but he was not about to just roll over.

But still, he needed to hire an assistant coach. Andre's list was still on the edge of his desk. He'd Googled the men and found them to be strong. They would do well for the right program. Unfortunately, that program wasn't Mozarkite.

Then there were the men he'd discussed with Dr. Fuller. One of them was particularly appealing. He was someone Dale had known for years, and while recruitment hadn't been his thing in the past, Dale felt he would figure it out in due time.

But how much time was due time?

And how much time did Dale have left?

Would another losing season lead to his dismissal?

Sure, he had four years remaining on his contract, but Dr. Fuller could always reassign him. He was certified to teach physical education but hadn't in nearly twenty years. She wouldn't do that, would she? Send Mozarkite's long-time football coach back to the classroom to teach Fundamentals of Basketball or, horror of horrors, Introduction to Square Dancing?

It was something to think about, but not at the moment. More than anything, Dale just wanted to go home and forget everything.

---

19

*D*ale let Chelsea into the backyard then went back inside to shower. In the three days since the press conference he'd heard nothing from Dr. Fuller. They'd passed on campus, but at such a distance that they had waved and gone on their way. Heaven Knight's article in the *Messenger* had lauded the President's foreword thinking, but also chastised her for not keeping Dale in the loop. The crowd at the Goldrush was solidly in Dale's corner, though Larry Bob had mentioned how beneficial it might be to have a "primetime recruiter" who could "pull in the big boys who washed out at Ole' Miss or Bama."

Dale realized that, sooner or later, he and Dr. Fuller needed to meet face-to-face. Should he be the person to set the meeting? He had thought long and hard on that the past couple days and concluded that the ball was in her court. Perhaps today would be the day. With that in mind, he passed on his usual coach attire in favor of a pair of khaki dress slacks and a navy sweater that Linda used to say made him look like a sexy version of Mr. Rogers.

The morning sky was gray and bleak, but temperatures were mild for a winter day in Mozarkite. Dale hadn't bothered to go out a few minutes early and start his truck, and when he got in, his heated seat wasn't yet warm. It was one of those first-world comforts that he'd come to appreciate, along with sixteen sports channels and curbside pickup at the Chili's restaurant on the highway. While he was waiting for the truck to warm up, he flipped through the five radio stations he had preset. The local station was giving hog prices, two of the others were blaring twangy country music from the seventies. A Kansas City sports talk station with a blowtorch signal was already talking Royals baseball. The fifth, a public radio station, was in the midst of a fundraising drive. Dale was turning back to one of the country stations when he saw Chelsea bolt out from behind the house. If she saw him, she didn't act like it. Her sights were set on the open road. Dale backed the truck out and took off, keeping up for several blocks until Chelsea darted down an alley and between two more homes in the middle of a block. The last Dale saw of her was when she turned the corner at Melkerston and Grand Streets. With the trail cold, he drove aimlessly for ten minutes.

And then he spotted her. Standing on the front porch of a brick rancher not much different from Dale's. The home belonged to Bubber Slate and his wife Tamara. As Dale pulled into the drive, Chelsea spotted him and started wagging her tail.

"Let's go home, girl," Dale said just as the door opened and Bubber appeared. They knew each other, but not well. Bubber was the farm loan specialist at County Savings Bank. Dale had never needed a farm loan, thus had never needed Bubber's services. Bubber and Tamara were Lutheran, so they never crossed paths in church, either. In fact, about the only time that Bubber and Dale came into contact was when they both happened to be making last-minute grocery stops at the Piggly Wiggly.

"Coach, what are you doing here?" Bubber appeared more surprised than he sounded. His eyes grew wide and he actually took a step back before seeming to remember that he was standing on his own porch. Chelsea jumped on him as if greeting an old friend. Bubber petted her, then pushed her away.

"I followed her here," Dale said, pointing at Chelsea. "Is this where she's been coming?"

"Is she yours?

"I guess so. She was Linda's, but she's mine now. And yours too, apparently."

"I assumed she was a stray. I let her come in out of the cold. She stays for a bit, then moves on."

"So, you haven't been tying her on my porch?"

"Is that what's been happening?"

"I can't remember how many times she's run off over the past few months. I appreciate you taking her in. I'm surprised that Tamara didn't recognize her as Linda's dog, though. They saw each other regularly, at Junior League and those library tea parties."

Bubber rubbed the back of his neck. His face flushed.

"Coach, Tamara and I aren't married anymore."

"Oh, gosh, Bubber, I'm sorry. I hadn't heard. Are you doing okay?"

"Well... yeah. It's been seven years."

Seven years?

"You and Tamara have been divorced for seven years? How could I not have heard that?"

"We tried to keep it hush-hush. The kids were surprised and a little embarrassed. Of course, now they're off on their own, so it's not as big a deal."

"Does Tamara still live here in Mozarkite?"

"Van Buren. She still works for Vernon Heckling's accounting office here in town, though, so you probably run into her now and again."

"Seven years? Man, I'm so sorry, Bubber. I guess I get so wrapped up in the team and family and all."

Bubber waved him off. "Don't give it a second thought, Coach. Do you want to take your dog with you?"

"I might as well. She'll probably be back, though. She seems to have some kind of innate sense on how to escape our back yard. Let me know if she shows up again, will you, Bubber?"

● ● ●

"ANDRE JAMESON IS ON LINE ONE." Rosie's cheerful announcement from across the hallway caused Dale's gut to knot up. He had expected to hear from Dr. Fuller before Andre, but it was three-thirty in the afternoon and there had been no word.

"Hello, Andre."

"Coach, how are you doing?" Andre's cheerful greeting was nearly drowned out by background noise.

"I'm pretty good. Where are you?"

"Oklahoma City. I'm leaving the airport to head downtown. Would you believe I'm doing color commentary on the Rockets game with the Thunder tonight?"

"The NBA? Wow, Andre, that's impressive."

"It's a one and done gig, but who knows what it could lead to."

"I'll tune in for sure."

"Thanks, Coach, but that's not why I called. I was wondering if you had made a decision on the assistant coach position."

There it was.

"I haven't, Andre. It's been busy as heck around here the past couple weeks. Between finalizing next season's schedule and talking to prospective recruits, I've barely had time to think."

"I hear you. Things get crazy. How about little Max? Are you making time for him and Susan?"

Actually, he had not, and he felt guilty about it. It had been three weeks since their lunch date at Applebee's. Susan had cajoled a spot for Max in one of Mozarkite's best preschools, a place operated by one of her high school friends. They had also joined a moms' and kids' play group that got together every couple weeks. Dale was invited to go bowling with them the previous weekend, but he'd had a phone call planned with the parents of a linebacker from some little high school up in Callaway County. He heard later that Max had bowled a fifty-one, which sounded pretty good.

"That little boy could probably use a grandpa in his life."

Andre's words hit harder than he'd likely intended. He had no idea about the guilt Dale felt sometimes, back when Susan was a little girl. The dance concerts he missed to travel with the team.

Coaches' meetings that superseded parent-teacher conferences. Linda would gently remind him of his priorities, and he would promise to do better, but he didn't. At some point she stopped reminding him.

"He's really growing up fast," Dale said, changing the subject. "I see him as a tight end or maybe a running back, depending on how fast he is."

"I pushed my kids away from football, though David played anyway," Andre said. "The girls both play volleyball. Sammy is into soccer."

"Why would you push them away? Is it the concussion thing?"

It was, and as Andre spoke of his NFL friends who were coming to grips with issues related to head trauma, Dale tried to think of things he could say to downplay the issue. Safer helmets, rules that protected players from hard hits. Some of the new stuff was looked down upon by coaches and fans, especially the safety factor, which some said made the game too soft. Dale had been part of that faction, until he witnessed firsthand one of his boys, a defensive end, struggle to come back from a concussion. Maybe pushing Max toward football was a bad idea.

But soccer?

"Hey, Coach, I've only got a couple minutes, but I was wondering if you still have that list of coaching candidates that I put together at your house last month."

Dale acknowledged that he did. He didn't acknowledge that he'd only given the names cursory consideration.

"Just throw it away."

"What? Why, Andre? I haven't made a decision yet. Any one of those guys might still be in the running."

Not true, but you never knew what might happen.

"They've all found other jobs. One of them will be coaching the offense for Jack Morrisey at North Central Oklahoma. Jack plans to coach for another couple years and said the new coach will be considered for the spot when he hangs it up. That was too much to pass up."

"Really?" Dale sat back in his office chair, surprised by this turn of events. "I spoke to Jack not too long ago. He didn't say a word about retiring."

"He's been saving for years to buy a house in Florida. From what I heard, he put in an offer on a condo in Sarasota."

Dale tried to imagine Jack Morrisey on a beach, but the only images he could conjure up included a clipboard and headset.

"Thanks anyway, Andre. I'll get to work this week narrowing down the candidates. There are some good men in the running."

The line was silent for a moment, and Dale thought they'd been disconnected. He almost put his phone away when Andre spoke again.

"Hey, Coach, what are you doing tomorrow?"

"Same as always. There are some administrative things that are due. A phone call or two. Why? Are you passing through?"

"As a matter of fact, yes. Can we get together tomorrow morning? Eight-thirty?"

"Want to join me for breakfast? The guys at the Goldrush would be over the moon if Andre Jameson walked in."

"No. I've got something else in mind. Can you give me the entire day?"

What?

"Tell me what's going on Andre. Is this another meeting with Dr. Fuller, because if it is, I'd rather not—"

"No, sir. Just you and me."

"Andre, I'm too busy to block out a whole day. How about we—"

"C'mon, Coach. Give me this. How much have I asked of you over the years?"

The truth was, not much. Andre had given much more than he had accepted in return, from unpublicized donations of new uniforms to occasional mentions of the school on TV and radio. What little the world might know about Mozarkite Junior College likely came from Andre Jameson.

"Where do you want to meet? My office?"

"I'll pick you up at your house. Eight-thirty sharp. Dress like you're going out to dinner at a nice restaurant."

"There aren't any really nice restaurants in Mozarkite. Just a few chains. And the Goldrush."

"Dress like it anyway. See you tomorrow."

Dale disconnected, then punched in another number.

"Hi, Dad."

"Hey, Susan. I was wondering if you and Max might want to go out to dinner tonight?"

"I don't know, Dad. Max isn't thrilled about Applebee's. And he thinks the Goldrush smells like old men."

"I was thinking about pizza."

"You? Mr. Meat-and-Potatoes? Get real."

"Yes. I've been wanting to try that place in Poplar Bluff that the kids like so much."

"Kids? You mean the guys on your team, Dad? I have no idea what pizza place that would be."

"No, kids. Little kids, Max's age. That place with the big mouse on the sign."

"Chuck E. Cheese?"

"Yes, that's the one."

The line was quiet for several beats, before Susan said, "You want to go to Chuck E. Cheese?"

"Yes, I've wanted to try it."

"Are you aware that it's full of bright lights and games and screaming kids?"

"That's what I figured, it being for kids and all."

"Okay," Susan said, her voice becoming suspicious. "I don't know who you are, but you need to give my dad back his phone before I call the cops."

"Do you want to go or not?"

"You'll make Max's week, Daddy. We'll see you in two hours."

20

"More coffee, Coach?" Patsy said as she swept by with plates for a nearby table.

"He's already had three cups," Welder Tommy noted. "If he's like me, he'll be pissing all day."

"He's not like you," Larry Bob said. "For one, Coach has a daughter. That means he's not a virgin."

"Are you going down that road again?" Tommy squared around as if he were expecting trouble. He would get it all right, but not the physical kind. Larry Bob would verbally mince away at him, like he'd done many times before.

"Sex is a road you haven't been down, Tommy, so yeah, I guess I am."

"I already told you that me and Ellen Biggerstaff did—"

"You didn't do shit with Ellen Biggerstaff, Tommy. You just keep throwing her name out there because she's dead and can't defend herself."

"We did so do it. We was out at—"

"It's okay, Tommy," Dale said. "Don't let him get under your skin."

"You must be nursing one heck of a headache, Coach," Plumber

Dick observed. "Because you usually laugh at them two as much as the rest of us do."

"Did you get into some of my stuff?" Uncle Homer asked.

"Your stuff?"

"You know," Homer pantomimed taking a drink. "My *stuff*."

"You know better than that," Larry Bob jumped in. "Coach is refined and college educated, like me. He doesn't drink piss water from a still."

"You're looking to get your ass whupped right here, Larry Bob." Still smarting from the jokes about his sexual past, Welder Tommy rose to his feet, looking for any reason to bust Larry Bob a good one.

"Sit down, boy," Uncle Homer growled. "Can't you tell when somebody is kidding?"

Tommy sat back down. He wore the forlorn expression of a little boy who had just been sent to his room.

"I hope you've got an easy day in front of you," Uncle Homer said, turning back to Dale. "Maybe you can hide out in your office."

"I'm tied up all day, actually, and it's not alcohol that's making my head crack. Susan and I took Max to Chuck E. Cheese last night.

Plumber Dick let loose with a low whistle. "The place with the rat on the roof?"

"It's a mouse. Yes, that's the place."

"I went in there to get myself some pizza a couple summers ago. You woulda thought I was an alien from the moon or something."

The table became silent. Uncle Homer looked at Larry Bob. Larry Bob looked at Dale. Dale looked at Welder Tommy. Tommy looked confused.

"Did you," Larry Bob said, drawing his words out slowly. "Did you, by chance drive your van?"

"Sure, I did. I had a leaky shower stall to fix at the Thompson's place. You all remember them, right? Leroy Thompson? Worked the evening shift at Tractor Supply? He got transferred to the store in Poplar Bluff and moved over there."

Larry Bob continued his pseudo investigation.

"So, you were driving your work vehicle, a white panel van?"

Dick said he was.

"And you went to a pizza joint that caters to kids?"

"Yeah."

"In the middle of summer?"

"That's when the Thompsons needed me to fix their shower. Yeah."

Larry Bob chewed on his words for a few moments before throwing up his hands. "I can't imagine why they would treat you strangely, Dick. A middle-aged man driving a white panel van. They should've seen immediately that you were someone special."

"I thought so, too, but nope. They got me my pizza, put me at a table in the back corner away from everybody, and left me there."

Dale knew it was time to leave.

● ● ●

BY THE TIME Andre rang the doorbell, Dale had already returned home and changed into a gray pair of slacks with a green sweater that he hadn't worn in two years. He felt guilty for not having time to go look for Chelsea, but he was becoming increasingly frustrated with her, anyway. If she came home before he returned from whatever Andre had planned for them, she would have to wait outside in the cold.

They engaged in small talk while Andre steered his rental sedan through Mozarkite. Dale considered asking where they were going, but figured in the end that if Andre wanted him to know he would tell him. As they exited the city limits Dale could see the light towers from the football stadium in the distance.

"Lots of memories under those lights," Andre said, following Dale's gaze.

"I remember when we put them up," Dale replied. It had been his fifth season, right after they played in the championship game. Locals thought that a school with a football program on the rise should have the option of playing night games. They initially played several each season, before it became clear that most visiting teams hated bussing to town to play a night game, then having to turn around and drive home through the night or spend money on hotel rooms. It hadn't been a great idea, but Dale got the point Andre was making.

When Andre steered the car onto Skeet Club Road, Dale couldn't hold back any longer.

"Are we going to the airport?"

"We are. Are you up for a quick trip?"

"Did Dr. Fuller tell you to dump me out from ten-thousand feet? Is this her way of getting rid of me?"

Andre's laugh was loud and melodious. It took Dale back to practices many years ago when his star player had kidded and joked his teammates toward peak performance. "Even if she had I would have said 'no way.' This is my idea. President Fuller knows nothing about it."

"So, what are we doing?"

Andre steered the car down a paved drive that led to the tarmac. "I'm working. You're along for the ride."

There were four planes in the area where they parked. Dale recognized one of them as belonging to Seymour Shaver, a local who had gotten rich operating a hunting lodge up in the hills south of town. That left three. A couple of two-seaters and a larger jet with *Cessna* emblazoned on the side, along with the name of a leasing company. A nattily-dressed pilot stepped out as they approached. That had to be the one.

"When was the last time you were in a plane?" Andre asked as they parked.

"I went with Linda to Tampa a few years ago. She won a trip from the national firm she represented before going independent. We flew on TWA."

"Then you haven't flown in a long time, Coach, because TWA has been gone for years."

Dale shrugged. "I guess so."

They approached the Cessna. Andre introduced himself to the pilot who appeared star-struck by his famous passenger.

"And this is Coach Dale Fox. He's responsible for helping me get where I am today."

Dale was touched by the acknowledgement. The pilot gave him a quick once-over, then returned his attention to Andre. "We'll be ready to take off in ten minutes, Mr. Jameson. Same flight plan as you discussed with my bosses?"

Andre said it was, then motioned for Dale to follow him. "Wait until you see this."

The first thing that hit Dale was the scent. Leather. It had a freshly-cleaned smell to it, like a new car. And when he saw what the jet looked like inside, well, it was simply more than he could take in.

"Unbelievable."

Andre nodded. "I remember the first time I got on one of these. It was after the Oilers drafted me. I kept thinking that sooner or later somebody was going to figure out that I was just old Andre from small-town Arkansas and pitch my black ass off the plane."

"It's more like a... restaurant. Or some private clubhouse." Not much impressed Dale, but the Cessna? It was impressive. Leather seats facing each other over small tables in the front. Longer seats, more like sofas, in the rear.

"The bar is stocked and there are snacks in the cabinets in back," the pilot said. "If you don't see what you want, let me know."

"We'll be fine," Andre said. "Coach, how about we grab those big seats in the back?"

● ● ●

IT WAS DAZZLING.

Dale tried to play it off, but he knew as they sliced through the morning sky that he was out of his element. When Andre excused himself to make some phone calls, Dale relaxed into the comfort of the buttery leather sofa with a bowl of pretzels and a Diet Coke. He gazed out the window at scenery that was wintry brown but greened up as they flew. They were heading south, that much he could tell. He knew that some big college coaches had jets at their disposal.

Whether it was true or not, he wasn't sure, but the thought of being able to fly around the country to meet recruits left him dizzy.

And a little sad.

Dizzy because of the glitz and glamour of it all.

Sad because he had hoped, years before, that he would be among that highest echelon of coaches who helmed major programs.

Even in the beginning, as an assistant coach at a small bootheel high school, he'd dreamed of leading a top-ranked team out of the tunnel and onto the field, cheered by tens of thousands of loyal fans.

Then, as an assistant at Mozarkite, watching and learning from his predecessor, imagining the possibilities until he was certain he could succeed as a head coach. The dream had lived on.

Then came the chance to be head coach. And playing in the national championship game in his fifth year. He was just thirty-seven at the time. Young, even for a juco coach.

The offers came, but they were not what he hoped they would be. Assistant coach positions at mid-level universities, at least a half-dozen, from the South and Midwest. Schools of all shapes and sizes, but with one thing in common. They were places that tended to churn through coaches. Dale had thought at the time that he was better off staying at Mozarkite, continuing to build a program that won championships. Eventually the call would come from a major university. Sure, it would probably be as an assistant, but he had already proven that he could rise from assistant to the head job. He did it once, and he could do it again.

The chance never came.

Neither did a championship.

Mozarkite had remained competitive. They won ten games a couple times, eight games a few times more. But when the calls came, they came to Dale's colleagues at other schools. A few accepted the kinds of jobs he had turned down. Several flamed out quickly. A couple had established a foothold that led to better things.

And yes, he had envied them.

"Gentlemen," the pilot said through an overhead speaker, "we're about to land in Gainesville."

Gainesville.

Florida.

Dale checked his watch. They'd made the trip in two hours. Andre stuffed some papers into a briefcase, snapped it shut, and returned to the seat across from Dale.

"We're breaking a big news story, Coach." Andre pointed toward the cockpit, then put his index finger to his lips as he held up his cellphone so Dale could see the name on the screen. "You're familiar with this person?"

"Of course. Who wouldn't be?"

Andre tucked the phone away. "He's being introduced in two hours as the new coach of the University of Florida. We're getting the first interview."

◊ ◊ ◊

As THE PILOT pulled the plane close to the small terminal, a gaggle of people appeared at a nearby fence.

"Reporters," Andre said. "They're hoping to find out who the new coach is."

Several of the ten or so clustered at the fence recognized Andre.

"Are you involved in the search for a coach?" one shouted.

"Are you part of the new staff, Andre?" another asked.

"Who's that with you?" called another.

"I'm here to join some friends for a day of fishing out on Newnan's Lake," Andre lied smoothly. "This is Coach Dale Fox. He's not interviewing for the Florida job, at least as far as I know." Andre turned to Dale. "You aren't, are you, Coach?"

Embarrassed by the sudden attention, Dale shook his head.

"Coach Fox was my juco coach. Sorry if we disappointed you."

The press fired off more questions that Andre volleyed nicely as he led Dale to a waiting car. As they exited the airport, Andre checked the rearview mirror several times.

"Just making sure none of them followed us," he said as he set the cruise control on fifty-nine. Twenty minutes later, after circumnavigating Newnan Lake and a conservation area, they pulled into the driveway of a nondescript ranch-style house in the little town of Windsor.

"It belongs to the friend of a friend," Andre said as he rang the bell. Coach Rodney Troy answered the door and pulled Andre into a bear hug. Dale would not have been more surprised if Lee Harvey Oswald and John Wilkes Booth came to the door in scuba gear. And then, when it was apparent that Rodney Troy knew of Dale and his team at Mozarkite, Dale thought he might pass out.

"Good to meet you, Dale," he said as he showed them to a cramped living room. There was no one else around, other than a freelance camera operator, a woman from Orlando hired to shoot the interview. Andre got situated and wasted little time getting started. Dale watched from behind the camera.

Rodney Troy had the unique quality of coming across as both smooth and sincere. Dale knew his past. Born and raised in Louisiana, linebacker at LSU, then a year on the Dallas Cowboys' taxi squad before moving into coaching. He was Andre's position coach in Houston before moving to the college level. Florida would be his third gig. In fifteen years, he had done nothing but win. Florida had been through its share of coaching changes in recent years, and Dale knew that Rodney Troy would be seen as the answer to the doldrums the program had recently endured.

The interview was short, just a half-dozen questions, and after Andre wrapped it up and sent the camera operator on her way, he motioned for Dale to join them in the living room. Rodney Troy immediately focused on him, beginning by expressing his sympathy at Linda's passing. How a major college coach knew this was beyond Dale, but he thanked him for his concern.

Then the talk steered back to football. Coach Troy talked about what all had transpired to bring him to Florida. Then they talked x's and o's. Coach Troy shared some ideas he had for the Florida offense, even bouncing a few thoughts off Dale. It felt both real and surreal at the same time. Just a few weeks earlier, Dale had watched from his La-Z-Boy as Rodney Troy's former team won the Cotton Bowl to cap off an eleven-win season that few predicted. Now he was asking Dale's opinion on a couple of plays he planned to use against the likes of Alabama and Ole Miss. He was cool, calm, collected, and Dale nearly forgot that the man was going to be introduced to the world as Florida's new coach in a matter of minutes.

Unbelievable.

"Are there any players up your way that I should know about?" Coach Troy asked.

The truth was, there were none he could recommend. He tossed out a couple names, but stopped short of any full endorsements

"That boy you had at quarterback, the one out of Little Rock. What about him?"

Dale shook his head. "Jeff Devereux. He might make it at a Division Two school, but even that's a stretch."

Coach Troy smiled conspiratorially. "Million-dollar arm, ten-cent brain is what I'm hearing."

"You might be overestimating the arm," Dale replied. "And come to think of it, you might be overestimating the brain."

They laughed together. Two coaches talking about football. It was the same regardless of whether it was Pop Warner or the NFL. Dale noticed how Andre sat back and allowed them to chat without interrupting.

"I don't send many to the big schools anymore," Dale said suddenly. It was a display of candor that he had not anticipated until it was out of his mouth.

Coach Troy nodded slowly. "Why not, Dale? Your conference has its share of studs. Why not Mozarkite?"

Dale considered what he could say to defend himself and his program but realized how hollow it would sound. He was speaking to a man who had been successful for fifteen years by adapting and growing. He took a few questionable players along the way, including a couple of high-profile cases, and they hadn't tarnished his program or reputation.

But Gainesville, Florida wasn't Mozarkite, Missouri.

Fortunately, the doorbell rang, saving Dale from having to explain his approach to coaching. It was a representative from the University of Florida, there to pick Rodney Troy up and deliver him to his press conference.

◊ ◊ ◊

DALE ASSUMED they were on their way back to Mozarkite, so when the pilot started circling, he looked out the window hopeful of getting a look at the surroundings he recognized. Instead he saw a metro area.

"Nashville," Andre said, glancing up from his paperwork. "Just a quick stop."

It was a little after three when the pilot pulled up to a small gate at Nashville International Airport. Andre again had arranged for a car. The guy never missed anything.

"Another interview?" Dale asked Andre as he navigated along a road called Briley Parkway. Skyscrapers appeared on the horizon; an indication they were headed into downtown.

"You could say that," Andre answered cautiously. "I have someone I want you to meet. He's interested in being your assistant coach."

Dale's defenses were on full alert. "I'm working on that. I don't need help."

Rather than answer, Andre pulled into the parking lot of a closed and shuttered fast food joint. Weeds growing through cracks in the parking lot indicated that the place had been abandoned for quite a while. He shut off the car and turned to face Dale.

"Do you know what it's like to play for you, Coach?"

Dale blinked several times. Andre's tone was direct, pointed even. Not angry, but very straightforward.

"I think so. I mean, I never really asked my players, but a lot of them stay in touch, so..." Dale's voice trailed off. He'd never given it any thought. He was, after all, a football coach. He wasn't there to mollycoddle or placate his players. He was there to win football games.

Of course, he hadn't been doing a lot of that lately.

"I'm not talking about most of your players. I'm referring to your black and brown players. How many boys of color have you had on your teams across the years, Coach?"

"I don't worry about skin color, Andre. You more than anyone should know that. If you can play, you can play."

Andre shook his head. "How many?"

Dale shrugged. "I have no idea."

"Yes, you do."

"Well..." Dale thought back. "Before you there were... McCracken and... that kid from Springfield that washed out... I can't remember his name. Then there was you and Tate. Since then... Bixby, Warren... Rideout... there were more, I'm sure. Why are you bringing up race, Andre? Are you saying that I'm racist?"

"Twenty-five years. How many players? A thousand? More?"

"Probably more than that." Dale felt his face flush. "I never – never – turned away a boy because of his skin color. All I ask is that you play hard and fit into the community."

"And that's the problem, Coach. Don't you see that?"

"I don't know what you're talking about."

"Take Tate and me. We were the only black kids on the team. You made it clear from the start that we needed to fit in. To do that we had to basically turn our back on our heritage."

Dale waved him off. "That's ridiculous. All I asked is that you live up to our code of conduct."

"A code of conduct that was easy enough for a kid who grew up in a town like Mozarkite, but Tate? He was from West Memphis. Have you been to West Memphis, Coach?"

"I've... been through it. Nice enough, I guess."

"The street he grew up on was as far removed from Mozarkite as it was from the moon. And me? I grew up in a poor black farming community in Arkansas. We talked different, ate different, churched different, listened to different music. I had to leave all that behind."

"Nobody asked you to leave anything behind. You chose to."

"But why did I have to, Coach? Why did I have to act white to fit in?"

Act white?

Act?

White?

"I'm offended that you would even suggest that, Andre. I gave you the opportunity that helped get you where you are today."

"And I appreciate that. But I also know that, somehow, I would've found my way." Andre turned to gaze at Dale. "I would have made it even if you hadn't given me that chance, because I believed in myself."

Dale wanted nothing more than to get out of the car and find his own way home. Andre was being shallow in his observations. Black kids were welcome on the Mozarkite team. The few he'd recruited had done well enough, except that kid from Springfield. He bucked the system and was dismissed. There was no doubt he was harassing Brooks Metcalf's daughter. Brooks came to Dale personally, imploring him to get the kid to stay away. And the boy's reaction when Dale had told him? That in itself was enough to warrant dismissal. Brooks's daughter had been pursuing him, the kid angrily proclaimed. She'd come by his dorm room several times and even spent the night with him once. It was lies. The player's roommate would not corroborate the claims.

But the others? They fit in just fine.

"Coach, the word on the streets is that, if you're not a small town white boy, you best steer clear of Mozarkite."

"Bull."

"If you don't believe me, ask some of the high school coaches. They know their players, what they're thinking and saying."

"Not necessary."

"Are you saying you don't believe me?"

"I resent you bringing me on this trip just to show me what you think are my shortcomings."

"I'm not trying to show you anything, Coach. I'm trying to help."

"I don't want your help, Andre. Let's go back."

"I love you, Coach."

"I'll pay for my own ticket. Just take me to the airport."

"I love you, and I love Mozarkite. I don't want you to fade off into the sunset and be forgotten."

Ouch.

That one twisted like a dagger.

Because if there was one thing Dale had felt during his visit with Coach Rodney Troy, it was that his career had peaked.

And was now in decline.

And he'd grown complacent.

And satisfied.

Being a big fish in a little pond.

Because, wasn't it better than being a fish with no pond at all?

"I want you to meet a young man named Brandon Yarbrough. He's an intern with the Tennessee Titans. He wants to be your assistant coach."

"Never heard of him."

"Prepare to be bowled over."

◊ ◊ ◊

THEY WERE SHOWN into an impressive conference room in the equally impressive corporate home of the Tennessee Titans. A receptionist offered them soft drinks, then said that their wait should be short. Two minutes later, the door opened, and Brandon Yarbrough hurried into the room.

He was young, not much older than the Mozarkite players. He was tall and wiry and looked nothing like a football player. He had a full head of curly black hair, and when he pulled off his Titans' ski cap, the curls seemed to pour out.

"Coach, I'm Brandon. Sorry to keep you waiting." The kid offered his hand. Dale shook it. He nodded hello to Andre, but didn't appear awestruck by being in the presence of a hall-of-famer. Then he sat down across the table from them. His eyes were brown and piercing. He looked directly at Dale when he talked.

"I want to be your Assistant Coach. I want more than anything to come to Mozarkite and help you build a championship team."

"What makes you think you can adapt to small town life?" As soon as the words were out of his mouth, Dale remembered his earlier conversation with Andre.

"When it comes to football I can fit in anywhere," Brandon replied. "I grew up in Louisville and hung around the university team as a kid, until they chased me away."

"The coaches who were at U of L at that time still remember him," Andre said. "One of them said that Brandon knew more at twelve years old than some of the assistant coaches."

"What did your parents think of you hanging around a college football program?" Dale asked.

"Dad worked two jobs. Three, if you count driving a cab when my uncle was sick or drunk. He never cared what I did." Brandon paused, and a somber expression came over him that he pushed aside. "Mom wasn't around. It was just me, my Dad, and my big sister, Daphne."

Dale asked a few questions, but mainly listened as Brandon Yarbrough shared his life story. As a player he topped out at junior varsity. Flunked out of college twice before hitting his stride at Morehead State, where he was a self-described 'walk-on assistant coach.'

"They started me running the video camera, but by senior year I was coaching the backfield."

From there Brandon moved to paid gigs with Coastal Carolina and Virginia. "Low-level coaching positions," he readily admitted. "They didn't have much use for a guy who never really played the game. An acquaintance introduced him to the General Manager of the Titans who offered him an internship in marketing.

"Unpaid, but I got by. I'm used to living on the edge anyway."

What Brandon loved most was recruiting. "I've kept in touch with people along the way. In Virginia and Carolina, even back in Kentucky. I get to know kids, friend them on Facebook, follow them on Twitter, that kind of stuff." He stared up at the ceiling for a moment, then leaned forward. "Coach Fox, I can find the players you need to win."

It all sounded too good to be true. Brandon Yarbrough talked a good game, but plenty of people did that. When the rubber met the road, would he be able to deliver?

"I don't just take any player," Dale said. "We have standards at Mozarkite that go beyond what other schools set."

"All the better. I like a challenge. Are you willing to work with kids who have a past?"

"Did you not hear what I said?" Dale said sternly.

"I'm not talking about bad people, just kids who made a mistake or two along the way."

"If they can't meet our standards, they don't make our program." Could he be any clearer? If young Brandon Yarbrough was interested in short-cutting his way to a head coaching job he was barking up the wrong tree.

"When do I start?"

Dale took a deep breath. "You've not been offered a job. Quite frankly, I find you to be cocky, abrasive, and short on real football knowledge."

Dale's assessment did nothing to dim the young man's enthusiasm. He reached into his backpack and pulled out a tattered spiral notebook. After flipping through a few pages, he started sharing insights about the current state of the Mozarkite offense, including player names, positions, strengths, and weaknesses.

"Today's players like offensive formations like the pros use," he said. "Your quarterback, Devereux, for example, he played in a more wide-open offensive scheme in high school. Good quarterback, but he struggled to adapt. If he'd gone to a school like South Tennessee, he would have been all-conference."

"You have no idea what you're talking about."

"You don't think he's very smart, do you, Coach?"

Dale considered the question. Andre tried to suppress a smile.

"He's not a dumb kid. He just wasn't the quarterback for your system. But you didn't know that because you didn't have time to do the recruiting you needed to do."

"But you would've known."

"I won't play the same offense you play. We'll be more up-tempo. Fast and loose. Kids are attracted to that kind of game."

"How good are you at following directions?"

"It depends, Coach. Whose directions?"

"Mine. Or any head coach you work for."

"Are you open to discussion, or do you hand down the law and that's that?"

Dale wanted to answer that he was open to discussion, but a glance at Andre made him reconsider.

"I guess you could say that I'm in transition." Dale placed his arms on the table and leaned forward. Brandon Yarbrough did the same. "Young man, do *not* make me regret this decision."

21

*D*ale's office phone jangled. A relic from the 1980's, it was probably one of the last ones on campus that did. The others beeped or made other high-tech sounds to announce a call. Dale's still jangled, and he liked that. Maintenance had come to replace it several times, but he always chased them off. It wasn't that he was particularly old-fashioned. He was, but that wasn't the reason he stuck with the old green phone. He had always liked the jangle. It brought back some of his most cherished memories.

The call from Professor Parker three decades earlier, letting him know he would be assuming the head coach position.

The time a representative from juco's national headquarters called with the news that Mozarkite was ranked first in the nation.

The phone had jangled when he received word that Andre was first-team All American.

And when Andre was the NFL's fourth overall draft pick.

And when Andre made the Hall of Fame.

It also jangled with the news that Linda had died. That might have ruined it for some, and the melancholy it brought upon Dale might eventually lead him to request an update, but for now it was what he had, so he grabbed the phone from its cradle. Office

Assistant Rosie Halliburton would usually be on the line, announcing who was calling, but Rosie was on another of her smoke breaks.

"Coach? It's Lamont."

Dale sat back and tried to recall whom he knew named Lamont.

Former players?

Nope. There were several Larrys, a couple of Lonnies, but no Lamonts.

Co-workers?

Again, a Larry or two, even a Lawrence who used to teach in Sociology.

Neighbors? Church members? Regulars at the Goldrush?

No. No. No.

"How are you doing, Lamont?" Dale decided to fake his way through until the caller said something that triggered a memory.

"I'm sorry it took me so long to get back to you. I came down with strep and couldn't shake it for nothing."

"Sorry to hear that, Lamont. I guess you're healthy again?"

"Yeah, finally. It cost me several weeks of work, though. The good news is, your wife's computer is ready."

Bingo!

Lamont was Hurley, the college tech guy. Was he Lamont Hurley or Hurley Lamont? Did it matter?

"I wondered what was up, Hurley. Every time I went by your office the door was closed."

"Yeah, I've been miserable. The good news is, I lost twenty-six pounds. Do you want me to drop off your computer? I'll be over that way."

"Yes, please. And if I'm not here, leave it in my mailbox."

"I sure will. By the way, I changed all the access passwords. Mrs. Fox had several, but they're all the same now."

"Great, Hurley. Thanks again."

"Don't you want to know what it is?"

"What?"

Hurley took a deep impatient breath. "The new password."

"Oh, yeah. What is it?"

"Linda."

Dale was disconnecting when he had another thought. "Hurley?"

"Yes, Coach?"

"Did you find anything?"

"Like what?"

"Anything I should know about? You know, before I actually turn it on?"

"I didn't really look, Coach. I just reset the passwords and checked for viruses. There are some photographs in a folder on the desktop, but I can't say that I took much notice of what they were."

● ● ●

DALE WAS hip-deep in preparing his remarks for the upcoming press conference when the office phone jangled again. It was Rosie, finally back from her trip to the little smoking shack behind the gym that most referred to as the Butt Hut.

"Cassie Whitman is on line three."

"What does she want?"

Rosie exhaled and sounded like Hurley had earlier. "I didn't ask her, but I suspect that she's interested in getting to know you better. You go to the same church, right?"

Dale said they did.

"You've been a widower for a few months. She's single and alone. I guess some would classify you as a catch."

Dale felt his face flush and was glad Rosie couldn't see it. He tried to come up with a witty response, but couldn't, so he pushed the flashing button on his phone.

"Coach Fox." He used the same tone of voice that he used when addressing strangers. Cassie wasn't a stranger, but she wasn't exactly a friend, either.

"Hi Coach... Dale. It's Cassie from church."

"Hi, Cassie. What can I do for you?"

Cassie was flustered and it showed. It took her several starts and stops to ask if he would like to come for dinner at her house the following Monday. He felt a pang of sympathy for her. He still remembered how many times he had picked up the phone and started to dial, only to get scared and quickly hang up, before working up the courage to ask Teri Jones to prom back in eleventh grade.

"That would be nice, Cassie. Can I bring anything?"

For the third time that day the caller took a deep breath. Dale wasn't an idiot. He knew that Hurley and Rosie Halliburton had sighed in exasperation. They were, in their own ways, mocking him. Cassie? She sighed with relief that it was over. She had done what she intended to do, call him and invite him to dinner, and it probably felt good. That made Dale feel good.

"No, Dale. I'll have everything prepared at seven. Feel free to come any time before then."

◊ ◊ ◊

THE GATHERING WAS CONSIDERABLY SMALLER than the press conference the month before to announce Andre's new affiliation with the college. Wally Westmoreland arrived first to set up for a live remote on Country 104. Two newspaper reporters, old-timers from neighboring counties, sauntered in together a few moments before the one o'clock start time.

Then there was Heaven Knight.

Dale had not heard much from her recently. At some point she had dyed her hair pink. He considered commenting on it but didn't. She nodded when she entered the conference room, then took a seat on the front row, opened her laptop, and started typing.

Press conferences were nonexistent under the leadership of Professor Parker. Margaret Fuller changed that. She called a half-dozen in the first nine months she was on the job. Grant announcements, construction projects, and faculty awards had been among her reasons for gathering the local scribes. Typically, the Athletic Director would open a press conference if it involved athletics, but since Dale was both Athletic Director and the person making the announcement, President Fuller would do the introductions.

And introduce she did.

President Fuller dug back through the annals of time to dredge up all of Dale's accomplishments and accolades.

Runner-up for a National championship, three-time conference Coach of the Year, four juco All-Americans, nine former players in the NFL. She mentioned everything. What she left out, thankfully, that all of those things happened more than a decade in the past. She was obviously ecstatic that Dale had gone beyond the local area to hire a new assistant coach and wanted the world to know that she was in his corner. Dale appreciated it, though it was embarrassing.

Brandon Yarbrough was kept out of sight in an adjoining class-room during the introductions. It was President Fuller's idea, some-thing she'd seen the big schools do when introducing a new coach. Wally Westmoreland was confused, interrupting President Fuller as she was making her final introduction of Dale to inquire if 'the new guy' had missed a plane or something. Dr. Fuller remained unfazed by Wally's question as she chugged ahead and turned the podium over to Dale.

Dale wore the same khakis and shirt from when Andre took him on their road trip two weeks earlier. He was still struggling with the washer and dryer, and the outfit was one of few that would not need ironing before being worn again. He approached the podium, cleared his throat, and began by thanking President Fuller for her support. They had avoided one another in recent weeks, and Dale was ready to move past that. He didn't like being at odds with anyone, least of all the person who signed his evaluations, so he was lavish with his praise of the President before moving on to his introduction of Brandon Yarbrough.

The reporters seemed impressed that Brandon had spent time with the Tennessee Titans. They and the Kansas City Chiefs were the teams most locals followed. Older folks usually sided with the Chiefs, who had been around longer, while those under thirty leaned toward the Titans. Both were a three-hour drive from town. Dale also took a moment to throw some shade Andre's way for brokering the meeting that led to the hire, then said, "I want to welcome our new Offensive Coordinator and Recruiting Director, Coach Brandon Yarbrough."

Brandon bounded in as if he had just won the lottery. Dale had not seen him since that day in Nashville and was caught off guard by how young he looked. Wally Westmoreland was too, obviously, because when he was given the chance to ask the first question, he blurted out, "What are you? Seventeen?"

Brandon laughed easily before sharing more of his past. Dale noticed that Heaven Knight's attention perked up when he started talking. Could the sharp-clawed reporter have a romantic future with the new assistant coach? That could certainly improve the team's coverage.

The dream ended with a splat.

Heaven Knight's first three questions came in rapid fire succession.

"Why should Mozarkite fans believe that you can out recruit the other conference schools?"

"You were an unpaid intern for the Titans, right, Coach Yarbrough? That's not even a real job, is it?"

"Missouri is a hotbed of football talent, but you've only been in the state as a tourist, right, Coach Yarbrough?"

Brandon was momentarily knocked back on his heels, but to his credit, he came back swinging. He shared some of the same anecdotes from his past that Dale had heard in Nashville. He described his approach to selling recruits on Mozarkite, Missouri, comparing it to his previous work in Kentucky's Appalachian region. And he dropped a few names. Not in a way that came off as bragging but to make his points. He'd learned recruiting from one person whose name was easily recognized. He had been schooled on talent evaluation by a former NFL assistant. The coach of a perennial Top-Twenty college team had helped him design offensive schemes. Brandon came across as young and confident and ready.

Then the wheels fell off.

The question came from one of the old-timers from a neighboring county. It was innocent enough, something about whether Brandon was a proponent of a pass-heavy offense. The young coach's answer was non-committal, along the lines of waiting to see what kind of players he had. All was good, or so it seemed, until Heaven Knight raised her hand and proceeded to pin Coach Brandon Yarbrough to the mat.

"Do you prefer a pass-oriented offense or not?"

"Again, it depends upon the personnel."

"But all things equal, what offense would you prefer to run?"

"Those decisions are made by the entire coaching staff. Not just me."

"I'm asking your personal opinion."

And off Brandon went, describing his perfect offense, a rock-and-rolling traveling circus of passes, trick-plays and razzle dazzle. "Players love it," he exclaimed, getting caught up in the moment. "Our fans will love coming out to see an offense that sends guys into motion and throws downfield. It's an offense that scores lots of points, and I certainly think our fans will get a kick out of lots of points."

Dale's stomach clenched. They had discussed offense schemes, among other things, in a handful of calls over the past couple weeks. He knew Brandon's preferences but had insisted no decisions be made until they could sit down face-to-face. And here he was, telling the world, or at least that part of the world that listened to Country 104 or read the newspapers in Mozarkite and surrounding communities, that the Polled Hereford offense would be action-oriented and pass happy. Dale moved to step in and set the record straight when a side door opened, and Andre Jameson entered. He was, as always, dressed as if he were about to go on TV. He tried to be inconspicuous, but how could he accomplish that in a room containing two coaches, a college president, three newspaper reporters, and Wally Westmoreland?

He couldn't.

Wally was the first to react, his voice rising to the timbre he used when he called games on Saturday afternoon.

"Listeners, you won't believe who just walked in! None other than

Mozarkite's own Hall-of-Famer, the one and only Andre Jameson. This press conference should get interesting real quick, folks. I'm going to turn this microphone around and put it up real close to the front so you don't miss a thing!"

As Wally repositioned his mic, President Fuller returned to the podium. Brandon stepped back to give her room as she introduced Andre and asked if he wished to speak. Dale had no idea that Andre was coming and wouldn't have agreed to the press conference if he had. There was nothing he could do, as the cow was already out of the barn.

Or was it the horse? It didn't matter. Whatever wasn't supposed to be out of the barn, was out.

Andre greeted the small gathering warmly. His appearance, it turned out, was unplanned. At least not by anyone at Mozarkite. In fact, he thought the press conference was earlier in the day and was planning on stopping in for a quick hello on his way to speak at a business gathering at Lake of the Ozarks. But speak he did. He lauded Dale for hiring Brandon, then waxed effusive about the young man and what he could mean to the college. So lavish was his praise that Heaven Knight raised her hand and asked Andre if he was positioning Brandon Whitman to be the next head football coach at Mozarkite.

Suddenly aware of how far he'd gone, Andre grew pensive. He said all the right things. Coach Fox could and should coach for as long as he wanted. The program was in good hands. Yada, yada. His intent, he explained, was to let everyone know how big a catch young Brandon Yarbrough was.

That was all.

There were a few more questions before President Fuller thanked the media for attending. It was over. As the press made their way out, Andre made his way toward Dale.

"Coach, please know that I—"

"Not now," Dale said sharply. He had his eyes glued on Brandon Yarbrough who remained on the edge of the stage, looking about nervously.

"Coach Yarbrough, come to my office."

Brandon knew he'd screwed up.

§ § §

BRANDON TOOK his reprimand with humility and grace. He readily admitted he had overstepped and apologized repeatedly. Then, when Dale ran out of steam, Brandon asked if he had the green light to hit the recruiting trail. He did, so he left and Dale headed home.

§ § §

THE DESKTOP APPEARED unchanged from when Dale handed the laptop off to Hurley. He went to the *W* file and clicked on it. It opened just as it had before Christmas. The same subfiles appeared, labeled by year. He clicked on the past year. It was still password protected. He started typing.

L-I-N-D-A

Nothing.

l-i-n-d-a

Still nothing.

L-i-n-d-a

That did it. The password screen disappeared. The file opened and a dozen thumbnail pictures appeared. He was about to click on one to expand it when the front door opened and Susan called out.

"Dad? It's me."

"I'm in the kitchen."

Dale was closing the laptop as Susan came in.

"You're using Mom's laptop," she said as she passed by and went to what had always been the snack cabinet. She pulled out a Little Debbie Oatmeal Creme Pie.

"I had the college's tech guy unlock the passwords for me."

"What did you find?"

"Nothing yet. I was making sure it still works. What brings you over so late?"

"It's only eight-fifteen. Max is spending the evening with Evan at the Holiday Inn in Charleston."

It was the first time Evan had seen his son since Christmas. That was too long in Dale's opinion. He also knew that Evan had not been sending support money for Max's care. He was about to ask when Susan jumped in first.

"I heard your new assistant coach on the radio today."

"How about me? Did you also hear your dear old Dad?"

Susan waved at him dismissively, took a bite of her cookie and spoke with her mouth full. "I grew up hearing you on the radio. I like the sound of your new coach, though. Yarbrough, right?"

"That's right."

"I like his ideas for the offense."

Dale harrumphed. Susan caught it.

"I guess you don't."

"He needs to learn that we have a way of doing things."

"Maybe. What's he like?"

Dale looked up at her. "What do you mean?"

Susan took a deep breath. A condescending one, like Hurley and Rosie Halliburton. Not like Cassie Whitman. "What's. He. Like?"

"He's a kid. A kid who likes football."

"Is he tall? Short? Good-looking? Married?"

Ah. There it was.

"He's a kid. Nothing else matters."

Susan took another deep breath. "Dad, I need your help with something."

"He's a kid, Susan. Too young for you."

"That's not what I need help with. It's Max."

Dale came to full attention.

"He needs to see you more often."

"What happened?"

"Nothing, Dad. Well, everything. He lives alone with me. He goes to a daycare where he's surrounded by women. He almost never sees Evan, and when he does it's like buddy-buddy instead of father-son.

He needs a man in his life." Susan paused, smiled at Dale, and said, "He needs you."

"I was a terrible father, Susan. What makes you think I'll be any different?"

Susan reached across the table and stroked his arm. "You weren't a terrible father. You were just... the only kind of father you knew how to be. And besides, I was a girl. Max needs a man's guidance and example. I want you to be that man."

Dale felt a tingle of affection from his daughter's kind words. But still... "Things haven't changed. I'm still coaching. It takes most of my time. I'm afraid I can't commit to something like—"

"He needs you. Who else is there?"

Dale shook his head. "I took him to Chuck E. Cheese."

"That was weeks ago, Dad. He needs more."

"Susan, I'm too busy to—" Dale's cellphone buzzed on the table in front of Susan. She picked it up before he could protest.

"Coach Fox's phone," she answered cheerily. Dale watched his daughter's facial expression as she listened to whoever was on the other end.

"He can't get to the phone right now. Can I help you? Coach Yarbrough? He probably does. Hold on. Let me see if he's available."

She flipped on the phone's speaker and held it up. "Heaven Knight from the *Messenger*."

"Hello, Miss Knight."

"Coach, I was wondering if you might be able to give me Coach Yarbrough's cell number."

"Maybe. What did you need to talk to him about?"

The line was silent for a few seconds. When she spoke again, Heaven sounded less confident. "I... wanted to ask some follow-up questions about his position on your staff."

"I'll have to find the—" Dale stopped speaking when he saw Susan hurriedly bring an index finger to her lips. She shook her head and raised both hands.

"I'm not sure I can get my hands on Coach Yarbrough's number,"

Dale said. "Can I give him a message to get in touch with you the next time he checks in?"

"That'll be fine. Thank you."

"She's not after his number to ask follow-up questions," Susan said as soon as Dale disconnected. "She's interested in getting to know him."

"What do you mean?"

"Dad, is he good-looking?"

"I... guess you could say that. It's not something I really considered."

"And he's single, right?"

Dale nodded.

"Mozarkite's pretty small, and Heaven Knight's looking for a man. Not one of the usual suspects. She wants to get her claws into Coach Yarbrough before someone else does."

"That's ridiculous, Susan. You said you were listening to the press conference. Did you hear the way she went after him?"

"Yes, and I also heard the way he handled her hard questions. He's smart, Dad. Smart and eligible."

"I don't think so."

"Did you hear how her voice changed? She was all in charge until you asked why she needed Coach Yarbrough's number. Then she started babbling like a high school girl."

"It's hard to imagine the two of them together."

Susan punched Dale's arm playfully. "Why don't you let me be the judge of that. Invite Coach Yarbrough to supper when he's back in town. I'll cook and we can all get acquainted."

"I don't think it's a good idea for me to be fraternizing with my assistant coaches."

"Oh, yeah," Susan laughed. "Now you start worrying about that, after twenty-five years of breakfast with Uncle Willis. I'll tell you what, Daddy-o. You get the man here, and I'll whip up a dinner that'll make him want to stay in Mozarkite for the rest of his life."

Later, when Dale opened the door to walk Susan out, they found Chelsea tied to the porch, as always.

"She's been gone for nearly a week," Dale said. "I keep filling in the holes, but she digs them again. I'm not sure what to do anymore, so I just let her go."

"Dad." Susan raised up on tiptoes to peck him on the cheek. "Think about what we talked about, about you and Max."

"I will."

"And let me know if you find anything on Mom's computer that I should know about."

Dale tensed. "Like what?"

"Work stuff. Deals she had going, contacts. That kind of stuff."

Dale stretched and yawned. "I will, but it will be tomorrow. I think I'm going to call it a night."

22

*D*ale glanced up from the laptop and saw it was already two in the afternoon. The chores he'd set aside for that Saturday had been ignored. He had been looking through the photographs in the *W* file for four hours. A few questions had been answered, but even more had arisen.

The Sweet Breeze Inn in Gulfport, the folks who had sent the huge display of carnations to Linda's funeral? Linda had stayed there at least two weekends each of the past five years. There were photographs from all over the property. Linda at the pool. Linda in a bar. There were several of Linda enjoying dinner with a couple that Dale did not recognize. Those pictures raised another question: who took them? It was obvious that the tables in each shot were set for four. Who was number four? Was he *W*? Was he even a he? Maybe *W* was one of Linda's many girlfriends. But who? Whomever *W* was, he or she was familiar to Linda and the other couple. All displayed easy smiles or mugged happily for the photos. It was obvious that they were good friends.

But not friends of Dale's.

The captions gave away nothing more than the dates of the get-togethers. Dale had dragged out his old calendars to cross-check.

Several were football weekends. Others were weekends he was recruiting out of state. A few appeared during times when there was nothing on his calendar, so he checked Linda's old desk calendars. A couple dates were identified as real estate seminars, but most were blank.

And the one that intrigued Dale the most? It was a shot of Linda. Alone, also at the Sweet Breeze Inn. She was dressed in a slinky black dress. She was radiant and sexy in a way he'd not thought of her in a long time. And she was looking directly into the camera lens as she blew a kiss.

She was not wearing her wedding ring.

Linda never took off her wedding ring.

That sent Dale back to the photos. How had he missed it? She wasn't wearing her wedding ring in any of the pictures.

He continued working his way through the files. One photo from three years earlier included the women he'd seen with Linda in the picture he'd found in her coat pocket, the one inscribed by *W, Things get a little crazy on date night.* Instead of fancy drinks they were holding beers. The women were in swimsuits. Linda was the prettiest and most fit of the four, and she was wearing a red two-piece Dale had never seen before. Still no sign of *W*.

Dale had just clicked on the file from four years before when his cellphone buzzed.

"Hi, Dale. It's Cassie Whitman."

"Cassie, how are you?"

"I'm well, Dale. Sorry to bother you. I was wanting to find out what kind of pie is your favorite."

"Pie?"

"Yes, for dinner Monday night."

He had completely forgotten.

"Uh... Cassie, I guess I like... I'm going to have to cancel, Cassie. Something has come up."

The line was silent. Dale felt like a heel.

"I was about to call you. I hope you've not gone to the market yet."

"Actually, I have. I bought a chicken and some other ingredients...
but it's okay. I understand that things come up at the last minute."

"I'm really sorry. Maybe another time?"

The line was quiet again.

"Cassie? Maybe another time?"

"Perhaps. Thank you, Dale... Coach."

◊ ◊ ◊

IT WAS HALF-PAST midnight when Dale turned off the computer and
climbed the stairs to bed. He didn't bother to set the alarm for
church. He wasn't feeling very churchy and preferred not to run into
Cassie Whitman. Did others know about Linda's secret life? If so, how
many? What did they know? Did anyone know who *W* was? Could
one of them actually be *W*?

Dale had spent the last twelve hours feeling as if a secret closet in
his home had opened and spilled out its sordid contents. He was
struggling to get his head around what the contents were and what
they meant. Over the past decade Linda had taken trips to Mexico,
the Caribbean, Bermuda, and even Cuba. She traveled to the Northeast for a fall foliage tour and the deep South for a historic plantation
tour. She cruised on ships and rode the rails on passenger trains. She
had backpacked, backtracked, and been sidetracked. She breathed
air from mountain tops and the depths of caves. There were pedi-
cures, manicures, and massages, some alone, others in tandem. She
lived. And lived some more. And documented each and every stop,
being sure to include photos and descriptions, but never disclosing
the identity of the person on the other side of the camera. The
elusive *W*.

And Dale had been oblivious.

Completely and utterly oblivious.

And that gave him a feeling of loss the likes of which he'd never
known. The woman he had buried several months before. The
woman he thought he knew better than anyone, well, he had not
really known her at all.

Linda Fox was a different person.

And the hardest thing to cope with was the sense of despair that came with realizing that the Linda he never knew might be the Linda he would have most liked to have known.

No, Dale decided as he crawled into bed, not knowing the Linda in the photographs wasn't the hardest thing to cope with. It was second.

First was not knowing the person whom she'd chosen to spend those moments with. He turned out the lights certain of little, other than one thing.

He was going to find out who the hell *W* was, and how he or she had come to know his wife in a way that he never would.

23

*H*ad President Fuller been devious enough to have cameras installed in Dale's office over the previous three weeks, she would have found plenty of justification to fire him for cause.

Nothing got done.

He arrived late, locked himself in his office with Linda's laptop, and left early. Phone calls weren't returned until absolutely necessary. Meetings were missed. Time usually spent checking up on the classwork of football players was wiled away looking and relooking at the photographs of Linda enjoying her other life. When Uncle Homer called to find out why he'd not been at the Goldrush, Dale gave him an excuse about being too busy. He did the same when Larry Bob called. Patsy even offered to bring by a plate of chicken and dumplings, but Dale declined. All he wanted to do was look at those pictures, hopeful of some small clue as to the identity of *W*.

Brandon Yarbrough was putting in enough hours for both of them. He had traversed the South, from Arkansas to Mississippi and Florida, then up the coast to the Carolinas and Virginia, before hitting Kentucky and Tennessee. Fourteen prospective players had already been identified for next season's squad. All Brandon was waiting for before pulling the trigger was Dale's okay.

Dale kept him waiting.

And finally, it became time to do something. Something that didn't involve those pictures of Linda. Dale always preached to his players the importance of putting first things first. He decided one afternoon after three weeks of staring at those damned pictures that it was time to put his own first things first. Sure, he would keep searching, trying to discover the identity of his wife's companion. But for now, if he was going to keep his job, he had to get back in the saddle.

The first step would be to actually cook something for dinner. He'd been existing on junk for three weeks. Salami and cheese sandwiches, frozen pizzas, and ramen noodles. Part of the reason was that he was lost in the kitchen. That would have to change. He picked up the phone and called Linda's office, which was now Susan's office. She answered.

"Is it really you?"

"Who else would it be?"

"We haven't seen you in ages. Max keeps asking what happened to Pop-Pop. I tell him you're a busy coach. You are a busy coach, right?"

It was apparent from her tone that Susan suspected there was something going on. She had her mother's intuition. Dale, it was turning out, had never intuited anything beyond the end of his nose.

"Yeah, I've been busy, but I wanted to see if you and Max want to come over for supper tonight."

"We would love to. What do you want me to make? Lasagna?"

"No. I'm cooking tonight. How does meatloaf sound?"

The line was silent for several beats before Susan said, "You're cooking?"

"That's what I said."

"Do you know how to turn on the oven? You have to bake meatloaf, you know."

Dale had no idea how to turn on the oven, but he remembered seeing the instruction book in a box in the utility room.

"I'll be fine. Come over at six."

"We'll be there. And, Dad, there's something I've been wanting to talk to you about anyway. Maybe after Max falls asleep we can chat."

● ● ●

DALE ENTERED the Piggly Wiggly armed with a recipe for *Zesty Saltine Meatloaf* he'd found online. Linda had always preferred the bigger supermarkets in town, HyVee and Thriftway, but Piggly Wiggly was only eight aisles. And if he couldn't find anything, Dale knew he could ask Mary Sherwood, the owner's wife, who'd manned Register One for fifty-seven years.

And best of all, he knew he was unlikely to run into anyone he knew. The Piggly Wiggly was rarely busy, and most of the folks who shopped there came from out in the country rather than Mozarkite proper.

He was headed down Aisle Two, *Condiments, Soup, and Canned Vegetables*, when his cart nearly collided with Cassie Whitman's rear end. She was bent over, inspecting the three varieties of green beans on a lower shelf, and Dale had been so intent on finding tomato paste that he didn't see her until the last moment. She straightened, turned, and smiled. Then the smile faded.

"Hi, Coach."

"Hi, Cassie. I didn't know you shopped here."

"I don't usually. I was on this side of town and ran in to get a couple things."

The moment became awkward as Dale searched for something to say.

"I'm looking for tomato paste."

Cassie nodded. "That's nice."

"I'm... trying to cook a meatloaf."

"Good for you. I hope it turns out well."

Cassie's farewell was as muted as her demeanor. Dale felt like an idiot. He was hoping they wouldn't cross paths in a later aisle. Fortunately, they didn't. But he did run into Bubber Slate in the checkout lane.

"Hey, Bubber."

"Coach." Bubber's tone was also muted. His eyes looked around uncertainly.

"Has my dog come by your place anymore?"

"Chelsea?"

"Yeah."

"Is she still getting away, Coach?"

"She disappears for days at a time. I'm not sure what I'm going to do."

"That's tough." They grew silent before Bubber said, "I guess I better get my groceries on the belt so Miss Mary can check them out."

●　●　●

DALE FELT BETTER than he had in weeks.

Zesty Saltine Meatloaf was a success, even though he was supposed to use ketchup instead of tomato paste.

Max asked for seconds. And he was wild about the sugary applesauce Dale had picked up.

"We usually use the no-sugar kind," Susan said casually. Dale could tell that she wasn't being judgmental.

Dessert was a hit, too. Strawberries and whipped cream. The strawberries were frozen, but with enough whipped cream nobody knew the difference.

"I don't think I've ever had applesauce and strawberries in the same meal," Susan kidded as they cleaned up later. Max had fallen asleep on the sofa after two games of *Chutes and Ladders*. Dale washed and Susan dried. He still hadn't mastered the dishwasher, but there was time.

"Where have you been the past few weeks?"

Dale considered how to answer his daughter's question. Should he share the photographs with her? What would she think?

"Recruitment season," was all he said. It was enough.

"Is Coach Yarbrough doing well?"

Dale said he was doing okay, though he was spending a lot of money on travel.

"Is there any other way to recruit?" Susan's question was both sarcastic and sincere.

Then, she took a deep breath and charged ahead.

"Can Max and I move back here?"

Dale stopped washing dishes. He dried his hands and looked at Susan. She wasn't kidding.

"Of course."

Susan waited, but Dale didn't have anything else to say.

"Don't you want to know why?"

Dale shook his head. "It doesn't matter."

"There was a meth lab in the house three doors down. They found it day before yesterday. You probably saw it on the news."

Dale hadn't.

"It was Wade Ricketts' cousin's lab. Wade knew about it."

Dale caught his breath. "It was probably operating while he was still on the force."

"Probably. It was too close for comfort. The area isn't bad but having something like that so close... it made me reconsider."

Dale smiled. "It'll be good having you back here. When?"

"Right away. This weekend."

● ● ●

AFTER SUSAN LEFT WITH MAX, Dale looked at his calendar for the following day. Nothing was scheduled, which wasn't a surprise, as he had not been returning calls or emails. His phone had eleven new voice messages. Eight of them were from Brandon Yarbrough.

"Hey Coach, it's Brandon. I'm in Ocala, Florida. There are two boys here looking to play football. One is a big lineman. Call me."

"Hey Coach, it's Brandon. I stopped in Valdosta to see that Smitkins boy

I wrote about in my email. He's looking at one of the Texas jucos, but I think I can sway him to come to Mozarkite. Give me a call."

"Hey Coach, Brandon again. I'm in Savannah. One of the Ocala boys committed to East Mississippi, but the other is still interested. Call me back, and I'll give you his information."

"Brandon again, Coach Fox. I'm in Orangeburg, South Carolina. There's a quarterback here who committed to South Carolina State but backed out at the last minute. He's been working in a butcher shop this year but wants to play football again. He's big and fast, and I think he can help us. Call me."

"Coach Fox, it's Brandon. I'm still in Orangeburg. I'm starting to wonder if your phone is working. We lost the other kid from Ocala. He's going to Stetson. The Smitkins boy in Valdosta is starting to lean toward going to Texas. We might still have a chance at the quarterback from Orangeburg, but we have to let him know something today, so please call me back."

The last call from Orangeburg had been three days earlier. Dale felt a twinge of guilt as he listened to the remaining calls, each sounding more desperate than the previous. He'd given Brandon Yarbrough a job to do, then followed up with zilch support. He checked his watch and saw that it was after ten, which meant it was after eleven back East. Still, he decided he would call Coach Yarbrough and catch up.

He didn't get the chance to dial the number. Coach Yarbrough was calling him.

"Coach Fox! Is it really you?" A seven-year-old on Christmas Eve wouldn't have sounded more thrilled.

"Sorry to have missed your calls. There has been so much going on and I just... well it doesn't matter. Is the quarterback from Orangeburg still interested in coming to Mozarkite?"

"Forget about him, Coach, he committed to a D-2 school in Virginia. What I found is even better."

"Tell me."

"Oh gosh, Coach, wait until you hear this." Brandon sounded breathless. "Let me close the motel room door so nobody hears me.

There's a parking lot full of drunks out here. I don't know if any of them are football fans, but you can never be too careful."

"Where are you?"

"Chattanooga. I was headed to Nashville and decided to stop in and make some calls. And, Coach, you won't believe what I found."

Dale waited while Brandon composed himself.

"Coach Fox, the Chattanooga Triplets want to come to Mozarkite."

24

PROSPECT SCOUTING REPORT
Prepared by Brandon Yarbrough, Assistant Coach
Mozarkite Junior College Football
Personal and Confidential

*P*layer #1: Carlos Kwan
    Position: Running Back
Height/Weight: 5'9" 210 lbs.
Hometown: Chattanooga, Tennessee
High School: Volunteer High School
Previous College: Arizona State University
Reason for Leaving: Grades. Not attending class.
Performance: Considered one of the top 25 running backs in the nation as a high school junior. Injured in third game of senior season and unable to return to team. Played seven games as third string running back at Arizona State. Projected to be a starter during sophomore year prior to dismissal.
Personal: Parents are first-generation immigrants. Father from Vietnam, Mother from Mexico. They own and operate a convenience

store in downtown Chattanooga. Plans to major in Physical Education.

Recommendation: Fast, strong, and quick. A likely starter at any Division One school. Carlos struggled with grades and will need academic help and support. He's a good kid who wants another chance. Outstanding parental support.

◊ ◊ ◊

PLAYER #2: John Smith
    Position: Wide Receiver
    Height/Weight: 6'1" 210 lbs.
    Hometown: Chattanooga, Tennessee
    High School: Volunteer High School
    Previous College: Arizona State University
    Reason for Leaving: Voluntarily Withdrew
    Performance: All-State Wide Receiver in high school. First-String Receiver at Arizona State. Named to PAC-12 All-Freshman Team.
    Personal: Parents are divorced. John lives with his mother, an attorney. Father is a Certified Public Accountant. Suspended from Chattanooga Scholastic Academy during sophomore year for various discipline infractions. Father of a two-year old daughter. Major is undecided.
    Recommendation: Will be an outstanding college player with the speed and size to attract attention from the pros. Past problems do not appear to have resurfaced.

◊ ◊ ◊

PLAYER #3: De'Shea Stephens
    Position: Quarterback
    Height/Weight: 6'5" 240 lbs.
    Hometown: Chattanooga, Tennessee
    High School: Volunteer High School
    Previous College: Arizona State University

Reason for Leaving: Voluntarily withdrew after confrontation with an Assistant Coach.

Performance: All-State Quarterback in high school. Redshirt Freshman at Arizona State.

Personal: Lives with father, who is a disabled military veteran. Major is social work or communications. Has had past arrests for drug use and possession.

Recommendation: Tall and fast with a cannon for an arm. Has all the tools to become a star.

25

"Have any of you guys heard of a kid named Carlos Kwan?" Dale tried to be nonchalant in asking the question. The last thing he wanted to do was jump start the Mozarkite rumor mill, something his Goldrush buddies were happy to do.

Welder Tommy guffawed. "What the hell kind of name is that? Is the kid Filipino or something?"

"Carlos... Kwan?" Larry Bob drew the name out slowly. "Must not be from here. Would I have seen him in court?"

"He's a football player," Dale explained. "Arizona State."

All four of Dale's friends were avid college football fans, often gathering in front of Uncle Homer's seventy-five-inch TV to watch the big boys after Mozarkite home games. Their rooting interests were united behind Mizzou. Beyond that, each had a favorite they rooted for, particularly when they were playing each other's favorites. Larry Bob followed Michigan; Uncle Homer had Southern Cal. Welder Tommy liked Texas. Plumber Dick, for some reason no one understood, was a Kansas fan.

Neither of them had heard of Carlos Kwan. All of them, though, had heard of John Smith.

"Son of a bitch is a plumber in Doniphan," Plumber Dick said testily. "He cuts into the work I get over there because he charges less."

"The John Smith I know teaches dance classes in Poplar Bluff," Welder Tommy said. "I did some work at his place when he opened. He's as gay as Larry Bob."

"I'm not gay and neither is he," Larry Bob interjected. "I did the paperwork for his permits. The man is married and has seven kids. And you're an asshole, Tommy. And that's worse than being gay any day of the year."

"All of you is full of beans," Uncle Homer said. "John Smith is the county roads guy over in Sharp County in Arkansas. I used to do some milling for him back in the day."

"That John Smith's been dead for thirty years, Uncle Homer," Dick said.

"The hell he has. I saw him in Walmart not more than a year or two ago."

"You went to his funeral," Dick insisted. "You made me and Tommy go with you."

"I remember," Tommy said. "After the funeral they wheeled him down the aisle of that little church and had him sitting up in the back when we passed by. Scared me so bad I couldn't sleep for a month."

"You're both wrong. That was..." While Uncle Homer paused to sort out the memory. Dale jumped back in.

"Different John Smiths. This one played football at Arizona State, too. Wide receiver."

No one recalled seeing him.

"There's another one, but I can't remember his name," Dale said. "They are all from Chattanooga, and all three went to Arizona State."

"Holy smokes, Coach, they're the Chattanooga Triplets." Larry Bob's statement brought nods of recognition from the others.

"Why didn't you say so, Coach?" Dick said. "Everybody knows the Chattanooga Triplets."

"Those boys were something," Tommy added.

"Have you seen that big quarterback? Uncle Homer said as he pulled out his cellphone. "Let me find that video."

It didn't take long for Uncle Homer to pull up a grainy YouTube video of De'Shea Stephens throwing a bomb to a receiver the high school announcer said was John Smith. The guys clustered around Uncle Homer to watch it three times, whistling and shaking their heads in disbelief.

"The Chattanooga Triplets," Larry Bob sighed. "I prayed to Jesus every night that they would go to Mizzou."

"Or Kansas," Plumber Dick said dreamily.

Dale was reluctant to say that he'd not heard of them.

"How could you have not heard of these boys?" Uncle Homer asked.

"Seriously, Coach," Tommy said. "Even Dick knows about the Chattanooga Triplets."

"They're a great story," Larry Bob said as he leaned back in his chair. "Three boys from different backgrounds who became stars at some old inner-city school that hadn't had a winning team in years. They got so close that folks in Chattanooga started calling them The Triplets. Coaches from all over were trying to recruit them, but they wanted to stay together."

"That's what made Mizzou back away," Uncle Homer cut in. "They didn't need another running back, so they only wanted two of them."

"Michigan said they didn't do package deals," Larry Bob said, taking back the floor. "Arizona State told them to c'mon down, so they did,"

While they knew quite a bit about the Chattanooga Triplets, Dale's buddies were not aware that they were looking to leave Arizona State. This saved him from having to explain his sudden interest. It did not save him from several minutes of good-natured ribbing for not having heard about them in the first place. Fortunately, he was able to escape their insults by stepping away to take a phone call.

"Hey, Coach Fox, this is Lanny Masterson over at County Savings Bank."

"How are you, Lanny. It's been awhile."

"Yes, sir, it has. I hope I caught you at a good time."

"You caught me at the perfect time. Uncle Homer Bennett was just questioning my intelligence."

"Homer Bennett's the last person who should be commenting on another person's intelligence. Coach, did you know he came in here waving a gun at my tellers three years ago?"

Dale hadn't known.

"He got upset when we told him to leave, so he withdrew his money and went to one of the other banks. We miss his money, because it was substantial, but my tellers can breathe easier. But, Coach, that's not why I called. Did you know Miss Linda had a safe-deposit box over here?"

Dale hadn't known that, either.

"She opened it last year. According to the log, she came in to access it a couple times a month. I figured you might want to come check it out. The fee comes due in a week, and you can let us know if you want to keep it or not."

"I'll be over today, Lanny. Thanks for letting me know."

When Dale returned to the table Uncle Homer picked up right where he'd left off.

"Tell me, Coach, since you haven't heard of the Chattanooga Triplets, have you heard of a guy named Peyton Manning? How about Johnny Unitas? That's an oldie you might remember."

The others laughed, and Dale knew he should go along with the kidding, but the thought that Linda had maintained a safe deposit box he didn't know about had unsettled him just enough to push back at his old friend.

"I remember both of them, Uncle Homer. Do you remember the time you got kicked out of County Savings Bank for waving a gun around?"

The laughter stopped. Fast.

It was apparent that Dale was, again, the only person who was unaware.

"That wasn't nice, Coach," Larry Bob said quietly.

"You leave our uncle alone," Dick snipped.

Dale looked from one face to another. They were stoic. Uncle Homer appeared wounded. Dale felt terrible.

"I'm sorry, Homer. I just heard and..."

"Walk with me, Coach," Larry Bob said as he got up from the table.

"Sit back down, Larry Bob," Uncle Homer said quickly. "I shoulda told him back when it happened."

The story was short and quick. And sad. Lanny Masterson's book-keepers had grown weary of trying to keep Plumber Dick's check-book reconciled, so they sought to have him declared mentally incapacitated. When Dick brought the paperwork to Uncle Homer, the old man was incensed.

"I went too far, but they were going after my boy," Homer explained. "Nobody goes after my boy."

Larry Bob had stepped in after Uncle Homer was taken to jail. The judge, who was a long-time consumer of Uncle Homer's hooch, was sympathetic. Uncle Homer was fined a hundred dollars.

"I pulled out every dime I had in that damned bank the very next day," Homer said.

"First time I ever realized the old man was loaded," Larry Bob laughed. "From then on, the fees I charged him tripled."

Plumber Dick, clearly embarrassed by the situation, remained quiet during the discussion. When Dale noticed, he said, "Dick, I'm sorry you went through that. It turns out that Linda had some business over there, but I'll go close it out as soon as I leave here."

"It's okay, Coach. I ain't worth shit at keeping a checkbook."

"Or much of anything else," Tommy said, drawing laughs and pulling their group of old friends back to reality. The barbs and insults were returning to normal as Dale took his leave.

◆ ◆ ◆

LANNY MASTERSON CAME out of his office to greet Dale as he entered.

"Homer Bennett is my friend," Dale said brusquely. "So is his nephew, Dick. You had no right to do what you did."

Masterson opened his mouth to explain, but Dale cut him off. "Take me to my wife's safe-deposit box. I'll empty it and let it go. I don't want anything to do with you or your bank."

Dale felt immediately better.

The feeling wouldn't last long.

After being escorted by a secretary to a small room, Dale pulled out the lone chair and placed the box on the table in front of him. He was about to open it when Lanny Masterson knocked on the door and entered without waiting to be invited. With him was a young man Dale didn't know, a bank security guard in a too-tight uniform.

"Coach, I need to have that box back right now."

"I haven't looked at it yet."

Masterson nodded at the guard who then swept by and took away the box before Dale could stop him.

"What are you doing?" Dale said, getting to his feet.

"Our attorney advised us not to let you have the box until we are certain it's personal and not business." Masterson pointed to the door. "Take it to the vault, Sonny." The security guard exited, and Masterson said, "Coach, I have to ask you to leave."

❂ ❂ ❂

"Do you need help getting your stuff back here this weekend?"

It was a pleasant spring afternoon, and Susan's visit was a welcome respite from the rest of the day. They sat on the porch swing and enjoyed a breeze.

"I hired two high school boys with pickup trucks. It shouldn't take long. We'll store the furniture we don't need and bring the rest here."

Once that was settled, Dale told her about the safe-deposit box. "I visited with Larry Bob after I left the bank. He thinks it'll be easy enough to get it released. I'll need you to go with me as a representative of your mom's business. Between us, they'll have to release it."

Lanny Masterson's actions incensed Susan even more than they had Dale. Hearing about the way Plumber Dick was treated added to her furor. "I opened a savings account there after Christmas, but I'll go and close it tomorrow."

They were quiet for a few moments as Susan's anger subsided. Dale was reminded again and again how much Susan was like her mother. Their demeanors, their mercurial behaviors. Much the same.

"Have you ever heard of the Chattanooga Triplets?" He ventured.

"The football players? Of course. They were a great story."

"They want to come to Mozarkite."

Susan nearly fell out of her chair.

"Shut the front door! Are you serious?"

Dale assured her that he was.

"Dad, this is huge. Do you know what that would mean to your program?"

"We don't want them."

"Dad!" Susan exclaimed, throwing her hands in the air. "They're the freaking Chattanooga Triplets! Everybody wants them!"

"They've run into problems. We don't need that kind of player here. Brandon Yarbrough needs to understand that."

Susan rubbed her face. Her exasperation was as evident as her rage at the bank. "Did they murder anyone?"

"Don't be silly."

"What did they do that was so bad that Coach Dale Fox doesn't want them in his program?"

"Bad grades. One of them got in an argument with a coach. Another one got arrested in high school. Him or one of the other ones already has a child. They don't have the discipline needed to succeed here."

"Teach them discipline, Dad. Be the model they need."

"There's no time for that. We have football games to win."

"How's that going for ya, buddy?"

Ouch.

Dale was about to reprimand his sassy daughter when a car pulled to the curb. Dale moaned when he saw who it was.

Cassie Whitman.

Susan saw who it was, too. "Dad, she called me today. She's

bringing lasagna. You will accept it graciously, then you'll ask her to stay and eat with us."

"Susan, I don't want to—"

"Dad. You will invite her to dinner. She's lonely and looking for companionship, and, quite frankly, you could use some companionship, too."

"I've got plenty of friends."

"Uncle Homer and the boys don't count. You need a woman in your life."

Dale had more he wanted to say, but Cassie had already removed a pan of lasagna from the back seat and was walking up the sidewalk.

"Hi, Cassie," Susan said brightly.

"Hi," Cassie said tentatively. She stopped a few feet short of the front porch. "I made two lasagnas today and thought you might want one of them, Coach."

When Dale didn't respond, Susan elbowed him sharply.

"Thank you, Cassie. I'll have it tonight. Susan and Max will be here for supper, and I would like you to stay and join us... if you have time."

Hopefully, she wouldn't have time.

Cassie's face lit up. "I would love that!"

26

It was easy to forget sometimes how competent of an attorney Larry Bob Billingsley could be.

The guy who showed up at the Goldrush most mornings was a bit of a slob who didn't much care how he dressed or behaved. Add a six-pack of cheap beer to the equation, and Larry Bob could become downright offensive. Dale had heard the whispers about his friend. Some thought he drank too much or skipped work too much. Others claimed he didn't bathe regularly or take care of himself physically. All the claims were probably true, but when push came to shove, Larry Bob could lawyer as good as anyone Dale knew.

Particularly when he disliked his adversary.

And when Larry Bob led Susan and Dale into Lanny Masterson's office at the County Savings Bank, he was loaded for bear. The axe he had to grind with Masterson went back to his attempt to have Plumber Dick declared mentally incompetent. The Good Book encouraged people to forgive and forget. Larry Bob must have skipped that section.

"Over the next hour I'm going to tear you a new asshole, Masterson," Larry Bob said nonchalantly. "You will probably start crying. You may soil your pleated slacks. In the end, though, you'll apologize to Coach Fox for making him wait over the weekend to remove the contents from his late wife's lockbox. You'll apologize to Susan for having to be dragged away from work to deal with this crap. Then you'll sit your skinny ass down and write a letter of apology to Uncle Homer Bennett for slandering his reputation."

Masterson's face grew as red as a tomato. "You're out of your mind, Larry Bob. I did what was best for our bank. You can't come in here and say—"

"I can say any damned thing I want, provided I don't speak words that are untrue or defamatory. Since your reputation is already lower than a snake's pecker, I'm not worried about defaming you."

Susan snickered at that one. Dale looked on silently. While he was enjoying Larry Bob's onslaught, he had to get on the road if he was going to be in Chattanooga by three-thirty. Masterson was making another run at defending himself when his attorney, Chet Richie sauntered in.

"Stop talking, Lanny."

Masterson stopped talking. Chet turned to Larry Bob.

"I'm sure you've been stirring up a shitstorm, Larry Bob. It stops now." He pulled a folder from his briefcase and handed it over. "Here's a letter releasing the safe-deposit box. It includes an apology from the bank's board of directors for Lanny sending Coach Fox away."

"We want a letter of apology from this asshole for what he said to Coach about Uncle Homer."

"You're not getting it. Take what's offered and be glad you got that much. There is some legal precedent for Lanny's actions, flimsy as it may be. If you want to muck up the system by demanding an apology for what he said about Homer, you're going to have to take us to court."

Larry Bob leaned heavily on the table as he considered the offer. It was Dale who broke the silence.

"This is fine," he said. "I have to get on the road." Then, turning to Larry Bob, he said, "put everything in an envelope and give it to Susan. We'll look through it when I get back tomorrow."

● ● ●

DALE HAD WORRIED all weekend about how difficult it would be to keep his grandson entertained on the five-hour ride from Mozarkite to Chattanooga. He'd worried for nothing. Max fell asleep before they crossed the Missouri-Arkansas border a half-hour outside of town. He napped through Arkansas and into the Nashville suburbs where Dale pulled into a McDonalds with an expansive kids' play area. Between bites of a cheeseburger Happy Meal, Max played hard enough to fall asleep before they were through downtown Nashville. What a great kid. The only way he and Linda had gotten Susan to sleep in the car at that age was to spike her juice with cold medicine. The memory made him smile. What was perfectly acceptable thirty years ago could get a parent locked up today.

The Chattanooga trip was part pleasure and part fishing expedition. The pleasure part was a planned stop at Ruby Falls, a tourist destination Dale's parents had taken him to when he was Max's age. They would spend the next morning exploring caves before heading back to Mozarkite. It was Dale's attempt to fulfill Susan's wish that he be more of a presence in his grandson's life. Since they'd moved back to the house over the weekend, Dale already felt closer to Max. A bit too close at times, to be honest. He had forgotten how loud and messy kids were.

The fishing expedition? That would happen at Volunteer High School, where Dale had a meeting scheduled with the football coach to learn more about the Chattanooga Triplets. It would have been easy enough to let Brandon Yarbrough handle the meeting, but Dale wanted to know the truth before he made a final decision. Were the three players worth the hassle? Arizona State must've felt they were not, and Dale suspected he would agree.

Brandon wanted to attend the meeting, but Dale insisted it be just him and the boys' coach. Rebuffed in his effort, Brandon had swung north into Beckley, West Virginia, where a big high school lineman named Dellinger was getting attention from a number of schools.

Dale steered through one construction zone after another as he made his way into Chattanooga. Max woke up when they were a few minutes from the high school.

"These houses are kinda old," he observed.

Indeed, they were. The section of Chattanooga where Volunteer High was located could best be described as blighted. Dale was glad they would be back in the suburbs by dark. A few turns and another construction zone later, he pulled into the parking lot.

Volunteer High School was an old three-story building that would have been considered stately, even regal, seventy-five years ago. Its columns and façade were grayed with age and lack of upkeep. The one bright spot on the building's exterior was a large vinyl sign proclaiming Volunteer's football program the Tennessee Class 6-A State Champion from two years before. The parking lot was empty, as Dale knew that school had dismissed at three.

"Be sure to stay with me," Dale said as he unbuckled Max. "We shouldn't be long."

Coach Levon Pitts was a large man with a round face and sunny disposition. He met Dale at the front door.

"I suspected that was you," he said in way of a greeting. Then, looking down at Max, he exclaimed, "Is this one of your assistants?"

"Max, say hi to Coach Pitts." Then, to the coach, "Max is my grandson. We're going to Ruby Falls in the morning."

The two immediately hit it off. Max quickly figured out that the mountain of a man was a pussycat. Dale felt a kinship with Coach Pitts, who was a decade younger, likely in his late forties, and had the thick accent of the Tennessee hills. When they arrived at his office in the back of the school next to the boiler room, Dale saw they shared the same taste in décor. Old. Cheap. Spartan.

"That new assistant coach of yours is a firecracker, Coach Fox."

"We've not spent much time together yet. I hired him and sent him on the road."

Coach Pitts nodded. "My boys loved him, even the two who are headed up to Knoxville stuck around and visited with him. You hired well."

"I hope so. His ideas are a lot different from mine."

Coach Pitts motioned for Dale to have a seat, then did the same before pulling Max onto his lap and removing a coloring book and crayons from his desk drawer. Max accepted eagerly.

"I got three grandbabies who stop by now and again," he explained as he nodded at the coloring book. "And about your new boy's ideas, sometimes it's good for us to try new things, don't you agree, Coach Fox?"

Not really, but Dale didn't feel it was necessary to say that. Instead, he charged right in. "Your boys are interested in Mozarkite, Coach Pitts. I'm up in the air about them, given their pasts, but I wanted to visit with you first."

Coach Pitts rubbed his day-old stubble as he balanced Max on his lap. "Those three were the reason that fancy sign is hanging out front," he said after a pause. "They aren't perfect, but neither am I. Talent-wise, all three of them have the potential to go pro. And I'm not talking about barely hanging on. I think they can be stars. Especially De'Shea. That one has potential the likes of which I've never seen before."

Dale was not moved by the coach's lauding of their talent. "Tell me more about them as young men. You said they aren't perfect. I want to know what I would be getting."

"Coach Fox, you probably got reports on them, so you know about their pasts. Johnny Smith, the wide receiver, he got tossed out of the fancy private school up the road after a girl's parents from up there went to the Headmaster. Johnny was seventeen and the girl was fourteen. Johnny's parents could've saved him, but he wanted out, so he transferred here." Coach Pitts paused for a second to glance at Max before continuing. "He and the girl wound up having a baby together. John came over here and immediately found a home."

"Does he support his child?"

"His parents wanted to send money, but the girl's parents told them to butt out. Johnny wants to see the little girl, but so far, he's been unable to make that happen. I think he sees football as a way to make the kind of money he needs to fight for his little girl."

"Why did he leave Arizona State?"

Coach Pitts smiled. "Him, De'Shea, and Carlos are thick as thieves. When Carlos flunked out, Johnny decided to go with him. You probably heard that De'Shea got into it with a coach out there."

Dale acknowledged that he had.

"The coach said some unflattering things about Carlos. De'Shea heard him and called him on it. Rather than man up, the coach made a big deal, and De'Shea was let go."

"Did you get the coach's side of the story?"

"I don't need to. De'Shea Stephens is as honest as anybody you'll meet. If he says that's what happened, that's what happened."

As the conversation continued, Dale became more certain that Coach Pitts was the kind of man who would go to the mat for his boys. Infractions that should have resulted in harsh penalties brought wrist slaps. The longer he listened the more convinced Dale became that the Chattanooga Triplets would be more trouble than they were worth. Coach Pitts must have picked up on his colleague's reluctance. They were standing up to conclude their meeting when he said, "Coach Fox, sometimes we have to take a chance that we can make a difference in some kid's life."

"I feel we do that every day, Coach," Dale replied.

"Do you?" Coach Pitts' tone was direct. "Do you really take chances?"

It was that moment when Dale decided to enroll the Chattanooga Triplets.

27

*S*usan was at the house when Dale pulled into the driveway. Strange, in that it wasn't yet four in the afternoon.

Max was ecstatic to see her, though. He ran to her as soon as Dale freed him from the booster seat and wasted little time getting into his account of their trip to Ruby Falls. Dale was pleased by Max's excitement. He also noticed the occasional glance he got from Susan. There was a worried look in her eyes, but she was trying to conceal it. Just like her mama.

Then, another surprise. Susan had prepared dinner. Pot roast in the crock pot. Linda's recipe. A meal that Dale hadn't savored since her passing. Despite being two hours before his usual dinner time, his mouth was watering.

They talked over dinner, in between Max's anecdotes about Ruby Falls. Susan asked about the Chattanooga Triplets. Dale swore her to secrecy before letting her know that the announcement would be made the next day. The Chattanooga Triplets were coming to town to sign with Mozarkite Junior College. She was happy, but not that effusive type of happiness she usually displayed. Something was holding her back, but whatever it was would have to wait until Max went to bed.

So, they talked other topics. Dale asked how things were going at the office. Quite good, it turned out. Linda's business was in capable hands. Then Susan let it slip that she was taking back her maiden name. She would again be Susan Fox. It would work better in Mozarkite, she thought. Dale thought it would, too.

Max watched television while they cleaned the kitchen. Dale considered asking Susan what was on her mind but resisted. Max fell asleep on the sofa a little past eight. Susan carried him upstairs to bed. She was gone for nearly an hour, and Dale was starting to think she wasn't coming back down. Then she did. He waited for her to open up, but she didn't. They focused on some mindless sitcom for a few minutes before Dale had a thought.

"What did you find in Mom's safe-deposit box?"

Susan's face clouded. "Nothing much, really. A spare set of keys to her car. Cancelled checks from work. That's about it."

Susan was not telling the whole truth.

Dale had always been able to tell when his daughter was hiding something. From age four, when she'd fibbed about breaking his Coach of the Year trophy, to high school when she'd lied about being out with Darren Farber when she was supposed to be with one of her girlfriends. Susan liked to kid that, after being caught stretching the truth a few times, she'd given up trying.

Well, she was trying again.

"So, that's all? A set of keys and some old checks?"

She nodded. She knew better than to try to speak. If she spoke, she would give herself away.

"Hmm." That's all Dale said. Just, "Hmmm."

Susan started bawling.

"What is it, honey? You know you can tell me."

She shook her head and cried harder. She reached for the tissue box Linda had always kept on the table next to the sofa. It wasn't there anymore, and that caused her to cry more.

Dale was starting to wonder if he really wanted to hear what Susan already knew, but he decided he did. He needed to. It would be unfair to allow his daughter to shoulder whatever it was alone.

How bad could it be, anyway? He already knew she had enjoyed quite an interesting life without him. Somehow, over the days since his discoveries, he had started to come to grips with that reality. He spent his life working crazy long hours, traveling extensively, and spending every waking moment worrying about the safety, welfare, and performance of a bunch of twenty-year-old kids. Linda probably felt squeezed out. What else could there have been? More pictures of her having fun with her friends? More personal notes? Maybe Susan had discovered who *W* was.

"Whatever it is, Susan. Tell me."

Susan shook her head and continued to cry.

"It's about Mom?"

Susan nodded.

"I'm aware that she had some..." Dale searched for the best words to describe what he already had discovered. "...other interests."

His words seemed to ease Susan's angst. He waited while she pulled herself together. "There's a file," she pointed to the table next to the front door. "over there, under my purse. I wasn't going to show it to you."

Dale's heart started beating faster as he crossed the room and picked up a lone folder. Inside was a cover sheet written on letterhead from a law firm in a neighboring county, an outfit Dale had never heard of. A handwritten message, dated five days before Linda's death, consisted of two sentences.

Ms. Fox, please review and sign. We'll get things rolling next week.

It was signed by someone named Felicia. Her name appeared at the bottom of the letterhead, as an associate at the firm. Dale suspected he knew what he would find on the attached pages.

He was right.

Linda had been preparing to file for divorce.

After glancing through the divorce papers, Dale decided to share more of what he'd discovered. He pulled up the photographs as he shared with Susan some of what he had found. While she was perplexed by the discoveries, the inscription, *Things get a little crazy on date night!* that *W* had included on the picture of the four women in a bar, made her angry.

"Date night? Who was she dating?" She held up the photograph and looked closely at the background. "This obviously isn't Mozarkite. You don't think Mom was—" she paused, looked at Dale and continued "was Mom gay?"

Dale laughed despite the gravity of the moment. "Mom liked... no, she wasn't gay."

Susan blushed. Dale sensed an openness between them that had not been there before, something akin to the ranks closing in to protect one of their own. Susan was protecting him, and that sweet gesture caused something deep inside him to shift. They were a team now, he and Susan. She had his back.

"You had no idea?" she asked.

"Not a clue. You?"

Susan shook her head, then stopped. "She was capable of... you know... flirting to get her way. I saw it even back in high school, but never in a way that I thought of as coming on to someone. It was more like... you probably won't understand, but sometimes an attractive woman knows she can use her attractiveness to get what she wants." She paused, glanced at Dale, and said, "Does that make any sense?"

"Not really."

"Okay, let me give you an example. I was showing a house to a couple last month. They came in together to look. The next week the man came back alone. He was different than before. The second time he was trying to impress me, make me think he had lots of money, that kind of thing."

"Coming on to you?"

"Well... yeah. Sort of. But he was also kind of a jerk, so I rolled with it. I gave off the vibe that I was impressed by him, but my main goal was to get the deal done."

"Did you?"

Susan smiled. "Of course. Then he called me after the closing, wanting to know if I would have lunch with him." Susan made air quotes with her fingers. "To talk about some of his plans for developing land in town. I thanked him for calling, but said I wasn't interested, but knew some realtors who might be."

"You shot him down," Dale said with a grin. "Nice work."

"Thank you, Daddy. Anyway, I handled that exactly the way I'd seen Mom handle similar situations. She never had to go beyond flirting to get what she needed."

Dale held up the inscribed picture and said, "or maybe not."

Susan shrugged. "I'm so sorry, Daddy."

"Don't be," Dale said, waving her off. "She's still your mother. She's still the woman I married. I can't help but think that I had something to do with all of this."

Susan squeezed his hand. "Don't go down that road. It makes you sound like a weak man. You're not weak. If Mom chose to step out, she did it on her own. If there were problems at home, she needed to address them."

They continued to talk. Openly. Honestly. Dale found it difficult and immensely touching. He was connecting with his daughter. As the evening grew late, he couldn't help but wonder why he had not made this connection thirty years sooner.

Fortunately, it was not too late.

● ● ●

SUSAN WENT off to bed at eleven-thirty. Brandon Yarbrough would be in town the next day, for the first time in several weeks. They had a press conference planned to introduce the Chattanooga Triplets. Dale was still wary about the decision, but it was too late to turn back. After the events of the day he felt as if a steam roller had run over him. A quick glance in the mirror confirmed that he looked that way, too.

But still, before shutting his eyes, there was one more thing he wanted to do. *Had* to do, actually, if for no other reason, to bring closure to the issue of Linda's seeking a divorce. He went back to the kitchen and into Linda's tiny office, picking up the divorce papers on the way. He woke up the laptop, opened his email, and entered the address he found on the letterhead for the attorney named Felicia.

Hello, Felicia, I'm Dale Fox. I'm sure you're aware by now that my wife, Linda, passed away last November. I recently came across the paperwork you had prepared for her and wanted to make sure there was no outstanding balance for your work. If there is, you can email me at this address, and I'll pay it. Thank you, Dale Fox.

As he was hitting the send button, a message popped up indicating that Linda was receiving an incoming email. He had not checked her account in several weeks, and nearly didn't again, but it was there if he wanted to. All he needed to do was click on the alert.

He clicked.

The email was sent from someone named Helen Sturtz. Dale had never heard the name before, but unfamiliar names and faces were becoming commonplace. He scrolled down to the message.

Hello Linda, it's been awhile since Norman and I heard from you. After the few days we all enjoyed together at Hippie Hollow, we were hoping we might persuade the two of you to come visit us in Minnesota. There's plenty of room, plus we have a new outdoor hot tub!

Norman found this picture of the two of you and thought you might want it for your scrap book. It was wonderful getting to know you and we wish you and Wesley all the best.

Don't be a stranger!

Love, Helen

Wesley?

W?

W!

W's name was Wesley.

Dale knew no one named Wesley.

He clicked on the link at the bottom of the email. A picture appeared.

A couple, Linda and the man named Wesley, together on a beach. Nude.

Well, not Linda, not completely nude. She was wearing a bikini bottom. She looked great. And happy. And maybe drunk.

And the guy? Yeah, he was nude. And judging from the picture, he was proud of it. He had his arm around Linda.

And as Dale stared at the man's face and looked into his eyes, the mystery of *W* was no more.

He knew exactly who *W*—who *Wesley*—was.

He'd known him for years, though not as Wesley.

And while the hour was too late to do anything about it, there would be a moment of reckoning soon. Very soon. Maybe not first thing in the morning. After all, he had a press conference to attend.

But later.

The man named Wesley would have to answer to Coach Dale Fox.

28

Brandon Yarbrough brought the Chattanooga Triplets to Dale's office an hour before the press conference.

They certainly appeared harmless enough. Carlos, the quiet one, was short and as solid as an oak tree. De'Shea, the quarterback, was tall and lean and had a quick smile. And dreadlocks. Dale couldn't stand dreadlocks and considered saying something. John was the vocal one of the three. He looked Dale directly in the eyes when they shook hands, then promised to win a lot of games. He had dreadlocks, too. It was the first time Dale had seen dreads on a white kid. He thought they looked dirty and ridiculous.

The three were dressed in jeans and white t-shirts that would soon be covered with Mozarkite football jerseys. Brandon wore a nice pair of gray slacks over a form-fitting black t-shirt and black blazer. His hair had been cut since they'd last met. He looked good. He looked like a coach.

"Here's how this will work," Dale said crisply. "I'll make some opening remarks, then Coach Yarbrough will hand you your jerseys. Slip them on and allow the press to take a few pictures. Then we'll open it up to questions. Are you guys okay with that?"

They were, especially John. "We did this at Arizona State. All together, like this."

"Okay then, any questions?"

"Yes, Coach," De'Shea said, raising his hand. "Is there a good pizza place in town?"

"Hoppy's on the main drag," Brandon answered quickly as his eyes darted from Dale to De'Shea.

"No offense, Coach Yarbrough, but you're new here." De'Shea grinned as he called Brandon out. Then, turning back to Dale, "Coach Fox has been here forever. He knows where the best pizza is."

Dale smiled. "I do a weekly show during football season from a place on Main Street called Pizza Lube."

The boys nodded appreciatively.

"Do not," Dale continued, "go there for pizza."

This got a laugh.

"Seriously, fellas, there will be time later to figure out the best restaurants. You'll be eating most of your meals in the school cafeteria, anyway. Keep your focus on the press conference. There will probably be a half-dozen reporters at most. The local radio station and newspaper, two reporters from neighboring counties, and maybe a TV station from Cape Girardeau. It shouldn't last for more than twenty minutes."

The boys gave Dale the thumbs up.

"Are you ready?"

They were.

● ● ●

THE BOYS WERE READY.

Dale, not so much.

What tripped him up most? Was it the fifty-some media members crammed into the conference room? Was it the appearance of talking heads from ESPN and Fox that Dale had seen many times on TV?

Or was it seeing Susan standing in the rear of the room?

It was, he quickly decided, Susan's presence that brought Dale up short. Her being there made him think of last night, of what they discussed. He would never tell her that she shouldn't have come, never in a million years. She was there for him but did not understand what her presence did to him. His life was made up of compartments, and Susan being at the press conference brought two of those compartments together, making them overlap in a way that was unsettling.

So, he started the presser a few steps off-kilter. The appearance of several media giants pushed him further from center. Someone had tipped off the press as to what was happening. Was it Brandon? One of the boys? Dale vowed to find out and vent his full fury on whoever was the culprit, then realized how silly that was. Whether he liked it or not he had just entered the world of big-time football. Leaks went with the territory, so he would make the best of it. Still, he wished that he'd worn a t-shirt under his Polled Hereford polo. He could feel the sweat prickling his arms and chest as he ascended to the podium. He nodded a quick hello to President Fuller, who sat proudly on the end of the front row, next to a reporter from *USA Today*.

When Dale began his prepared remarks, the nerves abated. He lauded Coach Yarbrough for his hard work. He thanked President Fuller and the college trustees for their support, he commended the fans for their fervor. Then, he motioned for Brandon to open the door and escort in the Chattanooga Triplets. Cameras flashed as the boys entered the room. They were big news. Bigger news than Dale anticipated. They were used to the limelight, waving and smiling easily. They slipped on the Mozarkite jerseys and took up positions behind Dale. Brandon stood on the edge of the platform to their right. When Dale asked for questions, the shouts came from all directions, reminding him of the presidential press conferences he saw on the news. He pointed to the ESPN guy.

"Coach Fox, is this the biggest day in the history of your program?"

"No. That would be the day we played in the national championship game." He pointed to the *USA Today* reporter.

"We understand, Coach Fox, that you run a traditional offense that is heavy on the run. Will you adapt to better use the talents of the Chattanooga Triplets?"

"We're still discussing that. We've been successful doing things the way we've always done them and don't want to change for change sake." Dale pointed at Wally Westmoreland.

"Coach Fox, what was your first reaction when Coach Yarbrough told you these boys were interested in coming to Mozarkite?"

"I'm pleased any time a player commits to our school."

Dale took questions for fifteen minutes before calling on the *Messenger's* Heaven Knight, who sat patiently scribbling notes.

"Do you believe this will save your job, Coach?"

Even the big-timers seemed shocked by Heaven's brazenness.

"I've never had any indication my job was in jeopardy." Dale moved on to call upon someone else, but there were no hands raised. Sensing the drama of the moment, they sat back to find out what happened next. Seeing her opening, Heaven Knight followed up with another question.

"What role did Andre Jameson play in bringing these players to MJC?"

From behind him, Dale heard John Smith whisper, "He gave us all Porsches."

"What was that, John?" Heaven said quickly. "Did you say Porsches?"

The room was instantly abuzz. Dale tried to quiet them, but it took several moments. John answered loudly enough for all to hear, "I was kidding. No Porsches. We didn't even get to meet Andre Jameson, though we would love to."

The other boys nodded in agreement.

"So, no free gifts?" The ESPN reporter asked.

"Nope," Smith answered.

"That's not the way we run our program," Dale said forcefully. "We never have."

"Then how did you get these boys to come all the way out here?" The question, asked by a reporter from a Chattanooga newspaper, brought ripples of agreement from the others. Dale bristled at their response.

"These are not boys," he said, boring in on the reporter who asked the question. "They're young men who want to play football. They'll get that chance here, and if the lack of a bunch of TV and radio stations means they get to concentrate on football and academics, all the better for them."

And with that, Dale ended the conference. He returned to his office to wait while the conference room cleared. Twenty minutes later President Fuller knocked.

"Great job," she gushed before dashing off. "You got us more free publicity than we've ever had."

Susan was next. She poked her head in and said, "You kicked ass, Dad. See you at home."

Coach Yarbrough came by with the Triplets. "I'm going to show the boys around town, Coach. De'Shea wants to enroll in a couple online courses to get ahead." They tried to beat a hasty retreat, but Dale collared John Smith.

"Young man, comments like that one about the Porsche are the kinds of things that start investigations."

"Seriously, Coach, I was making a joke with the guys. I didn't—"

"It stops now." Dale said in a tone that invited no argument.

"It was stupid," Carlos said, directing the comment to his friend.

"We'll keep him in line, Coach," De'Shea said.

After they left, Dale relaxed in his desk chair for a few minutes, just to make sure the coast was clear. He was locking up the gym when Heaven Knight approached.

"What do you need, Miss Knight?"

"It might be out of line, but I wanted to tell you that you handled that very well."

"Are you speaking on the record, Miss Knight? You told me to assume we're always on the record."

Heaven Knight smiled at his rebuke. "I think you'll like what I write this week, Coach."

Dale crawled into his truck and left campus. He was torn between going home or driving around for a while. There was unfinished business; that was for certain. W needed to know that he knew, but perhaps it would be wiser to have that discussion another time.

So, Dale drove toward home. He was nearly there when he noticed a flash across the street two blocks ahead. He gunned the pickup, but by the time he reached the spot, Chelsea was long gone. And for the first time, he knew with absolute certainty where the dog was headed.

Dale put his truck into gear and drove to the law offices of his longtime friend, Larry Bob Billingsley.

29

There was usually no keeping secrets from the guys at the Goldrush, but Dale had succeeded for once. The Chattanooga Triplets were big news.

"Why didn't you tell us?" Welder Tommy asked as soon as Dale arrived.

Plumber Dick said, "I should've known when you started asking about them."

"I suspected," Uncle Homer chimed in.

"Bullshit, Uncle Homer," Tommy answered quickly. "You said it was too bad that Coach never got good players like them boys."

Homer cast a baleful look at his nephew, then said to Dale, "It wasn't quite like that."

Dale didn't care what Uncle Homer might have said. He had bigger fish to fry. The conversation for the next fifteen minutes was all about the Triplets, and people from surrounding tables joined in the merriment. Everyone was genuinely excited about Polled Hereford football. Not just the hardcore sports nuts, but everyone.

"When will tickets go on sale?"

"Can we get the Triplets to come to our club meeting?"

"I'm thinking about traveling to the away games this year, too, Coach. Those boys are going to be big-time pros, and I want to say I went to all their games."

The hubbub provided the perfect diversion for Dale to half-listen while thinking about what he had to do. When Larry Bob arrived a few minutes before eight, it was time.

"Where are you boys off to?" Uncle Homer asked as Dale and Larry Bob stood at the same time.

"We think we've figured out where Linda's dog's been going," Larry Bob answered. "It seems she has an affinity for snakes."

● ● ●

THEY RODE TOGETHER. Larry Bob drove and offered advice that Dale didn't need.

"Don't get physical."

"Don't threaten him."

"Don't get so close that he can punch you, but if he does, you have every right to defend yourself."

When they pulled into the driveway Larry Bob blocked the garage door so there would be no escape. "Let's get this done," he said.

They approached the front door and rang the bell. A dog barked inside. It was a bark Dale recognized. A few moments later Bubber Slate opened the door.

"Coach?" he said, glancing behind him. Then, when he spotted Larry Bob, Bubber's face turned white. He knew that they knew.

"Did Chelsea sleep well?" Dale said calmly.

"She—she came back in the night. I was going to call you, but it was late so..." Bubber's voice was shaky. He was trying to hold it together but was losing. "Come on in," he finally said.

Dale and Larry Bob stepped into the living room but turned down Bubber's offer to sit.

"Bubber, how long have you and Linda been..." Dale couldn't bring himself to say the words. *Having an affair* or *having sex* or *running around* sounded cheap. Especially when they were referring to his late wife. Instead he settled on, "going on trips together?"

"We never did anything like—"

"Cut the bullshit, Bubber. My client found pictures."

The way Larry Bob said it, calling Dale his client, brought a sheen of perspiration to Bubber's face. He sat down heavily on the sofa.

"We... we went on some trips. When Linda could get away."

"Is Linda the reason your marriage broke up?"

"Oh... no, Coach. I mean, we started going... it was after Tamara left."

"Your marriage fell apart, so you tried to destroy mine, too." Dale remained steady. He'd been through crushing losses on the football field where he'd maintained his composure, but this was pushing different emotional buttons.

"Coach, I didn't do anything. Linda was just... lonely."

"Nice try, Bubber," Larry Bob cut in. "There's not a judge on this circuit who'll buy that line. What else will you say? That she turned to you to find the love she used to have?"

Larry Bob's insulting tone raised up something in Bubber. His nostrils flared for a second, just long enough to say something that silenced Dale and Larry Bob.

"Maybe it was the love she never had."

Dale lunged. Bubber dodged. They turned to face each other again, on opposite sides from where they had started.

"You don't talk about my marriage," Dale spat.

Bubber raised his hands. "I shouldn't have said that, Coach. I'm sorry. The fact is, we were both lonely. For companionship. Nothing else. It never was like you're thinking."

"How do you know what he's thinking?" Larry Bob asked.

"Because it's what I would be thinking, too."

"Did Tamara fool around on you, Bubber?" Larry Bob countered.

"No. Nothing like that. Look, Coach, go on and beat the daylights out of me if you have to, but there was nothing sexual between us. We went places, had some fun, then we came home. Nobody got hurt."

"Except my client. His wife was about to divorce him."

Dale was starting to wish that Larry Bob would stay out of it.

"I knew about the divorce papers, but it wasn't because of me. Linda was miserable. She had been for years."

"I wonder what the folks down at the County Savings Bank will think when they find out?" Larry Bob asked.

Larry Bob was in full lawyer mode and didn't seem to notice the change in Bubber's countenance. The man seemed to melt into himself. Dale was starting to feel sympathy for the man.

Larry Bob, not so much.

"Those farmers who come to you for loans, Bubber. Once they hear that you tried to steal Coach Fox's wife away from him, they'll start taking their business someplace else."

Whether Bubber's pallor came from fear or guilt, Dale was uncertain. What he did know was that the purpose of the visit had veered wildly off course. Linda was gone, and no amount of fighting between him and Bubber would bring her back. He only wanted the man to know that he was aware of what had happened between them. Larry Bob was out for blood.

"And your Board of Directors, Bubber? What will they think? Coach Fox is one of the most important men in town, and you were diddling his wife while he was off trying to win football games."

Dale felt the burn as much as Bubber. *Trying* to win football games?

"Larry Bob, stop."

Larry Bob stopped. The damage, however, was already done. Bubber's face crumbled, and he started to cry. It was a sight the likes of which Dale had never seen. He had always considered Bubber Slate to be a man's man. A guy tougher than... well, slate.

"Larry Bob, you can't do that to me," Bubber pleaded.

"The hell I can't."

"They'll fire me. I'll never find another job in Mozarkite. I'll have to move."

"You should've thought of that before you started your trysts with Mrs. Fox."

"They weren't trysts, not like you guys are thinking."

Larry Bob started to speak, but Dale waved him off. "Why should we believe that you traveled all over the world with my wife and nothing happened? You've got to do better than that."

"It's the truth, Coach," Bubber blubbered through his tears. "Linda wasn't interested in me that way, and I wasn't interested in her."

"Yeah, right." Larry Bob spoke before Dale could stop him, trying to recover from being shushed.

"Larry Bob, be quiet." Then, to Bubber. "Just friends, huh?"

Bubber nodded.

"No sex?"

Bubber nodded harder.

Dale had one more question but was uncertain if he wanted to know the answer. He considered leaving without asking, actually turned to go, then turned back.

"Why not?"

They waited while Bubber composed himself. It took several moments for him to wipe away the tears, blow his nose, and get his voice back. Then he spoke.

"I'm gay."

Dale and Larry Bob stood in stony silence, taking in what they'd heard and trying to reconcile it with the man who said it. Dale couldn't believe it. They moved in different circles, but Bubber Slate had always come across as so much like everyone else.

Gay?

Bubber Slate was gay?

Bubber seemed to be reading his mind. "No one else knows. Tamara kinda suspected, I guess, but never really asked. Linda, though. She figured it out real quick, and once I told her the truth, she became my best friend. The trips, the short cruises, we went as friends. And Coach?"

"Bubber?"

"She never cheated on you. Not even once. She wasn't happy

about the way things were. She didn't like playing second or third fiddle to football, but she never cheated on you."

The room became silent for several moments, before Dale spoke.

"We'll be on our way now, Bubber." Dale glanced at Larry Bob before saying, "Not a word of what we've heard will go beyond this room."

Bubber exhaled and appeared to relax for the first time since they'd arrived. "What about Chelsea?" he asked.

Dale shrugged. "I guess we have joint custody."

● ● ●

THE SCENE on the sidewalk was like something out of an old western, except there were no horses. There were no cowboys, either. Just Uncle Homer, Plumber Dick, and Welder Tommy.

"Everything okay in there, Coach?" Homer called out, sliding his coat aside so they could see the pistol strapped to his hip. "The boys are packing, too, just so you know."

"That's the scariest thing I've heard in months," Larry Bob said. "The Bennett boys with guns. What the hell are you all doing here?"

"We followed ya," Dick said. "We figured you coming here had something to do with Miss Linda, and if someone was due an ass whupping, we wanted to be part of it."

Dale felt a surge of pride. And fear. Larry Bob was right. The Bennett boys had no business with guns. They were as much a threat to themselves as others.

"You guys misunderstood," Dale said. "We were taking care of some legal stuff related to Linda's passing. Financial stuff. Bubber was helping."

The boys skulked off, disappointed, it seemed, at not getting to brandish their guns. Bubber Slate's secret was safe. So, too, was Linda's. No one besides Dale, Bubber, and Larry Bob ever needed to know what Linda had planned to do.

It was time to move on.

But first...

● ● ●

IT WAS after six when Dale arrived home. He had stayed at the office to make calls to recruits who had heard about the Triplets' commitment to Mozarkite.

Brandon Yarbrough was sitting in Dale's La-Z-Boy.

He had Dale's remote in his hand.

And he was using it to switch channels on Dale's TV.

"Hey, Coach," he said cheerfully.

Too cheerfully for a guy sitting in Dale's La-Z-Boy.

"Coach Yarbrough." Dale answered. He glanced around the corner into the kitchen, but there was no one there. Just Brandon Yarbrough. In Dale's La-Z-Boy.

"Susan's upstairs. Max fell in a mud hole and needed a bath."

Dale nodded. "Okay." Then he stood there, in the center of the room. Waiting for Brandon Yarbrough to get out of his La-Z-Boy.

Brandon eventually got the message and apologized. He was relocating to the sofa when Max came charging down the stairs.

"I'm clean again, Brandon!" he said with the enthusiasm of any five-year old who had fallen into a puddle of mud. Then, spotting Dale across the room, he said, "Hey, Pop-Pop" with less enthusiasm. Susan appeared on the staircase. Seeing the two of them, Dale and Brandon, together in the living room did nothing to remove the smile from her face.

"I wanted to tell you, Dad, but didn't get the chance. Brandon and I have gone out a few times. I invited him over to meet Max."

Dale looked from Susan to Brandon, then back to Susan. Then back to Brandon. "I thought you were working late at the office."

"That, too," she said as she took a seat on the sofa. She sat in the middle, leaving some space between herself and Brandon. Not enough space for Dale's liking, but some.

"Susan helped me find a place to live," Brandon said.

"He's renting Jake Eskridge's place," Susan explained.

The conversation over the next hour was generic, pleasant, and, for Dale, awkward. Susan and Brandon appeared perfectly at ease.

Max was already enthralled with Brandon, and Brandon seemed to be one of those guys who could easily relate to a five-year-old without coming across as phony. He crawled about on the floor with Max as they played Hot Wheels, then stepped aside when Susan said it was Max's bedtime.

"Can Pop-Pop take me up tonight?" Dale felt a warm flush, and though he disliked the thought of leaving his daughter alone with Brandon, he was touched that his grandson had requested his bedtime-tucking services.

As they lay together on Max's narrow bed decked out with sheets from a movie Dale had never heard of, he thought of the future his grandson faced without a father in the house. It wasn't an insurmountable obstacle. Dale had often marveled at the Herculean efforts put forth by single moms and dads to help their children find success. And he had no doubt that Susan would do as good or better than all of them.

Still, he remembered her request that he be more of a presence in Max's life. His efforts so far had been lackluster; not because he didn't want to be a father figure, but more a matter of not knowing how. He had watched how easily Brandon crawled around on the floor and made motor sounds while he and Max played Hot Wheels. Dale had never done anything like that and thought he would look silly if he did.

And then he started to think about Linda, and what she would have wanted. His dismay at finding out she was unhappy with their marriage made him wonder if he really knew her at all. Maybe, maybe not. But he did know what she felt for Susan and Max. She wanted the very best for their daughter, even when money was tight, and she would want the best for Max. If Brandon Yarbrough was the best thing for Max, she would have welcomed him to the family with open arms.

That was where she and Dale differed.

Brandon was nearly a decade younger than Susan. He had barely started living his own life. He worked for Dale, and if there were to come a time when Dale needed to discipline the young coach, he didn't want to have to deal with the fact that he was family.

Then he realized how ridiculous it all was. Susan wasn't marrying Brandon. They'd only seen each other a few times. She'd said so herself.

Dale rubbed Max's back as he drifted off to sleep. How different would things be if Linda hadn't died? Would Dale still be in the house, or would Linda have requested he move out? Would she have remained in Mozarkite or moved away, possibly to someplace more exotic, like the destinations she visited with Bubber Slate?

Bubber Slate. Wesley Slate. W.

Dale grappled with how he felt toward the man. Angry? No, that wasn't it. There was some sadness, not so much for Bubber as for himself. Dale would never claim to understand homosexuality. As a kid he and his buddies had been quick to assign hurtful labels to boys who walked or dressed differently. Then, he remembered a seminar he wound up in at a summer coaches' conference fifteen years earlier, where the speaker talked about lifestyle choices among football players. He asked the coaches in attendance to raise their hands if they'd had gay players on their teams. Five hands went up, in a room of seventy-five coaches. Dale's hand was not one of them. Then the speaker informed them it was more likely that almost all of them had, in fact, coached young men who were gay. A few coaches were quick to disagree. Dale was certain the speaker was wrong, but now he couldn't be so sure. How many players among the hundreds he'd coached over the past quarter century were gay? How many, had they had a coach who understood and protected their rights, might have shared their secrets with him?

And if he was unaware that some of his players were gay, what other signals had he missed?

Because if Bubber Slate—burly, manly, golf-playing Bubber Slate —could be gay, then so could anyone else.

Dale knew that the sadness he felt was for Bubber having to live a life that was a lie. Linda had been his one release. Together, for a few days at a time, they had enjoyed life, free of the burdens of the real world.

And that was when Dale was able to put his finger on what he was feeling toward Bubber Slate.

It was envy.

PART II

30

Reality struck Dale between the eyes when he pulled onto Main Street and could not find a parking space within three blocks of Pizza Lube. He finally settled for a spot in the First Baptist lot four blocks away and wondered if passers-by might think he was defecting from Third Baptist.

There was no need to worry. The streets surrounding First Baptist were deserted. Locals weren't thinking about church. For three blocks Mozarkite was a ghost town. No people, only cars and pickup trucks. Dale cut down an alley that backed the Main Street businesses and pushed through a rear door into Pizza Lube. He was greeted with a wall of noise. The place was a madhouse.

He made his way to the front table where Wally Westmoreland was setting up his equipment. "Can you believe this many people want to see me in person?" he joked as he slid into his usual spot.

"The Triplets are here," Wally said, pointing to a corner table. "I announced a couple hours ago that they were coming. That's why we've got such a turnout."

So, the turnout was for the Triplets. Dale could deal with that.

Wally motioned with his chin to another booth. "And take a look over there."

President Margaret Fuller was seated at a table with Andre Jameson. There was a line, fifteen deep, waiting to get his autograph.

"The town went nuts when they found out Andre was here," Wally said.

Dale waved. Andre and Dr. Fuller smiled and returned his greeting. "I guess I'm not the biggest fish in the pond anymore." He mused under his breath.

"What was that, Coach?" Wally said as he adjusted his controls.

"Nothing. Is everything ready to go?"

It was.

◊ ◊ ◊

"SPORTS FANS, it's finally football season, and from downtown Mozarkite, this is The Coach Dale Fox Show. *I'm your host, the voice of the Mozarkite Junior College Polled Herefords, Wally Westmoreland. We're live in front of a packed house at Pizza Lube. If you're on your way down, think again. There's not a table to be had. Frankie and his boys have even set up tables on the sidewalk out front, and they're full, too. Nope, your best bet is to place an order for delivery, then sit back, turn your radio up, and get ready. The season Polled Hereford fans have waited months for has arrived.*

◊ ◊ ◊

WALLY WAS NEARLY breathless with excitement, and he wasn't alone. All eyes in the packed house were focused on their little production. The electricity filling the air was far different than anything they'd had the past dozen years. Fans had shown up with sky high expectations of the season ahead. Dale knew their expectations had a good chance of becoming reality. He knew the team was good. Very good. He also knew that their ability to win games would boil down to whether or not Brandon's recruits came to play. And none were more important to that success than the Chattanooga Triplets.

Dale remained calm as Wally enthusiastically led him through a series of questions.

Was the new offensive scheme Coach Yarbrough had installed working? It was working very well. Dale had attempted to slow it down early on but had eventually let Brandon take things in the direction he felt they should go. The offense would be fun to watch.

Which teams would be most challenging? Dale pointed out aspects of the other conference teams that would make them formidable opponents. Good defense, special teams that caused turnovers, and offensive juggernauts. He had spent several evenings reviewing game film with his assistants. They saw who was going to be up and who would struggle. The last thing he would do, however, was share that information with Wally and their audience. Let them believe that it would be a tough season.

Wally's questions became more specific. Were the Triplets as good as advertised? Dale refused to go there. Football was the ultimate team game, he explained. Individual players didn't win or lose games. What he kept to himself was that De'Shea Stephens had a cannon for an arm and the ability to see plays developing and adjust accordingly. He was brilliant on the field.

But if what Dale had heard through the grapevine was true, he was also starting to show up in places and situations where he didn't need to be. One of Police Chief Mike Mayberry's boys had been dropping hints in town that De'Shea was buying pot from Wade Ricketts' shady family. Others had heard that De'Shea was seeing Norman Snelling's sixteen-year-old daughter, Haley. When Brandon spoke to him, De'Shea denied both accusations. Brandon believed him. Dale wasn't so sure.

The names of the other two Triplets had remained out of the rumor mill, though Carlos continued to struggle in class as he had at Arizona State. President Fuller had gone as far as releasing one of her assistant administrators for ten hours a week to help Carlos. He was a good kid, just not very smart. On the field he could put a beating on any defensive player who was unprepared for his combination of speed and brute strength.

John was a hard kid to read. He was loud, funny, and profane, yet his teammates were naturally drawn to him. He was receptive to

Brandon's coaching, and together they had identified some flaws in his game that John worked after practices to remedy. He might not be the player his buddies were, but he wasn't far behind.

◊ ◊ ◊

"I'M BEING TOLD from back in the studio that we're getting lots of calls from folks who weren't able to get into Pizza Lube tonight," Wally said after he'd finished his questions. "Coach, folks want to know if we can have the Triplets come up here and join us on the Coach Dale Fox Show."

◊ ◊ ◊

IN THE PAST, Dale had preferred not to have players on the show. There were too many things that could go wrong on a live broadcast. A player might slip and use inappropriate language, or, even a bigger concern for Dale, they might come across as sounding unintelligent. Some players, even smart ones, often weren't particularly articulate, especially when answering questions they hadn't anticipated.

But Dale had occasionally bent his rule. Andre had come on the show at least three times while playing at Mozarkite. A number of his teammates had also been interviewed during the dream season. All-Conference players had appeared occasionally. So, while he would've preferred that the Triplets not come up, he had no basis for turning down the request.

◊ ◊ ◊

WE'RE BACK FROM BREAK. If you're just tuning in, this is the Coach Dale Fox Show on Country 104. We're live from Pizza Lube in downtown Mozarkite. I'm your host, Wally Westmoreland. Pizza Lube Manager Frankie Steele tells me there are a hundred and seventeen people crammed into the place tonight, folks! That's a record that might not be broken. We're hoping that Lefty Lott, the County Fire Marshal, is at his weekly poker game tonight,

because if he comes by here, he might shut down the place. Anyway, we're
pleased to have the three biggest names on the Polled Hereford roster with
us. The Chattanooga Triplets in the flesh! They've joined me on stage, and
I'll ask them a few of the questions our listeners have submitted.

● ● ●

DALE HAD INITIALLY PLANNED to remain at the table with Wally as he
interviewed the Triplets, but after it became apparent that it would be
too crowded, he reluctantly moved to a table off to one side where
Brandon and the other assistants were seated. He gave Brandon a
disapproving look when he noticed him nursing a beer.

"It's a craft beer, Coach," Brandon said, holding it up for him to
see. "You want one?"

Dale shook his head and turned his attention to Wally and the
Triplets as they moved past the formalities of name, position, and
college major. The boys were at ease in the limelight, particularly
John Smith who bantered back and forth with Wally as if they were
old friends.

● ● ●

"YOU'VE BEEN in town for a few weeks now. What do you think of
Mozarkite?"

The boys glanced at one another for a moment before Carlos leaned
toward the microphone.

"I like the movie theater."

The others nodded their agreement, then John pulled the mic closer and
said, "There are some cute girls, too."

The crowd skewed much younger and female than in the past. They
cheered their approval. Their response spurred De'Shea to join the banter.

"Does anybody know a place where a brother can get his dreads
tightened?"

And just as quickly as they'd roared at John's cute girl comment, the

Pizza Lube crowd went silent. De'Shea waited a few beats, then said, "I might be in trouble."

● ● ●

DALE ADMIRED the easy repartee the boys had with Wally. There couldn't have been a bigger contrast between the young streetwise Triplets and the obese country boy announcer, but it was working, and Dale found himself enjoying their give and take. Even when Wally started taking questions from the floor, it was easy to tell how much love there was for the boys and Polled Hereford football. If he could have pulled the plug and let the show end with that, Dale would have. But he didn't have control of the show as he usually did. That control had shifted to Wally and the Triplets, and they let things go one question too far.

● ● ●

"WE'RE NEARLY out of time, so I'll make this my last question. Fellas, you open the season against Granger College. They whupped the Polled Herefords last season by a score of fifty-seven to seven. They're ranked seventh in the nation in the preseason polls. You're ranked fourteenth. What do you expect to happen this Saturday?"

The boys glanced at each other. De'Shea offered a nearly imperceptible shake of his head, a sign he wanted one of them to take the lead. Carlos reached out for the microphone after a few awkward moments, then slid it over so it was in front of John. John eyed the mass of Mozarkite fans jammed into every table and booth and clustered four-deep at the bar. He waited until the place was nearly silent, then uttered one sentence.

"We'll kick their ass from one end of the field to the other."

Pandemonium ensued, and Dale's job instantly became more difficult.

● ● ●

Pizza Lube was still hopping when Dale stalked out the back door. He knew that Granger would hear of John Smith's prediction. The coach would share it with his players over and over until kickoff, rousing their anger at the upstart Polled Herefords. Brashness was something he detested and seeing it in a player who was yet to play a down for his team made him see red.

Cassie Whitman was waiting outside. They had been spending some time together over the past months, mainly dinner at her house or at his place with Susan and Max. Dale had found her to be smart, kind, and wanting to move faster than he was ready for, so he kept her at arm's length. Susan regularly scolded him for not realizing what was right in front of him.

"Hey, Dale."

"Cassie. How did you know to find me back here?"

"I knew you wouldn't want to fight your way through the crowd."

"Were you in there?"

"No, I listened at home, then walked up when you got close to the end. I was hoping we could go someplace. Maybe get a nightcap?"

Dale checked his watch. It was eight-twenty. "I've got a meeting with the coaches in forty minutes. That won't be over until ten-thirty."

"I can wait."

Dale didn't intend for his next words to come across as angry as they did. It wasn't Cassie who had just guaranteed a Granger ass-whipping in front of a hundred and seventeen pizza-eating, beer-swilling football fans and countless radio listeners. It wasn't Cassie who was being whispered about for using pot and dating high school girls.

It wasn't Cassie who was the reason for Dale's foul mood.

She was just the unfortunate one who caught the brunt of it.

"I've got a game in two days, Cassie," Dale snapped. "Do you understand how much work I have to do between now and then? Do you even have a clue?"

Cassie said nothing. She didn't have to. Her eyes said everything.

Dale's outburst had shocked and frightened her. He knew he should apologize.

Instead he doubled down.

"I think it will be better if we don't see each other until the season is over."

He didn't wait for her response.

31

*B*ack in the glory days of Mozarkite football, Monday morning patrons at the Goldrush would be buzzing about the previous Saturday's game from the moment the doors opened. Big plays were relived, debates ensued about which players would become NFL stars, and predictions were offered about where the Polled Herefords might be ranked in the nationwide polls that week. Conversations typically crossed from one table to the next, without regard to anyone's job, family name, or political party.

Dale used to relish showing up in the middle of it. He loved the way everyone turned to wave and say hello, how they congratulated him on wins and offered encouragement after tough losses. When he spoke, the place became quiet. Folks at the Goldrush used to want to hear what he had to say. There were several diners in town, but only the Goldrush had Coach Dale Fox. Patsy and her staff did all they could to keep things that way.

The Goldrush on the Monday morning following the Granger game was like that again. When Dale stepped inside, conversations ceased so that the Goldrush faithful could do what they'd never done before, not even during the glory years two decades earlier.

They stood and applauded. They applauded loud, and they

applauded long. Dale nodded his appreciation and motioned for everyone to sit, but they kept at it for several moments while he made his way to his table. His chair was open and waiting, just as it had been every day for years. Welder Tommy pulled it out and motioned with a flourish for Dale to ascend to his throne. He felt his face beginning to burn. It was a good feeling. Maybe not as laced with adrenaline as the postgame meeting with his team two days earlier, but still pretty darn good.

"I'll get you your usual, Coach," Patsy said as she sidled up with the coffee pot while the ovation died down. "I would've had it ready, but I figured you were in New York getting interviewed on *Good Morning America*."

"Thank you, Patsy."

"That boy was right, weren't he, Coach?"

"What boy, Plumber Dick?"

"That white one with his hair cut like the black one, the receiver."

"John Smith, dumbass," Larry Bob said. "How hard can it be to remember a name as simple as John Smith?"

John Smith had indeed been right in his previous week's bold prediction. The Polled Herefords had kicked Granger's ass from kickoff to final snap. The score, 41-7, didn't come close to telling the whole story.

"Your boys could've scored eighty if you'd let 'em," Uncle Homer said.

Dale had removed the starters halfway through the third quarter, when the score was 31-0. The second-string offense hung ten more points on an overmatched Granger team that rolled over and played dead a few minutes into the second half.

"And to think they were ranked seventh in the country," an old farmer at an adjoining table chipped in. "Where do you think you'll be ranked this week, Coach?"

Dale answered that he never thought about rankings early in the year. Truth was, he had studied the weekend's results and figured Mozarkite would easily slide into the top ten, maybe as high as sixth.

Granger had come in ranked seventh, and they had proven to be a mismatch.

Things were like they used to be in the Goldrush and around town. The excitement. The adulation. Dale had nearly forgotten how good it felt, like a warm shower after being out in the cold. He spent the next hour grinning a lot, eating a little, and answering scores of questions before he had to get up to leave.

"Where are you going so early?" Welder Tommy asked as Dale was paying his check. "It's only eight-thirty."

"Max starts kindergarten today."

◊ ◊ ◊

IT WAS Susan's idea that Dale accompany them to Max's first day of school. He missed those opportunities when Susan was a child, and while he was certain there was a good reason, he couldn't remember what it was.

Mozarkite Elementary School was built in the 1920's. The stately two-story building smelled of freshy waxed floors and breakfast burritos. Max was as excited as he'd been at Christmas when they walked through the halls leading to the kindergarten wing. Along the way several small kids and their parents acknowledged Dale and the previous Saturday's performance of his Polled Herefords. Two boys in Max's class were even wearing Hereford t-shirts.

Max's teacher was standing in the doorway when they arrived. She introduced herself to Max, then smiled and offered a familiar hello to Susan and Dale. Mrs. Doubleday was her name. Jill Doubleday. Dale knew her better as Jill Ferguson, her maiden name before marrying one of the Doubleday boys from Clearwater four or five years earlier. Dale and Linda went to the wedding.

"Are you ready for kindergarten, Max?" she asked.

Max assured her he was; then he went into an extended monologue about how he already knew letters and numbers. Mrs. Doubleday listened patiently, then gave Max an 'attaboy' for being so smart. It was apparent that parents weren't supposed to overstay their welcome, so Dale and Susan helped Max find his seat, then made their way back to the car. Susan was crying before they left the parking lot.

"I'm glad I have a house showing in a half-hour," she said as she blew her nose. "Otherwise, I would go back home and cry all morning."

They were returning to the house to pick up Susan's car when Dale's phone buzzed.

"Fifth in the nation this week, Coach Fox," Heaven Knight said in way of a greeting. "Would you care to comment?"

Yes, he would very much like to comment. He would like to say how good it felt to have the folks at the Goldrush stand up and clap when he came in. He would like to say how much better he'd slept Saturday night after a convincing win. He would like to say that he didn't think there was another team in the conference that could come within three touchdowns of his boys. He wanted to say all of that.

But instead, he said, "I'm grateful to the voters who have faith in our team. We'll still have to go out and play our best game to beat Danbury at home this coming weekend. They lost Saturday by seven, but they're a dangerous team. It'll be all we can do to keep up with them."

The call ended as Dale pulled into the driveway.

"Is that what you really think?" Susan asked as she gathered her things.

Dale smiled and shook his head. "Danbury and Northeast Kentucky are both down this year. If we play like we did on Saturday, we'll still be undefeated in two weeks."

Susan laughed. "Dad, are you getting cocky?"

"Truthfully, Susan, with this team, winning games is the easiest thing."

"What's the hardest thing?"

"I hope I'm wrong," Dale said, lowering his voice, "but the hardest thing might be keeping the Chattanooga Triplets out of trouble."

he good vibes continued through the next two games, both Mozarkite routs. The latest poll ranked them third in the nation. Storefronts throughout downtown had purchased Polled Hereford flags to display. Jenny, a clerk in the college's bookstore, had mentioned in passing that team gear was flying out the doors.

"It's a good time to be a Hereford," she'd said.

It was indeed a good time to be a Hereford. At least until Heaven Knight's number showed up on Dale's cellphone Friday afternoon.

"Coach Fox, have you got a couple minutes?"

Her voice sounded different. Maybe it was the phone connection, but something in the way she spoke brought Dale up short.

"I do."

Dale could hear the sound of paper rustling on the other end of the line. It was rare to get a Friday phone call from the press. Most of their stories for the week were already published. He worried that Heaven Knight was calling with something he would rather not hear.

"Coach, do you know Haley Snelling?"

Yep, it was definitely something he would rather not hear.

"Not personally. She's Norman Snelling's daughter, right?"

He knew darn well she was Norman's daughter.

"Yes. She's a junior at Mozarkite High."

"Okay."

"Coach, I saw De'Shea Stephens pick her up in front of the high school this afternoon."

"Okay." It was better, Dale assumed, to say less than more. He'd heard rumors, but rumors surrounding a star athlete were nothing new. During his two years in town, Andre Jameson had been the subject of several tongue-wagging stories, particularly as his visibility increased. As best as Dale knew, they'd been nothing more than that. Rumors.

When Dale didn't elaborate, Heaven continued. "I've had three people contact me over the past couple weeks who thought I needed to know that De'Shea and Haley Snelling have something between them that might go beyond friendship."

"Did those people provide specifics, Miss Knight?"

"They didn't even leave their names. The calls came on the phone in my office, which is an older model that doesn't have caller ID, so I have no way of knowing who they were."

Dale thought about what he should and could say. Brandon didn't believe there was anything to the rumors. Still, he wasn't sure what direction Heaven Knight was going to go with the information. He wanted to ask her but knew that might only make her dig deeper.

"My assistant coaches have daily contact with the players, Miss Knight. I would like to think that if there's something going on that shouldn't be – with De'Shea or any player – that they're on top of it."

"Haley Snelling is sixteen, Coach."

"I understand what you're saying, Miss Knight."

"Are you going to look into it?"

"I look into any issues that impact my players, Miss Knight. The question is, are you?"

Heaven Knight was silent for a moment. Dale let her take her time, hopeful he would get a response he could live with, at least until after Saturday's game.

"My publisher will not let us run with sources who don't identify themselves, Coach. I have to support that position."

Whew.

"But please know that I'll be looking into this much deeper starting next week."

As the call concluded, Dale recalled the words that Heaven Knight's predecessor, Randall Shockley, had spoken to him at Linda's funeral. Speaking of Heaven Knight, he'd said, "She's her own person. She has excellent investigative and reporting skills."

Dale suspected that he was about to find out.

● ● ●

WITH SUSAN and Max off on one of their mom-and-kid-group play dates, Dale was on his own for supper. As he left campus, he considered what was in the fridge at home before opting for something from Mozar-Burger. It had been the first place he and Linda ate in town, on the night following his interview with Professor Parker. It was a slushy late winter evening, and they'd talked about how small and unwelcoming Mozarkite seemed while munching on the best cheeseburgers and tater tots they'd ever had. By the time the food was gone, they'd decided that, should a job offer come, they would turn it down.

So much for that.

Dale pushed the button and waited. A few moments later, the carhop's voice poured out of the tinny speaker.

"Help you?"

"Double cheeseburger, tater tots, large lemonade."

"Coach Fox, is that you out there?"

"It is. Who is this?"

"It's April, Herschel's daughter. He's coming out to see you."

Dale sat back and waited for Herschel Cumberford to make an appearance from inside the tiny shack where Mozar-Burger's delicious food was prepared. Herschel had remained an ardent supporter of the football team, even during the lean years. He probably wanted to talk about the next day's game. Everybody wanted to talk about the next game. McCrackenville was coming to town. They were undefeated just like Mozarkite.

They were ranked first in the nation. Mozarkite was third.

"Hey, Coach!"

"Herschel, how are you?"

"I'm sky-high, let me tell you. I don't think I'll be able to sleep a wink tonight. Louise and me are going out to the field an hour before the gates open so we can get our usual seats."

"A lot of people are doing that, Herschel. I hope that's early enough."

Herschel's brow furrowed in concentration before he said, "Heck, I may tell Louise to go on out there tonight and hold our spot, then."

They shared a laugh at the ridiculousness of the statement. Like many Mozarkite husbands, Herschel rarely *told* Louise Cumberford anything.

"What I came out for was to ask if you like chicken sandwiches."

"I do."

"Good," Herschel said, a grin spreading across his face. "Because starting Monday our chicken sandwich is gonna be called the *Coach Fox Chicken Sandwich*!"

"That's awfully kind of you, Herschel, but aren't you forgetting that I always get the double cheeseburger? Linda always did, too."

"Yeah, I know that, but two years ago I went and named it after Dale Earnhardt, Jr." Herschel pointed at the menu. "Ain't you never noticed? It's written right there."

It certainly was. *The Dale Earnhardt Jr. Double Cheeseburger*. Dale had been coming to Mozar-Burger so long that the menu was no longer necessary.

"Well, I'm honored to get the chicken sandwich named after me then, Herschel. Thanks."

"You betcha, Coach. Heck, when you win the national championship this winter, I might even consider bumping Dale Earnhardt Jr. to the chicken sandwich and naming the double cheeseburger after you."

"That's something to shoot for, then, Herschel."

"Dinner's on the house, Coach. April will have your burger and tots out in a minute. And I told the boys in back to throw in some extra tots."

Dale was enjoying the attention and the extra tots when a white sedan pulled into the stall next to him. Bubber Slate nodded. Dale nodded back, then had an idea.

"Bubber," he called after rolling down his window. "Do you have a few minutes to visit?"

When Bubber said he did, Dale invited him to come over to the truck. The two men shook hands, then Dale recited Bubber's order into the microphone. Chicken sandwich, fries, Diet Coke.

"Add his to mine," he instructed April. They exchanged small talk while they waited for Bubber's order to arrive. Mozarkite football was discussed of course, but so were Cardinals baseball and Bubber's plans for the upcoming deer hunting season.

"How's Chelsea these days?" Dale asked as Bubber dug into his chicken sandwich.

"I guess she knows that you're busy with football, Coach, because she's been staying at my place pretty much all the time. You want me to bring her home?"

Dale said he didn't. "She'll know when it's time."

They were quiet for several moments while Dale built up the nerve to broach the subject he'd intended to discuss. Before he got around to it, Bubber beat him to the punch.

"Coach, do you want to know about the things Linda and I did?"

The question had a creepy quality to it that Dale knew was unintended.

"Tell me about the nude beach."

Even in the dimly lit cab of the truck Dale could see Bubber's face getting red.

"That was a mistake. I felt self-conscious the whole time."

"You looked pretty happy in the picture."

"I drank away the shame. We were supposed to be there for three days, but we left after one. Linda and I both agreed it was ridiculous." Bubber slurped his Diet Coke before adding, "Coach, the kind of people who go to those places have no business going to those places."

"Tell me more."

"We always got rooms with two beds. I know that probably seems pointless, with me being... anyway, that's the way we wanted it. We had fun, but more than anything we were two lost people helping each other along."

"I had no clue Linda was lost."

"Yeah," Bubber said slowly. "We talked about that some. Linda never felt you deserved all the blame, Coach. She got so wrapped up in her own work she used to say that you guys grew apart without either of you realizing it. She just happened to be the first to figure it out."

Bubber was right. Dale hadn't figured it out. He'd not taken time away from his own world to consider the one he shared with Linda. And now it was too late.

It wasn't too late, though, to live that secret part of Linda's life through Bubber Slate. The man wasn't an adversary. He was, Dale decided, a kindred spirit. They'd both loved the same woman. In different ways, certainly, but loved her, nonetheless. They talked for the next hour, sharing Linda memories while cars came and went from the Mozar-Burger. And over that hour, Dale felt something change inside. The suspicions he'd had since coming across the pearl necklace were gone. So, too, were the feelings of jealousy and anger.

Linda was gone. Gone way too early. But that was the way life was sometimes. Dale missed her, but he would move on. Talking with Bubber was helping.

"Hey, Bubber," Dale said as Bubber polished off the last bite of his sandwich, "Did you know that you've just eaten a Coach Fox Chicken Sandwich?"

"I did not. Did you know, Coach, that you just had yourself a Dale Earnhardt Jr. Double Cheeseburger?"

"I didn't until about an hour ago."

Bubber smiled and reached for the door handle. "Well, there you go."

33

---

ello everyone, from sold-out Crowley Field in Mozarkite, this is Polled Hereford Football. I'm Wally Westmoreland, the voice of the Polled Herefords, and boy is it a big day.

The season opened three weeks ago with a 41-7 win over Granger College here at home. After that, the Herefords went on the road to win convincingly at Danbury and Northeast Kentucky, setting the stage for today's battle of the undefeated. It'll be Coach Dale Fox's third-ranked Polled Herefords against the top-ranked Minutemen of McCrackenville Community College. Stay tuned here to Country 104 for all the action coming your way after these messages from our sponsors.

● ● ●

THE BOYS WERE sky-high as Dale concluded his pregame remarks. Their euphoria wasn't due to anything he said. He hadn't pulled out an old Vince Lombardi speech or anything like that. They'd been that way all week, following the previous Saturday's 60-13 win over Northeast Kentucky that had seemed to put to rest any lingering doubts about how good the team could be. They'd prepared all week with an intensity Dale hadn't seen since the Andre Jameson years. He was reluctant to admit it, but he'd become concerned after Thursday night's practice that they were too charged up. What might happen if McCrackenville smashed their way to a quick touchdown, or if De'Shea or one of the ball carriers fumbled on the opening possession? After tossing about in bed, Dale had decided it didn't matter. The team was good, they were focused, and they were ready. McCrackenville better look out.

As always, he glanced up into the stands as he led the team onto the field. His eyes instinctively went to Linda's seat, which was now occupied by Stubby Proctor and his wife, Carol. He glanced down a few rows and spotted Susan sporting an old Polled Herefords jersey. Max should have been with her, but Evan had decided he wanted to spend a weekend with his son, so Susan had to acquiesce. Max had been excited all week about the game, and Dale wished he could've been there and had even hoped that Evan might bring him. He hadn't. They were ninety minutes away at Silver Dollar City.

Max was probably the only person from Mozarkite to miss the game. The stands were jammed. Twenty-two hundred and seven people in a stadium designed for two thousand. Fans filled every seat and stood behind rope barriers that ringed the end zones. The press box was stuffed with local and out-of-town reporters, including a representative from the Fox Sports regional affiliate. Heaven Knight was in her usual spot. Eleven cameras were placed around the playing field. The air was cold for September, and everyone was bundled against the chill. Dale spotted Larry Bob, Uncle Homer, and the boys, seated in their folding chairs behind the rope in the far end zone. Uncle Homer nodded, then opened his parka enough for Dale to see the cans of PBR he had snuck in.

De'Shea slowed as he passed Dale. They rarely spoke to one another, and Dale was surprised as his quarterback leaned close and said, "You ready, Coach?"

"I'm ready, De'Shea. How about you?"

De'Shea patted him on the shoulder. "Shit's about to get real, Coach. I'm always ready when the shit's gettin' real."

● ● ●

Mozarkite wins *the coin flip and elects to receive the ball at the beginning of the second half. The kick goes to McCrackenville's Andy Tolbert. He's at the twenty-five, the thirty, and across midfield to the forty, thirty, twenty, and touchdown McCrackenville. Tolbert avoided being tackled several times while showing off that speed that has the big schools' attention. The extra point is good. It's seven-zip McCrackenville and we're just twenty-seven seconds into this game.*

● ● ●

Dale admonished the players to keep their heads up as they came off the field. The quick touchdown had stunned the home crowd into silence, but there was plenty of game left. Brandon gathered his unit around as he gave them their marching orders. The kickoff was returned to the twenty-seven, where the Chattanooga Triplets and the rest of the offense would begin work.

And then, after two plays, their work was done. De'Shea's handoff to Carlos was mishandled, and suddenly McCrackenville had the ball on the Mozarkite twenty-four. Two running plays and a short pass later, they were up by fourteen. When Dale heard Brandon barking at his offensive players, he stepped in.

"You'll be fine," he said in his easy manner. Brandon's eyes were lit up. He seemed flustered at Dale's intrusion. The players, particularly De'Shea, appeared at peace.

"Shit's really real now," he said with a shrug. "We got this."

De'Shea was right.

● ● ●

Quarterback De'Shea Stephens *takes the snap and goes down on one knee to let the clock run out. And that's your ballgame! Your third-ranked Polled Herefords have just stunned the McCrackenville Minutemen by a score of 47-14. De'Shea had an outstanding day both rushing and throwing*

the ball, showing the world why many project him as a future NFL star.
We've got Raymond Peabody, our Country 104 morning deejay on the side-
lines waiting to get a word with De'Shea.

◊ ◊ ◊

DALE SHOOK hands with the McCrackenville coach and was heading toward the locker room when he saw one of the guys from Country 104 coming his way with a microphone.

"I'll catch you in the locker room," the guy said as he rushed past. "Wally wants me to grab De'Shea."

"I'd prefer you not talk to players on the field," Dale called out. The guy didn't hear him, so Dale turned to Brandon. "Coach Yarbrough, follow him and make sure De'Shea doesn't say anything to get himself in trouble."

"I'm on it, Coach."

The whooping and yelling were off the charts as the team stormed into the locker room. Dale caught snippets of their conversations that ran the gamut from talk of the team possibly being ranked first in the nation to short phone calls with girlfriends and family. Several, including Carlos Kwan, came over and hugged him.

"Sorry for the fumble, Coach" Carlos mumbled.

"It didn't hurt us, Carlos. And congratulations on your grades. I heard yesterday that you're passing all your classes."

Carlos beamed, and Dale could see the pride the young man was taking in his success in the classroom. His misgivings about the Triplets might have been premature.

Or maybe not.

"Coach, can we talk?"

Brandon had come up behind them.

"Sure, Coach Yarbrough. What's up?"

"In your office, please."

Dale motioned for Brandon to follow him. When they were inside with the door closed, Brandon said, "De'Shea just announced to everyone on the radio that he's sponsoring a party at a bar over in Swanson."

Dale felt his insides clinch.

"Are you sure you heard correctly?"

Brandon nodded. "Ten tonight. A joint called Hap's Place."

Dale knew of Hap's. It was the lone bar in Swanson, a run-down community of maybe nine hundred people just across the Arkansas line. Hap's had a reputation for serving liquor to underage kids. Of course, De'Shea was twenty-one, legal to buy a drink anywhere he wanted. And it was Saturday night after a game, a night when Coach had traditionally relaxed the team curfew.

"Maybe no one will show up," Dale said.

Brandon shook his head again. "It's already burning up social media. Hap's is setting up tables out back around a bonfire. Do you want me to go?"

"No. I think that's the last place any of us need to be."

● ● ●

DALE'S CELLPHONE buzzed at one-fifteen in the morning. He was not surprised.

Caller ID said it was the Mozarkite County Sheriff's Office. Again, no surprise.

"Coach, it's Nick Coates. Sorry to call at this late hour."

"What's up, Sheriff Coates? Are you hearing of trouble over at Hap's Place in Swanson?"

"No, sir. The locals seem to have that under control."

Dale took a deep breath. Had they dodged a bullet?

Nope.

"It's bigger than that, Coach. There's been a fire out at the Ricketts' place. It appears that one of your players might've set it."

34

MOZARKITE MESSENGER
Sunday Sports Edition
Quarterback Arrested After Big Win
By Heaven Knight

"It was the best of times; it was the worst of times."
Charles Dickens' opening line from *A Tale of Two Cities* was a fitting description of the day experienced by the Mozarkite Junior College football team.

The best of times? That's easy. The Polled Herefords routed the top-ranked McCrackenville Community College Minutemen 47-14 behind the strong arm and leadership of Arizona State transfer De'Shea Stephens. The game was essentially over at halftime when Mozarkite went to the locker room with a 37-14 lead.

The worst of times came later in the day. Much later, on a narrow backroad near the Missouri-Arkansas line where a fire just before midnight destroyed a family's century-old homeplace. Quarterback De'Shea Stephens is charged with setting the blaze.

George Ricketts is the family patriarch. He grew up in the old farmhouse and hoped to pass it on to his sons, Wade and Doyle. He was emotional when describing what he witnessed.

"I woke up and saw flames shooting up across the field and knew right away it was the old place. We were just getting ready to start fixing it up for Wade and his girlfriend to move into. It's a terrible thing."

Wade Ricketts, George's son, has recently returned to farming after being dismissed by the Mozarkite City Police Department. It was his suspicion that led sheriff's deputies to arrest Stephens.

"That boy (Stephens) has been pestering our family since he got to town," Wade Ricketts said. "He's always coming around asking if we know where he can get pot or drugs or stuff. He thinks that because I was on the police force, I might know about that stuff."

Police issued a warrant for Stephens' arrest after finding tire prints in an adjoining field that matched those on Stephens' automobile. Stephens is currently being held in the Mozarkite County Jail awaiting a bail hearing that will likely be held on Monday.

Mozarkite Coach Dale Fox announced early this morning that Stephens would be suspended from the team, pending an investigation.

35

_D_ale set aside the newspaper when Susan came in the front door. She made a beeline for him, her eyes blazing with fury.

"You had no business talking to Brandon like you did last night."

"And you have no business talking to me like this," Dale shot back. "And it was stupid of you to spend the night at his house, especially without telling me where you were."

"I'm thirty-five years old. I don't have to tell you where I am."

"You do if you're going to live in my house."

"If this is how it's going to be, Max and I'll move back out."

Susan stomped upstairs before he could respond. Yes, he had read Brandon the riot act late the night before, on the front steps of Brandon's house, the one that Susan had helped him find. He had it coming. De'Shea was proving that everything Dale had worried about could happen when a team recruited players with unsavory reputations. And when Brandon mentioned that De'Shea had twice broken curfew, well that really set him off.

What he hadn't expected was an argument from Brandon.

"How can you believe anything that involves the Ricketts clan?" he'd snapped. "De'Shea told me that Wade Ricketts and his brother have been calling him every racial slur in the book, and I believe him."

"He's been buying grass and who-knows-what-else," Dale responded in an even louder voice. "What do you expect to happen when he's mixed up with that kind of mess?"

"We have no proof of that," Brandon answered, lowering his voice to diffuse the situation. "All we know is that—"

"You're too close to the situation, Coach Yarbrough." Dale's tone left no question that the discussion was over. "You allowed your emotions to get in the way. I gave you responsibility for keeping tabs on those boys and you failed."

Dale had just finished telling Brandon that he was being suspended when Susan emerged from the house. He lost it all over again. The conversation grew louder. Neighbors, wondering what was going on at three in the morning, started coming outside or turning on their porch lights.

"I'll let you know when you can return... *if* you can return," Dale said as he stalked off.

◆ ◆ ◆

"I've never posted bail for a player and I won't start now."

De'Shea's eyes grew frightened as Dale made his declaration. They were in a tiny conference room next to the three cells that comprised the Mozarkite County Jail. De'Shea was the only prisoner. He appeared terrified.

"I can't come up with it on my own, Coach."

"Not my issue at the moment. I came here to get your side of the story."

"Can I make a phone call first?"

"You've put the reputation of this team on the line. My reputation, too. Tell me what happened, then you can find someone to post bail."

De'Shea began talking. He and Wade Ricketts had a history, but there had never been any sale or purchase of illegal substances.

"I'll piss in a cup right now if you want," De'Shea said.

Dale didn't want. He told De'Shea to keep talking.

Wade and Doyle Ricketts had targeted him soon after he arrived in Mozarkite. Wade had physically bumped him in McDonalds, then made a big deal out of it, as if it was De'Shea's fault. Doyle had been telling kids at the college that De'Shea was trying to buy meth. The brothers had shouted obscenities at him from their pickup trucks as they passed. De'Shea, if he was to be believed, had resisted the urge to fight back.

Until the previous night.

The owner of the bar in Swanson, Hap's, had approached De'Shea with a deal he felt was too good to pass up. Announce you're coming over to party, bring over a big crowd, and the drinks will be half-price for everyone. De'Shea admitted that he liked the idea of being the center of attention, so he accepted the offer.

"I thought it would be a good way to make friends," he said, daring to glance up for the first time. "Coach, do you have any idea how hard it is being one of the only black guys in town?"

Andre's words about having to fit in came flooding back. Still, throwing a party across the state line? That was taking things way too far.

De'Shea readily admitted he had been drinking, but only a few sips of beer. That jibed with what Sheriff Coates had reported, that De'Shea was below the legal limit. It was still enough to allow the Ricketts boys to goad him into a fight. Spurred on by the crowd, he'd followed them to the parking lot. Once outside, the brothers had inexplicably got in the truck and left.

If only it could've ended there.

They returned a half-hour later, De'Shea continued. And when they taunted him again before jumping into Doyle Ricketts' truck, De'Shea and fellow Triplet John Smith pursued them. They drove down backroads for several miles before Doyle Ricketts made a sudden turn into a fallow field. De'Shea conceded it was stupid to follow, but he'd had enough. He claimed that he never caught them, that their truck was faster in the dirt field than his car, so he gave up and returned to Hap's. He was on his way back to Mozarkite later that evening, alone, when a deputy sheriff pulled him over.

"How could you be so stupid?" Dale asked. His question brought tears to De'Shea's eyes. Dale had seen and heard enough. Crocodile tears wouldn't work. They never had.

❖ ❖ ❖

JOHN SMITH'S story aligned with De'Shea's. The Ricketts boys had repeatedly challenged De'Shea. He and De'Shea pursued them through the country but turned back. There was no fire, at least that they'd seen. At the end of the night De'Shea left the party by himself, headed back to Mozarkite.

Dale was finishing his meeting with John when Larry Bob Billingsley called.

"Need any help?"

"This is what happens when you recruit the wrong kind of players," Dale said in a tone as surly as he felt.

"It's the kind of stuff that happens when the Ricketts clan gets involved," Larry Bob said. "They'll say anything to make themselves look better."

"Their family home is burned to the ground, for God's sake, Larry Bob. Are you forgetting that?"

"The place was vacant for twenty-five years, Coach. Who's to say that Wade and Doyle didn't torch it themselves?"

Dale didn't need Larry Bob telling him how to do his job. Or what to believe.

"If De'Shea hadn't gone out there, none of this would've happened," he said before cutting the call short, only to have another one come in. This one was from Sheriff Coates. It was bad.

Investigators had found an empty gas can and matches in De'Shea's trunk.

"How long before he goes on trial?"

"Probably two months, maybe more," the Sheriff answered.

36

*D*ale showed up at Hap's Place at ten-thirty. It was an hour before a weathered Budweiser sign on the door said they opened, but there was a car in the lot out back, so he entered through a rear door into a small kitchen area. A bent-over old man was stacking glasses in a pass-through that separated the kitchen from the bar area. He didn't see Dale enter, and nearly jumped out of his skin when he spoke.

"Are you Hap?"

The old man removed his foggy glasses and cleaned them with the hem of his dirty white apron while he squinted in Dale's direction.

"Who wants to know?"

"I'm Dale Fox, the football coach at Mozarkite."

"Then, no, I'm not Hap."

The guy was evasive, or at least trying to be. He seemed to think he was pretty good at it, too. They remained at an impasse for several moments. Dale wouldn't plead for information, so he maintained steady eye contact until the old guy spoke again.

"Hap's my boy. We run the place together. He comes in later."

"Were you here last night?"

The guy nodded. "I saw your players, that's for sure. Drinking and carrying on. Strutting like peacocks. 'Specially that big black one with the ghetto head of hair. Him and that white boy who wears his hair like the blacks, they thought they was pretty special, I'm telling you."

Dale disliked the old guy. He was smug and quick to make accusations. He was also the only person who was available to talk to, so Dale soldiered on.

"You must've expected there would be plenty of people and plenty of drinking. You told De'Shea that you would provide half-price drinks, if he invited all his friends."

"Who the hell is Dee-Shay?"

"Our quarterback. The kid you just described."

"The coon or the white one?"

If the old man was trying to bait him Dale was not going to bite.

"Not the white one."

"You're full of shit if you think we would ask some Tennessee spook to invite his friends to our place. We serve the blacks because we have to, but the day that me or my boy start inviting them to come in will be my last on earth."

"How much did he have to drink?"

"Hell if I know. A lot. Him and that white boy he runs around with kept ordering beers and shots. I bet I took a half-dozen of each over to their table."

"And you saw them drink them?"

The old guy looked at Dale as if he were nuts. "No, some of 'em they poured down their pants," he scoffed. "Of course, I seen 'em drinking. I was going to cut them off, but when I tried that big coon gave me a look like he wanted to kill me. A little later they left with those older boys from over your way."

"The Ricketts' boys? Wade and Doyle?"

"I believe that's their names. The place was so damned crowded that I couldn't say for sure."

● ● ●

"I'M HAVING trouble reconciling what I've heard with your report," Dale said as he sat across from Sheriff Nick Coates in a conference room at the county courthouse. "You said that De'Shea wasn't over the legal intoxication limit, but the man who owns Hap's said he was drinking all night."

Sheriff Coates briefly looked through the stack of paperwork he'd brought with him before speaking. "Maybe the shock of what all was happening sobered him up."

"Is that even possible? I always assumed that once the alcohol was in your bloodstream traces would remain for quite a while."

"Traces, yeah, but his blood alcohol content had likely dropped since he left the bar. He was out in the open air, and if the accusations are right, he was very active. Who's to say that he hadn't gotten sobered up by the time we found him?"

Dale waited for Sheriff Coates to say more, but he was done. The Sheriff was a good man with a reputation for fairness and square dealing. If there was some kind of ruse being pulled by the Ricketts boys or the bar owner, Coates would never be a party to it. All he would go on was the evidence.

And the evidence was pretty damning.

37

The office phone rang all morning. Dale's cellphone, too. He allowed both to go to voicemail as he prepared for his meeting with President Fuller. It was a meeting she'd requested, one Dale felt was unnecessary. In addition to being football coach, he was also Director of Athletics. That title gave him the authority to make decisions about athletes. What Margaret Fuller could add to the conversation was beyond him. He'd said as much, earlier that morning when she'd called on his way to work. It did no good, though, as she made it clear that he was to make no final decisions until they spoke.

The previous day had been tense around the house following his encounter with Susan, until she left with Max early in the afternoon. He assumed they had gone to Brandon's place, but didn't know for sure and didn't want to leave the house to check. Fran Tompkins called around seven to see if Susan was there; she mentioned that she was expecting her to drop off Max. That meant it would be just Susan and Brandon. Was his own daughter siding against him? There'd been no time to dwell on it, as he had to figure out what to do with De'Shea.

Twenty-seven voicemails were on the office phone, another nine on the cell. ESPN had checked in three times. Fox Sports twice. NBC Sports, CNN, and the Washington Post. De'Shea had name recognition that stretched far and wide. One reporter offered five-hundred dollars for an exclusive with Dale. Another offered twenty-five hundred if Dale could get him an exclusive with De'Shea. It was ridiculous.

There was a call from Pastor Mark. The Third Baptist congregation had prayed for Dale the previous morning. A couple more calls of support also were left.

Most unsettling were the messages from haters. They didn't identify themselves but made it clear that they thought De'Shea was nothing more than an inner-city thug who deserved what was coming to him. One suggested lynching. They were ugly and vile and made Dale's stomach hurt.

The short walk from Baker Gym to the President's Office was usually a pleasant one, but Dale noticed the looks he received from students and staff he passed on the way. De'Shea's actions were big news in Mozarkite, thanks to Heaven Knight's article in the *Messenger*. He'd become a hero of sorts to a community that was hungry for one. Sadly, the adulation was misplaced.

Dr. Fuller's secretary motioned for him to go right in. The President's countenance was grim. She was as excited about Polled Hereford football as anyone. She'd forgone her usual business attire for a Herefords sweatshirt the previous Friday. Dale had caught a couple glances of her the next day, cheering on the team from her usual seat. He remembered what she'd said about football being a school's front porch. Well, Dr. Fuller, he thought, as he situated himself in the chair across her desk, our front porch is a mess at the moment.

She was considerate enough to first ask how he was doing. Dale kept his answer short. It wasn't about him. He wanted to get down to business.

"Tell me what we know," she said.

So, Dale did. He unpacked it all. De'Shea's version of the events, what he learned from the old guy at Hap's, and finally what Sheriff

Coates had included in his report about the gas can and matches in De'Shea's car.

"I learned from Coach Yarbrough that De'Shea has also broken curfew twice over the last month."

"Does Coach Yarbrough know where De'Shea went when he broke curfew?"

"He suspected to meet his girlfriend. We've heard he's seeing Norman Snelling's daughter.

"Who is Norman Snelling?"

"He owns the rock quarry out on Willow Springs Road. The family is pretty well off."

"Have you spoken to Mr. Snelling about this?"

Dale hated to admit that he hadn't. "It didn't seem pertinent to the situation at hand," he said quietly. "Compared to being arrested for starting a fire, running off to see a local girl is pretty small potatoes."

"Not if she's a minor," Dr. Fuller said sharply. "De'Shea could end up with considerably more trouble than an arson charge."

Dr. Fuller made a good point. Dale could have kicked himself for not pursuing the rumor.

Dr. Fuller appeared greatly troubled. She took notes but stopped occasionally to wring her hands in despair. She shook her head several times, making Dale wonder if she was doubting his report. When he finished, he sat back and waited for her to speak.

"What are you proposing?" she finally asked.

Dale was ready for the question, though he didn't like the way she phrased it. Professor Parker would never have asked what he was proposing. "I give you responsibility to oversee athletics, and I expect you to do your job," the old man had said numerous times over the years. "You make the decisions and I'll support them." Now, here was Dr. Fuller asking what he was proposing. It got into his craw. He knew he should let it slide but couldn't.

"I'm not *proposing* anything, Dr. Fuller," he said brusquely. "I'm telling you how I intend to respond to a student who repeatedly broke the rules."

Dr. Fuller picked up her notes, perused them for a few moments, then said, "Stop with the histrionics, Coach Fox. I don't make decisions in a vacuum, and neither should you. What are you thinking?"

"There's a pattern of disregard for rules that started before he came to Mozarkite. He was convicted of drug possession in high school. He had a confrontation with one of the coaches at Arizona State. Since he's been here, he's missed curfew, he made that inappropriate announcement on the radio about the party in Arkansas, he was seen drinking to excess. Now there's evidence tying him to arson. I'm suspending him from the team."

Dr. Fuller appeared alarmed. "They're charges, Coach Fox. He's not been found guilty of setting that fire. Where is he now? Still in jail?"

"He bailed out last night. I assume his father took care of it."

Dr. Fuller placed her head in her hands, then rubbed her temples. "I can't agree with your decision."

Dale said nothing.

"Since the beginning of the semester alone, we've had five students who attend class on this campus who were charged with crimes ranging from petty theft to spousal abuse. They remain in their classes as they await their days in court."

"They're not on the football team."

"They're students," Dr. Fuller shot back. "The same as De'Shea Stephens."

"De'Shea is free to continue his classes. He just won't be permitted to participate in football."

"What about his scholarship?"

"He'll lose that," Dale answered quickly. "He'll be responsible for paying his tuition."

Dr. Fuller sighed. She glanced at Dale, then turned to her desktop computer and punched some buttons. "De'Shea Stephens's father is a disabled veteran. The family is of very limited means." She locked eyes with Dale and said, "What if he can't afford to remain in school?"

"Perhaps that was something he should have considered when he missed curfew or went to Arkansas with his buddies." Dale knew he sounded callous, but facts were facts.

"Don't you care about the gray areas, Coach Fox?"

"Gray areas can keep a person from doing the right thing, President Fuller. I have to stick to the facts. I was against bringing those boys to campus from the start. Unfortunately, they've proven me to be right."

Dr. Fuller's nostrils flared. Her voice took on a challenging edge. "You seem proud of being right."

"Far from it. I've prayed for those boys, as I do all my players. It was a bad fit, unfortunately."

"Let's talk about this more tomorrow," Dr. Fuller said abruptly as she pulled away from her desk. "I have other issues that need my attention."

"The decision is made as far as I'm concerned," Dale said as he got up to leave.

● ● ●

HE DIDN'T EXPECT Heaven Knight to be outside the administrative building. He spotted her out of the corner of his eye and continued walking as she came alongside him.

"Coach Fox, were you in a meeting with President Fuller?"

"It's not any of your concern, Miss Knight." Dale continued walking.

"Have you made any decisions regarding De'Shea Stephens?"

"I'm not ready to say." Still, he kept moving in the direction of his office in Baker Gym.

"Sources say that the decision is in President Fuller's hands, Coach Fox. Can you confirm that?"

Dale stopped walking.

"De'Shea Stephens is suspended from the team until the arson case is cleared up."

He immediately regretted saying it. He regretted that he hadn't yet talked to the other coaches. He especially regretted that he hadn't broken the news to De'Shea.

Heaven Knight appeared startled by the revelation. She fumbled in her purse to pull out her cellphone, flicked on the voice recorder, and said, "You're saying that De'Shea Stephens is kicked off the team?"

Dale considered backtracking. There was no formal record of his comments due to Heaven Knight's rookie error of not having her recorder ready. He could always say she made it up. No one would know.

Dale would know.

Heaven Knight would know.

"De'Shea Stephens will no longer be part of the Mozarkite football program. He'll be free to continue attending class as a student, but his participation with the team is over until he is cleared of the charges against him."

"What if that takes six months?"

"It shouldn't take that long."

"What if it takes two months?"

"Then he can return in two months."

Heaven started to ask another question, but Dale waved her off and continued back to his office. Once there, he searched his cellphone contacts for De'Shea's number. He didn't have it. He had never had to contact his star quarterback, having turned that responsibility over to Brandon. He searched through his contacts until he came up with the name of a kid who started on the defensive line. He called, but the kid didn't know where De'Shea was, nor did he have his number. He tried three more players before finding one who had the number. By the time he placed the call to De'Shea twenty minutes had passed.

"This is De'Shea. Leave a number."

"De'Shea, it's Coach Fox. Call me back ASAP."

Dale waited. Fifteen minutes passed.

De'Shea didn't return the call.

An hour, still no De'Shea.

When he dialed the number again, De'Shea answered.

"De'Shea, it's Coach Fox. I left a message for you. We need to—"

"I already heard. The lady from the paper told me. I'm packing."

"You don't have to leave school, De'Shea. You're off the team, but you can still—"

"I can't afford to stay here, Coach. I'm headed back to Chattanooga, as soon as the judge says I can leave the state."

The young man's tone was calm. Respectful, even. Dale almost wished he were angrier. Maybe that would have absolved the guilt he was feeling for talking to Heaven Knight first. No player should find out through an outside source that he'd just been cut.

"Well..." Dale stammered, "if there's anything I can do, be sure to give me a call."

De'Shea didn't answer, and Dale felt like a fool for what he'd said. The last thing De'Shea Stephens needed was help from him.

The call ended awkwardly, and mercifully, a few moments later. Dale leaned forward in his chair, placed his head on his desk, and worked to regain his senses. Yes, De'Shea had been in trouble before. Yes, he missed curfew. Yes, he had put himself in a situation where he could rationally be accused of setting fire to an old farmhouse. He was, simply put, not the kind of player Dale wanted or needed on his team.

So why was he feeling as if he'd been hit by a bus?

Part of it was the way De'Shea learned of his decision. But that wasn't all of it. The young man had a troubled past, but he'd never been disrespectful toward Dale, other than his affinity for cursing. The last grade report Dale had seen had De'Shea earning B's and C's. Not exactly Ivy League caliber but given how much responsibility the kid had on the football field, the grades were pretty good.

Should he have given him a second chance? Would it even be a second chance? More like a third or fourth, right? Coach Yarbrough had given him two second chances after he missed curfew. Dale wondered if he should have personally pulled him aside after he invited the world to the beer bash across the state line, maybe told him to steer clear of stuff like that.

But De'Shea was twenty-one years old. A man. He had to make his own decisions. And by making his decisions he had to accept the consequences.

It was those conclusions that allowed Dale to get a couple restless hours of sleep that night. He hoped the situation would blow over, and he could get on with football. Getting on with football was tantamount. He gave the boys Monday off to prepare for midterms, so tomorrow would be their first time back together. No De'Shea. No Coach Yarbrough.

Somehow, he would make it work.

38

MOZARKITE MESSENGER
Tuesday Sports Section
Chattanooga Triplets Band Together, Quit Team
By Heaven Knight

*H*istory has repeated itself.

Late last evening, after receiving word that their friend and teammate De'Shea Stephens had been suspended from the Polled Hereford football team, running back Carlos Kwan and wide receiver John Smith announced that they were leaving the program. A similar occurrence took place a year ago at Arizona State University after Kwan was ruled ineligible because of issues with grades and class attendance.

Stephens, the team's quarterback, was arrested early Sunday morning following a party at a rural Arkansas bar. He was charged with arson after tire tracks led investigators to connect him to a fire that burned down an abandoned house in rural Mozarkite County.

Armed with that information, Mozarkite Head Coach Dale Fox suspended Stephens from the team indefinitely.

"The college must not believe people are innocent until proven guilty," Stephens' friend John Smith told the *Messenger*. "De'Shea is not the kind of person who does vindictive things like he's being accused of."

Smith went on to speculate that the incident was racially motivated, noting that the owners of the home that was set ablaze had been verbally abusing Stephens since soon after he arrived in town.

"If anybody had a reason to fight back it was De'Shea," Smith said. "He was called the n-word and worse by those brothers. I heard it, Carlos heard it, and plenty of other people heard it, too."

Answering to speculation that Stephens's actions were motivated by excessive alchohol, Smith was adamant. "He bought plenty of booze because he could. Beer and stuff was half-price, and De'Shea has a big heart. He wanted to pick up the tab for people who might not be able to buy it on their own."

Other than acknowledging to the Messenger that Stephens was suspended from the team, Polled Herefords Coach Dale Fox did not respond to repeated phone messages. MJC President Dr. Margaret Fuller said she would not comment on issues related to personnel or individual students but did promise a thorough investigation.

In a related story, it was learned just before going to press that Mozarkite Assistant Coach and Recruiting Coordinator Brandon Yarbrough has also been placed on indefinite suspension. Yarbrough was not available to comment.

Additionally, it was announced by the Junior College Press Association that the undefeated Polled Herefords will enter their game this Saturday against South Tennessee ranked first in the nation following their convincing victory against McCrackenville this past weekend.

39

*A*ny lingering enthusiasm from Saturday's big win was long gone when the team showed up for practice Tuesday afternoon. Dale had them gather for a quick pre-practice meeting. It was pointless. Every kid seated on the grass in front of him was aware that the Chattanooga Triplets were gone. Many had been at the party. Those who weren't had heard about it. Several had been asked to give their accounts to the sheriff's department. Still, for closure's sake, Dale gave a summary of what had happened, then asked if there were questions.

There were.

"Can De'Shea come back if they drop the charges?"

Dale said he could but would have to answer for his behavior first.

"Could John and Carlos come back if they decided to?"

If they were still enrolled and attending classes, they would be welcomed back.

"What if the people who said De'Shea did it were lying?"

That was for law enforcement to figure out.

When there were no more questions, Dale announced who would be taking over the positions the Triplets had held for the first four games of the season. The young man assuming De'Shea's spot at quarterback looked as if he'd seen a ghost.

"You are four-and-oh and ranked first in the nation. Do not lose sight of that. It takes more than three players to make a team great. Practice like the championship-quality team you are, and we'll go out there Saturday and make believers of everybody."

As the players split off with their assistant coaches, Dale wondered if they'd bought into his challenge. From his usual vantage point, near the home team bleachers, he watched as the offensive and defensive units sleepwalked through drills. The enthusiasm, the confidence, the fire, all gone.

No, he decided, they hadn't bought in at all.

֍ ֍ ֍

PRACTICE WAS WINDING down when Dale spotted President Fuller. There was someone with her, a man in a dark suit who appeared to be worried about his shoes getting dirty on the turf. Dale knew him, but not personally. His name was Jeffrey Lewis Teague, and he was the college attorney. Unlike everyone else associated with MJC, Teague wasn't local. He was part of a firm in Cape Girardeau. They represented the interests of the university up there, as well as three or four community colleges in the area.

They tried to remain inconspicuous, huddling close to the bleachers at the far end of the field, but the players quickly spotted them. They pointed and whispered among themselves. Dale picked up his bullhorn, and shouted, "Focus! You are the top team in the country!"

Nothing changed. The players kept whispering between plays. Even the assistant coaches cast nervous glances toward the sidelines. Dale was reminded of a line his old friend Willis Tompkins sometimes used when players weren't focusing.

This practice has done gone to shit. Let's call it a day.

In a silent salute to his buddy, who was probably at home watching TV with no idea where or who he was, Dale blew his whistle and ended practice. After the players and coaches had left the field, he started the slow walk toward where Dr. Fuller and Lawyer Teague were waiting.

"Hello, Dr. Fuller, what can I do for you?"

And then she told him.

MOZARKITE MESSENGER
Wednesday Sports Section
Coach Fox Placed on Leave
By Heaven Knight

*M*ozarkite Junior College Football Coach and Athletic Director Dale Fox has been placed on administrative leave effective immediately.

The announcement, made via written statement last evening by MJC President Margaret Fuller, states: "Dale Fox has been placed on administrative leave with pay, effective immediately while the Mozarkite Junior College administration investigates and assesses his ability to fulfill the requirements for the positions of Head Football Coach and Director of Athletics. This investigation is anticipated to take up to sixty days and will conclude if further action is warranted, up to and including termination."

When reached at her residence last evening, President Fuller had no other comments, citing confidentiality. Two members of the

Mozarkite football team who wish to remain anonymous told the *Messenger* that President Fuller and a middle-aged male appeared at the team's practice yesterday afternoon. Further investigation concluded that the male was Jeffrey Lewis Teague, 47, an attorney with the Cape Girardeau law firm of Meyer, Fleming, and Troost. According to the firm's website, Teague serves as the attorney of record for several higher education institutions in the area, including Mozarkite Junior College.

Turmoil has swirled around the Polled Hereford team over the past several days as Quarterback De'Shea Stephens was dismissed from the team after being charged with setting a blaze that consumed the homeplace of a long-time Mozarkite family. Two other players, Carlos Kwan and John Smith quit the team after Stephens's suspension was announced. The three players make up the "Chattanooga Triplets" and had been instrumental in the team's rise from also-rans to number one in the most recent junior college football rankings.

President Fuller's announcement went on to state that Assistant Coach Brandon Yarbrough will be serving as Interim Head Coach. Yarbrough was currently serving a suspension imposed by Coach Fox for reasons the *Messenger* has not been able to confirm. Reached at home, Yarbrough said that he would be meeting with the team this afternoon in an effort to regroup and prepare for their weekend game against South Tennessee Community College. It will be the first time in the Mozarkite football program's long history that they will play a game as the nation's top-ranked junior college team.

Coach Dale Fox did not return repeated calls for comment.

41

Dale used the back door to gain access to Larry Bob Billingsley's office. He felt as if he were skulking around like a criminal. Larry Bob's secretary wouldn't be in until eleven, having been conveniently dispatched to a neighboring county to file some paperwork. Larry Bob was already at his desk. That morning's copy of the *Messenger* was placed on his blotter, open to Heaven Knight's article.

They skipped the jokes and insults that were a usual part of their relationship. Larry Bob shook Dale's hand, and for a moment Dale thought his long-time friend might come closer for a hug. Thankfully, he didn't. A lot of men found the whole hugging thing to be easy and acceptable. Dale and his friends at the Goldrush weren't among them.

"Thanks for seeing me."

Dale took a seat in one of the two worn leather chairs in front of Larry Bob's messy desk. The room smelled of stale coffee and tacos. The night had been fitful, and Dale was bone tired. And scared.

"I'm honored to help, Coach." Larry Bob said as he grabbed a pen.

"Please, Larry Bob. Call me Dale. Right now, that's who I am. It's all I am." The words seemed as if they were coming from someone else, and Dale wondered if he sounded as defeated to Larry Bob as he did to himself.

"You'll always be Coach to me, so deal with it." His words were kind, but it was his grin that helped soothe Dale's frayed nerves. "Anyway," he continued, "I put together a list of four solid labor attorneys for you to consider. Two are in St. Louis, one's in Little Rock but is licensed to practice here in Missouri. The fourth one's in Springfield. They have good reputations and records of winning their cases. I've ranked them for you to—"

"You're my attorney, Larry Bob."

When the heavyset man looked up from his hand-scrawled list, Dale realized for the first time that his eyes appeared weary. Larry Bob had a reputation for drinking too much and gambling too much. His legal work was sometimes questioned by clients and opposing counsel alike.

None of those people knew Larry Bob as Dale knew Larry Bob.

"Seriously, Coach. You should consider someone who does this every day."

"I've already considered it. You're my attorney."

"Coach," Larry Bob sighed, "I implore you to give this some thought. I'm just an old ham-and-egger in little old Mozarkite. I'm okay at divorces and wills, but this is big."

"Will you take my case or not?"

The two men gazed at each other for several moments before Larry Bob cracked a smile.

"I've already gotten started. Let's get your job back."

They shook hands again, because it felt like the thing to do. There was no discussion of fees or retainers. Dale didn't feel the need to go there. His friend would treat him fairly. More importantly, he would pour his heart and soul into the case. Those out-of-town attorneys might have more experience, but Dale would just be another in a long string of clients. Larry Bob? Dale would get everything he had, and that was good enough for him.

Dale twiddled his thumbs while Larry Bob read through the letter Dr. Fuller and the attorney had presented him after practice the day before. It was ten minutes before he set it aside and said, "They're saying you were insubordinate. You were specifically told to hold off on doing anything about De'Shea, but you did anyway."

Dale shrugged. "They may have a point." He filled Larry Bob in on the details of his Monday meeting with Dr. Fuller. He was considerably more sheepish when he recounted what he'd said to Heaven Knight from the *Messenger*.

"That's where I screwed up. She insinuated that I didn't have the authority to make the final decision on De'Shea's status, and I spoke faster than I should have." Dale looked down at his feet as he said, "The worst thing is that I mishandled things with De'Shea. He shouldn't have gotten word of his suspension from a reporter. He's not a bad kid."

Larry Bob pulled himself out of his chair, huffing and puffing from the effort. "First of all, never say you 'screwed up.' Get those words and that sentiment out of your vocabulary right now, understand?"

"Okay."

"Second, this isn't a matter of if De'Shea Stephens torched that old rat trap or not. Personally, I wish a Ricketts or two would've been tied up inside the old place when it burned down. They're a bunch of thieves and liars, and their deaths wouldn't amount to anything more than addition by subtraction, if you know what I mean."

Dale knew.

"The case you're hiring me to handle, Coach, is this one." Larry Bob grabbed Dr. Fuller's letter and waved it around. "They don't mention De'Shea or Brandon Yarbrough. They only say you were insubordinate."

"Maybe I was... a little bit."

"There ain't no 'little bit' in the law, Coach. It's black and white. It was insubordination or it wasn't. They're going to try to prove it was. My job is to prove it wasn't. Now, back to your meeting with President Fuller. Was she recording the conversation?"

"Not to my knowledge."

"I'll have to find out for sure, but we'll assume she wasn't. Do you recall at any point her telling you specifically not to suspend De'Shea Stephens?"

"Not in those words. She said that she didn't agree with my decision, then at the end she said we would talk about it more the next day."

Larry Bob jotted more notes. "Have you traditionally made these types of decisions without advice or direction from the administration?"

Dale repeated what Professor Parker used to say, about it being Dale's responsibility to oversee athletics and how the Professor would support his decisions.

"Has Dr. Fuller indicated in the past that the decision-making process would change?"

"Never. We discuss things more than I did with Professor Parker, but she's not made any changes that I'm aware of."

"Good," Larry Bob nodded as he continued to take notes.

"How long will this all take, Larry Bob? Any chance I can be back on the sidelines for the South Tennessee game Saturday?"

"Nope. No chance at all. We'll request a hearing in front of the college's governing board. They have two weeks to respond to our request, then another two weeks to set a date and time."

"That's four weeks," Dale said glumly. "That will leave just one more game this season." The thought of missing his team's games was like a knife slashing through his stomach. Dale had prided himself on not missing a game or practice in his entire tenure at MJC. He had coached through three bouts of the flu and, fifteen years earlier, with a ruptured appendix.

"It's going to be the longest four weeks of your life, Coach. You can't set foot on campus or go to games."

"Should I stay at home all the time?"

"That's your decision. If you want to come to the Goldrush in the mornings, c'mon up. You're not suspended from life, just coaching."

Dale wasn't sure if he wanted to be seen in public or not. He wasn't sure of a lot of things.

"How's Susan taking this?" Larry Bob asked.

"Did you know she was dating Brandon Yarbrough?"

Larry Bob did. According to him, everybody did.

"She told me last night that they had agreed to take some time off from seeing each other. I could tell it hurt her very much, but she didn't like being in the middle. We had a disagreement this past weekend after I gave Brandon a dressing down for how he'd been handling De'Shea and the others.

"The boys at the Goldrush have your back, too. Uncle Homer said to tell you to hang tough."

Dale appreciated his friends' support.

"But," Larry Bob said, "there are folks who think you overreacted by kicking De'Shea off the team. They're going to say you cost Mozarkite a championship."

"I'm prepared for that."

"Are you? Are you really, Coach?" Larry Bob sat forward in his chair, placed his flabby arms on the desk, and said, "I'm going to be blunt. For the past twenty years you've been the biggest celebrity Mozarkite has."

Dale told Larry Bob to cut it out, but he didn't.

"I'm serious. You've been above reproach as far as most folks are concerned. Even when the team stopped winning, you weren't criticized. You achieved a status around here that none of the rest of us will ever experience, but that's about to change. There will be people who side with the college and others who side with De'Shea and the Triplets. They'll say Mozarkite was close to becoming a place people would know about, and you let your pride get in the way of that. They'll say they don't want you to ever walk the sidelines again. They'll turn their back on you and curse at you. They'll write letters to the paper about you, and you know the worst thing, Coach?"

Dale didn't.

"There's not a damned thing you can do about it. You'll have to take it. There's no fighting back, no putting anyone in their place. You've been the big man in this small town for a long time, and there will be folks who want to knock you off your pedestal."

Larry Bob leveled his gaze on Dale, his eyes boring into his long-time friends, and said, "Now, are you ready to fight for your job?"

42

MOZARKITE MESSENGER
Sunday Sports Edition
Herefords Eke Out Victory
By Heaven Knight

ollowing a week of controversy, the Mozarkite Junior College Polled Hereford football team returned to the gridiron Saturday at the home field of conference rival South Tennessee Community College. While the offense without the Chattanooga Triplets struggled to move the ball, the defense stepped up to the challenge in a 14-3 Hereford victory. It was the first win for Mozarkite Interim Head Coach Brandon Yarbrough, who took over earlier in the week when Coach Dale Fox was placed on leave.

The once mighty offense of the Herefords, now 5-0, scored just one touchdown in the contest. The second was provided by the defense, when an intercepted pass was returned for a score in the third quarter. Yarbrough was quick to praise his defense but wanted everyone to know the win was a team effort.

"It would've been easy for this team to roll over and play dead, but they came out hard from the start," Yarbrough said. "The offense avoided making critical mistakes, while the defense played like world beaters."

South Tennessee lost their third consecutive game and fell to 2-3 on the season.

The Polled Herefords maintain their top ranking in the junior college poll this week, despite the loss of three key offensive starters. They will have their hands full next week when they travel to Iowa Western for another conference showdown. Iowa Western beat the Herefords 41-7 last season and, despite being unranked with a record of 1-4, Coach Yarbrough expects a tough game.

"Their offense can be explosive," Yarbrough told the *Messenger*. We have to go up there and be ready to play."

43

Stopping by the Goldrush was a mistake.

Dale knew it was a mistake before he made it to his table. The buzz he had heard as he approached the front door instantly died. The place became dead silent. He considered retreating back outside, but that would look weak. He didn't want to look weak, so he maneuvered his way through the clusters of tables to his usual spot. Uncle Homer was the first to recover.

"About damn time you showed up."

The boys didn't say anything at first. Plumber Dick's mouth opened and shut like a fish trying to breathe out of water. Welder Tommy just stared. Larry Bob looked up from the newspaper, nodded, and went back to reading.

"How ya doing, Coach?" Uncle Homer asked before returning to his plate of runny eggs and toast. The rest of the crowd seemed to drift back to their private conversations.

"I'm all right, Homer. You?"

Homer nodded that he was okay but didn't speak until his mouth was empty. "They were talking about you," he said, gesturing toward the surrounding tables.

"Mostly good, I hope."

"Some of it. Frank and his bunch think you screwed up. A couple tables think you should be fired, but the rest of the crowd is behind you."

Dale glanced across the diner at a table occupied by a large swarthy man in a seed corn cap. Frank Cozzey and his tablemates returned Dale's gaze. Their eyes seemed hard and unforgiving, but Dale wondered if that was his imagination playing tricks on him.

"Frank," Dale mouthed from across the room. Cozzey stared but didn't respond.

"Maybe I should go," Dale said.

Larry Bob spoke for the first time. "The hell you will. Order your food and eat slow. Don't let the doubters get to you."

Patsy came over and squeezed Dale's shoulder. "Usual, Coach?"

"Yes, please."

"The boys won anyway," Plumber Dick said after Patsy had left. Tommy tried to shush his brother, but Dick was already finished with his observation.

"They sure did," Dale replied. "Good to hear."

"Woulda won by fifty if you'd been there," Dick said.

Dale laughed, then caught himself when he noticed the attention he was getting. Several people smiled when they heard him laugh. Others stared. Were they wondering how he was able to laugh after kicking De'Shea out of school?

"Did you hear that Coach Yarbrough invited the Triplets to come back to the team?" Uncle Homer asked.

Dale hadn't. He eyed Uncle Homer, half-expecting him to admit it was a bad joke. It wasn't.

"One of the boys who plays defensive line helps cut hay for Willie Murphy," Uncle Homer explained. "He told Willie that he got a text from the Kwan kid, the running back. They turned him down. Said there was no way they wanted to be here in the middle of the shit-storm surrounding your situation."

"Don't say anything, Coach," Larry Bob cautioned. "You never know who's listening, especially the way some of the rats around here are jumping ship."

With that admonition the conversation turned to other topics. Dale listened but didn't speak. When he was finished eating, he paid his bill, took a look around, and walked out.

❁ ❁ ❁

"SHERIFF COATES, what can I do for you?"

Dale held the front door open to allow the sheriff to step inside. He glanced up and down the street, then shrugged and came in.

"Coach, that lady President up at the college told me that any and all information I have regarding De'Shea Stephens's case goes only to her. You're not to be kept in the loop any longer."

Dale rubbed his neck and looked Sheriff Coates up and down. "And that's why you came by? To tell me that you can't tell me anything?"

The Sheriff grinned. "You've been around here a lot longer than President what's-her-name, and if there's something I think you need to know; I'm going to come tell you. She ain't the boss of me, Coach."

"I appreciate that, Sheriff."

"And there is something I wanted to tell you. It concerns some of the rumors going around, the ones about De'Shea Stephens spending time with Norman Snelling's daughter, Haley. Have you heard those rumors?"

Dale had.

"They're not true, at least not the way people want to think they're true. De'Shea did spend quite a bit of time at the Snelling house, but mostly it was with Norman."

"Why would Norman spend time with a college boy?"

"It's not common knowledge, Coach, but Norman is a recovering addict. He started with meth but wound up using cocaine. He was busted on a trip out West about four years back. Most folks aren't aware of all that, and I ask that you help keep it that way. It could be bad for Norman's business if word got out that he used to be a user."

"I'll not say anything."

"Thanks, Coach. It turns out that De'Shea's father and Norman were in the same army unit years ago. One thing led to another, and Norman has been mentoring De'Shea while helping him stay clean."

Dale's breath caught. "Does he have a problem? De'Shea, I mean?"

"He used to, back in high school. The stuff was easy to get for an athlete, so De'Shea started using in tenth grade. He stopped his senior year but fell back into it last year after leaving Arizona State. He and Norman meet two or three times a week. In fact, what nobody knows is that it was Norman Snelling who bailed De'Shea out of jail."

Dale could barely believe what he was hearing.

"Norman already told me that if this thing goes to trial, he and his wife and daughter will be character witnesses for De'Shea. Norman says he trusts that boy a whole lot more than he does the people who are spreading rumors that De'Shea is dating Haley."

"Do you know if he has stayed clean?"

"According to Norman he has. He told Norman that he had a sip or two at the party the other night, but only to fit in. And alcohol was never a problem for him, anyway."

"Did he tell Norman anything about the fire?"

"Only that he didn't do it, but frankly, Coach, the evidence is pretty overwhelming. He was at the scene of the fire at some point in the evening, he'd had at least two confrontations with the Ricketts boys, and then there was the gas can in his trunk. He swears it wasn't his and that he didn't know it was back there, but that's what people always say when backed in a corner."

The Sheriff put his hat back on and prepared to leave. "I'll be sharing this same information with the college president later this afternoon. I wanted you to know as well. I've always respected you as a coach and a person and want you to get a fair shake.

"One more thing, Sheriff?"

Sheriff Coates nodded for Dale to proceed.

"You've made law enforcement a career. You've seen a lot. Between you and me, do you think De'Shea set that fire?"

"If it weren't for the gas can, I would say no. That bit of evidence will be what puts most any jury in the mood to convict."

◆ ◆ ◆

DALE FOUND solitude to be unnerving. Not those short moments, like the couple hours he'd enjoyed after getting home and relaxing before Linda finished her day. Those were fine. It was the thought of long-term aloneness with little to do. He'd seen his father suffer through it for the last eighteen months of his life at the nursing home back in Dale's hometown. Long, unending days of mindless television interspersed with halting conversations about doctor visits and medications. Thankfully, his father's isolation had been tempered by dementia. Others that Dale saw in the same facility were not only alone, but fully aware of the extent of their situation. Was he about to become just like them? Susan was at work. Max was at kindergarten. Since being placed on leave the week before, Dale already found his days becoming longer. And lonelier.

So, when he answered the door about ninety minutes after Sheriff Coates departed and came face-to-face with Cassie Whitman, Dale was happy for the unexpected visitor.

Then he remembered their last conversation, just before the start of the season. He'd blown her off. She hadn't deserved that, and he should've done something to make things right. He hadn't, though. He'd shoved it to the back of his mind to leave room for football.

Well, so much for football.

"Susan said you might need a friend."

Dale considered telling her that Susan was wrong. He had Larry Bob and Uncle Homer and the boys at the Goldrush. They were his friends. The words were about to come out of his mouth when he realized they weren't true anymore. Larry Bob, over the past week, had transitioned from friend to lawyer. Homer was his friend, but not the kind of friend you knew you could confide in. And the boys? Well, they were the boys.

A few months earlier, he would've stopped by Willis and Fran Tompkins' place. The reason, he would say, was to check on his old friend, Willis, but more and more it had been to lean upon Fran's wisdom and friendship. Willis had grown increasingly needy in recent weeks, though, and Fran was focused by necessity on her husband's health and comfort. That was as it should be.

So, yeah, as much as Dale hated to admit it, he could use a friend.

"It's good to see you, Cassie. Please come in."

$\bullet \ \bullet \ \bullet$

CASSIE WAS STILL THERE when Susan and Max returned home at six-thirty. Max, oblivious to his Pop-Pop's issues, filled them in on the latest news from Miss Doubleday's kindergarten class at Mozarkite Elementary School while Susan pulled together a supper of spaghetti and meatballs, salad, and warm Italian bread. Nothing was said about Cassie's presence, though Dale thought he caught a couple looks pass between her and his daughter. The conversation was light, focusing on the real estate market, Cassie's work, and local gossip that didn't include Dale. They were finishing dessert and had excused Max to go watch TV when someone came to the door. Susan excused herself to answer. When she returned a few moments later, her eyes were blazing. She tried to hide her anger, but that had never been easy for Susan.

"Who was it?"

"Stubby Proctor."

"What did Stubby want at this time of night?"

"He was here to get your truck back."

Dale hadn't considered the possibility that his loaner pick-up might be reclaimed. He'd driven Stubby's program trucks for so long that it was part of his regular, everyday life. He got up from the table.

"I guess I need to get my stuff out."

"Stubby's gone, Dad. You can keep the truck."

Dale stopped and turned back to his daughter.

"It's okay," Susan said, taking a bite of cheesecake. "I took care of it."

"What did you say?"

Dale gasped at Susan's bawdy and vulgar response. Cassie didn't. Cassie laughed. She laughed hard. Her laughter wiped the anger from Susan's face. She started to laugh, too.

"You've helped that man sell a lot of pickups over the years, Dad. For him to come by the week after you're put on leave, well, he got what was coming to him."

"I agree," Cassie said, still laughing. "I would love to have seen the look on Stubby's face when you told him to..." Cassie would never say the same words Susan had used, but that didn't stop her from enjoying the moment.

"Focus on the things that matter, Daddy," Susan said as she got up to cut him another piece of cheesecake. "And don't forget that some of what matters most is sitting right at this table."

◆ ◆ ◆

SUSAN LEFT them alone after dinner, and by the time Cassie went home at ten-thirty, Dale had apologized for his past behavior. Cassie had accepted. She'd opened up about some of the stuff from her past, about how so many people had assumed that she'd cheated on her ex-husband, Frank, when, in fact, she hadn't. Dale found some of his own struggles mirroring Cassie's and realized that her response to those struggles might help him.

They also spent some quiet moments between the conversations. Cassie had slid closer to him on the sofa and placed her hand on his knee as she leaned in. She seemed to crave the closeness, and Dale found himself needing it just as much.

They kissed, Dale's first with anyone other than Linda in nearly forty years. And it was good. Sweet and tender and soft and perfect for the moment.

And they laughed, and that felt almost as good as the kissing. Dale hadn't laughed much recently, and as they recounted Susan's colorful sendoff of Stubby Proctor, he felt the release that came from laughing with a good friend.

And despite everything that was swirling around his life, as Dale walked Cassie to her car and kissed her goodnight on the curb, he couldn't help but feel that it had been one of the most enjoyable evenings he'd experienced in a long, long time.

44

"Folks are missing you down at the Goldrush."

Dust particles floated in the mid-morning sunlight streaming through the windows of Larry Bob's office as the two men took their usual seats.

"Not all of them, I'm sure." Dale answered.

Larry Bob chuckled. "Yeah, not everybody, but enough. Sorry to call you down here unexpectedly, but we received some new information that's going to hit you right between the eyes."

Dale stiffened. "Good or bad?"

"It depends how you look at it. A couple of the Ricketts boys' buddies came forward with new information about the fire after Sheriff Coates leaned on them pretty heavy the night it happened. De'Shea Stephens wasn't involved."

"Then he needs to be reinstated to the team."

"That's what you're going to tell Heaven Knight. She's coming by in twenty minutes for a sit-down interview."

Dale started to get up, but Larry Bob stopped him.

"I know, Coach. You've made it clear that you have nothing to say publicly, but your side of the story needs to get out."

"I don't talk publicly about player issues, Larry Bob."

Larry Bob reached for the latest edition of the *Messenger*, opened it to the *Letters to the Editor* section, and placed it in front of Dale. "Have you seen this?"

Dale had. The Herefords suffered their first loss of the season the previous weekend, in Brandon Yarbrough's second game as coach. It was an ugly defeat to a team with more losses than wins, and the locals were starting to weigh in on the situation. Of the fourteen letters the *Messenger* printed, eight implored the college to get the Triplets back on the football field. Three others were pro-Dale, sharing their belief that he'd gotten a raw deal for doing his job. The other three were of the opinion that since Brandon Yarbrough had brought the Triplets to town he should be given the head coaching job permanently.

"Talk to Heaven Knight. Let people hear from you," Larry Bob said.

● ● ●

HEAVEN KNIGHT WAS business as always as she entered Larry Bob's conference room, though Dale thought he detected a sympathetic glance when she shook his hand.

"I'll be listening and taking notes of everything that's said," Larry Bob said brusquely as they took their seats around the table. "If anything gets printed that wasn't said here, I'll sue you and the *Messenger*. So, make sure you—"

"Don't threaten Miss Knight, Larry Bob," Dale cut in. "She'll be fair."

She nodded at Dale, pulled out a small recorder and sat it on the table, and said, "Coach Fox, you've undoubtedly heard about the witnesses who came forth regarding the fire on the Ricketts place."

Dale indicated that he had.

"Does that change your opinion of De'Shea Stephens?"

"No."

Heaven Knight blinked several times. Larry Bob placed his hand on Dale's arm, but Dale shook it away.

"It doesn't change my opinion of De'Shea because I've never defined him by one incident. It was always my hope that he was innocent and could eventually return to the team. If I were coaching today, I would invite him back immediately."

"Did De'Shea Stephens get a raw deal from you and the college?"

"I can only answer that from my perspective. I can't speak for the college, but we dealt with the information we had at the time. The evidence was strong enough to warrant an investigation. Now that evidence has been refuted. It's not unlike someone being arrested for a crime and then proven innocent. Sadly, it happens sometimes. I wish it hadn't happened here."

"Do you feel the situation was racially motivated?"

Dale thought about the question for several moments. If he answered honestly, it might prove to be a powder keg. Sadly, there were people in the area who refused to accept others because of their skin color.

Screw 'em.

"Wade and Doyle Ricketts are narrow-minded bigots. I've personally heard Wade use racist language to describe a local family. Several guys on the team reported hearing both Ricketts boys refer to De'Shea in racist terms so yeah I'd say race played a part in what happened."

"There are some people close to the team that say you never fully supported De'Shea Stephens. Was your decision racially motivated?"

"I wasn't fully on board with some of our new recruitment efforts, but not for racial reasons. Mozarkite has traditionally recruited players with clean backgrounds. It worked for us for the most part, but times are changing. As President Fuller likes to remind me, we are a junior college football program. We need to be more open to accepting student athletes who might come with some baggage. That baggage never includes a person's race or economic background, though."

"The college is asserting that you were insubordinate in your interactions with President Fuller. Is this true?"

"Don't answer that," Larry Bob said quickly. Dale ignored him.

"That will be for the college Trustees to decide, but I believe I did what needed to be done at the time."

"I've just received an email from President Fuller," Larry Bob said, squinting to read the message on his cellphone. "Coach Fox's hearing will take place two weeks from today."

Heaven Knight began scribbling notes. "Will it be open to the public?"

"That will be up to Coach Fox," Larry Bob answered. "And that's all the time we have today."

45

"Coach Fox, I want to begin by saying this meeting is completely off the record. No one on the college's Board of Trustees knows I asked you here, nor will they ever know."

President Margaret Fuller had contacted Dale the afternoon before with the suggestion of a private meeting. He'd wanted to turn her down but thought differently after they spoke for a few moments. She'd chosen a private room in the rear of a stately old restaurant in Blytheville, Arkansas, sixty miles from Mozarkite. Far enough away to blend into the steady stream of mostly senior citizens who entered and left.

"I didn't tell Larry Bob I was coming." And he hadn't. He felt a pang of guilt for that but not enough to spill the beans. He wanted to hear what President Fuller had to say.

She was dressed casually, in jeans and a gray sweatshirt. Her hair was pulled back in a ponytail. Dale had chosen jeans and a flannel shirt. They ordered lunch, then after the server left, got down to business.

"Coach, you have three years remaining on your contract. I'm certain that I can get the college board to approve paying your full salary for two of those three years in return for your announced retirement."

It was a move Dale had expected.

"Does that mean you will rescind the insubordination charge?"

"You retire and it goes away. There's no need to proceed."

Dale took a sip from his water glass, then wiped his mouth with his napkin.

"No."

The hopefulness on Dr. Fuller's face disappeared.

"If I'm not cleared it will always be like a cloud hanging over my head, Dr. Fuller. I won't have that."

The President shook her head dismissively. "People don't care about that, Coach Fox. Give it a month and it's forgotten."

"Not by me."

"So, you would let your pride get in the way of earning two years' income? What if you lose and receive nothing?"

Dale scoffed. "It's not about the money, Dr. Fuller. I could have retired five years ago. My pension is vested, my wife did well in real estate, and we squirreled away a little along the way. It's more than that. Much more. It's about integrity and my legacy at the college. This has threatened both of those."

"Well then, Coach, I guess there's nothing else to discuss." President Fuller took a sip of water, stood up, and slipped on her coat. "I've got a football game to attend. I've already paid for lunch, so feel free to stay and enjoy it. The Trustees and I will see you Monday morning."

After she was gone, Dale pulled out his cellphone and scrolled down until he found the number he was looking for. His call would go to voicemail and be retrieved later, but that was fine. The call needed to be made, and the time to do it was at hand.

"This is Brandon Yarbrough. Leave a message."

"Coach Yarbrough, this is Dale Fox. I'm calling to see if you might have time this evening for me to stop by. There are some things I need to say to you. I can be there at seven, if that works. Also, I wanted to wish you good luck with today's game. Go get 'em, Herefords."

● ● ●

THE MAN HAD every right to turn him away at the door, but he didn't. Brandon welcomed Dale warmly, took his coat, and got him a glass of water. He seemed unaffected by the tension that should have existed between them.

"Sorry to hear the boys lost," Dale said after they were seated.

"The defense started breaking down in the second half," Brandon said, "but we saw some good things on offense. They're getting better every week."

The silence that followed was awkward. For Dale, at least. Brandon sipped a Bud Light and allowed his former boss a few moments to sort through why he'd decided to come. Dale would've preferred to keep the subject focused on football, the one topic the twenty-something kid and the old man had in common. He would've liked to dig deeper. Where were Brandon and the coaching staff seeing improvement? Had they been able to keep morale up after four consecutive losses? Which players were playing hurt? What others had stepped up to fill in when needed?

But those questions could wait. They would have to wait. Dale had come to Brandon Yarbrough's home for different reasons.

"Brandon, I want to apologize for the way I spoke to you that evening."

There was no need to specify what evening. Brandon knew Dale was referring to the night everything went down with De'Shea. Brandon took another sip of beer, his eyes focused on a spot on the wall behind where Dale was seated. Dale could see he was thinking about the apology.

"I should've told you about De'Shea skipping class."

"Maybe, but that doesn't matter now. You did what you thought was best, and I jumped all over you for it. Please accept my apology."

Brandon nodded his head slowly. "I accept your apology, Coach, and thank you for being humble enough to offer it. By the way, I went to visit De'Shea and the others. I invited them back, but they said there was no way in hell they wanted to see Mozarkite ever again."

It would've been easy enough to leave it at that, but there was something else.

"I appreciate the way you treat and respect Susan and Max. I've not done a very good job of filling the void left in Max's life when his parents split up, and I was a little jealous of how easy that seemed to be for you."

Brandon smiled. "I really like Susan. We're different in a lot of ways, but very much alike on things that matter. And Max? You've got quite a grandson there, Coach. I adore him."

"Would you mind calling Susan tomorrow and asking her out?"

"I can't do it, Coach. She specifically said it was best for us to keep our distance until everything with the team is settled. I don't want Susan to be put in the middle."

"There won't be any middle after tomorrow," Dale said. "Whether I'm reinstated or not, I want to see more of you in Susan's and Max's lives."

They left it there, with Brandon uncommitted to breaking the promise he'd made to Susan. As Dale drove home that evening, he did something he hadn't done in quite a while. He prayed. Not for himself, but for Susan and Max. And Brandon. And Cassie. And the guys at the Goldrush, and Heaven Knight at the *Messenger*, and the boys on the football team. He prayed for Dr. Fuller and the college's Board of Trustees. Then he prayed for the Chattanooga Triplets who had come into his life and shined so brightly for such a short time. Whether he would ever have another group of young men like them was impossible to say, but he found himself thinking back to what they'd brought to Mozarkite and realized that, whatever happened in that college conference room on Monday, they'd changed his life for the better.

46

*D*ale and Larry Bob arrived five minutes early. Over the past several days, Dale had tried to imagine what it might feel like, being in the Trustees' meeting room while they discussed his future. He'd imagined a packed gallery, most supportive, a few not, but filled to capacity, nonetheless.

It was nothing like that.

The room was arranged like many where public meetings were held. A raised dais with seating for seven dominated the front, a seat for each of the six Trustees and one on the end reserved for the college president. They were already seated, quietly sifting through paperwork and whispering among themselves. President Margaret Fuller was standing off to one side, huddled with the attorney, Jeffrey Lewis Teague.

And the gallery? There were approximately sixty seats, but only about twenty were occupied. The first row on each side had been roped off.

"We sit here," Larry Bob said, pointing to the front row on the right. Dale nodded at people he'd known for years. Four of the six Trustees were long-time friends. He attended church with one and had fished with another. Susan and Cassie were seated behind the front row, within arm's reach. Dale was surprised to see Fran Tompkins seated further down the row. He squeezed her hand and asked about Willis as he passed.

The next row had been taken over by the Goldrush boys. Uncle Homer sported a suit from forty years ago. Dick and Tommy had on their work clothes. They gave Dale the thumbs up when he made eye contact.

Seated behind them was the biggest surprise of all. Bubber Slate. He nodded at Dale. Dale nodded back.

On the other side of the aisle were two men Dale didn't recognize, out-of-towners in tailored suits. Behind them were a mismatched collection of curiosity seekers and press. Heaven Knight was alone on the back row.

The Trustees' Chairperson, Connor Hempstead, called the meeting to order at nine on the nose. Connor owned four automotive garages in the area and had been a friend of Dale's since the years when he still did the repair work himself. The Trustees were three men and three women. They wasted no time getting down to business.

"We're here to conduct a hearing into the actions of Coach Dale Fox, an employee of Mozarkite Junior College. I see Coach Fox is here, along with his counsel, Larry Bob Billingsley. Are you ready to proceed, gentlemen?"

Larry Bob labored to his feet. "We are, Mr. Chairperson."

"Damn right they are!" Uncle Homer's whisper wasn't a whisper at all and brought a harsh rebuke from Connor Hempstead.

"Coach asked that these proceedings be held publicly, which is his right. What won't be tolerated are outbursts of any type." Hempstead's eyes bored into Uncle Homer as he continued. "Am I making myself clear?"

Uncle Homer didn't respond, which surprised Dale. It was rare to see the old man shut down, but Connor Hempstead had done it.

That was the moment when Andre Jameson made his appearance.

Heads turned when the creaky conference room door announced

his arrival. Mouths gaped open, including a couple mouths of Trustees, as Andre surveyed the room. He was still a huge deal in Mozarkite, a famous person they all knew, a big fish in their small pond who'd become an even bigger fish in ponds bigger than any of them could fathom.

Andre started up the aisle, then paused. His eyes moved from one side of the room to the other, and it was evident that he knew what his choice of seats would say about his position on the issue at hand. He stood still for a few moments, then moved into the row occupied by the Attorney Teague and the well-dressed out-of-towners. Dale felt his composure start to ebb.

"Don't worry about it," Larry Bob whispered.

Dale worried anyway. There had been no thought that Andre might return to Mozarkite for the hearing. They'd had their moments in recent months, but he still considered his former star player a friend.

"This hearing will determine," Connor Hempstead continued, "if Coach Dale Fox was insubordinate in his interactions with his supervisor, President Margaret Fuller. If it is proved that he was insubordinate, the Trustees will determine appropriate recourse, up to and including termination of contract for cause. Are there any questions?"

There were none, so Hempstead continued. "Jeffrey Teague is representing the college today. As stated previously, Larry Bob Billingsley appears with Coach Fox. At this time Mr. Teague will share his opening remarks."

Jeffrey Lewis Teague, it turned out, had a talent for using many words to say very little. His opening remarks went on for a half-hour but boiled down to one point: President Fuller had instructed Dale not to take action on De'Shea Stephens, and he had disregarded her instructions.

Larry Bob was next. His suit didn't adequately fit his ample girth, particularly in the butt. The extended seat time had caused the entire rear to pucker into his backside. Plumber Dick actually guffawed when he saw it. Welder Tommy did too, after Dick pointed it out. They received a stern look from Connor Hempstead.

Despite his ill-fitting suit, Larry Bob did a commendable job. Short and to the point, he highlighted why Dale hadn't been insubordinate. His main points centered on three things:

President Fuller never specifically said not to dismiss De'Shea.

Dale had made similar decisions in the past without consulting administration.

Dale's long and storied history as an exemplary employee of the college.

As soon as Larry Bob was seated, Chairperson Hempstead called on Attorney Teague to present his witnesses.

"President Margaret Fuller, please."

It quickly became apparent that the conference room arrangement, while fine for board meetings, was clumsy and inadequate for hearings. President Fuller moved to a podium that faced the Trustees. Both attorneys would be behind her and the other witnesses while they answered questions. There was some initial discussion of rearranging, but in the end, things were left as they were.

Jeffrey Lewis Teague started by reminding President Fuller of the date of her meeting with Dale, then asked her to recall their conversation. Dale followed along closely, finding his boss's account similar to his, other than one key fact.

"Did you specifically ask Coach Fox not to take any action regarding De'Shea Stephens's standing with the team?" Lawyer Teague asked.

"Yes, I did. I told him to wait until the next day."

When it was Larry Bob's turn, he rose to his feet and moved to the side of the room in order to make eye contact with President Fuller. Fortunately, he had adjusted the seat of his pants so that his posterior was no longer outlined in flannel.

"President Fuller, did you record the meeting with Coach Fox?"

"No, but I took notes."

"And in those notes, did you write down exactly what was said between you and Coach Fox?"

"Not exactly, no. I summarized what was said, along with my personal thoughts and recommendations."

"Do you have those notes with you, President Fuller?"

She pulled them from a folder she had on her lap. "Right here."

"Please read what you wrote about Coach Fox's alleged insubordination."

President Fuller read through her notes for a few moments, then said, "Right here, I noted that he had not yet spoken to a local resident who might be able to shed light on the matter."

Dale knew she was referring to Norman Snelling. Larry Bob did, too. No one else, did, though. Nor did they need to.

"Had you specifically told Coach Fox to talk to that individual?" Larry Bob asked.

"No, but I thought it would be helpful. The individual might have had information relative to De'Shea Stephens's situation."

"Does that have anything to do with your allegation of Coach Fox being insubordinate?"

"Not directly, no."

"Then respectfully move on, President Fuller. Don't waste our time with additional unfounded claims."

Larry Bob's brusque manner appeared to have an impact on the college president. She spent several more moments flipping through her notes.

"I asked Coach Fox what he was proposing in regard to the student, and he said, 'I'm not proposing anything. I'm telling you how I intend to respond."

Larry Bob moved closer. He was now within six feet of President Fuller. Dale expected Connor Hempstead to order him back, but he didn't. "And what did you say to that?" he asked.

"I told him that it was better not to make decisions in a vacuum. I don't do that, and said that he shouldn't either."

"Do you think that Coach Fox was being insubordinate when he said that?"

"Very much so."

"Did you tell him that he was being insubordinate?"

"I was trying to keep the conversation positive."

"What did you say next, President Fuller?"

"As I already explained, I asked Coach Fox what he was thinking about doing in regard to the student issue. He said he was considering suspending De'Shea Stephens from the team and taking away his scholarship. That struck me as quite harsh, given the decision was based on allegations rather than facts."

"But Coach Fox was not suspending the player from school, only from the team, right?"

"It's still quite harsh. It's my job as President to watch out for the welfare of our students. They should be deemed innocent until proven guilty."

"So, you would have preferred the student remain on the team, despite being jailed on a charge of arson?"

"Innocent until proven guilty," President Fuller said again.

"What if the charge had been sexual assault? Would you feel the same, President Fuller?"

Larry Bob's question was greeted with murmuring from the gallery. Connor Hempstead asked for silence, then motioned for President Fuller to respond. She didn't appear to relish having to continue.

"This wasn't sexual assault. It was arson."

Her answer came across as weak and uncertain, but Larry Bob let it slide. "What else was said?"

"It was apparent that Coach Fox felt strongly about the decision to be made, and I felt it was best to delay it, so I said we would talk more the following day. Coach Fox grew belligerent at that point. He said something to the effect of the decision already being made as far as he was concerned."

"Did you tell him the decision was not made, President Fuller? Did you tell Coach Fox not to make a decision until the two of you got back together?"

"I assumed that he understood."

"You stated that it was apparent that Coach Fox felt strongly about the decision. You even said he grew belligerent. Did you become emotional at all, President Fuller?"

Margaret Fuller shifted uncomfortably at the podium, turning so her attention was redirected at the Trustees rather than Larry Bob.

"Perhaps, at one point. Coach Fox was talking about right and wrong and how he disliked dealing with gray areas. I might've been pointed in my response."

"So, you were both somewhat emotional," Larry Bob responded.

"I was doing what I felt was best for the student."

❦ ❦ ❦

THE TWO GUYS in suits turned out to be experts on employment law. They stated their shared beliefs that the case was cut-and-dried. Dale was insubordinate. Like Jeffrey Lewis Teague, unfortunately, they used a lot of words to say it. Dale noticed one of the Trustees, a former librarian named Mable Francis, start to nod off as the second expert droned on. Larry Bob must have noticed it as well, because he passed up the opportunity to question them.

That was the extent of the college's case. Two hours and fifteen minutes. Chairperson Hempstead called for a lunch break.

❦ ❦ ❦

WHEN THE BOARD RECONVENED, a new face had found his way into the room. Larry Bob hadn't told Dale that he had requested the presence of the college's former President, Dr. Daniel Trebelhorn Parker. Had he known, he would likely have objected. Professor Parker retired on June 30 of the previous year, conducted a massive auction of all of his century-old home's furnishings on July 1, and departed Mozarkite for Naples, Florida, on July 5. He'd not returned since, and Dale didn't like being the reason he had to leave sunny Florida.

Professor Parker looked the same. Slight of build, sharp, flinty features, an unruly shock of white hair, and a mole above his right eyebrow that some speculated had a pulse of its own. As soon as the hearing was called back to order Larry Bob took the floor and called on Professor Parker to testify.

The board appeared as surprised by his appearance as Dale. During Professor Parker's forty-year run as MJC President, the Trustees had faithfully done his bidding. Dale had heard that there were only four votes in those forty years that were not unanimous. In all four instances, the wayward Trustees who had cast dissenting votes were voted off the next time their names were on the ballot. Such was the legacy of Professor Parker.

But things had changed over the past seventeen months. A new President had arrived, and the Trustees had used that as an opportunity to assert their rightful place as caretakers and decision makers. The sight of Professor Parker making a beeline for the podium caused several of them to sit up straighter. The unspoken message was clear: the old dictator was in the house, and he wasn't to be trifled with.

Larry Bob skipped any introduction of the Professor's credentials. It would have been laughable. In Mozarkite, there had been God, then Professor Parker. Some might have complained about his heavy-handed, dictatorial style, but they always did it in whispered tones.

"Professor Parker, describe Coach Dale Fox as an employee."

"Hard-headed at first, but after a few years he settled down. I trusted him completely."

"When it came to the football program and athletics in general, did you give Coach Fox latitude in decision making?"

"He had complete autonomy. I was too busy running the school to do his job too."

Larry Bob paused to let the Professor's answers sink in. Dale thought he was about to ask another question but seemed to think better of it and sat down.

Jeffrey Lewis Teague hadn't been the college's attorney during Professor Parker's reign. Had he been, he would've known better than to question the Professor's age and mental acuity. By the time he was finished, Daniel Trebelhorn Parker had handed Jeffrey Lewis Teague his ass on a plate. Uncle Homer actually stood and applauded until he was shushed by Chairperson Hempstead.

It was Dale's turn to approach the podium.

Larry Bob went easy on him. Dale recalled the conversation much the way President Fuller had described it. Yes, he had become testy at one point. He was used to doing his job the way he'd always done it, and suddenly he was being told something different. Had he felt he was being insubordinate? That question was more difficult. Privately, he doubted he would have made the decision had he not encountered and felt challenged by Heaven Knight. The answer he and Larry Bob had rehearsed, while technically true, skirted the issue of Dale's authority being challenged.

"I never heard President Fuller tell me specifically not to move forward in my dealings with the player," he said.

"You don't like President Fuller very much, do you, Coach?" Lawyer Teague had recovered from the verbal shellacking he'd received from Professor Parker. He'd nearly jumped from his seat when his turn came, reminding Dale of a prize fighter who found himself trailing his opponent late in the fight.

"I respect Dr. Fuller. She's done plenty of positive things since she arrived."

"Is it hard for you to take orders from a woman, Coach Fox?"

"I've lived my adult life in a home where I was the only male. I was married to Linda Fox, who most everyone here knew very well. I've taken orders from women most of my life."

That response garnered laughter from several in the gallery. Two Trustees cracked smiles as well. It wasn't intended, but Dale would take it. One person not smiling was Jeffrey Lewis Teague.

"You find this humorous, Coach? Is that your feeling toward the hearing in general? That it's just a minor inconvenience? Something to laugh about?"

"Not at all."

"You're a very important person here in Mozarkite, aren't you, Coach?"

Dale thought about the question for a few beats. He tried to come up with a way to sugarcoat the truth, but in the end, he went with what came to mind.

"I used to think so. Not so much anymore. I've learned a lot over the past year about myself and about things that I had and took for granted."

There wasn't a sound in the room. No voices, no shuffling of paper, not even a cough or sneeze. Those gathered knew some of what Dale had experienced over the past year. The loss of his wife, his daughter's divorce and relocation back to town. The arrival and departure of the Chattanooga Triplets was just one more thing among many.

Dale remained glued in place at the podium. He had no idea what Lawyer Teague might have for him next, and he really didn't care. Suddenly he was very tired and wanted nothing more than to go home, sit in his La-Z-Boy, and mindlessly watch television.

But there was still work to be done.

"Coach Fox, if a player spoke to you the way you spoke to President Fuller that day in her office, how would you react?"

Dale hadn't seen that one coming, yet come it did. Like a haymaker at the last minute of the last round. He started to speak, stopped, thought, then spoke haltingly.

"I would feel... disappointed."

And that was it.

● ● ●

THE BOARD RECESSED to consider their decision. Dale and Larry Bob clustered with Susan and Cassie in an empty office down the hall. They'd been there for over an hour when someone knocked on the door, opened it slightly, and asked to come in.

"Sure, Andre, come in."

Andre Jameson entered the room and closed the door behind him. He hugged Susan, said hello to Cassie, then turned his attention to Dale.

"I was asked by President Fuller to be here."

Dale said nothing.

"They wanted me to speak as to the direction the football program has taken in recent years and about how you've been given too much autonomy."

Dale still didn't speak.

"I showed up intending to say that no employee should be able to contradict the wishes of the college's President. I was ready to go."

"What happened?"

Andre leaned against the wall, looked toward the ceiling, and said, "I remembered how you dealt with Chester Hyland."

Dale nodded. He remembered.

"Chester was with two other guys who held up the old Casey's Convenience Store that used to be downtown," Andre said, speaking to the others. "Coach found out about it and kicked him off the team." He turned to Dale and said, "Do you remember what you said to Chester, Coach?"

Dale did. "He could remain a student but would have to sit out football until the case was decided."

"There are some folks who are trying to find a racism angle to this whole De'Shea Stephens thing, but you dealt with him the same way you did Chester Hyland twenty-some years ago. And Chester was as white as the fifty-yard line."

It was true. Every bit of it. Still, Dale felt conflicted.

"True, Andre, but I want to be honest with you. I had issues with De'Shea and the others. Not issues of skin color but concerns about their pasts. Rather than work my way through those issues, I let them affect the way I dealt with them. Because of that I was unfair to one of my assistant coaches and to the player himself." Dale paused, swallowed, took a deep breath, and said, "De'Shea deserved my support. He didn't get it."

◊ ◊ ◊

FOUR HOURS HAD PASSED since the board recessed. It was supper time and Dale was getting hungry. Following Andre's visit, he had invited

Larry Bob, Susan, and Cassie to accompany him to grab a quick bite at Pizza Lube.

"I suppose I still have a couple free pizzas owed to me," he said.

Larry Bob recommended they wait. Susan offered to run out for sandwiches, but Dale wanted his little support group to remain together. Stomachs growling, they spent the next forty minutes speculating as to why the decision was taking so long.

"Is it really such a complicated thing?" Dale wondered aloud. "Either I was insubordinate, or I wasn't."

"You weren't," Cassie answered quickly.

"Why is President Fuller allowed to join them in their deliberations?" Susan snipped. "I don't think that's fair at all. She's had all this time to influence their decision."

"She is the college president," Larry Bob said. "Technically, she and the Trustees are on the same side."

Their conversation drifted, meandered, and circled back over the next twenty minutes, until five minutes before seven, when Larry Bob's cellphone began playing the Macarena song. He answered, listened, said okay, and put it away.

"They're reconvening in five minutes."

◆ ◆ ◆

"COACH FOX, our Trustees have reached a decision."

Dale wasn't sure if he should stand like the defendants in court or stay in his seat. He glanced at Larry Bob, who motioned for him to remain seated.

Many of the people who had attended the hearing had returned to the gallery following the recess. The out-of-town experts were long gone, leaving Jeffrey Lewis Teague with a row to himself. Plumber Dick and Welder Tommy were nowhere to be found. Uncle Homer was present, and it appeared by his disheveled appearance that he had remained in his seat, dozing through the recess. Dale suspected he'd brought along a hidden pint of liquid comfort to help him get comfortable.

Bubber Slate had returned as well. They nodded at one another when Dale entered the meeting room. Dale suspected that Bubber felt beholden to him. He hoped they could move past that. They did, after all, share custody of Linda's dog.

Connor Hempstead and the other five Trustees appeared weary. Connor's tie was askew and the skin around his eyes was dark. Dale could tell it had been a difficult afternoon and suspected that didn't bode well for him.

"Coach, it is the finding of this board, and I want to emphasize that the final vote was unanimous, that your actions on the day in question constitute insubordination."

Chairperson Hempstead paused to let his words sink in. Dale had wondered how he would feel if the board decided against him. Now he knew. He felt... nothing. They'd made their decision and that was that. For some silly reason, he remembered the legend of how Charles Manson had hurtled from the defense table toward the judge when his verdict was handed down. He'd never seen the movie and didn't know if it was true. If so, Manson had to have been much younger and closer to the judge than Dale was. If he decided to lunge at Connor Hempstead, he would likely fall heavily upon the builder-grade maroon carpet, about twenty feet short of his intended target. Just the thought threatened to bring a grin to his face, an urge Dale suppressed. It was for the best, because Heaven Knight had moved into a position off to the side and had started taking his photograph as soon as Connor Hempstead made his pronouncement. He could imagine the next day's headline: *Coach Guilty of Insubordination, Smiles at Decision.*

After a few moments Chairperson Hempstead said, "As I stated during opening remarks this morning, the Trustees are charged with determining what recourse should be taken regarding your actions, up to and including termination." Hempstead paused again, then said, "In light of the circumstances, and the latitude you were given in the past by Professor Parker, the Trustees have decided to place a letter of warning in your personnel file. Coach Fox, should another incident of insubordination be documented, you will be terminated from your position with the college." Hempstead paused, set aside his reading glasses, and looked down his nose at Dale. "Do you understand, Coach Fox?"

Dale started to speak, but Larry Bob cut him off. "I'll not have you talking to my client, a long-time resident of this community, like a five-year-old, Connor. He was coaching this team when you were still drinking tequila you and your high school buddies stole from Manny's Mexican Restaurant."

Chairperson Hempstead's forehead flared red. His eyes bored into Larry Bob's. "You'll refrain from frivolous charges that have no base in reality, Mr. Billingsley. And you'll address me as Mr. Chairperson or Mr. Hempstead in this meeting."

"Or what, Connor? You'll have me removed? Too late for that, bud. And regarding the tequila, are you forgetting who represented Manny in that case? You boys came into that juvenile courtroom crying like a bunch of babies with diaper rash burning up your asses. How much did your Daddy have to pay to get that taken care of, Connor? Two-fifty, wasn't it? That was one expensive bottle of tequila."

Connor Hempstead was livid. He remained in his seat, but Dale could see the way his arms were flexing beneath his sport coat. The other Trustees looked on helplessly, waiting to see what their chairperson might say next. Heaven Knight continued to flash away but had turned her camera on Hempstead. Larry Bob had turned the final moments of the hearing into a spectacle of dramatic proportions.

It took Connor Hempstead a couple minutes of deep breathing, flexing his arms and twisting his mouth to get calmed down. Dale wondered if he was debating rising from his lofty perch and whipping Larry Bob's ass. Larry Bob remained in his seat, a passive look on his face, waiting for the Chairperson to move ahead. Whether it had been a planned response or Larry Bob choosing to enjoy a moment of folly by cutting a man down to size whom he thought was acting too big for his britches, Dale couldn't say. It was good drama, though.

"Anyway, as I was saying, the Trustees will put a letter in your file,

Coach Fox. The Trustees' secretary will make sure you get a copy of it. Otherwise you're free to return to work and resume your responsibilities as Athletic Director and Football Coach effective tomorrow morning at—"

"Does that mean he can coach next weekend's game?" Dale was surprised Uncle Homer had refrained from having his say as long as he had. His tone when he asked his question was downright genteel, if not a bit slurred.

"Yes," Chairperson Hempstead said wearily, "Coach Fox can return to practice tomorrow and can coach the last game of the season this weekend."

What the ovation that followed lacked in quantity was more than made up for by enthusiasm. Susan, Cassie, Uncle Homer, and Bubber Slate stood and applauded the decision. The Trustees looked as if they were ready to bolt for the exit. When Dale looked at President Fuller, though, he was surprised to see her wink and offer a smile.

They were going to be okay.

47

"*We're back at Crowley Field where we've just witnessed a stunning upset. Your Polled Herefords defeated seventh-ranked Gales City College by a score of nine to three. Hi again, everyone, this is Wally Westmoreland, the voice of your Polled Herefords, and what a memorable day it has been. This final game of the season will go down as one of the best in the storied history of this proud Polled Hereford team, so good that I don't know where to begin.*

Mozarkite was undefeated and ranked first in the country after four weeks, then came a series of unfortunate incidents that resulted in the departure of the Chattanooga Triplets, followed by the suspension of long-time Hereford's Coach Dale Fox. Assistant Coach Brandon Yarbrough, suspended one week earlier, returned to assume the position of interim head coach as..."

◊ ◊ ◊

DALE FINISHED SHAKING hands with Gales City's coaches and players, then followed his exuberant squad toward the locker room at the end of the field. At midfield, he took a quick glance in the direction of Linda's seat, just in case. But of course, she wasn't there. A few rows away he spotted Susan and Max. And Cassie. They were beaming. Max waved. In the past Dale would not have acknowledged such a show from the bleachers, but that was the past. He paused to grin, wave back, and mouth *I love you* to his grandson.

At the end of the bleachers, standing in the same ominous spot where she'd been the day she came to inform him of his suspension, was President Margaret Fuller. She was in full Polled Hereford attire, and her hair was tied back in the same ponytail she'd sported the week before at the Blytheville restaurant where they'd met for lunch. Dale angled toward the sideline in her direction, coming to a stop a few feet away. President Fuller was grinning. So was Dale.

"So," he said, "what do you think?"

"As boring a game as I've ever seen," she said, her eyes twinkling in the late afternoon sun. "And one of the best afternoons of my life."

They remained there for a few moments. The quiet was awkward, and Dale considered beating a hasty retreat. They'd not crossed paths in the four days since he'd returned to work. He had heard she was at an out of town meeting most of that time. Probably for the best. Still, they needed to start communicating or the future would continue to be difficult.

"It felt good to be back," Dale said quietly.

"It was good to see you back," she replied.

More silence, before Dale said, "I have some changes to make."

"Really? Like what?"

Dale shook his head. "Like just about everything. The way I am as a father and grandfather. The way I am as a friend. The way I coach, the way I relate to my players." He paused, smiled wistfully, and said, "the way I relate to my boss."

He could see this touched something in her. Dr. Fuller blinked several times, then reached for his hand.

"Are you up to all that change?" she asked.

Dale squeezed her hand. "I suppose I have a few months to figure that out."

EPILOGUE
NINE MONTHS LATER

"*It's a beautiful late summer day here in Mozarkite, a perfect setting for the Polled Herefords' opener against Northeast Kentucky. I'm Wally Westmoreland, the voice of the Polled Herefords, and you're listening on Mozarkite's own Country 104.*

"*It's a new and very different season for your Polled Herefords, following a year of dashed expectations, turmoil, and a six and five record. It's good to be back with you, and I hope you're as excited for this season as I am. So, sit back and enjoy every game here on Country 104.*

"*The stands are nearly full for this home opener. Expectations are high, and the fans are decked out in their Polled Hereford gear. You can hear the Mozarkite Marching Band in the background playing the school fight song, and here come your Polled Herefords onto the field right now, led by their new head coach, Brandon Yarbrough.*"

● ● ●

IT WAS the kind of game major colleges play early in the season. Guarantee games, they're called, when big schools pay smaller schools sizable sums to come to their sold-out stadiums and get their brains beat out. The final score was sixty-seven to three in favor of the home team, about what was expected. From his spot at the edge of the tunnel leading to the home team locker room, Dale watched the winning team stream by, careful to keep their eyes down to avoid having to engage the adoring crowd that had gathered to shout out words of congratulations and adulation.

It was Mozarkite. Sort of. But on a much larger scale. Much, much larger.

The head coach was the last to pass by. He was surrounded by members of the state highway patrol ready to clear a way should any of the adoring fans choose to get between them and the locker room. Like the players, the coach kept his eyes straight ahead. Mostly. He did look up a couple times when his name was called, and it was at one of those moments that his eyes met Dale's. There was a flash of recognition, but little else. He kept running. And the moment was over.

Fans began to peel away, happy to have gotten within a few feet of their heroes. Dale knew it had been a longshot, but still he'd had to come. The ride ahead was long, and it was best to get going, so he started to follow the others. That's when he heard someone call out his name.

"Coach Fox?"

It was one of the state troopers.

"He asked me to come get you."

Dale followed the trooper through the tunnel, past a barrage of signs and banners reminding players of their team's past achievements while extolling them to future greatness.

"Wait here, please," the trooper said before briskly scooting away.

Dale waited. A half-hour came and went. Then, after forty-five minutes, the same trooper returned. "Come with me, Coach Fox."

The trooper led the way into the home team locker room. It was beyond anything Dale had ever seen. Lockers spaced apart to allow plenty of room for directors' chairs emblazoned with the school mascot to be situated in front of them. Large screen televisions against one wall, with oversized leather couches placed just so. The only similarities to the Mozarkite locker room were the pervasive stench of postgame sweat and the piles of perspiration-soaked uniforms on the floor. The players, except for a few stragglers, were gone.

The trooper pointed to an open door. "Right through there, Coach."

Dale entered an office any Fortune 500 CEO would envy. The carpet, school colors, of course, was immaculate. A conference table off to one side could seat at least twenty. There were two big-screen televisions beyond them.

And in the center of it all, a large desk.

And behind the desk sat a man whose face Dale had seen hundreds of times on ESPN. He came across in his interviews as warm and folksy, but Dale had heard rumors that he was nothing like that. He was about to find out. The coach stood, smiled warmly, and came across the room to shake Dale's hand.

"Coach Fox, welcome to campus."

Dale had rarely found himself speechless, but it was nearly too much to consider all at once.

It wasn't the surroundings that overwhelmed him.

Or the coach.

It was what he had come to do. What he needed to do.

Dale knew he needed to do it, and the man standing in front of him somehow knew it too.

"He played a great game," Dale said, for wont of having something better to say.

"It was a good starting point. We'll see how he does when we get to the meat of the schedule, but I suspect he'll be outstanding. Do you want to see him?"

Dale smiled wistfully. "I need to see him."

The coach motioned to the large conference table, invited Dale to take a seat, then left the room, quietly closing the door behind him. It would be the last time they were face to face. Ten minutes later the door opened again.

De'Shea Stephens stepped in.

The dreads were still there, the strong, agile body was the same, but he seemed different. Dale saw it in his eyes. He looked older, wizened.

And understandably, skeptical.

And suspicious.

Dale stood and took a few tentative steps in the direction of his former quarterback.

"Hello, De'Shea."

"Coach," he said evenly.

Dale had thought long and hard about what he would say if they were ever face to face again, but nothing sounded right. He was about to toss out a compliment about the way De'Shea had played but knew it would sound hollow.

"De'Shea, I'm sorry."

The young man blinked several times but didn't respond.

"You needed my support and you didn't get it. You needed me to believe you, and I didn't."

De'Shea blinked some more, then spoke. "Some people say I cost you your job."

"They're wrong, De'Shea. I retired. It was my decision. I guess you could say that my unwillingness to change with the times cost me my job."

They stood there for a few moments, the former coach and his former player. Dale considered offering his hand, but in the end decided it was a meaningless gesture.

"Well, I'll let you get back to your teammates," Dale finally said.

He had to pass De'Shea to reach the door. They came within a few feet but did not look at one another. Then, as he was about to step out, De'Shea said, "Coach told me what you did."

Dale turned and looked at De'Shea.

"He told me that you called and recommended me. I appreciate that."

"You're going to be a star, De'Shea. And after what happened in Mozarkite, after what I did, it was the least I could do."

The silence grew awkward before De'Shea spoke again.

"How are you doing, Coach?"

Dale offered a slight smile. "Learning how to live life, De'Shea. Trying to focus on what's important for a change."

De'Shea nodded, then waved toward the locker room. "Do you miss it?"

No one had asked Dale that question. Not yet, anyway. And he hadn't yet taken the time to think it through.

"I'm scared of the future more than anything else, I guess. I'm sixty years old and have no idea what's coming at me. Life has always been defined by seasons. Football, spring practice, summer practice. Now…" Dale didn't know what else he could say, so he shut up. Then, he knew.

"Thanks for seeing me, De'Shea."

De'Shea smiled and offered his hand. "Coach, I forgive you."

And that was enough, except for one thing.

"Thank you, De'Shea. Can I ask one favor? Will you call me Dale?"

De'Shea appeared confused by the request. "Just Dale?"

"Just Dale."

● ● ●

THEY WERE WAITING for Dale in the shade of a centuries-old oak tree on the edge of campus, a few blocks from the stadium.

"We got tired of waiting and went to get a Coke," Max said in way of a greeting. "We got one for you, but it's hot now."

Dale laughed at his grandson's forthrightness. "It's okay, buddy. I'm not thirsty. Are you ready to get back on the road?"

"How far do we have to go?"

"We won't get there tonight, but tomorrow we'll get on the ship, and you are going to have the time of your life."

The cruise was Dale's idea.

Taking Max along was his idea, too.

Inviting Cassie? That was all Susan. Dale had protested initially. It was inappropriate for two single adults to cruise together, especially when one had his grandson along. Susan had laughed at him, then got on the phone and confirmed there were two adjoining cabins available.

"One for you and Max, the other for Cassie."

Dale couldn't tell if his daughter was toying with him, then when she spoke again, he knew she was.

"Of course, you know how soundly Max sleeps. And Cassie's room would be right next door. And there is a door between the two, so..." Susan batted her eyes mischievously. Dale blushed, but he liked the idea of spending time with Cassie.

"So, are you going to call her?" Susan asked.

He had. And Cassie said yes.

As they returned to the car, Cassie reached out and took his hand. Dale let her.

"I received a text from Susan about the Mozarkite game."

"Really?"

"Um-hmm. Do you want to know the score?"

Yes, he did. Very much.

Didn't he?

Did he?

In the end, Dale decided that it could wait.

He wasn't Coach anymore.

He was just Dale.

And that was okay.

AUTHOR'S NOTE

People sometimes ask me if there is any truth behind specific events and places in my books. In a word, yes! Plenty of the places and lesser events are real. For example, in the book you've just read, there are a number of real-life references. Here are a few:

Dale Fox. Yes, he's real. Sort of. Actually, he's many people. He's the retired coach I worked with at one school and the administrator I worked with at another. He's a librarian and a social studies teacher. He's a bus driver I knew and an assistant superintendent friend. The more time I spent with Dale the more I came to appreciate his struggles. That's when I realized there's also a little of me in him.

Though *Mozarkite* is a fictitious town in Missouri, it's not unlike a lot of communities of similar size. Diners and coffee shops are still an important destination and the local school teams can pack the house on any given night. People read the local paper from front to back, but, like Dale and Fran Tompkins, often start with the obituaries. I'm glad I was able to spend much of my career in small Missouri towns like Perryville, Owensville, and Tipton.

Mozarkite Junior College is a creation of my imagination. The last time juco football was played in Missouri was by Kemper Junior College in Boonville, Missouri in the late 1990's.

There are a few locations mentioned that are real; too many to name, really. Some that I remember as I write this are *Cape Girardeau*, *Poplar Bluff*, *Caruthersville*, *Charleston*, *Monett*, and *Potosi* in Missouri, and *Piggott* and *Blytheville* in Arkansas. I think real names help give a story credibility.

Father Clark Smith raves about *Booche's Hamburgers* in Columbia, Missouri. They're real. Booche's has been a Columbia mainstay since it opened as a pool hall in 1884. The burgers are served on wax paper instead of plates.

The therapist who gave the elusive *W* his massage moved away to *Anna Maria Island*, Florida. That's our beach. If you like old Florida charm without a lot of traffic, chain restaurants, and insanity, come for a visit.

As Cassie struggles to ask Dale to dinner at her house he is reminded of how he had to work up the courage to ask Teri Jones to prom in eleventh grade. That was from my personal past. It was senior year and yes, her name really was Teri Jones. She had auburn hair and freckles and was very kind. Best of all, she said yes. Sadly, we lost Teri back in 2005.

Remember when Dale ran into Cassie at Piggly Wiggly? He was buying the ingredients for a recipe called *Zesty Saltine Meatloaf*. Yep, it's real. When I was young and single I set out to impress a young lady by cooking for her. Zesty Saltine Meatloaf seemed easy enough. Toss the ingredients into a pan, then use wax paper to hold every-thing in place while you roll it up. Dale's meatloaf turned out better than mine. His only mistake was substituting tomato sauce for ketchup. My mistake? Not removing the wax paper. I never tried the recipe again, and as best I recall didn't earn a second date.

I'm not above slipping a few real names into my books. I love using surnames, like Bennett and Schaefferkoetter, from places I've lived and worked. This time I purposely used the names of two friends. *Chuck Smith*, the guy who brings his Rottweiler to Rotary meetings? He's a friend of mine, a former college and pro football player with an interesting life story that gets even better when you find out that his alma mater, Yankton College, is now a federal prison camp. Chuck went to school there before it became a prison, I think. Regardless, he does not own a Rottweiler nor take one to civic group meetings. Yet. And *John Dellinger*, the promising lineman that Coach Brandon Yarbrough visits in West Virginia? John is the husband of my editor, Judy. They grew up in West Virginia but call Michigan home these days. John mentioned a couple years ago that he would like to see his name in a book.

So, there you go.

AFTERWORD

It's Paul again, back to ask a special favor. Did you like *Missed Signals*? If so, would you mind heading over to Amazon and leaving a review? Why? Well, reviews don't mean a lot to the big boys and girls of the publishing world, but for authors like me, they move mountains. I don't have a big advertising budget or a major publishing house behind me. What I do have is readers like you, people who find my books, buy them, read them, and enjoy them. Your review can convince others to take a chance on my writing. It's easy and won't take more than two minutes. While you're there, I hope you'll check out my other books.

It would make me very happy to hear from you. The best way is to go to my website and sign up for my newsletter. When you sign up you'll receive my eBook, *Hope Less – A Grebey Island Short Story*. It's a prequel to my first book, *Harvest of Thorns*. You'll also receive special offers, such as becoming part of my Review Team, a group of folks who receive my new books for free in return for an honest review when the book debuts. My website is paulwoottenbooks.com.

Thanks for reading! Please read more and tell your friends about my work.

ACKNOWLEDGMENTS

To everyone who read my previous books, thank you!

Thanks to my editor Judy Falin Dellinger and her husband John.

I appreciate my beta readers! Your help is huge.

I love my family, and it keeps growing. Four grandkids now. I'm proud of you guys.

Robin makes my world go around.

And thank you, Lord, for giving me the time, interest, and ability to write these words. Without you, I'm nothing.

ALSO BY PAUL E. WOOTTEN

Harvest of Thorns - Grebey Island Book One

Shunned

The Resurrection of Hucklebuck Jones

Some Summer - Grebey Creek Book Two

Christmas Class Reunion